MW00329641

West Wind Clear

V. M. Knox

Book Reality

Helping Writers Become Independent Authors

Copyright © V. M. Knox 2022
Published: 2022 by The Book Reality Experience

*

ISBN: 978-1-922670-59-5 - Paperback Edition
ISBN: 978-1-922670-60-1 - EBook Edition

All rights reserved.

The right of V. M. Knox to be identified as author of this Work has been
asserted by her in accordance with sections 77 and 78 of the
Copyright, Designs and Patents Act 1988.

This book is a work of fiction and any resemblance to actual persons,
living or dead, is purely coincidental. Although a number of details
within this novel allude to actual historical events and individuals, no
actions, intentions or opinions of the characters reflect, or should be
inferred to reflect, actual motivations or actions undertaken by actual
persons.

No part of this publication may be reproduced, stored in retrieval system,
copied in any form or by any means, electronic, mechanical, photocopy-
ing, recording or otherwise transmitted without written permission from
the publisher. You must not circulate this book in any format.

Cover Design by Brittany Wilson | brittwilsonart.com
from an original concept by Luke Buxton | www.lukebuxton.com

For all the unsung heroes of the Intelligence Corps

Also by V. M. Knox

The Clement Wisdom Series:

In Spite of All Terror
If Necessary Alone
Where Death and Danger Go

Sydney 1941

1

5th December 1941

Clement stepped from the harbour ferry onto the gangplank and descended to the platform. It was a journey he always enjoyed; the fresh salty air, the sparkling blue waters of Sydney Harbour and the jaunty little double-ended ferry boat that brought him from Geraldine's house on the river to the birthplace of the Dominion of Australia, Circular Quay. Although, today, the trip would be his last. Beside him was Geraldine Naylor, the widow of Reginald, his former colleague and friend. Clutching his suitcase in one hand, Clement took Geraldine's arm and they walked along the platform towards the terminal building. A short gust of wind swept off the water, its effect instantly cooling and helping to alleviate the warmth of the day. Handing their tickets to the collector at the gate, they walked out to the street beyond. A few cars were parked outside the ornate, four-storey Customs House opposite. Further along the foot-path, Clement could see Reg and Geraldine's son, Charles Naylor, waiting for them on the pavement.

The young man crossed the street and hurried towards them.

'Charles, good of you to come and see me off,' Clement said.

'Not at all, Clement. It's such a lovely day and being out of the noisy machine shop is a treat. Let me take your suitcase,' Charles said, reaching forward. Kissing his mother's cheek in greeting, they walked towards the long, overseas terminal adjacent to the quay. The harbour glistened in the morning sunshine. Berthed beside the wharf was the grey-hulled ship that would take Clement to Canada. The bow, with its massive anchors, loomed above them. It was the biggest ship that had been in port for some time and its presence dwarfed the surrounding buildings. Clement could see several gantries loading supplies and equipment for the journey ahead. The ship was to take Clement and hundreds of Royal Australian Air Force personnel across the Pacific to Vancouver. Thereafter for him, he'd travel across Canada by train before another sea crossing back to England. He stared at the four-funnelled ship and felt the thrill, the mix of excitement and apprehension. The Pacific Ocean was a different place since his journey out to Australia five months previously.

While the war in Europe had not abated, now, from

all accounts, the Japanese were showing signs of impending hostilities. But he couldn't stay. His war was elsewhere, and he'd promised both Johnny and C, Sir Stewart Menzies, the Head of the Secret Intelligence Service, that he'd go to the Shetland Islands in the Northern winter. It was the reason he'd been permitted to come to Australia to inform Geraldine personally about Reg's death. Clement's gaze settled on the massive Sydney Harbour Bridge beyond, its arched span towering over the city that clustered around the shores of the harbour. In the early afternoon light, the imposing structure seemed to silhouette the vessel like a halo, overshadowing even the enormous ship waiting at the wharf.

Clement swallowed, trying to suppress a growing feeling of unease. He couldn't fully explain it. He didn't believe it was apprehension for the perils of the oceans in wartime, although they were considerable. Nor was it at leaving Geraldine and Charles with whom he'd stayed for the past five months. He held a genuine fondness for them, especially Geraldine; they shared many memories of Fearnley Maughton, the village in East Sussex where they'd both lived before the war and where Clement had been the vicar for twenty years. He liked Geraldine but he didn't love her. No one would ever replace his beloved, late-wife Mary. But he did like Australia, although he acknowledged he hadn't seen anything other than Sydney and Gladesville, the suburb where Geraldine and Charles now lived. Their sturdy brick house fronted the Parramatta River, the name given to the upper reaches of Sydney Harbour, and it had a wonderful view of the small city from the sitting room windows.

While Sydney was profoundly smaller than London, in the five months Clement had been there, he'd developed an appreciation for the place. The people were polite and friendly; there was an almost naïve honesty that was missing in larger cities like London. It reminded him a little of village life but on a grander scale. He looked across the harbour again at the small ships sailing there then gazed up at the cloudless sky, the bright summer sun making his eyes squint. The intensity of the vivid blue was not remotely like an English sky. His gaze settled on the stone buildings around the harbour front. Old warehouses, four storeys in height, and commercial enterprises clustered around the foreshore. Among them, terraced houses overlooked the busy Circular Quay. It was all pristine and, more notably for him, unscathed. He prayed it would remain so but the evening radio news broadcasts had told them of the escalating threat of war with Japan. In Clement's mind, he saw the carnage of the relentless Nazi bombing Britain had endured and he prayed that Australia would be spared such devastation. He felt a shiver course through him, his gaze again on the undamaged buildings around him. For now, at least, no sandbags lined the streets here, neither was there any bomb damage. In fact, looking around Circular Quay, if Clement didn't know a war raged in the Northern Hemisphere, he would never have guessed. Not that the Australians were oblivious to the conflict.

The country had followed Britain in declaring war on Germany and Italy and had sent thousands of troops to fight in distant lands. It had, numerous times, caused the delay in his returning home. Whenever he'd packed his suitcase to leave, he'd been bumped from the passenger list at the last minute. Yet, despite the heightened awareness of Japanese aggression, this time, he believed he'd be on his way. His thoughts turned to Shetland and what *C* wanted him to do there. He dreaded the thought of the North Sea in winter. The weather there would be about as different to his current location as could be imagined.

They slowed as they approached the crowd of well-wishers gathering behind some barricades on the platform. Only those travelling were permitted to cross behind those barriers. Clement reached for his papers, then taking his suitcase from Charles, turned to face Geraldine.

'It seems rather congested from here on, so perhaps I should leave you here.' Clement thrust out his hand to Charles who grasped it firmly. 'Thank you, Charles. Look after your mother.'

'You don't need to worry about that, Reverend Wisdom.' Charles flashed a brief smile, the gesture awkward and without joy. Clement knew why. During their many talks of an evening, Charles had expressed his gnawing guilt at having a restricted occupation which prevented him from joining up with other men he knew. Clement caught his eye. 'What you're doing is helping to keep our ships at sea, Charles. It's just as important as any other occupation.'

'I suppose so. Making ship's engine parts means I'm not ever likely to be on the front line.'

'Glad to hear it!'

'Do you have the chess set?' Charles asked.

Clement tapped his suitcase. 'Thank you for it. I'm sure it will get much use on the long journey ahead.' He turned to Geraldine. 'Thank you so much for putting up with me all this time. I'm embarrassed at how long I've stayed.'

'Not at all, Clement. Our pleasure. And not your fault. It's to be expected that fighting men would take precedence. But truth be told, I've enjoyed your time with Charles and me. A little touch of home. I'm so grateful to you for coming all this way.' She paused, her gaze on her hands. 'I know you did your best for Reg. And knowing that he lies in the graveyard in Fearnley Maughton is a real blessing. So many women have no idea where their husbands' bodies lie.'

Clement saw the woman's eyes well up.

'But enough of my troubles,' she said, sniffing. 'I know you miss Mary as much as I miss Reg. One day this madness will be over and, God willing, we'll both be alive to see our village again. I'm sure it won't have changed that much.' She hung her head. 'Somehow, I knew Reg had died. I can't tell you what it means to me that you were with him at the end.' She looked up and smiled. 'It helps, Clement. Knowing you were there.'

The memory of Reg's death flashed in Clement's mind. He hadn't told Geraldine any details. He couldn't. Reg's death had been brutal, but it wasn't the only reason for concealing the truth; that mission, like everything Clement did for the Secret Intelligence Service was classified and could never be repeated, even to the closest relative.

'May the peace of God be with you.' Clement placed his suitcase on the ground then kissed Geraldine on the cheek. 'I should go. I don't want to miss it after waiting all these months for a berth. Goodbye to you both. And thank you again for putting up with me for so long.' Clement picked up his suitcase then turned and strode towards the barrier and the waiting guard. Showing his ticket and papers to the man, he made his way towards the gangway.

A crowd of embarking RAAF stood waiting to board, the gangway congested, their excited voices raised and raucous. Clement hung back, allowing the young airmen to climb aboard first. Beside the gangplank, next to an official in civilian clothes, were two military policemen and for one second, Clement wondered why they were there. He glanced back over his shoulder. Geraldine waved, her handkerchief in her hand. Clement smiled to her, then he saw Charles escort his mother away. Goodbyes were never easy. Inching forward, he held his papers ready to show the official.

The man stepped forward, his gaze on Clement's clerical collar. 'Papers, please!'

Clement handed them over.

The official turned to the military policemen. 'This is him!'

'This way, thank you, Reverend,' one of the military policemen said. Stepping forward, he took Clement's papers and ticket.

Clement blinked several times. 'Is there a problem?'

'If you'll come this way, Reverend.'

The other policeman reached forward and took Clement's suitcase from his hand.

'Am I being detained for something?' Clement protested, aware of the men's slightly intimidating presence beside him.

'If you'll just come with us, sir,' the first policeman said.

Clement walked between the two large men along the wharf towards a flight of stairs at the end of the long two-storey overseas terminal building. He glanced back over his shoulder but other than a few raised eyebrows, no one on the wharf had taken much notice of him. Taking the steps, the men escorted him up; one in front, the other behind. He glanced at the assembled crowd below, his eye searching for Geraldine or Charles. But he couldn't see them. At the top, the first man opened a door and Clement stepped inside what appeared to be a waiting room. It was decorated in the art deco style and spoke of another era when ships and journeys meant elegance and frivolity. Only one person was there. He stood when Clement entered. He was tall, well-built with dark hair, thin lips, and a broad, amiable face and wore a well-tailored suit and a mackintosh coat. Clement had no idea who he was. Yet despite the pleasant countenance, there was a seriousness to the man's expression. Clement heard the door close behind him, the two military policemen disappearing down the stairs.

'I cannot think why you have apprehended me. I have all the necessary papers to make the journey. Is there a problem?'

'Major Wisdom?' the man said, stubbing out a cigarette.

Clement caught his breath. That the military policemen had called him *Reverend* was no surprise in view of his clerical collar, but that this man had used Clement's military title was unexpected. 'I am.'

'Allow me to introduce myself. I'm Commander Rupert Long. I'm Director of Naval Intelligence and in charge of the Combined Intelligence Operations Centre here in Australia. And we need your help.'

'I'm sorry. I'm due back in London. I work…'

'We know who you work for. In fact, Sir Stewart Menzies contacted me yesterday and told me you'd be here.' Long smiled. 'I've been informed you have a *Most Secret* security clearance. Other duties are on hold for a while, Wisdom. There's a war on, you know.'

'I am aware of that, Commander.'

'However, what you may not know, Major, is that a war here, in the Pacific, is imminent. We have a situation on our doorstep and your name has been put forward.'

9

'By whom?'

Long laughed. 'I was told you were a proper old gent. The reverend disguise is a goodie.'

'That's because I am a reverend, Commander.'

'And, from all accounts, a minister with certain skills I need right now.'

'What's this all about?'

'In a nutshell, Major, the Japanese are coming. Faster than many expected. And Singapore is in the firing line. The Far East Combined Bureau, the Intelligence and Cryptology Centre in Singapore is to be relocated to Colombo but, typically, only those directly assigned to them are going. Anyone else must find their own way out. This is a dangerous situation, Major. The FECB have direct access to the Government Code & Cypher School in England. Sir Stewart has informed me you know of that facility, so you will see why the FECB are in a hurry to leave.'

'I don't know anyone in Singapore nor anything about the place.'

'It's possible you do.'

Clement waited. He didn't know what or who Commander Long was referring to, but he sensed he was about to learn.

Long went on. 'We need you to identify someone and, when you have, get him out. This is top priority, Wisdom. We need this particular someone.

'And who is it?'

'Captain John Winthorpe.'

Clement's eyebrows rose involuntarily. 'Johnny's in Singapore?'

'By that remark I'll take it you know him. He's carrying some top-secret intelligence, so we need to get him out. And Sir Stewart Menzies, no less, said you could do the job.'

'He isn't going with the others of FECB to Colombo?' Clement asked feeling that Commander Long was holding something back.

'No. He must escape another way. FECB personnel amount to about fifty people with tons of secret files and equipment. If they were targeted, Captain Winthorpe could either be killed or taken prisoner. And flying Captain Winthorpe out was considered too dangerous. Should his aircraft but engaged and shot down, we would lose not only him but also what he's carrying.'

'What do you want me to do?'

'Good man! First, we must get you to Melbourne. You need to meet some people. After that you'll fly to Darwin. Then it's by boat to Singapore. There just isn't a huge amount of time, Major. I just hope it won't be too late.'

'What do you mean, too late?'

Long paused. 'Menzies has told me you've signed the Official Secrets Act in England?'

'That is correct.'

Several seconds passed before Long spoke again. When he did, his voice was low and quiet. 'As we speak, the Japanese Fleet are steaming down the east coast of

Indochina. Any day now, it is expected they will invade Siam and Malaya, as well as other sites around the Southwest and Southeast Pacific. And they're not finished yet. It's been a busy twenty-four hours, Major, and we suspect it is only going to get busier. You would recognise this Captain Winthorpe? Perhaps I should say, would he recognise you?'

'Of course. I've known Johnny for years.'

'Good. Everything now depends on speed.' Long indicated a door on the other side of the room and together they left the bygone era waiting room and descended the steps to a car parked on the land side of the terminal. Through the barriers Clement could see the last of the passengers boarding. He sensed he wouldn't be returning to England any time soon and Shetland would have to wait. Clement opened the car door and climbed in.

'By the way, Wisdom, I didn't ask; can you swim?'

'I grew up on the English coast so while I'm not a strong swimmer, I can swim, if needed.'

'Good. I don't need to worry about you drowning then.'

Clement stared at the old buildings clustered around Circular Quay and the back streets in the area known as The Rocks. He couldn't begin to think why he would be swimming. But whatever it was they wanted him to do would obviously involve a sea crossing. The car climbed up a steep hill where warehouses lined both sides of the road. Charles Naylor worked in one of the machine shops around the wharfs, but Clement didn't know which. It was, however, a typical waterfront area, with old warehouses and workmen's public houses with names like *The Hero of Waterloo* that seemed more at home in England than in Australia.

The car drove on through city streets, the elegant, triple-storey government buildings and double-storey commercial premises of Sydney's business district giving way to factories as the car approached the airport; a large flat area with a small shed-like structure at the end of a narrow road. The car pulled up and Commander Long got out. Clement reached for his suitcase and followed Long into the building.

Through the glass partitions, he could see the tarmac, but he couldn't see any aeroplanes. He'd flown only twice before, and he wasn't looking forward to his third flight. He didn't really know how far away Melbourne was, but he knew Australia to be a huge country and distances would be great.

'This way, Wisdom. We don't need tickets. There's an RAAF plane waiting to take us.'

'How far is it?'

'Just a couple of hours. Ever flown before?'

'Yes. Uncomfortable and very cold.'

'I'll remind you of that when you're back from Singapore. It's pretty close to the equator there, you know. Hot and wet this time of year.' Long strode towards a door and holding it open, they stepped outside. A warm wind blew into Clement's face as they crossed the tarmac, the heat reflecting off the metal building and rising from the tarmac making it shimmer in the hot afternoon temperatures. He glanced at the sky as they walked directly to the waiting aeroplane. Far out to the west clouds were gathering. Most days during the brief summer he'd experienced in Sydney, it stormed in the afternoons. Clement rather liked it; it cooled the heat of the day making the evening temperatures balmy and everything felt washed and clean. But he wasn't sure about flying in a thunderstorm. Long clearly didn't see it as a problem. Clement checked his watch. Two o'clock. Perhaps they would be well away from Sydney when the afternoon storm struck.

Clement climbed the small ladder into the aircraft. He thought it the same as the one he'd flown in before when he and Johnny had flown from Cambridgeshire to Hampshire earlier in the year. But if it was the same type of aeroplane, this one was set up for passengers not parachutists. Settling into his seat in the rear of the plane, he buckled his seat belt and stared through the porthole. He had no idea what the future held.

The plane moved forward and taxied some way out onto the airstrip before stopping; the engines roaring, the feeling of contained power making the aeroplane throb. Then it lurched forward, thundering along the strip before lifting off. He looked out the window as the sparkling waters of Botany Bay disappeared from his view.

Clement settled back as the plane climbed higher. Soon they were above the clouds, the threatening thunderstorm no longer on his mind. He would have liked to know more about what they wanted him to do but the aeroplane's noise was sufficient to make conversation difficult, if not impossible. Besides which, whatever it was, Clement knew it would be top secret and not for the ears of pilots to overhear. In the seat across from Clement, Long leaned his head against the small glass window, his eyes closed. Clement's gaze returned to his own window. He watched the sun setting in the west, the gathering clouds below him turning pink at the edges in the afternoon glow.

It had all happened so quickly. One minute he was standing on the quay about to board a ship to Canada, the next he was on an aeroplane bound for Melbourne. But the biggest surprise was that Johnny was in Singapore. He tried to visualise the tropical island, but he knew almost nothing about it. He'd read that the small island off the tip of the Malay peninsula was considered to be impregnable. There was, reputedly, a large British community there and it was the foremost British Military base in Southeast Asia. He also remembered that Johnny had told him that he'd been born in Singapore. Was that why Johnny was there? Clement didn't know if Johnny had spent any time there in his youth and had no idea about the whereabouts of the man's parents. Regardless, the island was considered a British bastion. That the Japanese were threatening to invade it seemed unimaginable. Clement thought about the FECB. He hadn't known that the GC&CS had a far eastern branch. That they were evacuating didn't bode well for Singapore or the future of the British garrison there. Nor, in fact, for Johnny Winthorpe.

2

Melbourne, Australia - 5th December 1941

Clement stared out as the plane circled to land. The airport was small, more an airfield than an airport and from what Clement could see, it didn't appear to be a military installation. In fact, cows grazed in adjoining fields. The plane landed then taxied towards a hangar. Five minutes later, Clement and Long alighted.

The first thing Clement noticed was the temperature. It was cooler and the tarmac didn't radiate heat. He checked his watch; it was just after four. Long strode ahead of Clement towards a car parked beside a hangar. A young woman wearing a Naval uniform got out of the driver's seat and, coming around the car, opened the rear door. Smiling at him, she took his suitcase and placed it into the boot. Clement climbed in, Commander Long beside him.

'I expect you have a few questions, Major, but I'll ask

you to keep them to yourself until we get to the barracks.'

Clement nodded.

The young women got in and they drove away. He kept his eye on the passing scene. Unlike Sydney, Melbourne seemed more widespread, the town centre built on either side of a large, brown river. Crossing it, they passed a park of considerable size then moments later, drove through a gate, the car stopping outside a three-storey, grey stone building covered in Virginia creeper. A flight of steps led to the front door.

Long leaned forward to speak to the driver. 'Can you arrange a room for Major Wisdom in the barracks?'

'Of course, Commander,' the young woman said.

'Major, you can stay here tonight. It won't be luxurious but at least you don't have planes bombing you. Not yet anyway.' Long checked his watch. 'Are you hungry?'

'I am rather.'

'We can eat in the Mess soon, but first I'd like to introduce you to someone. Leave your suitcase with Leading WRAN McManus, she'll see it gets to your accommodation and will let you know where to go.'

Clement smiled at McManus. Under normal circumstances he wouldn't dream of asking a woman to carry his suitcase, but he could see the girl was that capable sort of young woman which nothing appeared to daunt. He followed Long up the stairs and into Victoria Barracks.

They walked along a corridor, crossed a courtyard and went into a red brick building at the rear. On the first floor, at the back of the building, Long pushed open a door. Inside was a small, cluttered office where a man sat at a desk, his head down. He appeared to be pouring over a page of scribbled notes. The man looked up as he as Long entered.

'Nave. This is Major Wisdom from London. Clement, this is Commander Eric Nave, Royal Navy, but on permanent secondment to us and currently involved in code breaking activities.'

Eric Nave stood. 'I'm pleased to meet you, Major.' Nave looked across at Long, a quizzical expression forming on his face.

'Ah!' Long said. 'The clerical collar. Don't let that fool you, Nave. Wisdom here is with MI6, Special Duties.'

'SIS? Oh, yes! Of course. Now I understand.' Nave seemed to be threading thoughts together.

Clement wished he could, although he believed he soon would.

Long went on, 'I thought, Eric we could have dinner together and you can tell Major Wisdom a little about what you're doing?'

'Of course. I'll let the others know.'

'That can wait till tomorrow. Tonight, it'll just be the three of us.'

'As you wish, Cocky,' Nave said.

Clement thought Eric Nave seemed the quintessential academic. Even the strange nickname he'd used for Commander Long had been said without the slightest disrespect intended and neither had Long chastised him for it.

'We'll see you in the Mess, Eric,' Long said.

'Yes, Cocky. I'll just finish up here.'

Long led Clement downstairs and into the Officer's Mess. It was a pleasant room and could easily have been in any British Military establishment in England rather than on the opposite side of the world.

'Drink before dinner?' Long said.

'I wouldn't say no.'

'What's your poison?'

'I never used to drink much. Sherry or the like. But living in Sydney for the past five months has given me a taste for cold beer.'

'You do surprise me. I was in England once. Went there after Naval College. Took a year for me to get used to room temperature beer.'

Clement smiled.

'Ah! Here's Eric.'

Nave sat down and Clement listened as Long told him about what went on in Victoria Barracks. Clement was surprised to learn that at one time, the barracks had held the Australian government, until the nation's capital had been relocated to a place called Canberra. Nowadays Victoria Barracks housed the Royal Australian Naval Signals Intelligence Unit and Nave, along with some clerks, had been installed there as a cryptographer where he was receiving Japanese messages via the RAN radio intercept stations based in Canberra and Darwin. From those early days, the unit had developed into the Special

Intelligence Bureau where Nave had continued to work on Japanese codes.

Long leaned back in the chair. 'We have a small group here, Wisdom. It's taken a while for the powers-that-be to agree to the formation of the Secret Intelligence Bureau, but here we are, even if a bit late. And with some others now working with Eric, we've moved on from commercial codes to the Japanese Diplomatic and Naval codes.'

Clement also learned that Commander Eric Nave, who had been born in Australia, had spent time in Japan and spoke Japanese fluently having been posted there to learn the language and customs. But with his relocation from Far East Combined Bureau based in Hong Kong to Singapore, he'd developed a serious illness and the doctors had forbidden him to return to the tropics. The British had wanted him at the Government Code & Cypher School at Bletchley Park in Britain but with the assistance of an Australian Admiral, Long had been able to keep the intelligent code breaker in Australia.

'Major,' Long began, 'Eric's made real inroads into the Japanese Diplomatic and General Operational codes. But recently there have been a few unexpected changes. Never a good sign. The Americans too are interested in these as well as the British. They're now calling the Japanese Naval code, JN25 and its new variant, JN25B. Eric will tell you more about it tomorrow. Suffice to say for your purposes, a rather brilliant mathematician in GC&CS has made some considerable progress with it and we are keen to see what's been learned.'

'And Johnny has this information in Singapore?'

'That's about the size of it. Contrary to circulated belief, particularly in Singapore amongst the British garrison there, I believe the Japanese will prove to be formidable opponents. Not at all the apathetic or second-rate soldiers we've been led to believe. We know from our network of Coastwatchers around the Pacific that they already have a wide and intricate intelligence network established throughout Malaya and Singapore as well as in the Dutch East Indies and the islands further to the east. And all this was set up before any impending hostilities. Very clever really. Then, around August this year and because of growing fears about Japanese expansionist policies, the Americans and the Dutch began imposing embargoes on their oil supplies. The Japanese understand the need for reliable supply lines and if they cannot get sufficient oil from traditional sources, they will simply take it by force. Between us and Singapore, Clement, is the complicated network of thousands of islands collectively known as the Dutch or Netherland East Indies. Most are inhabited and not necessarily friendly with us. I mention this labyrinth of islands because there are several Dutch oil refineries operating there. You can understand now, Major the strategic significance of these islands to the Japanese. And the British in Singapore lie between where the Japanese currently are in Indochina and the Dutch East Indies. Singapore for them is either a stepping-stone or a fortified barrier and one they must take if they are to get to that oil. Moreover, it would also seem they have not heard of the Geneva Convention. They have a secret police force known as the Kempeitai who are as ruthless as any Gestapo Unit. To complicate the issue, the Dutch East Indies indigenous population isn't especially friendly to European faces. And, generally speaking, they have a limited loyalty to the Dutch. But while the Japanese are beginning to take a keen interest in this part of the Pacific, there is one island of strategic importance for our purposes that belongs to the Portuguese. And that is Timor.'

'So it's neutral?' Clement said.

'It should be, but Lisbon is a long way away and the Japanese won't care too much about neutrality, if they want something, they take it. For now, the leader there is predisposed to us, but unfortunately, most of the indigenous populations elsewhere will support whoever pays them the most. Or who gives them what they want. In a way, it's understandable. These are poor countries. We have a very extensive network of Coastwatchers in place around the South Pacific, and have had for some time, but it's fragile. It relies on secrecy and volunteer tele-radio operators and once their full-time jobs no longer exist or the Japanese get too close, they'll be gone and so will our reliable intelligence source. They use a code system and one frequency for transmission but for an experienced codebreaker, it may not take long to crack it.'

'And you're sure the Japanese are coming south?'

'Eric, tell Major Wisdom the intercept you noted a couple of weeks ago.'

Nave leaned forward; his voice measured. 'On the 19th of November, Major Wisdom, I decoded a message from Tokyo to all Japanese Embassies. It was to alert all their diplomatic staff to where the forthcoming attacks would take place. This was done so that they could destroy their code books and sensitive correspondence in advance of any strike. The relevant message would be inserted into a news broadcast but in the form of a weather report. If the Japanese intend to attack the United States, the message would read, *East Wind; Rain*. If they intend to attack the Soviet Union, it would be *North Wind; Cloudy* and if they intend to attack British territories the message would read, *West Wind; Clear*. Yesterday, I decoded the *West Wind; Clear* broadcast.'

'Dear Lord! Do we know when?'

'No. But it won't be long,' Long said.

3

Melbourne - 6th December 1941

Clement walked into Eric Nave's small office at nine o'clock. Grouped around Eric Nave's desk were six men and four women. Long introduced them.

'Clement, Eric Nave you've met. This is Professor Room, Lt Commander Merry, Lt Miller, Jim Jamison, and Lt Commander McLaughlin formerly of FECB Singapore. Miss Copeland, my private secretary, Miss Eunice Robinson and Miss Esmé Berridge, who both work for Eric, and Miss Alice Ferguson our recent arrival from Singapore who is assisting Professor Room and is one of our few Japanese linguists. I also hear she is a dab hand at Morse code and the Japanese version of it, Kana Morse. Everyone, this is Major Clement Wisdom. And don't let the clerical collar fool you. He's trained in guerrilla fighting techniques with Special Duties in England.'

Everyone nodded and smiled.

Clement took the only unoccupied seat in the cramped space.

Long stood before them. 'As I said last night, Clement, we have a situation in Singapore. We estimate that the Japanese could be on the island sooner than expected. Of course, the Royal Air Force is in Malaya and there is the British garrison in Singapore. I have also been informed that Churchill has sent a Naval Task Force comprising the brand-new battleship HMS *Prince of Wales*, the battle-cruiser HMS *Repulse*, the aircraft carrier *Indomitable* and four destroyers. Two of these ships arrived in Singapore four days ago. The *Indomitable* unfortunately ran aground in the West Indies, so isn't there yet. That leaves the fleet which is there rather unprotected except by RAF bases in Malaya where there are no Hurricanes or Spitfires. While it is expected the Japanese will attack by sea, it is possible a small force could invade from the north through Malaya. But the Japanese would have to wipe out the RAF in Malaya first. Worst case scenario, they could be in Singapore inside two months. Fighting would be fierce and at close quarters. FECB is based on the northern coast of Singapore, at the Naval base in Seletar, so it was deemed prudent for FECB to leave. This will take a little time, but I understand arrangements are currently being made.

'Will they be coming here?' McLaughlin asked.

'No. Our Communications Commander has declined their kind offer to come and take over from us both here and in all our intercept stations. While it would have been useful for them to be here, he believes we are quite capable of doing all that needs to be done.'

Jamison let out a stream of air from his lips. 'Egos! They'll get us all killed.'

'I am trying to unite us into one intelligence-disseminating unit but as Jamison says, personalities on all sides get in the way. So no, FECB is not coming here. They are going to Colombo, I believe. Personally, I think it's an interim move, but we shall see. However, we have learned that anyone not on the active FECB muster has been told to get themselves out of Singapore. To this end, we are to welcome a whole raft of new people to assist us. Miss Ferguson, here, is one of the first to arrive.'

'Although I didn't work at FECB, Commander.'

'Indeed. Miss Ferguson grew up there and speaks many languages. One of which, happily for us, is Japanese. However, among the people trying to leave is an Englishman, a Captain John Winthorpe, who is known personally to Clement here. Any intelligence you intercept concerning Singapore is to come immediately to me. I need to be constantly updated about events on that island, day and night. The minute something happens there could define what we ask Major Wisdom to do.'

'Cocky, things are changing daily. How do we reach Major Wisdom with any updated intelligence?' Nave asked.

'He'll go to Darwin first then to Timor. We can contact him through the intercept station *Coonawarra* in Darwin or through David Ross in Dili. But we don't have long. If he doesn't leave in the next few days, it could be too late.'

Clement shook hands with the men and the women gathered around the table. He was beginning to understand what they wanted him to do and staying in touch with assistants and secretaries, so Clement had learned, cut corners, and almost always netted a better result.

That night Clement prayed for his future and for Johnny's. If Long's predictions were correct, the island wouldn't be in British hands for much longer. It was vital to get Johnny out as fast as possible, especially if this Kempeitai were anything like the Gestapo. Anyone of a high rank would be the among the first to be shot. But anyone from Naval Intelligence would undergo ruthless interrogation first. Clement closed his eyes and prayed for what lay ahead.

Rising, Clement washed and dressed then went to the Officer's Mess. Nave was there, sitting at a table in the corner. In Clement's opinion, Nave was an unassuming man, but evidently an intelligent one. Although in the Royal Navy, Nave, so Clement believed, was an odd mix of career Naval Officer and academic. Clement guessed him to be in his forties. He'd learned from Long that Nave had recently married and for the sake of his health was more than happy to remain in Melbourne pouring over codes and cyphers.

'Good morning, Eric. May I sit with you?'

'Yes, of course, Clement.'

Clement silently thanked the Lord for his meal; cereal followed by eggs and bacon. He lifted his knife and fork. Eggs and bacon! Such a treat! He thought of the rationing in Britain. It all seemed so far away, which he knew to be true, but this time the enemy wasn't Germany but Japan; a nation of people he knew little about.

'I understand you lived in Singapore, Eric?'

'Yes. Singapore is a wonderful place, Clement. Exciting and bristling with life. Although, I think it likely that the old days of the British living a life of indulged luxury in the Far East are over. They have created an attitude, even a torpor of superiority and complacency. I dread to think what may befall them. I've been deciphering the Japanese Diplomatic codes for some time but this Operational Code, JN25B is difficult. They modify it quite regularly but recently, as Cocky said, they've changed it. I need as much help as we can get from any source. It's not an easy thing. And too much for one man and a few assistants.'

'What exactly is Kana Morse?' Clement asked, remembering Long's description of Miss Ferguson's abilities.

'It's like Morse code but Japanese doesn't have a Romanised alphabet, so Kana is syllabic. Most Morse code operators can do it quite proficiently. It just takes a little practice. I simply need more of them.'

'From what Long said you're about to get more help.'

'Yes. I hope so but Jamison is right. Egos get in the way. I've never understood political rivalries. For all our sakes, we need to know what the Japanese are intending to do and more importantly, where they are. This isn't like the European theatre. In my opinion, the Pacific War will be won or lost at sea and the ocean is a vast place. Almost impossible to know exactly where the enemy is, let alone where they are going. They could be a few miles off your starboard bow but if they're over the horizon they'll never be engaged. And that could be disastrous. Intelligence is the key to knowing where they *will* be. That's the vital thing. Then getting the ship's captains to believe it and act on it.'

Clement thought he heard desperation in Nave's voice. Doubtless the man had experienced firsthand the stultifying effect of not sharing or, worse, not believing vital information. 'You must know a good deal about Singapore?'

'It's just a small tropical island with a lot of jungle. But its location makes it strategic. There are Chinese, Malays, British, Indians, Javanese and Dutch all crammed into an island about twenty miles across.' Nave looked up and stared into Clement's face. 'The weather is very warm, Clement. There are only two seasons: dry and wet. And you'll be going there in the wet season. It rains almost all the time and it's more of a deluge than a shower. It brings the mosquitoes out too, I'm afraid.

Best to keep your sleeves rolled down and wear long trousers. Drink tonic when you can. The quinine in it helps with warding off malaria.'

From the corner of his eye, Clement saw Rupert Long enter the Mess. Nave glanced at Long who was standing about fifteen feet away at the breakfast buffet. 'Be careful, Clement,' Nave said, then quickly added, 'what this Captain Winthorpe has is more important than anything or anyone else. He can't be allowed to fall into Japanese hands.'

'I'll do my best,' Clement said, watching Nave stir some sugar into his tea. In Britain, sugar was impossible to buy and cane sugar non-existent. While he didn't take sugar in his tea, he'd sprinkled it liberally on his cereal just for the taste.

Commander Long drew a chair out from the table and sat down beside him. 'Morning, Eric, Clement. Sleep well?'

'Not too badly, thank you, Commander,' Clement said.

'I've got you on this afternoon's flight to Darwin. This morning, you can spend some time with Eric. It could be as well for you to understand a little about what Eric does; nothing classified, just a general understanding. Come to my office at noon. We'll go over some details then.' Long finished his tea and left.

Nave and Clement left the Mess and walked straight to Nave's office in the red brick building at the rear. Nave closed the door and sat down behind his desk.

Clement sat on an old wooden chair, upright and distinctly uncomfortable.

Nave leaned forward. 'There isn't much I can tell you about it, Clement. I'm concentrating currently on the Japanese Diplomatic and Naval codes. As I said, the one concerning me at the moment is this JN25B7. It's used in about seventy percent of all Japanese Naval communications so you can see why we'd like to solve this one. It's a five-digit, double-enciphered code, with a superimposed numerical additive that's applied in a certain way and an indicator system. I say 'B' because there is an earlier version, simply named JN25 which we've renamed JN25A to differentiate. JN refers to the Japanese Navy, the number 25 is the one given to naval codes. The end letter refers to the code book in use and the end number is for the additive tables. It's quite extraordinary really. There are between thirty and forty thousand substitutions for the characters in the code books. Ten days ago, and sooner than usual, they introduced a variation to the code. So now we're calling it JN25B7 not JN25A7. Never a good sign when things change unexpectedly. Although, oddly, they have not changed the additive tables.' Nave suddenly paused; his eyebrows lifted. 'Could be their big mistake.' Nave looked up and smiled at Clement. It was as though he'd just remembered Clement was there, or so Clement thought.

'Well, I'll show you what I'm doing but I'm afraid it won't yield you anything of a practical nature. But, if there were trouble and your contact could only tell you about it, it may make sense to you if you have some knowledge of how it works.'

They sat at Nave's desk, Clement leaning over Eric's shoulder. But Nave was an expert and Clement's mind struggled to follow the man's workings. By the time the clock on Nave's wall struck midday, Clement felt more confused than if he'd never heard of JN25, A or B. He checked his watch and saw that Nave kept his wall clock running five minutes fast. 'I should leave you, Eric. Thank you for showing me your work.'

Nave stood. 'I hope it's helped. Good luck to you, Clement.'

Clement shook the man's hand. He felt like he'd met a kindred spirit in Nave but there was no time for building friendships. Another friend was in the thick of looming danger and Clement needed to leave. He smiled at Eric Nave then turned to exit.

Clement went to Long's office in the grey stone building at the front of Victoria Barracks. The door was open. Clement looked in. The Commander was standing, staring out of the window, his shirt sleeves rolled up and his braces in full view. His hands were in his pockets, and he was rocking slightly on his heels. Clement saw Long's cap on a stand in the corner. His naval jacket hung over his chair. Long was deep in thought. Clement knocked.

Long turned around. 'Ah! Wisdom. Won't you sit down?' Long lit a cigarette and offered the box to Clement.

'I've never developed the taste for them but thank

you all the same, Commander. When do I leave?' Clement asked.

Long sat down and drew a file from a stack on his desk. 'You'll fly out this afternoon for Darwin where you'll overnight. You'll be met by Sergeant Tom Archer who will take you to the hotel. Archer's a useful chap to know. He's with Signals and he'll go over the plan with you. The next morning, you and Archer will take a Qantas Empire Airways flying boat to Dili in Timor. One goes every day. Our agent in Dili is David Ross. He's ex-Navy himself and he'll meet you at the wharf there. After that John Whittaker, Ross's assistant, who is an undercover agent with the Royal Navy, and a radio operator, will arrange your onward movement.'

'Are these men aware of my mission?'

'In part, yes. They'll know where you're going, obviously, and that you're going there to collect someone but not why and no names. Need-to-know, you understand. Whittaker will get a signal to me when you arrive and once you've left. You'll need to be on high alert there. While the Portuguese Timorese are pro-us at the moment, it is a dangerous place. There's a Japanese Consulate there, only opened in October and we know they're attempting to purchase the island, which would make it impossible for us to operate there. There are also numerous Japanese spies and sympathisers passing on information in the area and strangers draw immediate attention. The flying boat's arrival will certainly be watched. Your cover is that you are a photographer for a Melbourne newspaper wanting to do a short feature about Portuguese Timor. You'll have a camera with you, but you'll need to keep it on you at all times, even at night. Photograph anything you think important or anyone who looks Japanese. Covertly, of course. Needless to say, Clement, you cannot be wearing your clerical collar. Once you're there, Whittaker will arrange your onward movement and you'll meet up with the team from Australia who are already on their way to Timor by fishing lugger.'

'How many?'

'You, Archer and two others.'

'When do I meet these men?'

'When you reach Dili, at Ross's place. As soon as Whittaker can arrange it, leave. It will take around twelve days to sail to Singapore and that is if there's no trouble. If you need to contact me, do so through Ross in Dili. Once you leave there, it isn't safe to transmit from ships, so you'll only be able to make contact via a landline. The number I'll give you connects directly with the Dutch Intelligence Unit in Bandoeng on the island of Java. Of course, you'd have to put into a port to make the call. I'll inform them that should they receive a call from you, they are requested to connect you to us here as a matter of urgency. Memorize the number, Clement, but only use it in an emergency.'

'Is it secure to use from the Dutch East Indies and Singapore, if I need to?'

'Yes. Once Bandoeng connects you to us here, it's secure and nothing you say or are told can be overheard.'

'Would you have a map of the area I could see to familiarize myself with the region?'

'Of course. I'll get Miss Copeland, my secretary, to arrange one for you, along with some tidal charts and weather forecasts for Singapore and the Dutch East Indies region.'

Returning to his room, Clement collected his suitcase then returned to the front door where Long was waiting. It surprised Clement that Long, himself, would be taking him to the airport. But Clement suspected that Long would have a reason. Once outside Victoria Barracks, they strode towards a parked car at the front of the grey stone building. In the street, a tram passed but Clement noted the destination board was blank. Only the tram number was there for any would-be passengers. Opposite, council workers were removing street signage and, in the park beyond, a tractor was ploughing up the lawns. It had all the hallmarks of a city preparing for invasion and war. At one time, Clement would have thought it was all a bit premature. But he'd seen how things in Britain had changed when the Nazis threatened invasion back in the summer of 1940.

Long opened the driver's door and climbed in. Clement put his suitcase in the boot then sat in the front passenger seat. The Commander started the engine and drove out of Victoria Barracks, into St Kilda Road. As the car drove away from the barracks, Clement watched the people walking nearby. He saw they'd developed a sense of urgency. People hurried. The tractor was still ploughing the park. And he noted as they drove through the city, shops and offices had drawn black curtains over the windows. It was all reminiscent of another time for Clement. He knew only too well the way fear manipulates life; the anxiety of the unknown but expected casting its gloom over a community.

Long hadn't spoken, which Clement thought uncharacteristic of the man. 'You seem distracted, Commander?'

'What's that! Oh yes. Worrying news. We are receiving information from many of our Coastwatchers around the Pacific about Japanese planes being sighted. It doesn't look good. Keep your eyes peeled, Clement. I can't stress just how important your mission is. Only abort this mission if you really must. We need Winthorpe and what he's carrying out of Singapore.'

Clement heard the urgency. While he would do everything he could to get Johnny out, Clement felt there was something Long wasn't telling him. He remembered Nave's whisper about being careful. Whatever Johnny was carrying, Nave and Long weren't sharing it with him.

'If time wasn't so important, I'd send you out to Swan Island for a run-through with weapons handling and field craft. As it is, I'll take your word for it that you can handle yourself in a crisis.'

'While I am getting older, as we all are, I've already had to test my survival skills too many times. So far, so good.'

'Glad to hear it.'

They drove into the airfield and Long pulled up near the hangar. 'Sergeant Tom Archer will meet you when you land and take you to the hotel in Darwin. He'll have everything you'll need for this mission and some more suitable clothes. Get a good night's sleep, if you can, Clement. You carry your own knife, I understand.'

'Yes. A Fairbairn Sykes. I'm never without it,' Clement replied knowing that Long could only have learned that from C in England.

'I'll leave you here, Wisdom. And thank you for helping us out.' Long reached for a bulky envelope on the car seat beside him. 'Inside is a camera and film along with the map you requested. I've also included relevant tide charts and weather information. In the small envelope is the direct telephone number for Miss Copeland, if you need to make contact. She has been informed that if you call, she is to assist you as a matter of priority. Only use it if absolutely necessary. Memorise it, Wisdom, then destroy it.' Long reached forward and grasped Clement's hand. 'I'll look forward to seeing you again here with Captain Winthorpe. God be with you, Clement.'

'And with you, Commander.'

As Clement walked across the tarmac, he could see the pilot sitting in the cockpit. He climbed the steps and entered the plane. He'd noted before how the air inside an aircraft always felt close. Putting his suitcase in the compartment near the cockpit door, he settled himself into a seat. Securing his seat belt, he closed his eyes; he knew the flight would be the longest he had ever taken and would need at least one refuelling stop halfway across the massive continent. Commander Long had told him he would arrive in Darwin around midnight. Clement laid his head back on the seat and thought of Eric Nave and his vital secret work as he waited for others to board. In Clement's mind he saw the myriad of numbers and facts Eric worked on day and night. Everyone had a role to play in this war, although he was grateful his wasn't cryptography. As Clement heard the aeroplane door close, he opened his eyes. Through the porthole he saw the steps being rolled away. Other than the pilot, he was the only person on board.

Settling himself in his seat, he waited for the aeroplane to take off. He marvelled it was all becoming second nature to him. Once above the clouds, he opened the large envelope Long had given him. Inside, he could see two thick folded documents he believed would be maps, and a camera with five rolls of film.

Lifting the camera from the packet, he turned it around studying the apparatus. It was quite small and would easily fit into his trouser pocket, the patterned leather around it felt comfortable in his grip. It had a view finder and two dials for rolling the film on and the shutter. Holding it to his eye, he focused the lens with his right index finger. He didn't think it would be too difficult to use. From the small plaque on the back he could see the name; Leica 1. With it were five rolls of 35mm film. Placing the camera and film into his pack to study later, he withdrew the maps. The first was a tide chart with phases of the moon. Leaving it, he withdrew the second map and spread it out on the seat beside him. He stared at the huge distance across the landmass of Australia, from Melbourne in the south to Darwin in the north, then the shorter distance from Darwin to the long strip of land that was the island of Timor. From there, whatever boat had been arranged would have to negotiate the seas where scattered islands of varying size were spread out across the Java Sea. He ran his finger along the sea lanes they would take, past the long stretch of Java and Sumatra on the west and the mighty chunk of Borneo on the east. Finally, Clement located the tiny island of Singapore at the tip of the Malay peninsula. Leaning back in his seat he felt a sigh rising. The daunting enormity of his immediate future was almost overwhelming; twelve days on a boat in hot, inclement weather with a team of men he didn't know.

4

Darwin - 7th December 1941

It had already gone midnight when Clement stepped from the Hudson aircraft. The heat engulfed him like a blast from a furnace and rain was beating down. Drawing his jacket around him, he hunched against the deluge and ran across the drenched strip towards a building about twenty yards away, where lights were blazing in the darkness.

Opening the door, he went inside and shook the rain from his jacket and head. He was wet through. Standing in front of him was a young man, about thirty-something, or so Clement guessed, dressed in a loose-fitting shirt, wide legged shorts and a brimmed hat that had seen better days. He was the only person there. The young man walked towards him. 'Would you be Major Wisdom?' The man shouted over the terrific noise of the falling rain on the corrugated iron roof.

'I am. Sergeant Archer, I'm guessing.'

The sergeant beamed a row of perfect white teeth. He was of more than average height, with dark hair and skin that looked as though he'd lived in the tropics all his life.

'Got a truck outside. Let me carry that for you, Major. I've also got you some more sensible clothes in the truck.'

Leaving the tin-roofed building, they ran towards the parked lorry. Archer nodded towards the passenger door and Clement climbed in. Two seconds later, Archer was behind the steering wheel, Clement's suitcase, and another between them on the seat.

Archer released the brake and the vehicle drove forward. The lorry began to rock violently and rhythmically. Clement reached for the parcel shelf in front of him to steady himself. 'Is something wrong with the lorry?'

'Nah,' Archer shouted, his eyes never leaving the road. 'The tyres don't match, so it's a bit bumpy.'

Clement felt the vehicle stumble along. He wasn't sure if it was tiredness from the journey or the ridiculousness of the situation, but he burst out laughing. He saw Archer turn to look at him, the bemused face spreading into a wide grin.

'I'm sorry, Sergeant. It just seems absurdly funny to me,' he said, his body lurching uncontrollably with the movement of the vehicle.

Archer glanced again at him, 'I heard you're a pom, Major. But you've got a good sense of humour. Goes a long way up here.'

'In view of what we're about to do, perhaps we

should refrain from the military titles. Could get us into all sorts of strife. I'm Clement, by the way.'

'I'm Tom.' And with that the sergeant beamed another wide grin, then thrust his right hand suddenly across his body, towards Clement. 'Nice to meet you, Clem.'

Clement shook the hand, the lorry limping its way over a rough and sodden dirt track.

Archer must have seen his mild concern over letting the steering wheel go on the slippery road. 'Don't worry,' Archer said. 'The tyres are in the grooves now. The road is dirt, or rather mud. We'll slide off soon when we hit the main road.'

'Is the hotel far?' Clement asked, wondering if this mission could end before it'd begun.

'Yeah, not far. It's pretty good for up here and you can have a wash and clean up. But we should go over the plans tonight. Tomorrow you and me are off to Dili on the flying boat. Noisy damn things. Can't talk easily and best we don't. Never know who's beside you.'

Clement listened to the young sergeant. He wanted to correct the young man's grammar, but he thought better of it. He glanced across at the inadequately dressed sergeant as the lorry hobbled and slid its way onto the bitumen heading for Darwin. He thought of British generals who would have reprimanded the sergeant for his attire. But there was something about Archer. Clement got the impression he knew his way about, not only around Darwin, but also around life. Archer was, Clement guessed, that kind of sergeant who is pragmatic, resourceful, and brave. Although a good deal younger, Archer reminded Clement of another resourceful sergeant; one who lay buried in the graveyard of his old church of *All Saints* in Fearnley Maughton, and one Clement would never forget.

Through the torrential rain and the darkness of the night, Clement saw the lights of the Hotel Darwin. From what he could see, it was a long two-storied building with a pitched roof and it looked rather grander than Clement had expected. Opposite was the broad dark expanse of Darwin Harbour.

Archer grabbed the suitcases and together they ran towards the front door of the hotel. Inside and on his right was a large area with green painted columns and a dance floor. Archer pushed open the glass doors and walked towards the bar at the end where a man was tidying up.

'G'day, Tom,' the man behind the bar said. 'Plane's late tonight.' His gaze shifted to Clement. 'You must be Mr Clement Wisdom. I hear you want to take some shots of our neighbours to the north.'

'That's correct,' Clement said.

'This is Bert Stephens, the publican,' Archer said.

Bert came from behind the bar and together they walked through the wide, green foyer towards the hotel reception desk. Bert reached for a key hanging on a board.

'You're a long way from home by that accent.'

'Yes, not sure when I'll get back. Best to make oneself useful in the meantime.'

'Here's your key. Room two is at the top of the stairs, first on your left. Breakfast is at seven here in the lounge.' The man pointed to several tables and chairs inside a room with a sign above the door proclaiming it as *The Green Room*. There, Clement saw numerous cane chairs were grouped around the dance floor. Beyond were some closed double doors that presumably led outside. The windows, which had louvered panels, were open, the panels pointed downwards to deflect the rain. Insect screens covered the windows and above their heads, long paddle-like fans swung back and forth, catching any cross breeze.

'Thanks, Bert. Can we get a drink?' Tom said.

'I suppose so. What'll you have?'

'Beer thanks, Bert. Clem?'

'I'd love a cup of tea, if you can manage it?'

The publican smiled. 'What is it with you pommies and tea? Don't answer. Yeah, you can have a cuppa.'

Tom led Clement to the lounge, and they sat down. Sitting on the chairs, Tom pulled a folded map from his top pocket and spread it out on the low table in front of them.

'We'll take off from Darwin harbour tomorrow morning at eight. The flight's a couple of hours. Can't be more precise than that. It's all weather-dependant. But it shouldn't be too much of a problem.'

'What about lightning? Is that a problem here?' Clement asked, remembering the Sydney afternoon storms.

'Lightning season is almost over. November to early December. So, it's pretty much gone. It's monsoonal now. Flooding is the big wet-season problem. But that won't affect us. We're going by flying boat.'

'And the team?'

'They left yesterday on a fishing lugger for Timor. There's two men; Mick Savage and Hugh Kearsley. Hugh's a pom. He's our signals expert. Mick is our sniper and explosives man. He's strong, tough and a good shot. They've got the weapons and some other surprises with them. Once we get to Dili, we'll meet David Ross. He's the contact there and then there's John Whittaker the radio operator. There's also plenty of Japs in the area.'

Clement leaned forward in the chair, his gaze on the island of Timor. 'Commander Long told me the Japanese have a consulate in Dili.'

'Yeah. And they're not there to chat. Japs are all over these islands,' Archer said, his finger tracing several islands around the immediate area on the map, then Papua New Guinea and the islands further east. 'If they've got their sights on Australia, they've done a good job in setting up bases and spies throughout the islands. And if they give the locals presents, the islanders will tell them what they want to know. We may not be at war with them yet, Clem, but it's coming, and they've been planning it for years, I reckon.'

Clement thought of Eric Nave and the *Winds Message*, as they were calling it, that Nave had intercepted in mid-November. 'I'm inclined to agree with you, Tom.'

Tom went on. 'Whittaker will arrange a fishing boat to take us to Singapore.'

'How long to get there?'

'About two weeks, Clem.' Archer suddenly sat back on the couch. 'You don't mind me calling you Clem?'

'Not at all, Tom,' Clement said, and he meant it. Archer and his ilk, no matter the country of their birth, were the bulk of the Allied fighting forces. Clement remembered reading that the first Duke of Wellington had called such men, the *scum-of-the-earth*. Clement preferred the *salt-of-the-earth* and when it came to fighting, Clement knew who he wanted by his side. Men like Archer who were not impressed by rank or privilege. In fact, Clement considered, it would have the reverse effect. He thought about the people of Australia he'd met; good, honest and hard working. But while he considered that Sydney was small and Melbourne smaller, Darwin was like a holiday camp. Everyone dressed casually and knew each other. In England, in a village, it was the same, but village life survived because of a rigid social order and formality, here it seemed to be the reverse. But it also increased the risk of information being spread. Clement recalled the publican knowing his cover. Secrets had to be kept, if they were to remain secret.

'Does Bert know what you do?'

'No. Bert likes to chat. So, I watch what I tell him.

Not that I'm saying he'd pass anything on. He's not a spy but it's best people like Bert just don't know what can get them into trouble.'

'Very wise, Tom. This boat journey to Singapore, can't it take any less than two weeks? I was told twelve days.'

Archer shook his head doubtfully. 'Same problem. Monsoons, cyclones maybe. While it could be possible to do it in less time, you have to have a bugger factor.'

'Sorry?'

Archer laughed, his perfect teeth gleaming. 'A bugger factor, Clem. Allowances for delays.'

'Right! So, when we get to Singapore, do we go into a harbour?'

'Probably easiest. Then you find your man and we leave.'

Clement nodded. They heard the publican coming towards them. Archer folded the map and returned it to his pocket. Clement drank his tea and Archer swallowed his beer.

'I'll pick you up at half past seven.'

'Thank you, Tom.'

Saying good night to the sergeant, Clement found his room. Removing his damp clothes, he hung them on a stand in the corner and lay naked on the bed. He thought about all that Archer had said. It seemed straight forward enough. The overhead fan whirred, the heat and the impending mission heightened the nerves and made sleep unlikely.

5

Darwin - 8th December 1941

lement stared at the fan above his head. His
heart was pounding from the heat, and he was
in a lather of perspiration. Sleep had been almost impossible and when he had drifted off, he'd
dreamt violently: images of Reg and the bitter cold of
Caithness in winter. He drew in a long breath. Through
the open louvers he could hear the early morning birds
chirping. He reached for his watch; just after five. A second later he heard someone thumping on his bedroom
door. Sitting up, he reached for his dressing gown and
went to open it. Archer stood before him, his face serious, his eyes wide.

'What is it, Tom?' Clement asked, immediately aware
that something terrible must have happened.

'They've bombed Malaya, Singapore and Pearl Harbour! All within hours of each other.'

'Dear Lord! You're sure?' Clement said, ushering

Tom into the room and closing the door to the corridor.

'Got the message about fifteen minutes ago. They reckon we'll be at war with the Japs any day now, Clem.'

'Right. Has Commander Long sent us any change of orders?'

'I've sent a message to Melbourne asking what they want us to do but I haven't received an answer yet. Regardless, you get yourself ready to leave.'

'Will do. I'll see you in the lounge in ten minutes.'

Archer left. Grasping the light-weight clothes Archer had acquired for him, Clement ran down the hall to the men's bathroom and, turning on the shower's cold tap, stood beneath the welcome chill. He closed his eyes, absorbing the coolness and allowing the water to cascade over his head. But the familiar, gloomy pall was descending. It was what he'd felt when Britain had declared war on Germany. Now, it was happening all over again. His mind turned to Johnny. Getting him out now had become complicated; and that was if he hadn't been killed in the bombing raid. Clement wanted to speak with Long. He knew Pearl Harbour was where the American Pacific Fleet was anchored. A significant bombing raid there could cripple America's ability to fight a sea engagement. Surely now the Americans would declare war on Japan and join with the Allies? And with the Americans would come much needed equipment and thousands of men. While this fact was heartening, Clement's immediate concern was for Johnny. Hurrying, he towelled himself dry then returned to his room to dress.

Packing what he thought he needed into one suitcase, he left the room and took both suitcases downstairs to the lounge. Archer stood as he approached.

'I would like to speak to Commander Long, Tom. Can that be arranged?'

'Maybe. But the phone lines will be jammed. We can send a radio message, but we may not get an answer for hours. I'm guessing he'll be pretty busy right now.'

'Of course.'

'Whichever way we try to reach him, getting through before eight could be a problem. Your decision of course, but perhaps we go anyway and contact him from Dili. Even if the Japs are moving south, they won't be in Timor just yet.'

'Right you are.'

Archer checked his watch. 'Let's get some breakfast. Don't know when we'll eat good tucker again. And you can leave your old clothes here with Bert, if you like. He'll look after them.'

Clement smiled. He was learning a whole new vocabulary.

Clement stood with Tom on Town Pier as the daylight increased. From this day on it would be a new era and the future was yet to unfold. Out on the silver bay, the Sunderland flying boat sat moored. It was a peaceful sight. Although Clement thought it unlikely it would remain so. At Clement's feet sat three sealed cardboard boxes Tom had said were necessities. The tide was low, the water about ten or more feet below the jetty. Out in the bay, Clement saw a man jump from the flying boat into a launch. A few moments later the motor started up and the craft slowly approached the pontoon where a small crowd had gathered.

Taking his turn, and clutching his suitcase containing the fragile camera in his left hand, he stepped into the launch. Tom carefully passed each box to the young man in the boat. As they motored out to the aeroplane, Clement glanced over his shoulder and out to sea. Rain clouds were gathering, blurring the horizon. Within the hour, the whole place would be deluged with water. Clement prayed it would hold off at least until they were airborne. When it did come, the day would be dull and the grey shroud that descended over the city would make visibility difficult.

Despite Darwin being small and remote, it was strategically important. Archer had told him about the numerous airfields around the small city and the military installations in the immediate area. Despite the low cliffs around the city, Clement considered the flat land, wide bays and beaches around the area would be a perfect place for an amphibious invasion of Australia. But he wondered if the Japanese appreciated just how vast the continent of Australia was. Invading Darwin was one thing but getting south to the capital, Canberra, another matter entirely and most likely only achieved by air. He looked across to the flying boat, the emblem of Qantas Empire Airways emblazoned on the fuselage.

The young man steering the boat beamed at them. If he was aware of impending war, it didn't seem to disturb him much. The launch slowed as they drew up beside the flying boat. The attendant stood and tied the launch to the moored aircraft. Passing the parcels and luggage to a waiting crew member, Clement and Archer, along with four men wearing light-weight business suits, stepped onboard and the crew went about their departure routine.

'I'm surprised it's still flying,' Clement whispered to Tom as they took their seats.

'Maybe they haven't heard yet. Besides, people still need supplies, and businessmen still do deals.'

'Really?'

'Timor has a lot of clay, sand and gravel. Just the sort of stuff needed to build runways.'

'Right. I think I'm beginning to understand Timor's importance.'

'I'm just glad the team arrived there yesterday,' Archer whispered. 'We must expect the Japs on Timor at the Consulate there to be waiting at the wharf to see who's arriving. Of course, they aren't at war with Portugal, but they'll still be watching us. Just as well we aren't carrying weapons. I'd keep that camera well hidden.'

'You think there'll be a problem?'

'Not really. Besides, they're only interested in the pilot. He supplies them with whisky, crates of the stuff.' Tom tapped the boxes at their feet. 'It'll rot your socks, but they seem to like it. Gets them drunk real quick!'

'Helpful.'

'Too right!'

Clement smiled. While-ever the Japanese officials on Timor consumed illicit whisky, he believed he and his team would be all right. But he did wonder how long that would last.

Clement stared through the porthole and watched the propellers beginning to rotate, each engine starting separately until all four roared with power. As the plane began to move, he watched the waters of Darwin harbour rush past his porthole, the plane bouncing over the small waves, the white spray splashing his window. It was a very strange experience to be moving so quickly over the water, yet, Clement conceded, it was exhilarating. Within minutes they'd lifted off and were climbing quickly. Below he could see the port of Darwin where ships of all sizes were moored, the small town built around the bay. He thought of the Japanese bombers. Darwin would be an easy target.

If Clement had thought the noise of the Hudson was bad, the flying boat was deafening. He stared through the window then checked his watch. Archer had told him the flight would take at least two hours. He closed his eyes.

Just before eleven o'clock, Clement saw the southern coastline of Timor below them. Large verdant mountains fringed the island with only a thin strip of beach along which were dotted several huts. Crossing the coast and flying over the extensive mountain range, they flew through turbulence and above the lush mountainous country to the northern coast. The plane circled low over the jagged mountains then descended quickly, landing on the pristine waters. From his window Clement could see the luxuriant green vegetation of the mountains and the crystal blue of the sea. It was mid-morning, and the day would be warm. The plane skidded along the surface of the bay like a swan landing on the Thames. As it manoeuvred towards the mooring, he saw people gathering on a nearby jetty.

Stepping from the aeroplane to the waiting boat, the heat and humidity hit him like a cricket bat and he audibly gasped. Tom Archer tossed his pack into the boat then lifted the boxes and stowed them carefully onto the dinghy's floor. Clement clutched his luggage, not wanting Archer to throw the suitcase in case the camera's delicate mechanisms were damaged. Looking up he saw two Europeans standing on the jetty behind a group of local Timorese. He knew at least one of these men would be David Ross. Clement sat on the seat beside Archer as instructed by the crew member.

'Whisky?' Clement whispered.

Archer nodded, then with a tilt of his head towards the jetty, indicated three shorter men with jet black hair standing separately from the local people and a little further back along the pier.

'Japanese?' Clement mouthed.

Archer nodded.

'Will they cause us any trouble?'

'Leave the talking to Ross.'

'Have you been here before, Sergeant?'

'Yep!'

Clement didn't probe further. If Commander Long had arranged for Tom Archer to go with him, Clement believed Archer would have experience of the area and its people.

Clement watched the people on the wharf. It was a tranquil scene. Some of the people were there for the plane's arrival. Others were fishing from the pier. And still others were just watching the event. The arrival of the flying boat was evidently a crowd attraction. He could see now why Archer had sent the team separately. No one could arrive by flying boat unnoticed. The tide was coming in so that the pontoon was not too far below the pier. Clement stepped onto the jetty and shook hands with Ross who suddenly embraced him.

'I've told the Japanese you're my brother,' David Ross whispered into Clement's ear. 'Best not to speak unless they stop you. Let me do the talking.'

'Don't worry, I will.'

They walked back along the jetty towards the three Japanese men, Ross laughing and asking questions about their non-existent relatives. He seemed to be avoiding the Japanese glares. Clement had never seen a Japanese man before and he curbed the urge to stare. They were quite short of stature, thin bodied with dark hair and dark eyes. They held a serious, almost impassive expression that was impossible to interpret.

Ross walked beside Clement, his arm wrapped around Clement's shoulder. 'Great to see you. How was the flight? Noisy damn things those flying boats, aren't they,' he was saying.

Clement muttered a response. Ross's arm remained around Clement.

The Japanese man at the end stepped forward. Ross, perhaps anticipating trouble said loudly, 'Tom, give that box to our friends here. Today's a day of celebration. My brother's come to visit.' Tom walked straight up to the man in the centre of the group and held out the box.

The man took it then handed it to the man beside him, his gaze remaining on Clement.

'What's Uncle George been up to lately?' Ross said loudly, ushering Clement and Archer towards an old car. 'Just get in or they'll dream up an excuse to question us about you.'

As the car drove away from the port, rain started falling. Driving through the township of Dili, the deep gutters were already drawing the torrents of water away from the crumbling bitumen. They drove into the hills, the road steep, and the rain heavy.

'It's a good thing it's raining. They'll be inside drinking this afternoon,' Ross said.

'Have my blokes made contact?' Archer asked.

'Yes. They arrived last night. Took a while for them to get over the mountain roads but they're here.'

'Has Whittaker found us a boat?'

'Yes. It's an old Japanese fishing boat run by an Australian who's lived in these parts for years.'

The car wound its way up a dirt road into the hills, stopping outside a house overlooking Dili harbour. It was more Portuguese than Colonial English in design and painted a dark shade of pink with semi-circular, terracotta roof tiles. A mature-aged, Timorese woman met them at the door with a tray of cold tonic waters. Taking a glass each from the tray, Ross led them into his study, a room that overlooked the sea and back towards the jetty. The flying boat was reloading with people, mostly women and children. Clement thought the news of the Japanese bombings would have travelled fast and every seat on the Sunderland booked.

The wide sea view across the water was quickly disappearing into the grey mists of monsoonal rain. Wide enclosed verandas looked out over the bay, keeping the house cooler than Clement had expected. At any other time, Clement would have said Timor was exotic and, in Ross's Portuguese house, even idyllic. But the Japanese consulate in Dili worried him. Their recent arrival and continued presence on the small island had the potential to make life difficult and not only for Clement's mission. If Ross continued to live in Timor, and the Japanese armies moved further south and took control of the small island, he could find himself a prisoner of war.

'Do you have a radio transmitter here, Mr Ross?' Clement asked.

'Yes. Like everyone, we've heard the news.'

'Can we get a message to Commander Long. I'd like to know if he has any further instructions for us?'

'John Whittaker, my assistant and radio operator will be here soon. He will have heard the flying boat arrive. While we wait, I'll get Anita, my cook, to bring us some food. I wouldn't eat the lettuce, Clement. It's washed in local water. Your stomach won't be used to it, and it could make you sick.'

'Anything else I should know?'

'Drink lots of tonic.'

'So I've been told.'

'And don't sleep on beaches,' Archer added. 'A mosquito bite can cause Malaria. If you catch it, you won't get over it, if it doesn't kill you first.'

A knock at the door saw a tall man with dark hair and glasses walk in. David Ross stood to introduce John Whittaker, undercover Royal Navy agent and wireless operator.

'You've heard the news?' Whittaker said, looking at Ross.

'We have. John, this is Major Clement Wisdom. He's been tasked with getting the important Englishman out of Singapore.'

Whittaker nodded to Clement. 'How do you do. What you may not know, David, Major Wisdom, is that the Japs have landed at Kota Bharu in Malaya and they're heading south.'

'What about the Royal Air Force?' Ross asked.

'Old fighter aircraft were no match for Zeros.'

'Destroyed?'

'Totally. The recently arrived British Fleet has put to sea. But the Japs are moving faster than anyone expected. And, with no aerial support, I don't like our chances. This extrication isn't going to be as easy as we first thought. You may not be able to get into Singapore harbour. Perhaps you should consider another point for the rendezvous. I'll try to make contact with Melbourne so you can get any amended instructions. As soon as we hear, you should leave.'

'Agreed. Is there a radio on board the boat taking us to Singapore?' Clement asked.

'Yes. But it's best not to use it unless absolutely necessary,' Whittaker answered. 'You can listen in from time to time but not too long. And transmissions can be triangulated, so you can be located.'

'And Tom's team? Do you know where they are?'

'In town. It was a difficult trip over the mountains last night. Roads are almost impassable due to the rain. They're getting some rest and staying out of sight.'

'If we cannot get into Singapore harbour, we're going to need canoes. At least two but three would be better. And fold-boats better still. Do you know where we could get some?' Clement asked.

'I'll get those,' Archer said. 'Just leave that to me, Clem.'

Clement stared at Archer's face. Something about the sergeant told Clement that he was a very useful man to have on your side. Clement looked at Whittaker. 'This fishing boat that will take us to Singapore, where is it exactly?'

'It's tied up further along the coast around Baucau. It's called the *Krait*. Its owner is a man named Bill Reynolds.'

'Oh! The *Krait*. We'll be fine,' Tom said.

'Do you know this boat, Tom?' Clement asked.

'Yeah. I've seen it in Darwin a few times. It's a good size. Should take us all, no problem. Bill's an Australian but he's lived in these parts for years. Knows it like the back of his hand. Doesn't need charts.'

Ross rummaged in his pocket for his car keys. 'There's an old Burns Philp trading store in town. They may be able to help with the canoes, Tom. I'll go with Archer, John. You stay here with Clement and try to get a message through to Melbourne. And I'll bring Savage and Kearsley back with us.'

'I should come with you, Tom,' Clement added.

'No offence, Clem, but you stick out like dog's balls, mate. You leave it to me. She'll be right.'

Archer left with Ross.

Whittaker was smiling. 'Don't judge him too harshly, Clement. The Australians have little regard for rank or ceremony. But, if I'm right, Archer will be a real asset to you. Men like your sergeant are rough diamonds, but diamonds nonetheless.'

Clement went with Whittaker to Ross's study. Manoeuvring the corner of a tall bookcase away from the wall, Whittaker revealed the radio room. Clement sat beside Whittaker as the man lifted the headset into place then shifted the dial.

'What do you want to say? Try to keep it short.'

'Will you transmit in code?'

'Yes. The Coastwatchers use a specific code called Playfair. We'll send in that and mark it as urgent.'

Clement thought for a minute then dictated the message to Whittaker. 'In view of current circumstances, we await new instructions. Request urgent response. Vicar.'

'Good.' Whittaker opened a book on the desk and encrypted the message. Ten minutes later he sent it.

Clement visualised Long in his office in Victoria Barracks, in his shirt sleeves, staring through his window towards the ploughed-up park and rocking on his feet. Clement hoped the radio receiving station wouldn't delay in getting his message to Long.

The reply came within thirty minutes. That surprised Clement. Long must have made any messages received from Whittaker top priority and told them to telephone anything from Dili through to him. Was that routine with a mission? Or was it just this mission? Clement pondered Johnny's extraction from Singapore. Intuition told him there was more to it than had been confided to him. Whittaker decrypted the answering message.

'Vital you go. Will send rendezvous site and time.'

Whittaker looked across at Clement. 'This person you're going to meet must be top priority!'

'Indeed. Do you think we'll get the information soon?'

'Given the quick response time to this message, I'd say yes.'

Clement wondered if Long was in direct contact with Johnny. If that was so, then Johnny was alive and either in hiding somewhere with access to a radio transmitter or Singapore was still in British hands. Keeping his eye on the clock on the wall in the radio room, Clement watched every minute of an hour tick by. Just after dark, the second message came through. '21st. Keppel Island Pier. Midnight. Green light; three on, two off.'

6

Sunset had come and gone. Its beauty was awe inspiring. An orange orb of fire had spilled its liquid glow over the sea, its spectacular size and colour astounding the senses, turning the land black and the sea and sky pink and gold. But once gone, a darkness like Clement had never seen before enveloped the land. Some hours had passed since Tom and Ross had left and Clement was beginning to worry about them. Outside, he heard several car doors slam. He looked across at Whittaker.

'I'll go,' Whittaker said.

Clement followed Whittaker to the doorway of Ross's study ready to push the bookcase back into place, if required. From where he stood, he could hear what was being said in the front hall. He reached for his knife.

'Everything all right, David?' Whittaker said somewhat loudly, Clement presumed for his benefit.

Clement sheathed his knife and stepped forward, joining Whittaker in the hall.

Ross, followed by Archer and three other men, two of whom Clement guessed would be Savage and Kearsley, stood in the front hall. The third man was tall and held the most eager expression Clement had ever seen. The man seemed to beam with excitement.

'Could you get through to Melbourne?' Ross asked.

'Yes,' Whittaker said. 'Anything going on in town?'

'Dili's a strange mix of excitement and panic, so I'm guessing people have heard the news about Singapore. Everyone's trying to hire boats to take them to Australia.'

'Any trouble with the Japanese?' Clement asked, his gaze still on the tall stranger.

'The Japanese Consulate is lit up like a Christmas tree,' Ross said. 'They're burning something. Smoke is hanging over the consulate like a shroud.'

'Any idea what?' Whittaker asked.

'Code books would be my guess,' Clement said, thinking of Nave.

Ross nodded. 'More than likely. No time to lose, Clement, if you're still going. What did Melbourne say? You can speak confidently in front of this man.'

Whittaker eyed the newcomer. 'The mission goes ahead but there's a new rendezvous site. And Clement and the team must be there on the 21st at midnight.'

'The 21st? And two weeks to get there means you must leave tonight.'

Clement studied the tall stranger. 'We haven't been introduced, I'm Major Wisdom.'

'Yes, sorry,' Ross said. 'These chaps are Mick Savage and Hugh Kearsley. And this is Major Ivan Lyon.'

Clement shook hands with them. 'Thank you for being part of this mission.'

Savage was tall, thin with blond hair and a sandy complexion. The type of man people describe as wiry yet are incredibly strong despite their slim physique. Clement saw that he stood a little behind Archer, his face down as though embarrassed. Kearsley was barrel-chested, of medium height, with a full head of mid-brown hair and intense brown eyes. From his uniform, Clement could see he held the rank of corporal.

'And you have another member of your team, Clement,' Ross said indicating Lyon.

Clement turned to face Ross. 'I cannot take passengers. Especially now it's so dangerous.'

'I think you'll want Major Lyon,' Ross said.

Lyon held out his hand for Clement to shake. 'How do you do.'

'No disrespect intended, Major but I meant what I said. I cannot take passengers.'

Ross smiled. 'Clement, Lyon is based in Singapore. Has been for five years. He's also an amateur sailor and has sailed around most of Southeast Asia.'

'I can be of use to you, Major Wisdom,' Lyon said. 'I've already done a bit of sabotage work in Indochina against the Japanese there.'

'You've met each other before?' Clement asked Ross.

'Not until this day. But I am aware of Major Lyon's activities in the region.'

'How it is you're here in Timor?' Clement asked.

'Having a look about. But I need to get back to Singapore. My wife and child are there. If Singapore falls, they'll be behind enemy lines. So, if you can take me, I'd be grateful.'

'Were you based there or in Malaya?' Clement continued.

'Singapore but I went frequently to the RAF bases in Malaya.'

Clement nodded but he suspected Lyon had more to tell him. He waited until Ross and the others went out to the veranda.

'Would I be correct in saying that your frequent trips, *looking about*, are more to do with watching the Japanese build-up in the South Pacific?'

Lyon faced him. 'They are already among us. It's just a matter of time before they are assembled.'

'Where were you recently?'

'I'd taken a friend's yacht to Fiji, then managed to get a berth out of there to Moresby and from there to Dili. I arrived here two days ago. Ross told me you were heading to Singapore and so here I am.'

'Are you being watched?' Clement asked.

'To be honest, I could be. But perhaps that's only because as a newcomer, they're curious.'

'Could they know you've been spying on them?'

'I'm not carrying any documents or a camera.'

'Doesn't really answer the question, Major.'

Lyon's eyebrows raised. 'It's possible they suspect me of something. But they couldn't prove it. Not that that would stop them, if they wanted to detain me.'

Clement nodded. 'I'd be interested to know anything you can tell me about where we are going and what we are likely to encounter.'

'Of course. Happy to. Just take me with you and you can quiz me all you like.'

They joined the others on the veranda. Clement glanced at his team; men whose lives were in his hands. 'Alright with you, Tom if we take the Major?'

'Yeah, Clem. She'll be right!'

'That's Australian, Clement, for, all is well,' Whittaker said, smiling.

'Very well. Perhaps it's best we use Christian names, if you don't mind, Major?'

'Of course. It's Ivan.'

'You should get going now, Clement,' Ross said. 'Before the Japanese discover Archer has availed himself of some of their equipment. Before you go, I'll give you some maps. I did an aerial survey of Timor some years ago with the flying boat captain. Didn't realise then just how useful they were going to be. Give them to Long once you're done with them.'

Clement looked across at Archer. In view of Ross's comment about the procured equipment, Clement thought it better not to ask Tom about it. Ross returned and gave him a folded map. 'Look at it later. Best of luck to you, Clement.'

'And to you, David.'

Clement shook hands with David Ross. Thanking him, they left Ross's tranquil house overlooking the sea and walked outside. The lack of twilight and the rapid onset of night in the tropics surprised Clement. In the darkness, and behind Whittaker's run-down car, Clement could see a lorry. Without waiting for an explanation from Tom about where or how he acquired it, Clement climbed into the car with Whittaker and Lyon. Archer, Savage and Kearsley went to the lorry.

The twisting dirt track heading north-east to Baucau was not for the faint-hearted. As they rose into the mountains, the slippery track following the escarpment narrowed, making the journey slower and more perilous than Clement would have liked. Every time they rounded a bend, he prayed they wouldn't meet someone coming the other way. Or indeed, that the rain hadn't washed the road away. Once in the mountains, the landscape changed from wide, verdant terraced fields to thick forests. The headlights illuminated huge trees with large girths that towered above them. After almost six hours they crested the hills and descended towards the town of Baucau.

'The town itself is a little away from the wharf, so we shouldn't be observed,' Whittaker said, his eyes fixed on the road ahead.

In the pre-dawn light, Clement could see the old fishing trawler moored in the bay. It was larger than Clement had envisaged but he frowned when he saw the Japanese flag flying from the stern.

Whittaker glanced at Clement. 'Don't let the flag worry you. Bill's just keeping the Japs happy.' Whittaker drove the car down towards the muddy beach and pulled on the handbrake. He flashed the car's headlights twice.

In the pale, early morning light, they saw someone climb from the fishing boat into a dinghy tied alongside and start to row towards the shore. Fifteen minutes later, it pulled up on the muddy beach.

'Bill Reynolds, this is Clement Wisdom. Clement's in charge of the mission, Bill. These men are Ivan, Tom, Mick and Hugh.'

Clement shook Bill Reynolds's hand. The man was older than Clement had expected. His skin was tanned from years of living in the tropics and his white hair was dishevelled. Sitting askew on his nose was a pair of glasses that had been repaired with a large blob of marine glue that had turned yellow with time.

'I understand you want to go to Singapore,' Bill said. 'Could be a bit tricky now. These last few weeks especially, I've seen more than a few Japanese planes overhead. Not attacking anything. Yet. Just reconnaissance, I'm guessing. Can be difficult customers. That's why I fly the *Rising Sun*. Better not to attract trouble.'

'It's good of you to take us.'

Archer now stood beside Clement. 'G'day, Bill. Can

you bring the boat to the wharf? We've got a bit of stuff to load.'

'I'll take one of you and the luggage back with me in the dinghy, then I'll bring her in alongside. Tom, you and your lads get the truck unloaded on the wharf.'

'Right you are, Bill,' Tom said.

'As quietly as possible, please Tom,' Clement said. He turned to face Lyon. 'Ivan, could you go with Bill and help him bring the boat into the wharf? I'm sure you'll be a lot more useful to him than me.'

'Of course, Clement. Happy to.'

Clement joined Whittaker, who waited by his car. 'Thank you, John for what you've done,' Clement said, shaking the man's hand. 'And please thank David again for me. May God be with you.'

'God speed to you too, Clement. I hope all goes well for you and the mission. And don't worry about Ivan Lyon. He's well respected and more than he seems. He's also quite used to evading Japanese patrols.'

'I suspected as much.'

Clement walked back to where Archer and the others were unloading. 'We didn't properly meet earlier,' Clement said in a muffled voice. 'Thank you both for coming along. I'm Clement Wisdom.'

'Mick Savage,' the taller of the two said. Squatting down, he jumped from the back of the lorry and made to salute. Clement stretched out his hand. Savage wiped his palm on his shorts before taking the offered hand. The young private had a firm grip but Clement could see his embarrassment. Evidently Savage wasn't in the habit of shaking hands with majors. But for Clement, such missions were not about rank or blind obedience. In a small team, every man had a job to do, and each man was an expert in his chosen field. He believed men were more inclined to watch each other's backs if they were on friendly terms.

'You're our sniper I understand.'

'That's right. Also, explosives and weapons handler.'

'Where were you posted before this?' Clement asked.

Savage stood, his frame almost rigid. 'Darwin, sir. Then Archer found me. Said he needed someone to go with a radio expert to the islands; to watch his back. That's when I first met Kearsley. We did a few trips together to Fiji, Rabaul, Moresby...'

'Hugh Kearsley, sir,' Kearsley said thrusting out his hand towards Clement. 'I was in the Middle East then about six months ago I was transferred with a Wireless Unit to Melbourne. Someone must have learned of my wireless experience because the next thing I'm in Darwin and visiting the Coastwatchers in the Pacific with Savage here on a regular basis. Once the operators were recruited, I went in and set up their radios. I also attend to any maintenance.'

'How long have you been in Signals, Hugh?' Clement asked.

'Since the beginning of the war, sir,' Kearsley replied.

'And in the islands?'

'Four or five months.'

'Have either of you been to Singapore?'

Both Savage and Kearsley shook their heads.

'What about you, Tom?'

'Nope,' Tom said reaching for a crate of ammunition, his voice raised just loud enough for Lyon and Reynolds to hear. 'But from what I understand, it's a fabulous life for those who can afford it.'

Clement glanced at Tom wondering if his comment had been directed at Ivan. Regardless, Clement was looking forward to hearing about Ivan's trips into Indochina and any encounters with the Japanese in particular.

Clement left them to finish unloading the lorry and walked out onto the beach where Bill and Ivan were dragging the dinghy into the water. 'What Tom said about the British in Singapore, is that true, Ivan?'

'It's Utopia for the planters and settlers. They make large incomes, have many servants and enjoy a privileged life.'

'How will they fare if the Japanese invade?'

'I shudder to think.'

Bill stood in the water then swung his leg over the gunwale. Sitting on the middle seat, he lifted the oars into the rowlocks as Clement and Ivan pushed the dinghy out into the shallow water. With Clement holding the little boat steady, Ivan loaded the luggage into the stern then climbed into the bow.

Clement watched as Bill began to row towards the *Krait*. Once the dinghy was clear of two other moored boats, Clement returned to the lorry and the increasingly large mound of supplies piling up on the wharf.

'What weapons have you brought, Mick?' Clement asked, his eye taking in the quantity of munitions.

'Four brand new Owen Guns and enough ammo for a small war. Some grenades, a few sticks of dynamite, some time-pencils and a couple of Limpets, just in case. Wasn't sure what you'd planned, so Archer said to get a variety of things.'

Clement glanced at Tom and smiled, Whittaker's words about diamonds ringing in his ears. 'Well, thank you, all, for being part of this team. Once we are under way, we'll have time to go over the revised plan for the rendezvous. For now, I think we just get the gear and ourselves on board and head for the open sea then get some sleep. Tom, were you able to get the canoes?'

'Yeah, I got them. Fold-boats. Easier to stow than canoes. Didn't know the Japs had them but they're perfect for us!' Archer grinned. 'Snatched them from under the Japs' noses. I knew they'd be asleep for a while. Put a sleeping draught into that case of whisky bottles before leaving Darwin. The truck belongs to them too.'

Mick and Hugh laughed.

'Won't they find it here and start asking questions?' said Clement.

'Even if they do, we'll be well away by then. No harm done.'

'And there'll be no local reprisals?'

'Shouldn't think so. They'll think it was the locals anyway. Besides, they're consular staff not commandos,

Clem. Well, let's hope they aren't.'

Clement wasn't so sure. He considered it unlikely that consular staff had a need for fold-boats. 'I'd be happier if it wasn't sitting here by the wharf when they find it. I'll drive it back into the town and walk back,' he said.

'Now that would alert the locals,' said Kearsley. 'I'll drive it back up the hill a bit and park it close to the edge of the road leading out of Baucau. With luck the rain should wash the mud out from under it and it may go over the edge. Oh dear! What a pity! Won't be long.' Kearsley disappeared into the darkness and Clement heard the lorry's engine start.

From across the water came the sound of the *Krait's* slow diesel engine approaching. Tying the black-hulled ship to the wharf, they loaded the fold-boats and munitions onto the deck as the daylight turned the waters from silver to blue in the morning sunlight. Half an hour later, as the first rays of sun streamed over the headland, Kearsley re-joined them. Untying the ropes that held the *Krait* to the wharf, and with the ship's engine on half throttle, they slowly reversed then motored away from the shore and out into the Wetar Strait.

Bill introduced his crew; José, Juan and Pedro, three local lads approximately twenty years of age. Neither Juan nor José spoke English but Pedro, the oldest of the three had a few words. As the *Krait* left Baucau behind them, Clement helped stow the equipment into the first of three for'ard holds. The first two were deep, having been intended for the storage of fish. In the one closest to the bow, they stowed the equipment including the fold-boats. In the second, Archer and Savage strung up three hammocks. The third hold held the radio and navigator's desk as well as three bunks, one of which was Bill's. Clement put his pack on the starboard bunk leaving the other for Ivan.

Clement watched Archer replace the hatch covers over the holds as the morning light began to break into the day. 'Thank you, lads. But now you should get something to eat and some sleep. We'll discuss the revised plan later when I've had time to think about it.'

'Like a cuppa, Clem?'

Clement smiled. 'Thank you, Tom. I would.' He watched Archer walk aft, past the covered engine compartment to where a wooden cupboard of sorts stood beside the stern and under a canvas canopy. The galley was nothing more than a gas burner on an open-air shelf with a cupboard below for the storage of pots and pans. Archer filled the kettle and set it on the stove. While it was simple and completely exposed to the weather, it seemed to work well enough and, from what Clement could see, Archer was in his element. Clement left him to speak with Bill, who was in the wheelhouse. He knocked on the door. 'Mind if I join you?'

'Not at all,' Bill said. 'Any problems with the Japs in Dili?'

Clement stepped inside and closed the door behind him. 'None that whisky doesn't fix, apparently. Which way will you take?'

'We'll go to the north of Atauro Island and stay away from the land. By tonight, all being well, we'll be in the Banda Sea. Then, it's into the Java Sea. I'd prefer we stay as far offshore as possible. But from now on, during the day I think one person should be on the look-out for Japanese planes. They fly low to see who's onboard. Can't have them seeing gleaming white skins.'

'Thank you, Bill, I'll arrange it with the lads,' Clement said.

'And Clement. I can sleep here in the wheelhouse. The bench can double as a bunk. Your radio operator can use the third bunk in the radio hold.'

'Thank you, Bill. I'm sure Hugh will be most grateful.'

Clement went aft to where Tom was pouring some tea into several enamel mugs. Mick and Hugh sat with Ivan under a large, raised wooden cover over the engine bay. Clement took one of the mugs of tea that Tom lined up along the engine housing. 'Bill has asked for one of us to be on deck as look-out for Japanese planes during daylight hours. And he is willing to sleep in the wheelhouse so, Hugh, you can use the third bunk next to the radio.'

Hugh smiled.

'Good idea,' Ivan said. 'Anything more from Melbourne?'

'No. The plan is still to go to Keppel Island Pier. We need to be at the site on the 21st at midnight. Do you know it, Ivan?'

'I do. It's on the southern side of Singapore Island. If

Bill keeps the ship in the open sea to the east of Blakang Mati Island, we can row the fold-boats past Fort Siloso then onto the pier from there. That way we should be shielded from any prying Japanese in Singapore Strait. I'm not saying it will be easy. The Japs, if they're there, will have look-outs posted all over the place especially around the military installations.'

'I think we should take all three fold-boats when we go. Will they take more than one person, Tom?'

'They can carry up to three men, but two with equipment is better.'

'Good. I brought some information with me that we should look at. I'll get it.'

Clement returned to the radio hold and retrieved the maps from his pack. Taking them aft, he spread them out on top of the engine housing, the mugs of tea holding the charts in place. 'Commander Long gave me the Singapore tide charts. If the estimation of twelve days is correct, then we should arrive on time for the rendezvous. But this doesn't allow for any delays or mishaps. By the 21st of this month, it will be a quarter waxing moon. So just enough light and not too much. The man we are collecting will flash a green light at exactly midnight, so we know where to land. He'll wait one hour only. If we fail to show up, or take too long to make the crossing, he'll leave and return the following night to repeat the process. But obviously a flashing light will draw attention, so this couldn't go on for more than day or two at most. While it all seems straightforward, it has been my experience that things seldom are. And especially so if we are now at war.'

'Will we all go? Or will some of us stay on the *Krait*?' Tom asked.

'I think it best we all go. Bill and his crew will remain in the open sea a little distance off the eastern tip of the island of Blakang Mati.'

'Are you familiar with paddling a fold-boat, Clement?' Ivan asked.

'I can row a canoe, but I've never paddled a fold-boat.'

'You'll be fine then,' Ivan said.

Clement looked around the faces. 'As the boats can carry two men each, I'll take Ivan with me. Mick will be in the second with the weapons and Tom with Hugh in the third. That leaves two places for the return trip; one for Captain Winthorpe, the man we are going to collect, with the other seat for any large equipment he may have with him. Mick will also carry the Limpets but each man, except Ivan, should have a gun and a grenade, that is, Ivan, if you are still planning to leave us once on shore.'

'I must, Clement. Sorry, but my wife and son come first.'

'I understand. Mick, I'm not familiar with the Owen gun you mentioned. Is it similar to a Sten?'

'Yeah. Only better. It's ideal for close quarters and will work in any weather over any ground whether it's water, sand or mud. Ideal for the jungle!'

'I'll get you to show me later, if you would, Mick.'

Savage nodded.

Clement went on. 'Please remember, however, that this mission is supposed to be silent. Weapons are only to be used in an emergency. Ivan, do you carry a weapon, if we encounter problems on arrival?'

'I have a knife and a pistol.'

'Good. That should be sufficient. While we're at sea, we'll take it in turns to keep a look-out at all times during daylight hours for Japanese aerial surveillance. And we should darken our skins with strong, cold, boiled tea. It will make us less obvious to overhead eyes. As I'm sure most of you are needing sleep, as I certainly am, we should draw up a roster and when not on watch, get some rest. Mick, you and Ivan bunker down and I will waken you.'

Clement drained his tea and Archer collected the mugs and rinsed them out with sea water.

While Savage and Lyon slept, Kearsley went to the foredeck to watch for aeroplanes and Clement went through the weapons with Archer. There were four Owen guns, each with six magazines of thirty rounds apiece, six grenades, two Limpets, two time pencils, four Enfield pistols plus ammunition, ten sticks of dynamite, ten detonators, a length of fuse and four knives.

'You are expecting to conduct a small war, Tom?' Clement said. 'We're supposed to collect one man in total silence, not take on the Japanese army single-handedly.'

'Sorry, Clem. But you never know what you may

need. Next time I won't bring so much.'

Clement looked at Archer. He wasn't expecting there to be a next time but one thing he had learned in this war was to always expect the unexpected. Clement went on. 'Each man should have a knife, a pistol and an Owen gun with one magazine attached to his webbing. As Ivan and I already have knives, Tom please see to it that you, Mick and Hugh have one each. You should also carry two magazines of ammunition for the Enfield pistol and one only for the Owen as machinegun magazines are much too noisy if attached to a belt. Mick, as our sniper, should carry more.'

'I'll take a grenade or two with me, just for emergencies,' Tom said.

'I don't want Mick to be weighed down with weapons. He should only take what he can carry silently.'

'She'll be right, Clem. Mick and me have got in and out of places carrying quite a bit of stuff without being heard.'

Clement glanced at Tom, but he didn't say anything. He'd been told that Archer was resourceful. Perhaps it was more light-fingered. In the end the same skill set was required.

'I should go up on deck now. I'll take over from Hugh. Get some rest and I'll waken you in four hours.'

Clement went on deck and sat on the step near the wheelhouse and the open hatch to the radio hold. It worried him that he didn't know these men. He thought of his former team in East Sussex; men he'd known for years. Although, he did acknowledge he hadn't known them as well as he thought he had. Regardless, he had served with many types of men before and from what he could judge, he thought the Australians would be a good lot. Secretly, he hoped Ivan Lyon would stay with them. The man had skills and local knowledge which would be useful. But the man's family was in Singapore and that alone precluded Ivan from any long-term involvement with his team. Clement walked for'ard. Bill had unrolled a battened shade cover over the boom. Clement sat near the bow, a pair of binoculars at his elbow. He glanced back aft. One of Bill's young crew was at the helm in the wheelhouse as the heat of the day descended in a milky haze around them. It wasn't raining yet but the sultry heat made the temperatures almost unbearable.

Through the open for'ard hatch, Clement heard Tom's voice. 'Another cuppa, Clem?'

'I thought you were getting some rest.'

'Yeah. I will. Just need to settle a bit.'

'I understand, Tom.'

Archer climbed through the hatch and disappeared aft to the improvised galley to make the tea. Pedro was there and from what Clement could see, he wasn't too happy about sharing his galley. Some minutes later Tom joined Clement on the foredeck and handed him the mug.

'Problems?'

'Nah! Pedro is the ship's cook. He didn't seem to like me using his stove at first. I told him he still is the cook.

I just make tea. Seemed to make him happy.' Tom sipped his tea then settled himself on the small anchor hatch cover. 'You're not like any major I've ever known. What did you do before the war?'

'I'm a vicar, actually.'

'Really! A vicar with knives and guns!'

'It's a long story. What about you, Tom?'

'Rouseabout. On one of the big stations in the Territory.'

'I'm not sure what a rouseabout does.'

'I do anything from rounding up cattle to digging fence holes to getting equipment and supplies.'

'I should've guessed,' Clement said, smiling. He sipped his tea. 'Are you married?'

'Me! Nah! No woman would have me. I couldn't stay bound to a house. Besides, I'm away droving a lot of the time. Just like my freedom too much I suppose.'

'And Mick?'

'He's from the south. Sydney, I think but he hardly talks about it. We just get on. You know how it is. Some people you do and others you don't.'

'What about Army discipline? Having to be in certain places and doing as you're told?'

Tom laughed. 'Don't mind rules if they make sense. Besides, I'm never bored. I get to go in and out of most of the military posts around the Territory and generally spend time on my own. So, what the army doesn't know doesn't hurt anyone.'

'And if there is a war and your freedom to move

about so freely is curtailed?'

'Maybe I'll just work for you, Clem.'

Clement didn't have the heart to tell Tom that he wasn't staying beyond this mission. Besides, he couldn't envisage Tom in the icy northerly climes of the Shetland Islands. He finished his tea and reached for Tom's empty mug. 'I'll get myself painted with the dregs. You should get some rest, Tom.'

'Right you are, Clem.'

Clement went aft and poured some left-over tea into his mug, allowed it to cool then covered his arms and legs with the liquid. He could smell the tannin on his skin. Combined with the oppressive tropical heat he thought the smell almost intolerable. Walking for'ard again, he quietly climbed down the small, steep ladder into the radio hold and, reaching into his pack, retrieved his camera.

'Time to change watch?' Ivan whispered.

'No. Sorry to disturb,' Clement said, retying his pack. Climbing back up on deck, he studied the camera and practiced using it, then loaded the film and took a practise shot of Bill leaning into the engine bay, the *Rising Sun* billowing behind him. Standing beside the wheelhouse Clement then took another shot out to sea. It was warm and the sea tranquil; it reminded him of trips to Eastbourne with Mary. He allowed his thoughts to linger over his late wife. How she would have laughed at his current appearance. He thought he must look unrecognisable with his tea-stained skin, wide-legged short trousers, and short-sleeved shirt. Winding the film on, Clement clicked the shutter again, taking a second picture of Bill, who was now standing on the aft deck. Ivan had joined him there and they were both engaged in chatting and staring out to sea.

Two hours later, Archer appeared on deck. 'I hardly recognise you, Clem. What a change! Your missus will think you've gone native.'

Clement smiled. 'You're right about that, Tom. But it's not your turn yet.'

'Can't sleep. I'll take over from you, Clem. You look done in.'

'Thank you, Tom. I won't say no, if you're sure.' Clement went to his bunk. Hugh was lying asleep, his skin shiny with sweat in the airless cabin. Clement stowed the camera under the sheet and against the bulkhead then removed his shirt, the hot humid air stifling in the enclosed space. Through the open hatchway he felt a slight breeze. But it wasn't sufficient to cool the tiny hold. He lay back on the bunk and stared at the timbers above his head, visualising the team in the fold-boats. As the occupants in the third boat in the group, Tom and Hugh would function as both the sentry party and covering party. Once they were in sight of the Keppel Island Pier they'd regroup with Archer and Kearsley taking the lead and beaching first, with both himself and Savage providing any cover from the sea. Once Archer and Kearsley had beached, they would find cover and remain on the beach adjacent to the jetty where the rendezvous was to take place. He and Lyon would then land and locate Johnny. Archer and Kearsley would act as covering party on the beach until he returned with Johnny and they would maintain that cover until he and Johnny put to sea. Savage would stay in his boat under the pier and remain there unless needed. If there were no problems, it should be straight-forward. Clement closed his eyes. Despite the heat and perhaps because of it, his body felt the exhaustion and he fell asleep.

7

Java Sea - 9th December 1941

Clement heard the noise. He stared through the open hatch. From what he could see of the sky, he knew the brief twilight was descending. It was late in the day, but the sound of an aeroplane approaching fast was loud and unmistakable, and it was getting louder. Jumping out of the bunk, he grabbed his binoculars and hat and headed for the deck. Lifting the binoculars to his eyes, he saw the aeroplane. He scanned the sky, but the plane seemed to be alone and heading straight for them. From that angle, he couldn't see if it was one of theirs or Japanese.

'Japs!' Bill shouted from the window in the wheelhouse door. Looking back along the deck to the stern, he nodded, as if satisfied that the *Rising Sun* flag was visible. Clement stood in front of the wheelhouse and watched the plane approach. The Zero fighter's speed was astonishing. Bill and two of his crew were waving.

Clement did likewise, one hand on his hat, pulling it down hard over his head. The plane flew over them then turned, banked, flew back overhead, then lifted into the sky.

'Will they report seeing us?' Clement asked Bill.

'Yes. But they won't be suspicious. They will have counted how many on deck and seen me and my lads. Although they will have counted you as one of them. Good thing Juan was in the engine room and below deck at the time.'

Clement watched the Japanese plane until it was a spec in the darkening sky. Despite Bill's words that the Japanese plane had been solely for reconnaissance, he didn't feel reassured.

'Do you know this Keppel Island Pier?' Clement asked Bill.

Bill nodded. 'It's a good place for a rendezvous. It's largely protected from the sea by Blakang Mati Island, the big island off Singapore's south-eastern coast.'

'Is there a surf to worry about?'

'No. You'll be able to beach the boats there, although it is quite rocky. There is some beach but not much. More at low tide, of course. But while it's protected from hazardous seas, it isn't well hidden from prying eyes. There are a couple of batteries along that part of the coast which will be heavily guarded now, I should've thought. It's quite possible you'll be seen. Depends, of course, on who's in the battery at the time. If it's the Japs, you've got problems.'

Clement thought about the rendezvous. Without up-to-date intelligence about the area and what was happening in the wider world, it was more than risky. If the Japanese controlled Singapore, they would be rowing into a hornet's nest. Speed and stealth would be the aim. 'Are there any uninhabited islands hereabouts?'

'There are over fourteen thousand islands in the Indies so, yes, there are a quite a few. What do you have in mind?'

'A practice run. Are there any nearby?'

'I wouldn't recommend it. Even though that was the first Japanese plane we've seen, it cannot be guaranteed they won't come back tomorrow. And three canoes adjacent to a near motionless fishing boat would arouse their interest.'

Clement stared out to sea. Protected by the surrounding islands, the Java Sea was calm, idyllic even. But no expanse of open sea is without its issues. Not only was there the threat of Japanese surveillance flights but the daily rain squalls were drenching, and the heat and humidity made the weather unpredictable and the seas dangerous. And from what he'd learned in Melbourne, the Dutch had submarines in the area. If they saw the *Rising Sun* billowing from the *Krait's* stern, they may engage it, or worse, sink them.

The days passed in hot monotony. The morning weather stifling and humid, and the afternoons wet and even more humid. The vessel, though, was moving at a good speed. Not enough, Clement believed, to attract attention but sufficient for a light breeze to cool a sweat-drenched body and air the cramped sleeping quarters below deck. All he'd seen of other vessels were numerous small local fishermen's luggers, their nets dragging behind the boat. During the early morning or late afternoons, Bill's crew dropped lines over the side to catch the evening meal. While Clement enjoyed the taste of the spicy fresh fish and rice that Pedro cooked, he knew they would soon become bored with a diet of nothing but fish and rice. He knew Tom had brought some tinned food along for emergencies. Tom had removed the labels and instituted a numbered system so that they knew what the tins contained. But so far, fish and rice was still being well tolerated by the men.

Mealtimes and the endless hours onboard gave Clement time to know his team. They seemed a genial lot even though their ranks were poles apart. Clement wished Ivan with his local knowledge could remain with them. Moreover, Clement liked him. There was a quiet affability about Lyon which exuded confidence and control. During the evenings, Clement retrieved the chess set Charles Naylor had given to him from his pack. He and Lyon had played several games already. Chess, for Clement, had mixed memories of his former friend, Peter Kempton, and Fearnley Maughton, but few games afford an opportunity to study how one's opponent thinks like chess. And even though chit-chat was limited, Lyon, so Clement learned, had been born in India but, like most children of British colonialists, had been sent to school in England.

The two Australians, Tom and Mick, though nothing alike in appearance seemed the perfect combination. They understood each other without fuss or indeed much dialogue. Mick, who cleaned the weapons and practised firing his rifle at empty tin cans on the foredeck daily said little, taking his cue from Tom but he was strong and co-operative. Clement had spent time with him practising using the Owen gun. He'd learned that Mick had grown up on a dairy farm just south of Sydney and was the youngest of six boys. With so many brothers, Clement wasn't surprised he was quiet. And Archer's resourcefulness had proved astounding, even to finding several Japanese fishing lanterns and tins of food, including raisins, doubtless stolen from the Japanese stores in Timor.

Hugh was the more distant among them and seemed to be the odd-man-out. Clement saw him standing on the deck staring out to sea, the binoculars around his neck, his gaze on the sky, watching for Japanese aeroplanes. Clement went to join him.

'Alright, Hugh?'

'Oh yes. Sorry, Clement. Dreaming I suppose,' he said, his gaze returning to the flat sea. He lifted the binoculars and scanned the skies.

'May I ask what about?'

'The tropics, I suppose. They are lovely. Idyllic even in this heat. But they're not home, are they?'

'I know I haven't been in England for six months or so, Hugh, but it isn't the place you remember. It's grim. There is little food and what there is, is rationed. And there's almost no petrol. Do you know I ate bacon in Melbourne? Unheard of in England now. And sugar. There's no rationing in Australia. I hope it stays that way. The U-boat packs and Luftwaffe have seen to it that England is starving. I think our nation is exhausted, by war and fear. It seems so never-ending. But it has had a curious effect. Some have remained afraid while others seem to be saying: do your worst, Herr Hitler. London theatres and music halls are still open and the young flock to them in droves.' Clement half laughed. 'Do you know even during the raids which have become an almost daily and nightly routine, some people no longer go to the shelters? They'd sooner die dancing than huddle in gloomy air-raid shelters and tube stations.'

'It's the centre of the world though, isn't it,' Hugh said and Clement knew it wasn't a question.

'When this mission is over, perhaps you should request a transfer back. Why did you leave?'

'I volunteered to go to the Middle East. It sounded exotic. And I should have gone with a group of lads to Crete, but someone decided differently. I ended up on a boat to Melbourne. And within a few weeks to Darwin. The rest you know.'

'You said you installed the tele-radios for the Coast-watchers around the Pacific islands; do you know Morse code?'

'Of course.'

Clement thought about his next question carefully then decided to take a gamble. 'And Kana Morse too, I suppose.'

Hugh turned to face Clement; his eyes wide but he didn't say anything.

'Perhaps it is your adaptability that saw you go in a different direction to your former colleagues,' Clement added. He visualised Eric Nave slumped over his desk at Victoria Barracks. 'You would not have been brought here unless your talents were needed. You should know that even in this small way, your abilities will greatly assist us to win this war.'

'Did you know Ivan before this mission?' Hugh asked.

'No. Why?'

'There's more to him than you might think.'

Clement nodded. 'I think you're right.'

A long silence settled between them. They both stood, staring out to sea. 'Have you done any undercover work before, Clement?'

'A little,' he said. 'Why don't you get some rest. I can take over from here.' Clement reached for the binoculars before Hugh could object.

'That is most generous. Thank you.'

'There's nothing much for us to do these next few days anyway.'

Clement watched him disappear down the open hatch to his bunk in the radio hold. He wondered if he should speak more with Hugh Kearsley. Something about the young man troubled Clement. He wondered if Hugh had wanted to chat further. Clement shrugged. There would be plenty of time for that in the coming days.

Clement checked the surveillance roster to see who was on duty next. He read Ivan's name. An hour later, Lyon came on deck.

'My turn, Clement.'

Clement passed the binoculars to Lyon. 'A word if I may, Ivan.'

'Of course, Clement. What troubles you?'

'Have you encountered Hugh Kearsley before?'

Lyon faced Clement. 'That is a very loaded question, Clement and one worthy of any interrogation officer.'

'Do you intend to answer it?'

Lyon laughed. 'Can I answer you with another question?'

'Perhaps.'

'Why did you include Kearsley in this mission?'

'In fact, I didn't choose any of them. Not sure who did. I've always suspected it was Commander Long, but it could be that Long allowed Archer to choose the men.'

'Only one way to find out.'

'And my earlier question?' Clement persisted.

'I've bumped into Kearsley before, although he may not remember it. It was in Rabaul. He is an exceptionally good telegraphist. He can also build and repair radio transmitters. This is largely what he was doing for the

Coastwatchers.'

'And he is proficient in Kana Morse.' Clement waited to see Lyon's reaction but there was none. 'And he knows where these Coastwatchers are located.'

'That would be a safe guess.'

'As would Savage.'

'Perhaps. But not necessarily.' Lyon beamed his wide almost naively angelic smile.

8

Java Sea - 12th December 1941

Clement turned in his bunk. The morning light was streaming through the open hatch. He glanced at Hugh, who, although he had his eyes closed, Clement guessed wasn't asleep. Clement stared at the beam above his head. He felt a growing sense of unease that he couldn't completely explain. In the three days since his enigmatic conversation with Hugh, he thought the man had become more distant. Clement acknowledged that he didn't know these men as well as he would have liked. He felt an unusual mix of emotions; but mostly he felt unsure. He questioned his own reasoning and regretted not chatting with Hugh further to find out what troubled the young corporal. He wondered if Hugh had wanted to confide something? But regardless of whether Hugh was awake now or not, any conversation they had in the radio hold would be overheard by the man on surveillance duty because the hatch was open. If he closed it, the small space would be unbearably hot. He was about to whisper to Kearsley when he saw Ivan's head in the open hatch above him.

'Can I have a word, Clement?' Lyon said.

'You're meant to be on surveillance duty, Ivan,' Clement said.

'I know but this is important. Would you come on deck for a few minutes? There is something you need to know.'

'Of course.' Clement swung his legs out of his bunk and climbed the ladder to the deck. 'What is it, Ivan?'

'Before leaving Timor, I received an order from Commander Long. I was to make my way to Surabaya in the Indies to extract an American there. When I learned that you and your team were heading for Singapore, I knew Reynolds would have to refuel at Surabaya and so decided, if you'd take me, we could combine our missions. I know I should have run it past you earlier, but I was afraid you'd say no and I wouldn't get back to Singapore to save my wife and child. I unreservedly apologise and hope you won't hold it against me.'

'You are correct, Major. I'm not happy about it.' Clement looked out over the sea. 'And yes, you should have mentioned it earlier.'

'I know, but I was worried, Clement, that you may not have taken me. And, as you recall, most of the boats in Dili which could have taken me to Surabaya, were taking women and children to Australia. The American I'm supposed to meet there needs to get to Singapore rather urgently.'

A heat haze had settled over the waters. Beside them, in the sea, a turtle lazily lifted its head and stared at the ship then dived into the tranquil waters. 'While I am not at all happy with your deception, I suppose if Bill is heading there anyway, it won't make much difference and an extra hand could be useful.' Clement paused but he noted Lyon didn't say anything. 'So this American will also be leaving the *Krait* in Singapore?'

'Yes. He's going to try to obtain passage to the Philippines on any ship he can get on to.'

Clement watched Lyon's face. 'Who is he?'

'He's an American code breaker, named Joe Watkins. He was visiting the Dutch Signals Intelligence Unit, known as Kamer 14, located at Bandoeng in Central Java. The Dutch SigInt group has been working on the Diplomatic codes that Nave is also working on. This particular American is engaged in Traffic Analysis and is one of only a handful of competent Japanese linguists we have, so it is vital that he does not fall into Japanese hands. He'll be in Surabaya on the sixteenth at the oil depot where Bill will refuel. I am to meet him in a bar on the waterfront and get him onto the ship as quietly as possible then leave for Singapore. Collecting him won't have any adverse impact on your mission, I promise you, Clement.'

Clement frowned. He didn't like surprises and he wanted time to think about the repercussions of Lyon's revelation. 'Do you really have a family in Singapore?'

'I do. And it is still my intention to leave you there. I haven't lied to you Clement. I did take a friend's yacht to Fiji, but it was a ruse. While I'm not a code breaker myself, I do work for SIS in Special Ops. I did take local boats to get to Timor, but it was Long who arranged it through Ross and Whittaker. I'm just trying to kill two birds with one stone for now. Especially if we are officially at war with the Japanese, we need to move quickly. And you are the only person who can recognise this Captain Winthorpe. Do you know what he's carrying that is so top secret?'

'No idea. I've just been told to get him out.' Clement was beginning to have reservations. Was Lyon's inclusion and his mission why Clement had felt Long and Nave had concealed something from him? But why would they? It didn't make much sense to Clement but while he didn't like the deception, he saw no reason why they shouldn't collect the American if they were to refuel in Surabaya anyway.

'Thank you, Clement. Very decent of you.'

Clement paused. 'Do you have any other surprises I should know about?'

Lyon shook his head. 'Sorry, Clement. I know I should have told you sooner, but I was afraid you wouldn't agree.'

'No more surprises?'

'No more surprises, I promise.'

As the days passed Clement knew his skin was tanning from the tropical temperatures, even without the daily application of cold tea. The afternoon storms brought relief in the form of a drenching shower. It also gave them a renewed supply of fresh water. Then everyone gathered on deck to feel the heaven-sent cooling waters. Clement gazed up at the endless sky, his eye searching for Japanese planes. But none had been sighted for three days now. He considered it was both a good and a bad thing. Good, if it meant the Japanese had no interest in them. Bad, if it meant the Japanese armies had advanced further than they thought.

Clement thought back on the agents in Dili, David Ross and John Whittaker. He prayed they were all right and still operating in Timor. He thought of the lorry Kearsley had parked on the road to Baucau and wondered if the Japanese had asked questions about it and the removal of much of their equipment. If the situation in the Pacific stayed unaltered for another two weeks, Clement knew they would be all right. It was the not knowing that caused him concern. Despite listening to local radio chatter, nothing of the Japanese advance had been learned. Clement knew anything to do with the war would either be restricted or encoded and therefore, for them, unintelligible. But several days had passed since leaving Timor, and he had no idea what the Japanese were doing nor where they were.

Bill Reynolds was in the wheelhouse when Clement stepped on deck to watch for Japanese planes.

'Any activity?' Clement asked as he collected the binoculars from Hugh.

'None.'

Clement glanced at ship's young crew. They were sitting around the deck, mending fishing nets stretched over their knees. Tom and Mick were on the foredeck cleaning weapons. Ivan had made a quoit set from some rope and was tossing the rope rings over a spigot. It was early evening, and the heat of the day was slowly abating. It was an ordinary sight and one he hoped the Japanese would see and dismiss the *Krait* from their random surveillance flights.

Bill lifted his head to the horizon and turned a full 360 degrees. 'We'll be in Surabaya tomorrow where we'll refuel.'

'Tomorrow?' Clement asked, his gaze flicking to Lyon who now stood smoking on the foredeck.

'Yes. We won't make it to Singapore without refuelling,' Bill said. 'There's an oil refinery there operated by the Dutch. And you'll most likely be able to find out some news there too.'

Clement nodded. From the corner of his eye, he saw Lyon nod towards the companion way that led below. A minute later, he followed Lyon into the radio hold.

'Clement, I have something to ask of you.'

Clement waited.

'While I'm not expecting trouble tomorrow, you and I should go through a few things before we arrive in Surabaya, just in case. If something does happen there, we should have a plan of some sort.'

'I agree. Should the team be present?'

'First, you and I should decide on the course of action. Once we've formulated it, we'll tell the others.'

'Understood. Do you know Surabaya?'

'Not well. I've been into the port a few times with yachts but not beyond the wharf area. Any contact between myself and the Dutch SigInt Unit was done by coded radio signals. Only once did I have to collect something and that was done by one of their number meeting me in a pub on the waterfront. Of course, that was before the declaration of war. Who knows how it will be now?'

'Where is the rendezvous with Joe Watkins?'

'In the pub I just mentioned. It's called *The Flying Dutchman*. I'm thinking you, me and Kearsley go into the bar leaving Archer and Savage outside. Then, if everything is all right and Watkins is there, we have a drink inside but no direct contact with Watkins. Could you sit separately and at a distance from Kearsley and me, so you can watch proceedings? Kearsley and I will finish our drinks then leave. Watkins will follow us out. If you could wait behind and leave a few minutes after Watkins just to make sure no one is taking an interest in us. Once Archer and Savage see you leave, that will be the signal for them to return to the ship making sure no one is following.'

Clement nodded. 'And if there is trouble?'

'Even though we may be at war with Japan, and the

Japanese have their sights on the oil fields there, it's unlikely they've moved this far south yet.'

'They'll have spies there though, I'm guessing.'

'Yes, which is why I'm asking you to be the last man to leave. You're new and should the Jap spies have photos or descriptions of us, they most likely won't have one of you. If there are any in the pub, you should remain and watch them for a few minutes before leaving.'

'Will you hold a briefing?'

'I'd rather not be too obvious, Clement. I don't want to involve Bill or his crew. It could make it difficult for them in future if the Japs connected us with Bill. Better you talk with Tom and Mick separately and I'll have a word with Kearsley. That way, we'll save time.'

'Right.' But again, Clement felt uneasy. He didn't like that everyone involved didn't really know what or where others in the party would be if there was trouble. 'Have you worked with Archer and Savage before?'

'No. But they seem able men.'

'So I've discovered,' Clement paused. 'Do you speak Japanese, Ivan?'

'I have some Malay and Chinese but not Japanese, unfortunately. Of course, Joe does but as soon as he speaks anyone would know he was American by his accent which would definitely raise a Japanese eyebrow or two.'

'I agree.'

Clement walked for'ard to where Tom and Mick were

stowing the weapons. Even though Lyon had said Clement was in charge, he knew he wasn't and for the first time since his involvement with the secret world, whether alone or with a team, he felt a level of confusion and uneasiness he'd never experienced. The pressure of leading a clandestine mission was relentless but working with men he didn't know added a dimension of uncertainty he didn't like. It made for sleepless nights and churning stomach acid. Tom closed the hatch on the weapons as Clement told them the plan Lyon had devised.

Walking aft, Tom and Mick went to the stern where Pedro was preparing the evening meal and Clement went to the wheelhouse to speak with Bill. He wanted to know more about the waterfront of Surabaya. Opening the door, he went inside. 'I suppose you've been to Surabaya many times, Bill,' Clement began.

'Oh yes,' Bill paused.

A low hum filled the heavy evening air. Clement glanced at Bill then reached for the binoculars by the helm. A Japanese Zero fighter was approaching fast. 'Japs!' Clement shouted from the wheelhouse door. He saw Tom and Mick rush for the engine room hatch and disappear below. Kearsley and Lyon were still below in the radio hold. Clement counted the crew on deck then watched the plane through the windows as it approached from the starboard side of the ship. It flew in low, the thunderous noise reminiscent of another plane, a Stuka that had strafed his village in England a lifetime ago. The

Zero banked, then rose high into the sky before turning again. Then it did another low run over the ship, as though trying to identify them. Lifting high, it circled again, the noise still loud above their heads, then Clement saw it disappear into the sky, returning to wherever it had come from.

Clement kept his gaze on the skies, but the plane did not return.

'I'll get the boys to lower the nets just in case they're interested in us,' Bill said. 'It'll slow our speed, but I think it's a good idea in view of the circumstances.

'As we get closer to Singapore, we should expect that they'll become more interested in us.'

'I just hope they continue to think we are local fishermen and leave us alone.'

'I agree, Bill. It should be all right,' Clement said, but his mind was on whether the Japanese had learned anything about them. He thought of Whittaker and Ross in Timor. Something troubled Clement about it but he didn't know what. Also, the revelation about the Surabaya rendezvous with the American worried him. Long hadn't mentioned it but, Clement rationalised, Lyon's mission would have been a separate operation and one Clement would never have learned about if Lyon had not joined them. Clement wondered if he'd believed Lyon too quickly. Were Tom and Mick even who they said they were? And what of Kearsley? Clement needed information. He thought of the four secretaries in Nave's office. But however much he wished to speak with Miss Copeland, there was no way of contacting her until he was in Surabaya and even then, any available time to place long distance telephone calls would be limited. For now, his questions would have to remain unanswered.

9

Surabaya, Dutch East Indies - 16th December 1941

Clement stood in the wheelhouse where, through the windows, he had a clear view of Surabaya port. He held the camera to his eye and pressed the shutter as the *Krait* slowly manoeuvred between other vessels, heading for the refuelling depot. Dutch Navy ships lined the quays and docks to their right and a submarine lay beside the wharf, its eerie shape and colour an instant reminder of a German submarine he'd seen in the English Channel in '40. Off to his left, several large ships sat beside the port's oil refinery. There wasn't a *Rising Sun* to be seen. Clement breathed a sigh of relief as he rolled the film on and took numerous pictures of the surrounding shipping and port structures.

'How long will you be refuelling?' Clement asked Bill.

'Couple of hours. Why?'

'I think we'd all like to go ashore.'

Bill nodded. 'Don't be more than two hours. I'll have

to move after that.'

Clement nodded then went to the radio hold. Going straight to his pack, he replaced the film with a fresh one and put the camera into the pocket of his shorts, then strapped his knife to his left arm and rolled-down his sleeve. He then went to the foredeck where everyone had gathered. Below him, in the for'ard hold, Tom and Mick had assembled the weapons and were waiting to pass them up to him. Clement reached for an Enfield pistol and some extra ammunition and secured it into his belt. He then put a grenade into his short's pocket.

'Is everyone clear about the plan?' Ivan asked.

Heads nodded.

'Where is this pub, *The Flying Dutchman* located?' Clement asked.

'It's on the quay about fifty yards further on than the Customs House. It has a large sign so you shouldn't have any difficulty in finding it,' Ivan said.

'Will we be able to see one another?' Clement asked.

Ivan pushed an Enfield into his belt. 'Not guaranteed, Clement. But everyone should constantly be checking where other members of the team are.'

'As I am the last to leave, I'll need to know where everyone is. I would ask you to be mindful of that as I may not have time to locate a missing member.'

'Understood, Clem,' Tom said.

Clement looked along the line of faces. He felt uneasy, the doubts resurfacing. Was he just being suspicious for no reason? Something plagued him. He left the group and went aft to take some photographs of the ships in port.

Archer joined him. 'What's troubling you, Clem?'

'Truth be told, Tom, I feel like a fish out of water.'

'Not ideal, given where we are.'

Clement couldn't help but smile.

'We're in your hands, Clem. As last man out, you can make or break it for us all.'

'Do you really believe that?'

Archer was silent for a second. 'She'll be right!'

But Clement wasn't convinced by Archer's optimism. 'Are you anxious about something, Tom?'

Archer glanced around him as though checking to see if they were alone. 'Just a gut feeling, I suppose.'

'Don't ignore intuition.'

Tom stared at his feet. It was a gesture Clement didn't associate with Archer.

'Just get the feeling there's another agenda here,' Tom said, his voice a mere whisper.

'If there is, it's not one I know about. But then I didn't know about the American until yesterday so I'm probably the last person to ask.'

'Are we walking into a trap?'

'Meaning?'

'Could we have been set up?'

'You mean by Lyon?'

'Or Ross and Whittaker. Or Kearsley for that matter.'

'I thought you knew these men?'

'I know Mick. And if Mick says Kearsley's dinkum

that's fine with me. But I think we both know that a good con man is convincing. That's the trick of his trade. And Mick could be wrong. As for the others…' Tom shrugged.

Clement paused; he hadn't considered Kearsley. But if Ross or Whittaker were traitors that would implicate Commander Long, and Clement couldn't imagine that. 'While anything is possible, sometimes you just have to go with your intuition. And take lots of precautions.' Clement tapped his left sleeve.

'I'll try to keep you in sight, Clem.'

'Thanks Tom. You just look after yourself. And keep your eyes open for people watching.'

Surabaya port sat at the end of a wide bay known as the Madoera Strait. Off to Clement's right was another, smaller island; the two land masses separated by a narrow channel. The entrance to the port was evidently deep, the water depth easily able to accommodate large shipping berthed alongside wharves. The bay was congested with vessels of all kinds. And the Dutch Naval installation was crowded with ships either in dock or moored nearby. Panning the bay with his binoculars, Clement could see the oil refinery ahead and off to his left. As instructed by Bill, the team stayed below and waited until the ship was tied up alongside the wharf. Minutes later, José and Juan jumped ashore. Clement watched them dragging hoses on board. He heard them shouting and understood the hoses were to fill the ship's water tanks.

Once the water hoses were in place, the massive and evidently heavy fuel hoses were dragged across the wharf. Bill supervised the refinery workers as they climbed on board. Clement's eye coursed along the wharf. From what he could see, no one just stood watching events. Numerous men were engaged in manoeuvring cargo. Still more appeared to be involved in the process of refuelling other ships. In fact, the wharf appeared to be in a perpetual state of organised chaos. As soon as the *Krait* was in position, the team assembled on deck.

Ivan and Hugh jumped ashore first. Clement watched them saunter along the wharf chatting. When they were about halfway down the wharf, Tom and Mick left. A minute later, Clement stepped ashore. It was a strange experience not having stepped foot on land for over a week and Clement felt mildly unsteady. He walked towards the waterfront offices then leaned on a bale of some unknown produce before walking along the wharf, his eye constantly on the four members of the team ahead. He saw Ivan and Hugh stop. Ivan appeared to be buying a newspaper from the vendor on the quay. Clement knew Lyon would want to see if Tom and Mick were in place before entering *The Flying Dutchman*. Off to Clement's right, he heard a splash. He turned. He could see Bill Reynolds and his crew busy on the *Krait's* deck, their attention was on the process of refuelling and filling the various tanks. Clement glanced around but no one seemed to have heard the unexpected noise, or if they had, were paying it scant attention. Checking the faces around him, Clement walked back towards the *Krait* his peripheral gaze on the water around and between the ships tied up alongside the wharf. Nothing appeared abnormal. Slowing, he stopped, pretended to tie his shoelace, and checked the water. Standing, he walked towards a ladder that descended from the wharf into the harbour. The ladder was covered in seaweed and was doubtless there for smaller shipping. But he saw no one in the water. Lifting his gaze, his eye searched for the team ahead. He could see Tom and Mick. Ivan and Hugh were some distance in front of them and close to the buildings that fronted the quay. Clement squinted. Ivan appeared to be carrying a rolled-up newspaper under his arm like a swagger stick. Clement took one last look at the murky-brown waters beside him before moving quickly through the stacks of cargo on the wharf, heading for a line of warehouses built in the white-painted, Dutch, colonial style. Nestled between two lines of warehouses was the public house, *The Flying Dutchman*. Clement saw Ivan and Hugh go inside. Tom and Mick were further along the wharf, chatting and smoking with two local workmen.

Clement slowed and checked the people around him. But everyone was engaged in loading or unloading cargo. No one was simply observing. More especially, no one was watching the entrance to *The Flying Dutchman*. Above him the skies were their usual whitish haze, and he knew it would rain soon. When it did, torrents of water would make moving around the wharves slippery and intensify the pungent waterfront aromas. Clement wiped the sweat from his forehead. Yet despite the ever-present heat he believed he was becoming accustomed to the humid weather. His heart no longer pounded from the sheer debilitating temperature. Passing the Customs House, Clement opened the door to *The Flying Dutchman* and stepped inside.

His gaze scanned the crowd in the room. None were local people. Most appeared to be Dutch refinery workers, all wearing the grimy workman's clothes from a long day's shift. Lyon and Kearsley were already seated at a table near the door. Clement ordered a beer then went to sit at a table against the wall. In the corner by the front window, sat four large men wearing the light clothes of office workers. Their faces were flushed pink and shiny with sweat. They were chatting loudly in what Clement supposed was Dutch, and numerous empty glasses had accumulated on the table in front of them. Clement could see they appeared to be oblivious to everyone else in the room. In the other corner, at the rear, sat three Japanese-looking men all wearing suits. They shared no conversation and looked distinctly out-of-place. Clement couldn't see anyone sitting on their own.

He wrapped his hands around the cold glass. Without turning his head, he could see the Japanese men in his peripheral vision. A drink of some kind was in front of each but they didn't converse, or touch their drinks.

Suddenly Ivan drained his glass and he and Kearsley left the bar. At the same time, one of the four raucous men in the corner stood and went to the bar, loudly proclaiming he needed the men's lavatory.

Clement realised in a second, this man was the American.

As Clement watched, he saw the American seem to gag, as though about to vomit. Holding his hand over his mouth, the man hurried outside.

Not three seconds later, two of the three Japanese men stood and hurried towards the door. Clement stood and rushed forward. With his drink in his hand and his face turned towards the windows, Clement bumped into one of the Japanese, spilling the drink over him. Clement reached for his handkerchief and began to mop the man's clothes as the other raced outside. Now the remaining Japanese seated in the corner, came forward. Pushing Clement aside, he left the bar.

Clement placed his empty glass on the bar. 'Do you speak English?'

The barman nodded.

'Do you have a telephone I could use?'

The barman indicated the rear of the room. Clement glanced back at the door. Through it he could see Tom and Mick still talking to the two workmen. Lyon with Kearsley and the man Clement presumed was Watkins were already walking slowly along the wharf. The suited Japanese men stood near the entrance to *The Flying*

Dutchman, but Clement couldn't tell if they were watching Archer or Savage or, indeed, Lyon and the others.

Clement went straight to the telephone and lifting the receiver dialled zero for the operator. Giving the number he'd memorised, he waited. Within seconds a man's voice with a strong Dutch accent answered.

'Can you connect me with Commander Long in Melbourne, reversing the charges, please. Major Wisdom speaking.'

'Hold.'

Clement heard the line crackle. The only other time he'd placed a long-distance call was from the vicarage in Fearnley Maughton to Somerset, which wasn't exactly long distance but the call had taken some time for the operators concerned to connect his call. Perhaps Bandoeng was using a tele-radio transmitter to connect the calls. Either way, he hoped the connection wouldn't take too much longer. He checked his watch. Two minutes passed before he heard the familiar sound of a ring tone.

'Hello?'

'Miss Copeland?'

'Speaking?'

'This is Major Clement Wisdom. I need to speak to Commander Long urgently.'

Clement glanced at his watch. He prayed Long was in his office. Ten seconds later he heard Long's voice.

'Wisdom?'

'I need some advice. Are you aware of a Major Ivan Lyon and an American named Joe Watkins?'

'Yes. I know Major Lyon and why he's in Java. A highly trustworthy man. He has orders to collect Watkins. Where are you, Major?'

'Surabaya.'

'Do not abort this mission on their account. Lyon is fine. As is Watkins.'

'Right.' Clement hung up and returned to the waterfront. He'd been on the telephone no longer than seven minutes in total. Pausing in the doorway for one second, he saw Lyon with Kearsley and Watkins walking along the waterfront. In front of Clement was Archer, still chatting to the oil refinery workers. Savage was a little distance away, smoking and chatting to two other local men Clement thought could be wharf labourers. Archer looked up and Clement caught his eye. He nodded to Archer, signalling that it was time to leave. As Clement walked away from the pub, his gaze fell on the Japanese men who still stood watching the waterfront. But he saw only two. Frowning, Clement's gaze searched the quay for the third man. He was nowhere to be seen.

10

Surabaya - 16th December 1941

Clement walked towards the workmen he'd seen Archer talking to, but his eyes shifted constantly, scanning and searching everything on the quay. Positioning himself near some cargo, he turned and studied the windows at the front of the buildings along the foreshore. At one, he saw a man holding binoculars to his face. It was the third Japanese from *The Flying Dutchman*. Clement waited. He wanted a photograph of the man, but he knew he was too exposed, and the camera would certainly draw attention. He stood and wandered down the wharf to see if Lyon, Kearsley and Watkins had boarded the *Krait*. He could see them now talking to two men in a uniform Clement didn't recognise. He decided they were most likely port or customs officials. Looking further along the wharf he saw Archer and Savage were now about halfway down. Clement stared. Something didn't feel right. He remembered the splash.

Glancing back, he saw the Japanese man was still at the window, the binoculars still focused on the wharf. Clement felt his pulse quicken. He hurried, his pace increasing. Dodging workmen with trolleys and stacks of fresh produce from the local markets, he caught up with Archer.

'Tom, come with me! Give everything to Savage except your knife.'

Clement pulled his camera from his pocket and shoved it into Savage's hands. Turning around, he quickly scanned the immediate scene. But time was against them. Moving rapidly and adroitly through the workers, Clement walked back along the wharf to where another boat, a small pleasure yacht, was tied up. Descending the wharf ladder, he jumped onto the ship and went straight for the opposite side. With his knife in his teeth, Clement climbed over the rail and lowered himself the three feet into the water below. Tom followed, slipping into the murky, tepid bay beside him.

'What's happened, Clem?'

'I think there could be a mine on our ship. But we don't have much time and an explosion now would be catastrophic with all this fuel about. It has to be aft, attached to the fuel tanks.'

'Can you be sure, Clem?'

'The *Krait* is wooden, Tom, and a limpet mine is magnetic. It needs metal to adhere to the hull. The only thing

I can think of that is metal and near to the gunwale would be the aft fuel tank. While I move there, you check the hull anyway and anything on the deck that is metal and within reach of the gunwale.'

Working their way along the side of the yacht towards its stern, they swam the short distance to the *Krait's* bow. The vertical prow loomed above them. Staying on the seaward side, Archer pulled his knife from its scabbard on his belt as they edged their way along the side of the *Krait* towards the long, overhanging stern.

With his knife between his teeth, Tom duck-dived into the water several times, disappearing from Clement's view. Clement continued to swim along the side of the *Krait*, his hand running over its wooden hull just below the water line. Finding nothing, he swam on to the stern then dived down and opened his eyes. While it was unlikely to be attached to the non-magnetic brass propeller blades, he checked them anyway. On surfacing, Clement stared at the seaward-side fuel tank. Nestled between the gunwale and the back surface of the aft fuel tank was the mine. Within a minute, Archer was beside him. 'Nothing there, Clem,' Tom whispered, hiding under the long overhanging transom of the ship. Clement pointed upwards. 'Attached to the side of this fuel tank.'

'Bloody hell, Clem! She'd blow us to kingdom come!'

'Quite!'

'Did you see a timer?'

'Yes,' Clement said. 'But not when it's set to go off. Don't want to be too obvious. Whoever put it there

119

placed it quickly and left. You wait here, I'll go back up on deck and attempt to prize it free. I just don't want to drop it into the water. It would kill everyone within a fifty-yard radius if I did.'

'Right.'

With the noise of the refuelling and the chaos on the wharf, Clement knew that neither Bill nor his crew would have heard the magnetic clunk when the limpet was secured to the iron tank. Nor would they have witnessed the man who placed it there. It faced outwards, towards the bay. And it wouldn't have been found even after they'd put to sea. Clement swam around the hull and back to the ladder. Climbing on board the *Krait* he went straight aft. Kneeling beside the tank, he checked the timer. It was set for six o'clock, approximately four hours' time. They would be out to sea by then where their deaths wouldn't be known about for days, if ever. Clement leaned over the gunwale to where Tom waited in the water. 'Set for four hours' time. But it'll need both our strength, Tom, to prize it free.'

Tom reached up and, gripping the gunwale, pulled himself over the edge and squatted there, his feet either side of the mine. Using both knives, they prized the bomb gently away from the fuel tank. Lifting it carefully, Clement carried it to the radio hold and warily placed it on the bench. He checked the clock again. Definitely set for six o'clock, four hours' time. Then he stood staring at the primer switch. The mine hadn't been armed.

'Not a wise idea to swim here,' Bill said, looking at

Clement through the open hatch.

'I'll tell you later. How soon before we leave?'

'Ten minutes.'

'As soon as you can, Bill,' Clement said then quickly changed his wet clothes.

Staying in the radio room for no more than a few minutes, Clement then went on deck where he could see Lyon still talking with the port officials. Kearsley and Watkins were sitting aft, near the galley. Returning to the quay, he could see Savage further along the wharf perching on a stack of timber. Skirting Lyon and the port officials, Clement re-joined Mick.

'Any problems?' Mick asked. 'Where's Tom?'

'On board already. There was a limpet attached to one of the fuel tanks.'

'Bloody hell!'

'Tom and I removed it. What's happened here?'

Mick pointed. Clement shifted his gaze. Lyon was still talking to the officials on the quay.

'Been there a while. Can't hear them though. Got the impression he knows them. Or maybe he's just good at...'

Clement perceived that Mick had stopped himself from swearing.

'...talking nonsense to strangers.'

Clement nodded. He kept his eye on Lyon and the two men. 'Bill says we'll be leaving in a few minutes. Pass me the camera would you, Mick.' Holding it close to his body, Clement wound the film on then turned, focused the lens on Lyon with the port officials and clicked the shutter. Clement handed the camera back to Savage. 'You go on board now and, thanks Mick.'

Clement wanted to see the men with whom Lyon was spending so much time. He walked towards the group then suddenly paused behind and about two yards short of Lyon. The port officials were both European. Stooping, Clement pretended to tie his shoelace and listened to their conversation. He could hear they were conversing in French. While his French was limited and learned during the Great War twenty years ago, he hadn't forgotten it completely. Two English names stuck out: the *Prince of Wales* and *The Repulse*. Both were British ships, and both had arrived in Singapore about two weeks previously. As he knotted his shoelaces, he turned his head back to where he'd seen the man with the binoculars standing at the window of one of the buildings along the quay. While he couldn't be certain, he believed the man was still there. He felt a cold shiver course through him. Even though he'd discovered the limpet, he couldn't shake the feeling that something else was happening. He stood, his gaze on Lyon and the men he was talking to. As he passed, Clement nudged Lyon's back then continued on, climbing aboard the *Krait* now eager to leave.

As he walked along the deck, he turned to see Lyon laughing and waving. The officials he'd been talking to were walking back along the wharf and away from the *Krait*.

Clement waited on the foredeck for Lyon to climb

aboard. Two seconds later, Juan tossed the shore ropes back up onto the wharf and the *Krait's* engine roared into life.

'Problems?' Clement asked as Lyon stepped aboard.

'Not sure.'

'Who were they?'

'Vichy French.'

11

Surabaya Port - 16th December 1941

D o you know them?' Clement asked Lyon.

'No. But they may know about me. I have
led a few raiding parties around Indochina, so
it is possible they are on the look-out for a tall Englishman. I think I managed to fool them though. Said we
were going to the Philippines. But I learned some very
bad news; The *Prince of Wales* and the *Repulse* have both
been sunk off the coast of Malaya. It doesn't look good
for Singapore. They said it will fall within weeks.'

'That's terrible news.' Clement glanced around the
quay. People were everywhere and he felt the overwhelming desire to be far away from Surabaya. 'While
you were busy with the Frenchmen, Tom and I removed
a limpet mine someone had placed on the side of the
Krait's aft fuel tank.'

'What!'

'It's set to go off tonight at six, so we need to leave as

soon as possible.'

'Where is it now?'

'Tom's watching it.'

'Dear God. It could blow us to smithereens.'

'We need to talk, Ivan but first we leave.'

As the *Krait* pulled away from the wharf, Clement thought back on what Commander Long had told him about the Dutch oil refineries and Singapore being considered a stepping-stone. Now he understood. If Singapore fell, Clement knew where the Japanese would be next, if they weren't already here in some form. But he couldn't shake the feeling that Major Ivan Lyon was playing another role.

Two hours later they were once again in the Java Sea. Hugh was on aerial surveillance, the binoculars around his neck. Ivan was reading a book on the foredeck and the American was chatting with Tom and Mick near the galley.

'Could we talk, Ivan?' Clement said.

'Of course, Clement.' Lyon slammed the book shut.

'Who is Joe Watkins, exactly?'

'An American working in the Philippines at the US Intelligence Unit based in Manilla.'

'Why was he in Java?'

'Visiting the Dutch Signals Unit in Bandoeng. But I've no idea if he did anything else while there.'

'You didn't ask?'

'No. My brief from Long was to get him to Singapore. More than that I don't know. It's all on a need-to-know basis, Clement. If you want to know more, I would suggest you ask Watkins. He may tell you, but I suspect he may not.'

Clement stared at José and Juan on the foredeck. They'd caught some fish and were gutting them ready for the evening meal. 'Did you learn anything from those Frenchmen in Surabaya?' Clement asked.

'Malaya is falling, Clement. They said the British airfields have been abandoned or taken by the Japanese. And the British forces in Malaya are falling back, along with thousands of refugees and all heading for Singapore. Of course, they said they were Free French and therefore on our side. But I suspect they are Vichy French. And the Vicky French authorities in Indochina have virtually opened the door to the Japanese and welcomed them in. My wife and child have almost no hope.'

'I'm so sorry to hear about your family. When was this, did they say?' Clement asked.

'Five days ago.'

Clement knew that the Japanese advance, if all indications were correct, would be swift and there was no telling how far south they'd come in five days. He hoped Singapore wasn't even now in the hands of the Japanese. He felt sure Long would have said as much during their brief conversation if that had been the case. He looked at Ivan, but he didn't see fear or even apprehension. Just the calm stoicism he'd come to associate with the major.

'I'm so sorry, Ivan. You must be very worried about your family.' Clement paused. 'But I think there's something you're not telling me. Am I right?'

Lyon looked out across the darkening sea. 'Why would you think that, Clement?'

'Firstly, I learn of another man we are to extricate. Then you inform me that the *Prince of Wales* and the *Repulse* are sunk and that you've learned this from men you suspect are Vichy French. Want to tell me what's going on, Ivan?'

Lyon kept his gaze on the distant horizon then nodded. 'My wife and child are in Singapore. And I do want to get there to rescue them from harm. However, I believe we have a spy on board, Clement. I've been tracking him all over the South Pacific.'

'Who?'

'Kearsley.'

'You have proof?'

'No.' Lyon leaned towards Clement keeping his voice low. 'Call it a process of elimination. Think of it this way; he knows all the locations of the Coastwatchers around the South, East and West Pacific and, more importantly, their transmission codes. He volunteered to come on this mission. He drove the lorry back up the road to Baucau and was away at least an hour doing that. Suppose he'd informed those Japanese on Timor before leaving Dili who then followed us to Baucau. By then Kearsley knew which boat we were taking and our destination. It's my opinion that they were waiting for us in *The Flying*

Dutchman. How else could they have known which ship to target and where to place the limpet? And they have established agents and consulates all around this area just poised to strike.'

'Do you think they knew about Watkins?'

'Dear Lord, I hope not.'

Clement glanced at Lyon. 'While I agree it doesn't look good, Ivan, it isn't conclusive proof of Kearsley's guilt.' Clement stared at Lyon. 'What are you intending to do?'

'It's my guess he'll abscond once we're close to Singapore. He'll return to his lair like the traitor he is.'

'And the limpet? It would have blown him up as well as us?'

'Perhaps that was why it wasn't primed. Perhaps he intended to prime it then jump overboard. Perhaps the Japanese will have a craft available to pick him up just after six tonight.'

'Then we'll watch him. I'll make sure he's on watch tonight at six.'

12

Java Sea - 16th December 1941

Clement joined Archer and Savage in the for'ard hold. Tom had placed the mine into a crate.

'Bill isn't happy about it,' Tom said. 'Especially as the boat is now full of fuel.'

'I'm not thrilled myself, Tom. Have you checked our munition supply?'

'Yeah. First thing Mick and I did.'

'And?'

'It's not one of ours.'

'Any markings on it?'

'Yeah, but I don't know what it means,' Savage said.

'Show me.'

Mick lifted the mine and indicated the initials on the reverse side.

Clement read the initials *M.D.1.*

'Do you know what that means, Clem?' Tom asked.

'Yes. It was made in England. I must ask you both

not to mention this to anyone. And that, I'm afraid, is an order.'

Tom and Mick nodded but neither man spoke.

Clement felt the hollow in his chest that always accompanied betrayal. It made no sense. Why would a British limpet have been stuck to the fuel tank of their ship? He had no answers. 'Anyone else know this?'

'Just you and us, Clem. I don't seem to have too many friends at present.'

'Can't understand why, Tom.'

Archer laughed.

'Until we dispose of it, I need you to stay with it. No one but you and Mick are to have access to it. All right with you?'

'Yeah. She'll be right. Can't go off, it's not armed. And I've removed the detonator anyway. Harmless as a fly now.'

Clement went to his bunk and found his camera. He wanted a photograph of the thing. He wasn't sure anyone would believe him without it. Returning to the for'ard hold, he took three photographs making sure the identifying markings were clear.

'When do we get rid of it?' Tom asked.

'Soon.' Clement climbed back on deck. 'Remember, Tom, no one is to have access to it other than you and Mick and it's not to be left unattended.'

'We won't leave it.'

Clement nodded. He stared out to sea. On every side all he could see was endless ocean. A wind had sprung up and Bill's crew were making sure everything was secured. He glanced along the deck and saw Ivan and Joe Watkins sitting on the engine housing. They seemed to be deep in conversation. While Bill was busy with his crew, Clement walked aft to properly meet the American.

'How do you do, I'm Clement,' he said thrusting his hand towards Joe Watkins.

'Nice to meet you, sir. I'm grateful to you for putting into Surabaya to collect me. Things are getting a bit scary around this part of the Pacific.'

'Things are probably not going to get any less scary around Singapore either, Joe.' Clement glanced at Ivan. 'You two met before?'

'Yes, at one of those ghastly diplomatic things in Manilla,' Ivan said.

'Yeah, well…' Joe interrupted.

Ivan continued. 'There were a lot of military people there. You know the sort of thing, Clement, I'm sure. But a British Officers' summer mess uniform never fails to impress the ladies. I'd sailed a boat there,' Ivan added.

Clement glanced at Joe. Ivan had stopped Joe from speaking and Clement wanted to know why. Despite Ivan's suspicions about Kearsley, Clement increasingly felt that Ivan wasn't what he seemed. 'And what is it you do exactly, Lieutenant?'

'I work for Uncle Sam. I can't really say anything more about it. Sorry, sir.'

'And you're going to Singapore?'

'Yes, sir.'

'To find passage to the Philippines.'

'That's right, sir.'

Clement couldn't quite decide if Watkins was being deliberately obtuse or whether he, like Clement, didn't really know who to trust. Leaving them, Clement returned to the wheelhouse to speak with Bill. 'Just to let you know, Bill, we'll dispose of the mine by dropping it over the side. But this afternoon, about five, I'd like to jettison some debris; broken timber, perhaps a mattress or something that will float for an hour or two.'

'Expecting a surveillance flight?'

'Most likely.'

'I thought it wasn't primed?'

'It wasn't. But it cannot be guaranteed that someone on board may have intended to arm it after we left port.'

Bill Reynolds was staring at him. 'You think we have a traitor on board?'

'Anything is possible. But if the Japanese see debris on the sea, they will think it exploded; regardless of whether or not a traitor exists; if they think the ship has sunk, they may give up their daily surveillance flights. So, it would help if they saw some wreckage on the sea. If we were to jettison it around five, that would put us ahead of the location when the surveillance flight flies over.'

'I'll ask the boys to arrange something. Perhaps Archer should just check it all first though.'

'Good idea. Thank you, Bill.'

Returning to the for'ard hold, he told Tom and Mick about the plan. 'I'll leave it with you.'

'She'll be right, Clem. We'll sort it!'

Clement returned to the radio room and his bunk. It was the only place he could think uninterrupted. That the limpet wasn't from their supplies didn't absolve Kearsley. Could the man have brought it with him? That it was British and not an enemy device was puzzling. And what of the Japanese and the Vichy Frenchmen in Surabaya? Could it all could have been arranged from Timor by the Japanese? Would that implicate Ross and Whittaker who, as far as Clement knew, were the only people there who knew their destination. If the Japanese knew about Watkins's inclusion, then it was small wonder there hadn't been any interference in Surabaya. The Japanese would think they'd all be blown up in the Java Sea and an evening aerial surveillance flight would confirm it. But why use a British limpet? To defray suspicion? Could it have been seized during a raid of some kind? He didn't know if the Japanese had such devices of their own. And who would have ordered it to be placed on the *Krait*? Was Joe Watkins involved in some way? And who was to prime it? Too many questions. And the familiarity between Joe and Ivan worried Clement. Ivan had said they'd met previously but something didn't seem right to Clement. He'd ask Joe about it later when they were alone. Were Archer and Savage as innocent as he hoped they were? He thought back on Archer's quiet chat with him prior to their visit to *The*

Flying Dutchman. Clement didn't believe Archer or Savage capable of such a degree of deception. Only once before Clement had felt as though something was happening around him that didn't include him and that was in the bitter winter in northern Scotland six months ago. He hoped he wasn't reading too much into it. But his intuition rarely let him down. What consoled him was that Long himself had confirmed Lyon and his mission to collect the American. But if one of their number was a spy, Clement needed proof not suppositions.

Rising, Clement returned to the deck and stood beside Bill in the wheelhouse. 'How far out from Surabaya are we?'

'Ten miles or so,' Bill said.

'I think we'll drop the limpet over the side now.'

'Armed or not, the sooner it's off my boat the better, as far as I am concerned, Clement.'

Clement went for'ard and found Mick. He along with Bill's crew had assembled a collection of demijohns, mattresses and saucepans with sealed lids along with numerous broken planks of timber. 'Good work, all of you.'

'And if they don't buy it?' Mick asked.

'Then we'll prepare a welcome for them they won't expect. But only if it's absolutely necessary. We'll dispose of the limpet now we're well out to sea. And Mick, please double check the arming switch is off and the detonator removed.'

'Already done, Clem,' Tom said, climbing on deck,

the limpet in his grasp.

The event attracted the entire ship's company, all gathering on the foredeck to watch the proceedings. Clement stood back, his gaze on Hugh Kearsley. But if Kearsley had placed the limpet on the fuel tank, he gave nothing away. Tom picked the mine up and tossed it into the air, the circular disc gaining height then falling into the ocean with a small splash. A chorus of cheers marked the occasion.

'When do we throw the pots and pans overboard, Clem,' Mick asked.

'Just after five. Until then you can stand down.'

Clement looked along the deck and saw Ivan sitting aft. Leaving Tom and Mick to play cards, he walked towards Lyon. 'Mind if I join you?'

'Please do. Quite a spectacle. Perhaps Archer should enter the Australian Olympics Team for discus throwing.'

Clement smiled. 'Ivan, is what you are concealing from me anything to do with our mission to Singapore?'

'Sometimes Clement you can be too astute for your own good.'

'We are all of us here putting our lives on the line, Ivan. And, I have *Most Secret* security clearance. It would help if I thought I could trust you.'

Lyon remained silent for a few minutes. Clement waited. He knew the routine. Silence is something most humans don't like much. In fact, the longer the silence the more likely it is that the less experienced person will feel intimidated and be the first to speak. Clement waited, the uneasy silence increasingly palpable.

When Lyon did speak his voice was only a whisper. 'My mission is completely unrelated and everything I've told you is true. Despite your security clearance, I cannot tell you what I'm looking into, but it has nothing to do with your mission. And, it is true that someone on this team is a traitor. But I will say this, Clement, and I'm only telling you to put your mind at rest; I said I worked for SIS. That is only partially true. You and I work for the same person, Sir Stewart Menzies. What you are doing will shorten the war; of that I have no doubt. What I am doing, regardless of who wins this war, will guarantee that Japan will not prosper in the post war period. I cannot say any more than this.'

Clement looked out at the sea. Heavy clouds were gathering off to the west. 'You think we will lose this war?'

'Not in Europe, especially now the Americans are with us. But I fear the Pacific War will be longer and have disastrous consequences for the Allies unless the Japanese Naval codes can be broken.'

'Why do you say that?'

'What I'm about to tell you is so secret, I'd be shot if they ever discovered I'd told you.'

Clement faced Lyon.

'About a year ago, a British merchant ship, the *Automedon* was captured in the Indian Ocean by the Germans. On board were some highly sensitive documents destined for the British High Commission in Singapore. These documents included some British War Cabinet discussions on the Far East. The minutes detailed that Britain would not be able to defend Singapore in the event of a Japanese attack. Moreover, it stated that Hong Kong and Borneo were indefensible. Needless to say, the Germans handed this information over to the Japanese. Hence their speed of attack in the South Pacific.'

'Dear Lord! Singapore will fall and all the troops there will either die or be prisoners of war.'

'And the *Prince of Wales* and the *Repulse* have been sunk. We have nothing to stop them. No aircraft carrier, not even one Spitfire or Hurricane.'

'Sitting ducks. And Hugh Kearsley?'

'I'm sorry to say it, Clement but he's your problem now. With the discovery of the limpet he may not make his move now until after we arrive in Singapore. Once there, I'm guessing he'll disappear as soon as we've landed.'

'And Joe Watkins?'

'What about him?'

'How do you know him?'

'As I've told you. I know he is based in Manilla with the US Intelligence team and that he speaks Japanese. But that's about it.'

'Who asked you to collect him from Surabaya?'

'Long. But the directive would have come from Sir Stewart. I'm guessing it was a request from the Americans initially to London then through FECB to Long in

Australia.'

'How sure are you that he is Joe Watkins?'

'You have a very suspicious mind, Clement. While I said I don't know him well, I have met him, just the once and rather briefly in Manilla. But that is Joe Watkins.'

Clement stared back towards the fading Dutch East Indies coastline. It was no more now that a thin grey line on the horizon. They'd made good progress, but he estimated the rain was only minutes away. Most days, Clement prayed for a thunderstorm which would keep the Japanese aeroplanes grounded, but this night he prayed that a surveillance flight would find the jetsam and dismiss the *Krait* from their searches.

Clement stood. Casting his eye along the deck he saw Archer and Savage still sitting aft and playing cards. Joe and Kearsley were at the radio at the Navigator's desk. Clement left Lyon and went to sit on the step beside the wheelhouse where he knew everyone would hear him. 'Could I have your attention please?' Clement shouted. 'Just after five this afternoon, we will jettison the debris. I expect there will be at least one surveillance flight around six o'clock tonight. If the floating debris doesn't convince the Japanese that we've sunk, they may come looking for us.'

'Anything you'd like me to do, Clement?' Hugh called from the radio hold.

'Yes. I'd like you to remain beside the radio, listening. And please don't leave it between five and seven o'clock this evening.' Clement looked at Watkins. 'I understand you speak Japanese, Joe. It would be good if we had advance warning of any chatter about us so I'd like you to sit with Hugh at the wireless and listen during those two hours.'

'Sure thing, Clem,' Joe said.

'How is it you speak Japanese?' Clement asked.

'Learned it state-side before the war.'

Clement nodded. There was more he would have liked to know about Watkins's activities but the least said in front of Hugh the better, especially if Ivan's hunch about Kearsley was correct. 'Would you mind being added to our daily aerial surveillance watch, Joe?'

'Not at all, sir. Happy to help.'

'Could you take a turn now?'

'Sure.'

Clement waited while Joe went for'ard with the binoculars. He watched Joe and Ivan but there was no interaction between them. Ten minutes later, Lyon closed the book he was reading and walked aft. Clement saw him standing with Pedro near the galley. While Tom and Mick assembled the items to be jettisoned, Clement joined Joe for'ard. 'Joe, once you are with Hugh at the radio-transmitter, would you please listen carefully for any references to us and by that I mean not just whether we've been sunk?'

'Anything in particular?'

'Any information about the ship, Singapore or Timor. But I would ask you please not to confide this information with anyone other than me. This would include

Hugh.'

'Sure thing, Clem. Any reason for that?'

'I don't want the team placed under any more stress than we already are. If Singapore has fallen to the Japanese, we are heading into a war zone. And I'd sooner not alarm the team unnecessarily. Is it still your intention to leave us in Singapore, Joe?'

'Yes, sir.'

'If it's in Japanese hands, might I suggest you return with us? If they are moving as fast as I've been led to believe, the Philippines may not be a safe place either.'

Clement checked his watch. It was just after two and there hadn't been any Japanese planes flying overhead. But, if the limpet had been placed on the ship by the Japanese, he believed there wouldn't be any before six o'clock. And, with Joe Watkins listening in to the wireless with Kearsley from five o'clock, it would be unlikely Kearsley could transmit anything of a traitorous nature.

Clement gazed aloft. The *Krait* had a gaff-rigged mainsail that was furled around the boom. A battened shade cloth was stretched over it and tied at various points along the rigging. Clement stared at the folded, red-coloured sail. If it were raised, he believed they could disguise the *Krait* sufficiently to confuse a Zero pilot who would be travelling at speed and may not make the immediate connection to their former appearance.

Clement went to speak with Bill. 'Do you think we could raise the sail this evening, Bill?'

'Too slow, Clement.'

'I have a mind that we should appear to be a different ship. Sails and a different number of crew visible this evening may help to confuse our enemy.'

'I suppose so. It takes about twenty minutes to raise it and stow the shade cloth.'

'Perfect. And four people on deck tonight until after dark. Can we cover the name?'

'I can do better than that. This ship was once a Japanese fishing boat named the *Kofuku Maru*. I still have the old name board stowed somewhere and we could paint a line of whitewash around the gunwale. I'll get the boys onto it now.'

'Any disguise would be helpful, thank you. And I'll ask Tom and Mick to pitch in too.'

'I'm not doing it just for you, Clement.'

'I understand, Bill. Regardless, it's appreciated.'

At five o'clock Clement went below to check on Hugh and Joe. They sat together by the radio transmitter. Hugh was turning the frequency knob. Wireless static was filling the humid air.

'Anything?' Clement said.

'Nothing yet,' Joe said. Clement glanced at Hugh but said nothing. While the identity of a collaborator was a lingering problem, Clement's immediate concern was the anticipated Japanese aerial surveillance flight.

At a quarter past five, Tom and Mick tossed an assortment of debris into the sea: two mattresses, empty demijohns, pots and pans with their lids sealed and several broken and splintered planks of timber. As each item floated on the surface, it left a trail of flotsam on the sea, the waves and current dispersing it over the shiny waters. Clement watched it, waiting for it to sink but everything stayed afloat.

Clement gathered everyone on deck except Hugh and Joe. 'You've all done an amazing job in disguising the *Krait*. But I'm expecting that we'll have company sometime around six. They'll be searching for the ship, and they will check us out even if only to eliminate us from the search. Only four of us will be on deck plus Bill at the helm: One of Bill's crew, Tom, Mick and myself. Everyone else will be below decks. Those of the team on deck will have a loaded Owen gun close at hand but not visible for obvious reasons. But we should only fire if fired upon. And even then, only if it is a matter of life and death. They may strafe us as a precaution or to see if we respond, so please keep alert, and resist the urge to retaliate. Wait for my command. No one fires unless or until I reach for my Owen gun. Understood?'

Heads were nodding.

'Tom, you take the foredeck, Mick at the aft near the galley. I will be amidships and Bill at the helm and Pedro at the galley. No one else on deck.

From the corner of his eye, Clement watched Ivan. While Lyon had been forthcoming about his inclusion on the *Krait* and the staggering information that the Germans had seized highly secret documents from the *Automedon*, Clement had no way of checking the veracity of any of it. Astounding as Lyon's revelations were, none of it affected their current situation. But together with all the other uncertainties, Clement knew he was in for a long night.

13

Java Sea - 16th December 1941

The light faded as six o'clock approached and the jettisoned debris had long since disappeared from view. Clement estimated that if it was still afloat, it would be about seven miles behind them now. He checked his watch again, eight minutes to six. He glanced through the open hatch to the radio hold where Joe and Hugh were sitting. If Kearsley were the traitor, he didn't exhibit any sign of impending alarm. Neither was he wanting to jump overboard. In fact, he didn't exhibit any signs of being anything other than a radio operator doing his job. Clement looked up into the evening sky. It would be dark within the hour and too late for any further surveillance flights. Clement turned to look at each member of his team. Anticipated anxiety is what he saw and felt as the allotted time neared. He studied each man carefully as they waited in position. Tom was sitting on the foredeck, a fishing net across his knees.

Clement knew an Owen gun lay beneath it. He glanced back at Mick. Mick had secreted his Owen next to the stove and only an arm's length away from him. Clement paced the deck near the wheelhouse. All eyes lifted to watch him. He checked his watch again; seven minutes to six. He scanned the skies then, seeing nothing, stuck his head into the radio hold again to check on Hugh and Joe. Hugh lifted his head as Clement peered into the tiny space.

'Anything?' Clement asked.

'Nothing,' Hugh said.

Joe was wearing the headset, his hand slowly turning the frequency dial, his head down and his brow creased, his concentration apparent.

Neither man spoke. Clement squatted by the hatch to gain Joe's attention. He tapped his wristwatch. Joe acknowledged the gesture, but his fingers lingered over the frequency dial.

Clement stood, gazing at the skies. All eyes on him.

Six o'clock came.

Clement's fingers tapped the rail around the wheelhouse, his nerves heightened and his pulse rate thumping. Everyone was tense. The minutes dragged by, but no aeroplanes appeared. Neither had Kearsley made any attempt to challenge him or jump overboard. As each minute passed, Clement dared to consider that the subterfuge had worked. He began to pace the deck again. Everyone sat, watching him, waiting for the order to stand down or reach for their weapons.

Clement drew in a deep breath; his mouth was dry and his heart rate pounded. He checked his watch again; five minutes past six. The expected flight hadn't arrived. He looked around the faces. Bill was already making preparations for the evening watch. He began to allow himself to breathe again.

Then it came. The unmistakable sound.

Clement looked up, his heart thumping, his gaze fixed on the sky. It came out of the west at speed, appearing like a black speck coming out of the setting sun. As it approached it banked and circled above them. Clement stood, his mouth dry. He waved to the aeroplane. No one moved. Clement quickly checked the team. All were watching him, waiting for the signal. As the aeroplane banked again it dropped low, then it came towards them at a frightening pace. Clement held his breath as the plane passed overhead. Looking up, he watched it climb high, then descend again passing so low that the noise was deafening. Then a burst of gunfire. Clement heard the spitting of bullets hitting water then the rapid thud of shots biting into the wooden deck. Everyone crouched low as the plane thundered overhead. A line of bullets dug into the deck near Clement's feet. He reached forward to where his Owen gun lay under a pile of ropes. All eyes were watching him. The plane lifted. 'If they fly over again at low level, we shoot!' Clement called. The aeroplane banked then lifted into the sky. Everyone waited, hardly daring to breathe.

'I thought we were done for! You've got nerves of

steel; I'll give you that, Clem,' Tom said.

'A close-run thing, Tom,' Clement said, still looking at the receding Zero. 'Meeting, everyone, aft.'

'I want to check my boat first,' Bill said.

'Of course. Then would you join us?'

Bill nodded then hurried to the engine bay and lifted the hatch. Clement could hear him and his crew checking the engine hold, then the water and fuel tanks.

Clement leaned over the radio hold hatch to where Hugh and Joe still sat at the wireless. 'Anything?'

Hugh held up his hand. 'Joe's listening to something now but I don't know what yet. We heard the shots. What happened outside?'

'A few shots fired but nothing serious. Tell Joe to stay here listening. Hugh, would you join us aft?'

'Of course.'

Clement sat on the end of the engine housing, the team squeezed onto the aft deck and engine housing around him.

'It appears as though we've got away with it, this time. Once we know what, if anything the Japanese are saying over the wireless, we'll know for certain if the disguise has worked. In the meantime, there is something I think you should know. It is possible, Ivan, your presence among us has put us all in danger. And put this mission in danger. It is my belief that you haven't been completely honest about your presence here and it's time you were.'

All eyes turned to Ivan.

Ivan shifted his feet; his eyes were wide and intense and squarely focused on Clement. Clement could see the man felt betrayed. Or was it something else? Was his hesitation traitorous guilt or because Ivan Lyon was concealing something else? Either way, if Major Lyon was indeed a loyal member of the British Army, this was his opportunity to prove it. Clement watched Lyon closely while keeping Kearsley in his peripheral vision. Despite Lyon's mission, it was Clement who was ultimately in charge and Lyon's continued presence with the team depended on his answer. Clement began to plan how they could off load Lyon and perhaps also Kearsley onto the nearest island, leaving them to their fates.

Lyon leaned forward and rested his elbows on the engine housing, his voice low. 'What I am about to tell you is highly secret. Clement is right, I haven't been completely honest with you. The Vichy French were asking all sorts of questions about where we'd come from and where we're going.'

'And what did you say?' Tom asked.

'I said we'd come from Fiji and were heading for the Philippines.'

'Did they believe you?' Clement asked.

'I don't know. I said I was a trader and that I did the round trip frequently. That bit is true. But I'm not sure if they believed it. They told me to take another route as the Imperial Japanese Navy was in the area. That's when they told me about the *Prince of Wales* and the *Repulse*. Chatting with me could have been solely to occupy me while they had the limpet attached to the fuel tank. But, as I suspected, they didn't know Clement. By keeping you separate, Clement, and you discovering the limpet, their plan hasn't worked.'

'Will they try again?' Mick asked Clement.

Clement pondered the question. 'While I don't think they will, we cannot guarantee they haven't passed on a description of the ship and ourselves to the Japanese secret police. It just depends on who's in charge when we get to Singapore. But you were going to tell us, Ivan what you're really doing in the South Pacific?' Clement said, aware that Lyon had cleverly steered the conversation away from the question.

Lyon looked around the faces present. 'They have become suspicious of me, or at least, a tall Englishman, and Clement is correct when he says they are taking an interest in me and therefore you too. I have been involved in a good many raids around the Indochinese coastline, boarding and sinking numerous Japanese ships. I am under orders from Churchill himself to collect whatever intelligence I can from these ships then scuttle them. The focus is on code books for decrypting the Japanese Imperial Naval codes. So, while it goes against my orders, I will tell you what I've been able to piece together about the activities of the Japanese Imperial Army and Navy. I've learned that there are not only numerous Japanese plants in the Dutch East Indies, but they are well established in New Guinea, New Britain, Timor, Fiji and in the French territories further to the east. These French territories, along with those in Indochina are particularly worrying. What you may not appreciate is that it isn't the former French government controlling these islands anymore. It is the Vichy Government. And that may as well be Nazi Germany. This has given the advancing Japanese Armies in Indochina a clear run through Vietnam and Cambodia and now they are in Siam and Burma, as well as south into Malaya. The Japanese have large and well-trained secret police known as the Kempeitai but there is another secret organisation of great power and ruthlessness. Rumour is that the Japanese Emperor's brother, Prince Chichibu, who heads up a secret organisation known as the *kin no yuri* or Golden Lily, is amassing anything of value from these over-run territories, especially in China and Burma, and what they have already stolen is said to be worth millions if not billions of pounds in gold and precious stones. The *kin no yuri* are ruthless when it comes to taking what they want. They may not be in charge yet, but once Singapore falls, they will control the whole of the Southwest Pacific. And the Americans in the Philippines and their other bases around the North Pacific, as we have seen, are not safe either.'

'And the oil refineries would be in their control too,' Clement added.

'Of course. I must get to Singapore; for my family but also to inform Air Chief Marshall Sir Robert Brooke-Popham who is in charge there. Egos and attitudes aside, and some other sensitive information that Clement knows about, it is my opinion that we are literally fighting a losing battle. And, quite possibly sailing into a hornet's nest.'

Joe poked his head out of the hatch and called to Clement. 'I've heard something. The pilot reported no sighting of the ship but some jetsam on the water then there was an encrypted message.'

Clement thought of Eric Nave and the JN25 code. 'Did you write it down, Joe?'

Watkins stared at Clement.

'A yes or no will do, Joe.'

'Yeah. I got it.'

'Would you please stay listening?'

'Sure.' Joe returned to the radio. Clement would speak with Joe later.

'It is imperative we get Captain Winthorpe out,' Clement said.

'Then we continue,' Ivan said. 'But you must be prepared to encounter further Japanese surveillance or resistance. This ship, whether they recognise it or not, could be impounded and see us all taken prisoner.'

'Do you think those Japs in Surabaya will tell others about us?' Tom asked.

'Almost certainly,' Clement answered. 'But so far, if they really believe the *Krait* has been sunk, and this is a completely different ship, it may buy us a few days. Let's hope it's enough.'

There was silence around the group for a full minute.

Clement looked around the wide-eyed faces. 'Under

normal circumstances, if this could be considered normal, I would say that your further involvement with the mission is voluntary. However, given where we are and what you've just learned, I don't think that's a viable option.'

'I'd be in anyway, Clem,' Tom said.

'Me too,' said Mick.

'And me,' Hugh added.

'Thank you,' Clement said. The mission, which was to have been a silent rescue mission from friendly territory, was now a vastly different prospect. While Clement would never have described himself as a superstitious man, he held very few real facts about their current circumstances and that always made him uneasy. As darkness fell, he went to his bunk to think and pray.

Lying back on his bunk, he closed his eyes, the sound of radio static buzzing in the background. Focusing his mind, he went through recent events. Given the level of interest in them in Surabaya, Clement asked himself who exactly was the person of interest for the Japanese and the French. In view of all that Ivan had told him, the obvious person was Lyon. But he couldn't shake the feeling that something else was going on. He thought back to Timor wondering if David Ross or John Whittaker had been interrogated and the Japanese had learned of the mission or Ivan's presence on the *Krait*. Opening his eyes, he stared at the rusty marks on the bulkhead beside his bunk. There were no answers, just more questions. More doubt, more uncertainty. He thought of the rendezvous and Johnny. What was Johnny carrying that was so vital? Ivan's activities in the region had doubtless brought him under suspicion but perhaps it wasn't, nor ever had been, about Lyon. Or, indeed, Joe Watkins. Perhaps it had always and only ever been about John Winthorpe. Clement thought again about the team of men he hardly knew; Hugh had driven the lorry back up the hill in Baucau. He may have alerted the Japanese to their departure. Ivan, despite what he'd confided, may not be what he purported to be. He had spoken to two men in Surabaya but Clement had no idea what had actually transpired between them or even if the men were Vichy French. Likewise Lyon had spoken to the barman, albeit briefly, in *The Flying Dutchman*. Could he have passed on a message to the Japanese men in the bar? Bill, who regularly sailed the area, could be flying the *Rising Sun* not to defray suspicion but because it was his true allegiance. And Clement had no idea about Bill's young crew, although he thought that option unlikely. These lads were local Timorese boys whose only ambition in life was a freshly caught fish and a sunny afternoon asleep in the shade. And as far as Tom and Mick were concerned their loyalties were, so Clement believed, to each other and the land of their birth; a country the Japanese almost certainly had on their list of countries to occupy. And Joe Watkins may have been simply in the wrong place at the wrong time.

Clement sat up and swung his legs over the side of the bunk. Climbing the ladder, he peered out the hatch to see where the team were. Each of them was either reading or playing cards. Satisfied each man was occupied, he returned to his bunk. He wanted to speak to Joe without being overheard by the others. A difficult enough thing to do on a ship the size of the *Krait* and its confined quarters but with Joe at the radio, he took the chance.

'Anything further, Joe?' Clement asked, keeping his voice low.

'No. But you're full of surprises, Clem,' Joe said, his voice equally quiet.

'Could I see the encryption?'

Joe handed Clement the sheet of paper. Clement stared at the numbers, all in groups of five. 'Is this JN25B7, Joe?' Clement said in a whisper.

Watkins's eyebrows lifted. 'Like I said, full of surprises. But no, it's an updated version. JN25B8.'

'They've changed it? When?'

'Last week.'

'But not the code book. You said JN25*B*8, so they've changed the additive table but they're still using the same code book.' Clement looked up at nothing in particular. 'Can you decipher it?'

Joe turned to face Clement. 'Not me. I'm an analysist not a code breaker. But what are you, Clem?' Joe kept his steady gaze on Clement.

'Someone who doesn't know much about anything,' Clement said.

'Well, if that's true, you're a pretty good guesser but I

don't know the content of the message.'

'Did you recognise the touch, then?'

'Are you sure you don't work for Uncle Sam?'

'Maybe I do some work for Uncle Sam's parent. Where do you think this message came from?'

'Signal was quite strong so most likely a ship.'

'An aircraft carrier?'

'Could be. But it could also be a nearby island. Regardless, Clem, I'm not a code breaker.'

'I'd like to keep it.'

'Me too.'

'Perhaps Captain Winthorpe will know more.'

'Your Captain Winthorpe is a code breaker?'

'Actually, Joe. I've never really known what he does. So maybe he is.'

Watkins smiled again. 'I'm glad you're on our side, Clem.'

What Clement had learned from Joe troubled him greatly. Not because of the change in additive tables, which were important to Long and Nave, but because the Japanese had transmitted an enciphered message. Why had the Japanese thought reporting on the ship required the message to be encrypted? Surely if it was a straightforward aerial surveillance flight to locate a ship that had been blown up, the message could have been sent in plain text or Kana Morse, which Hugh would understand. That it was deemed necessary to transmit in JN25B8, Clement believed gave their mission an added level of importance that even he hadn't attributed to it.

14

Java Sea - 17th December 1941

Clement stood beside Tom on the deck. Neither spoke. The day had dawned very hot. A low, white haze settled over the sea and the wind dropped ominously making the sea a pale silver lake. He couldn't see if any rain clouds were forming but he prayed they would soon. Thunderstorms kept aeroplanes grounded and made the high temperatures bearable. The thick, humid air settled on his skin and an eerie quietness had descended.

He'd made sure his turn as look-out for Japanese planes followed Tom's sunrise watch. He glanced around the deck before speaking. 'How well do you know Hugh, Tom?'

Archer lowered the binoculars and looked at Clement. 'Truth be told, Clem, I don't know any of you very well. You're wondering if we have a traitor on board. I've been wondering the same thing. And, despite everything

Major Lyon said last night, if I'm honest, he's just a bit too suave for my liking.'

Clement didn't respond but while he was inclined to agree with Tom's assessment, he had met many officers in the forces in England who were no different to Ivan. 'Have you checked the equipment recently, Tom?'

'Yeah. Mick and me checked the Owens after last night and cleaned them again. Even though they're good in wet weather, it's best to do it daily in humid conditions. Don't want them not firing at the wrong moment.'

'Quite!'

'You ever had to test your skills in combat, Clem?'

Clement rolled up his sleeve. The large, purplish scar of jagged, raised flesh from the wounds he'd received in Caithness were a permanent reminder.

'Struth! Close range. I'll take that as a yes,' Tom said. He lifted the binoculars to his eyes and scanned the now glaring white skies. 'Just so you know, Clem, I've been involved in plenty of brawls outside pubs but not a fight to the death and not with a Jap. Not with a knife either.'

'You'll be fine, Tom and with divine help, we won't have to worry. My hope is still that we can get in and out of Singapore without being seen.' Clement paused. 'And it would help, Lord, if the Japanese are not in control when we get there.'

'Amen to that, Clem,' Archer muttered.

Clement half smiled. He believed Tom would be both brave and courageous when the time came for, despite what he'd told Tom, he believed things would not go according to plan in Singapore. Clement suspected the traitor still held a trump card. Although, why it hadn't yet been played worried him. Perhaps whatever it was, it would identify the traitor so absolutely that there would be no room for doubt. Clement also believed there was only one place where this confrontation would take place and that was on Singapore island itself where the man had an escape route or where the Japanese would personally meet him.

Whatever plan Clement devised now; he knew it not only largely depended on himself, but he couldn't confide it to anyone, not even Tom. He also needed a reserve plan just in case things went horribly wrong.

'What makes you suspicious of a traitor being on board, Tom?' he asked, still scanning the skies.

'When Mick and me returned the Owens, we checked all the equipment. We found a tear in the canvas of one of the fold-boats.'

'What?' Clement said, hearing his own incredulity.

'Mick's repairing it now. It could have been damaged when the Zero flew over or in transit coming from Dili. Or it could've been torn to begin with, I just don't know. But it looks more like it's been cut to me.'

'Just one fold-boat?' Clement asked.

Tom nodded. 'But if it was someone on board, they could've been disturbed and may come back later to finish the job.'

'Who else knows?'

'Just me and Mick. And now you.'

'Any suspicions?'

'Well, not Mick. He was as surprised as me.'

'So, you think it was either Ivan, Joe or Hugh? Or me?'

'Not you, Clem. I reckon you're dinkum;'

'Dinkum?'

Tom laughed. 'True blue.'

'Doesn't help.'

'The real deal.'

'Right. And for what it's worth, Tom I think you're dinkum too.'

'She'll be right, Clem. Mick and me'll have your back.'

'I'm counting on it, Tom. Perhaps we should have a practice at assembling these boats anyway. We'll do it daily from now on. Just in case.'

'Good idea. That should stop him, whoever he is.'

No planes had appeared during Clement's two-hour watch. Passing the binoculars to Hugh, he went to the for'ard hold where Tom and Mick had slung their hammocks and where all the equipment was stowed. He wanted to know if Mick had been able to repair the fold-boat. Mick looked up as Clement climbed down the hatch.

'Tom has told me about the tear. Can you fix it, Mick?' Clement asked.

'Yep! Bill had some pitch and marine glues on board. It should hold.'

'Any damage to the other two boats?'

'No. Just this one.'

'Right,' Clement replied. 'Did Tom tell you I think we should practice assembling them daily from now on.'

Mick nodded. 'I'm not your guilty person, if that's what you're thinking,' Mick said. 'But I think I know who is.'

'Well?'

'Hugh Kearsley.'

'Why him?'

'I saw him down here a couple of days ago and again yesterday.'

'Did you actually witness him with a knife in his hand making the hole?'

'No.'

'That he was alone in this hold isn't conclusive evidence, is it? After all, you're here alone. You and Tom even sleep here.'

Savage nodded his head. 'Fair enough!'

'I would prefer it, Mick, if you were to keep your suspicions to yourself. We have a job to do, so, until we have absolute proof if there is a saboteur on board, this kind of speculation erodes team morale which can compromise the mission. Understood?'

'Understood. When that dries, it should hold it!' Mick said, gathering the tools and screwing a lid down firmly on the thick yellowish paste of congealed glue.

Clement left the hold and went to the wheelhouse where he could sit in a small degree of comfort and away from the men. He wanted to think. The damage had been found and repaired but it didn't bode well for the coming mission. If one of their number was intent on sabotage, they still had plenty of time to do it. He decided he'd check everything daily from now on.

Tom tapped on the window to the wheelhouse. 'Cuppa, Clem?'

'Thank you, I'd be grateful. Would you like some, Bill?'

'If Archer's making.'

Clement left the wheelhouse and walked aft. The men were sitting or lying around the deck, some under the shade cloth for'ard and some on the engine housing under the permanent cover. He checked his watch. It was just after noon and the heat was terrific. On the horizon he saw the storm clouds gathering. The clouds were forming into a gigantic circle of threatening power; dark grey at the base and snow-white at the top. They hadn't heard any Japanese surveillance flights this morning which Clement thought reassuring. He collected the tea then returned to the wheelhouse. Clement sat on the bunk-like bench. Bill had opened both port and starboard windows to the wheelhouse, but the air was still and breathtakingly hot.

'Makes me wonder why we drink tea in weather like this,' Bill said.

'My wife used to say it cooled the blood.'

'Is that true?'

Clement shrugged. 'She also used to say, "Tea in a crisis".'

'Not reassuring, Clement.'

Clement smiled. But his personal life wasn't any of Bill's concern. 'Did any of the crew leave the ship while in Surabaya?'

'José and Juan left for an hour or so.'

'Do you know why?'

'José suggested we top up the water tanks. I thought it a good idea. But the hoses are on the wharf, of course, close to the ship.'

'And he didn't leave to go into the town afterwards?'

'They both did. Said they wanted to buy some fruit.'

'And did they?'

'Yes.'

Clement finished his tea. The truth was that there was no evidence to show how the damage occurred and Clement began to consider it was more likely that the canvas may have been damaged before the boat came aboard. But regardless of whether the damage was sabotage or not, nothing would stop the rendezvous. It was what happened there that was important. Clement thought one last time about the men of his team. He'd done this before, in England, in Fearnley Maughton when he'd chosen his team for the Auxiliary Units. But those men he knew; some better than others it had to be said, but he did know them. These men he'd only recently met, and he knew only what they'd told him.

The rain when it came was relentless. The sheer volume of water kept the men below. During such a deluge, only the man on surveillance duty and the crew were on deck. Clement sat in the wheelhouse studying the charts of the myriad of islands that made up the Dutch East Indies. Over the rain and the familiar sound of the ship's plodding engines Clement heard the now recognisable high-pitched roar of an approaching Zero.

Clement looked up at Hugh, who was on duty in the pouring rain on the foredeck.

'Japs!' Hugh's voice shouted through the heavy rainfall and he pointed towards the sky.

Clement stood and stared through the window to where he could see the Zero as it flew out of the heavy grey mist. It was heading straight for them. Clement checked his watch. It was late in the day for a surveillance run; the reduced daylight and heavy mist making visibility limited. With the sound of the Zero increasing, Tom and Mick had lifted their for'ard hatch cover to watch the aeroplane descend out of the gloom. Clement hurriedly counted the men on deck. Six! One too many. The Zero pilot would surely count them.

'Hugh! Get below!' Clement shouted.

Hugh held the binoculars in his hand, his face staring upwards as though frozen in fright.

'Hugh! Take cover! Now, or the pilot will strafe us!'

Bill leapt from the wheelhouse and rushing forward grabbed the binoculars from Hugh's hands then pushed him down the for'ard hatch. Rushing back he tossed the binoculars to Clement then stood on deck outside the wheelhouse and stared into the oncoming Zero, his hand reaching for his hat and waving it vigorously.

Everyone held their breath as the thunderous sound passed overhead. It passed low, tipping its left-wing to see the men on deck. Clement, Bill and his crew waved back. The plane lifted into the sky then banked, returning for a second run. If it followed previous surveillance flights, it would fly over a second time then lift into the air. Clement returned with Bill to the wheelhouse and watched it approach again. This time, it circled above the ship several times; the wing tip low, the plane continuing to fly above them in a tight circle. Clement counted the minutes. It was taking too much time. He looked out and again counted the men on deck. With Bill in the wheelhouse that left four on deck. The correct number, now that Hugh was below deck. Why had the Zero taken such interest in them? Had they seen Hugh? The rain was heavy and the visibility not good. Perhaps the pilot wanted another look. The loud roar of the engine intensified again as it prepared for another pass. Clement stared through the front window of the wheelhouse trying to see the Zero. Then he heard the cracks; the familiar sound of strafing fire hitting the water around them.

'Bloody hell! Not again!' Bill shouted. Stepping out of the wheelhouse, he pointed his soaked sun-tanned arm towards the aft end of the ship where the Japanese flag hung limply over the stern.

The plane did another circuit swooping over them then lifted, making one final pass before flying away.

Clement waited until the Zero was not even a speck in the sky and Bill returned to the wheelhouse. 'Any damage, Bill?'

'I'll get the boys to check below but I don't think so. That was a close call, Clement,' Bill said. 'None of the bullets actually hit us. Despite our attempts at disguise, I'm wondering if they've put two and two together.'

Clement stared out over the vast ocean. 'Perhaps. How well do you know your crew?'

Bill's eyebrows shot up in surprise. 'They're all local lads from Timor. José and Juan are brothers and Pedro is their cousin. Why?'

'It's possible we have a saboteur on board.'

'And you think it's one of my crew?'

'No one is above suspicion, Bill. And it's not only your crew. It could be anyone on board. All I know is that the Japanese seem to be taking a very keen interest in us.'

'Well, it isn't me. And I certainly don't want my boat damaged. She may be old, but she's a great old ship. Easy to handle and seaworthy. Just the way I want it to stay.'

Clement stepped out onto the deck. He was drenched in seconds but he wanted to check the equipment and the radio. His mind was spinning. Rushing for'ard he lifted the hatch cover and peered in. 'Everyone all right?'

Tom and Mick looked up at him.

'Yeah. We're right, Clem.'

'The equipment?'

'All fine, Clem,' Tom replied.

'Hugh? You alright?' Clement shouted, the rain dripping from his face.

Kearsley nodded but Clement could see the fear that still gripped the man. Clement let the hatch cover fall and went straight to the radio room. 'Joe? Everything all right with you and the radio?'

'More by good luck than good management, sir.'

Clement replaced the hatch, making sure the cover was firmly in place to prevent any ingress of water damaging the vital radio valves.

'Everyone all right?' Lyon called from the hatch above. 'I was aft and climbed into the engine bay when that plane came over. No one hurt, I hope?'

'Everyone is fine, thank you, Ivan,' Clement said. 'We just need to put as much distance between us and Surabaya now. Perhaps it would be best if everyone stayed in their bunks for a few hours until sunset. Just in case they return. I'm sure we could all do with some sleep anyway.'

Lyon climbed down the ladder and lay on his bunk. Since Joe's arrival, Hugh had taken the third hammock in the for'ard hold with Tom and Mick, allowing Joe to be near the radio. Clement wasn't unhappy about it. He thought with Hugh bunking in with Tom and Mick, a man Hugh knew, it may help him to feel more settled. But something about Hugh's reaction to the Zero troubled Clement.

He listened to the rain falling on the deck as his mind processed facts. Since leaving Timor everything seemed to have gone to plan. Until Surabaya. Was it only after Surabaya that things changed? He thought of the limpet. He now believed it had been placed there by someone still in Surabaya on the instructions of the Japanese he'd seen in *The Flying Dutchman*. But how had they known the *Krait* would be in Surabaya? And what of the aerial surveillance flights? Was it the Kempeitai or this *kin no yuri* tracking Ivan across the South Pacific? Or had they learned of the mission to Singapore? Either way, the bomb would have killed them all. With the exception of Joe, though, they all could have been killed in Timor. Why wait till Surabaya?

15

Java Sea - 18th December 1941

Clement sat up and wiped the sweat from his face. He'd tossed and turned most of the night. The heat and stillness of the air below deck added to his discomfort. One thought plagued his mind. Why wasn't the limpet armed? While he couldn't think of a plausible reason, something told him it wasn't an oversight. He felt the pervasive doubt. It lingered around him like a shadow. And what had Commander Long and Eric Nave withheld from him? Was the mission to collect Johnny as important as Long had said? But that didn't explain the unarmed limpet. Clement thought back on the strafing runs from the Japanese fighters. Despite some of the bullets hitting the decks, no one had been injured and it had caused no or little damage. Clement frowned. The Zeros had almost been careful not to destroy them. Clement jumped down from his bunk.

'Tom!' Clement shouted.

'Here Clem,' Tom called from the for'ard hold. Clement went for'ard. Tom was sitting on a box, an oily cloth in his hand cleaning the Owen guns, his feet spread wide to maintain his balance with the ship's movement.

Clement glanced aft to see if anyone other than he and Tom were within earshot. 'Can you think of any reason why the limpet wasn't armed?'

Tom's hand stopped polishing the weapon. 'I put it down to inexperience.'

'Or maybe it was to be armed at some future time?'

'Struth! What do you reckon is going on, Clem?'

Clement was silent. He knew Tom was staring at him. If it was to be primed at some future time, when the ship was at anchor near Singapore, for example, there may not be a traitor on board and the damaged fold-boat could have been as a result of strafing or accidental. 'Can you keep this just between you and me?'

Archer nodded.

'And that includes Mick.'

'She'll be right, Clem.'

'I hope she will be, Tom.'

All Clement knew for certain was that the Japanese armies were moving south down the Malay peninsula but even this information was old and had been learned from unreliable sources in Surabaya. But while Singapore's fate remained a mystery, the unarmed limpet refused to be ignored.

He didn't believe the diver in Surabaya had forgotten

to prime it. It was to be used, of that Clement was sure. But at a later time. Why? Moreover, the surveillance flights hadn't stopped, even with the ship's new appearance. Clement gazed at the sea, the endless rolling oceans. Johnny. He was the key. Clement stared into the vast open sky. He almost held his breath as the thoughts came rushing to him. Could the Japanese know about Johnny and his secret? But they, like Long, needed him identified? If that was the case, they'd be watching and waiting. And as soon as Johnny was rescued, they'd strike. But it wouldn't be by blowing the limpet. The limpet was for himself and the others on the *Krait*. Johnny would be taken and interrogated. And for that he needed to be alive. A patrol boat would intercept them, Johnny would be taken along with the secret documents and then the limpet would be primed by one of their divers.

Clement felt the gnawing in the pit of his stomach that was always there when missions became complicated. He wondered if there was a way of exposing the traitor before arriving in Singapore. Clement gathered the team and Bill on the aft deck. He looked around the solemn faces. 'It has occurred to me that the Japanese, their agents and collaborators may be tracking us and that the aerial surveillance flights are just that. Moreover, it is entirely possible that the Japanese will be waiting for us at Keppel Pier, if they already control Singapore, or, if they don't, they will attempt to intercept us at sea either before, but more likely after the rendezvous.'

'How have you come to this decision?' Ivan asked.

Clement explained his reasoning. The group were silent for several minutes. Clement watched the faces. If a collaborator existed among them, he gambled that he would be the first to speak.

Joe leaned forward and rested his elbows on the engine cover. 'You could be wrong about all this. Maybe they were just playing with us this afternoon and they're not interested in us at all.'

'I would like to think so, Joe. And Mick has repaired a small tear he found in one of the fold-boats.'

'What!' Ivan said.

'Accident, Ivan,' Clement said, his eye on Joe. 'Probably done when loading them in Baucau.' He slowly scanned the men present, his eye looking for even the smallest twitch of guilt. But there was none.

'Right you are, Clem,' Tom said, standing.

'Before you go, I'd like to go through how we're going to do this,' Clement said, unfolding the map of the region on the engine bay roof.

'Do you want me to stay, Clement?' Bill asked.

'Yes, thank you, Bill.'

'Now that the mission isn't as straight forward as we previously believed, we will need to be on high alert and watching each other's backs. I will still take the first boat with Ivan, then Mick and Tom with the heavy weapons will be in the second and Joe and Hugh in the third. I had thought it best not to weigh each of you down with too much weaponry which could be troublesome with moving silently through any vegetation. However, now

171

that it is possible we may encounter problems landing or even once on the beach, I think we should each carry a machine gun with one spare magazine, as well as a pistol and knife. A grenade each would also seem prudent. But I want to make sure you understand that nerves will be heightened, and it will be dark. Not a good combination when men are heavily armed and on edge. So, I don't want anyone doing their own thing and disappearing in the dark; that will get you killed by either a Japanese sniper or one of us. Ivan, do you know this Keppel Island Pier?'

'Yes, Clement. The vegetation there is thick and extends down to the water's edge. The beach is more a narrow flat of sand, or rather mud. Less, of course, at high tide but quite rocky. If approached too quickly, the rocks could tear the bottom out of the fold-boats. The jetty there is long and made of timber poles sunk into the mud. The pylons wouldn't offer much in the way of cover for our boats. But it could be enough, given the hour. There are a couple of machine gun pillboxes about half a mile apart and a large battery, Labrador or Pasir Panjang, there also. There are rumours of tunnels connecting the pill boxes to the battery and munition stores, but I've never been into them. Rumour also has it that the tunnels connect underwater to the Battery on Blakang Mati, Fort Siloso but I don't know if any of this is true.'

'This Fort Siloso, where is it?'

'At the south-western tip of Blakang Mati. It, and the

one at Pasir Panjang guard the entrance to New Harbour.'

Ivan ran his finger over the island of Blakang Mati and Fort Siloso. Clement could see it occupied a commanding position to both the Singapore Straights and the entrance to New Harbour. The team gathered around.

'Is the land at Fort Siloso the same as our rendezvous site?' Clement asked Ivan.

'The Fort is sited moderately high above the water here, and it would be difficult to land there.'

Clement paused, his finger on the map. 'So, remaining in our fold-boats, we gather under this Fort Siloso and wait for each other. We stay there until we see the flashing, green-light signal.' He lifted his gaze and stared at Lyon. 'Where is this battery, exactly?'

Lyon pointed to an area of coast on the main Singapore island and about two hundred and fifty yards across the channel from Fort Siloso.

'Right. Once we have all seen the signal, we make our way towards the rendezvous site, gathering a little distance to the east and at the end of the Keppel Island Pier. Then Ivan and I will go in first. Hugh, you and Joe come in next with Tom and Mick acting as cover party from the end of the jetty. If there is no trouble and I can collect Captain Winthorpe, I'll signal with one flash. So, Tom and Mick, if you see that signal, you stay in your boat. Joe and Hugh, you land but stay at the shoreline as sentry party. Hugh, you remain in the boat. Once Joe and Ivan have left, and as I leave with Captain Winthorpe, Hugh, you act as cover, following as soon as Captain Winthorpe and I reach the end of the pier. We can then cover you leaving the area. Then we paddle across the strait and reassemble under the lee of Fort Siloso before returning to the *Krait*.'

'And if there is trouble, Clem?'

'Try to stick to the plan. Remember this is supposed to be a silent mission. If there is trouble or you hear firing, then land and find cover. That includes you too, Tom and Mick. Thereafter is anyone's guess. But we must stick together. Should we become separated, I will endeavour to wait for you, but it will all depend on what's happening. Once Captain Winthorpe is with me, should anyone be missing, I'll wait ten minutes only in the boat at the end of the pier. After that, you would need to make your own way back to the *Krait*. But I cannot hold the ship indefinitely.' Clement turned to Bill. 'Do we have an up-to-date weather forecast?'

'It's pretty much the same every day although the wind can, at times, be strong and that makes for higher waves and choppy seas. The moonlight will be limited too. No moon tomorrow so by the 21st, it will only be a sliver of waxing moonlight.'

'That's as I prefer it, thanks Bill.'

Clement looked at the faces of his team. 'Any questions?'

Everyone shook their heads. More detailed plans

were impossible, but Clement wanted them to feel included in the decisions.

As evening fell, Clement joined Bill on deck. 'Bill, was there a reason you refuelled at Surabaya?'

'It's en route to Singapore.'

'Is it the only port for refuelling?'

'Pretty much. Borneo's too far away and you have a tight schedule. It's also closer to where the Japs are likely to be.'

'Thank you. And I want to apologise again for putting you and your crew in danger. It's good of you to continue, given what's happened.'

'While I have no real allegiances to anyone, least of all a government, I don't much care for the Japanese. I've heard the stories of what they've done to the Chinese and others. Wouldn't wish that on my worst enemy.'

'Who is your worst enemy?' Clement asked.

Bill laughed. 'I don't really have one. At least, not yet.'

16

Clement rose with the sun. He wanted to speak with Kearsley. Since Hugh's reaction to the approaching Zero, Clement had tried to engage him in conversation but he hadn't been forthcoming. Moreover, he had become reclusive, preferring to spend his time with Ivan or alone. Clement didn't understand it. He decided that while time permitted, he'd try to get Hugh to talk about himself and what troubled him. Clement pulled on his clothes and went aft to the galley. Tom and Mick were already there.

'Hugh still asleep?' Clement asked.

'Not in the for'ard hold, Clem. I guessed he slept on deck. Or in the wheelhouse. He was last on surveillance duty last night so maybe he crawled into the engine bay not wanting to get wet.'

'I'll rouse him, if you want him,' Mick said.

'No. Let him sleep. Just let him know I'd like to see

him when he surfaces.'

'Right you are.'

Clement went back along the deck. Young Juan was in the wheelhouse and Ivan stood staring out over the sea on the foredeck, the binoculars around his neck. The morning was already hot, and a low humid mist had settled over the sea obscuring the sun. 'Morning Clement. Nothing to report.'

'Have you seen Hugh this morning, Ivan?'

'No. Perhaps he's having a long lie in. He had quite a bit to drink last night.'

'Really?' But Clement's gut told him something was wrong. Lifting the for'ard hatch, he jumped in. Three empty hammocks swung in the hold. He thought if Hugh had had as much to drink as Ivan had suggested, perhaps he'd been unable to climb into his hammock and slept on the floor. But he wasn't there. He knew Hugh wasn't in the radio room nor the wheelhouse. Walking back along the deck, he lifted the hatch to the engine room. It was a large space. In the centre was the long diesel-powered engine and around it there was enough room for a man to walk. At the rear of the engine bay was a low bench, sufficient to serve as a bunk but with the engine running and in the tropics, it would be hellishly hot. Frowning, Clement returned to the radio room where Joe was still sitting at the wireless.

'Have you seen Hugh this morning, Joe?' Clement asked.

'No. But there was a note for you on the bench here

this morning. I put it on your bunk for you to read privately.' Joe turned around and pulled the note out from under Clement's pillow.

Clement read it. 'Dear Lord,' he whispered the breath barely escaping his lips. The note said that on the night they'd left Baucau, while walking back to the wharf, Hugh had passed a local who'd spoken to him. The man had asked where he was going. Hugh had said he was leaving Timor for Singapore on a secret mission. In view of recent events in Surabaya, Hugh couldn't bear the guilt of having compromised the mission. It would most likely cause their deaths and he blamed himself for their current circumstances. The note concluded that, despite having basic training weapon skills, Hugh believed when the time came, he wouldn't be able to kill a man and so had decided to end his life. Hugh had dated and timed the note, so that they wouldn't search for him. His body would never be found. Hugh had slipped into the sea in the early hours of the morning and would now be many miles behind them.

Returning to the deck Clement saw Tom and Mick aft. He walked towards them. 'Did you hear anything unusual last night?'

'What do you mean, Clem?' Tom said.

'Tom, would you gather everyone on the foredeck. Tell them I need to speak to them.

'What's happened?'

'Just gather everyone, please.'

Five minutes later they assembled on deck.

'I need to speak to you all,' Clement began.

'We aren't all present, actually Clement. Hugh isn't here,' Ivan interrupted.

Clement looked at the expectant faces. 'I have the very sad duty to inform you that Hugh committed suicide last night. I have a handwritten note here which he must have left beside the radio last night. He believes he compromised the mission because he spoke to a local on the night we left Baucau. Apparently, Hugh told this person that we were going to Singapore. In view of events in Surabaya, he believes his actions have jeopardized the mission.' Clement searched the faces. Shock was what he saw but he knew if he mentioned that Hugh was having reservations about his involvement with the mission it wouldn't be long before the young man would be posthumously accused of cowardice.

'What? Why would he do that?' Mick said.

Clement studied the anxious faces. 'It's important that we stay focused on our mission. I'm not asking you to forget Hugh but for all our sakes, I'm asking you not to read too much into this. It is a tragedy when someone is lost. It is a greater tragedy when someone feels they cannot reach out to others. His was a simple error and we have no definite proof that his indiscretion is or was the cause of the Japanese surveillance flights or the behaviour of the Japanese men in Surabaya. It may all be circumstantial. I will be holding a service for Hugh this evening at sunset if any of you would like to attend.'

'Good idea, Clement,' Ivan said.

'One man down for the mission. Not ideal,' Tom said.

'We'll manage. But in view of this, Tom, you will operate the third boat alone. Everything else remains unchanged. All right with you?'

'She'll be apples, Clem.'

Clement cast his eye over the men, he saw grim faces and uncomprehending expressions. They'd been a team of six, now it would be five, and three once Ivan and Joe Watkins left the team in Singapore. Clement prayed Johnny was armed and could paddle a fold-boat.

The afternoon passed with almost no conversation. Tom and Mick played cards. Bill's young crew were sitting quietly chatting between themselves on the aft roof over the engine bay. Clement decided to take the last surveillance shift. He collected his pistol from the pack on his bunk, checked his knife then put a torch into his pocket and went on deck.

Ivan passed the binoculars to Clement. 'How is everyone?

'Grieved.' There was a long pause.

'So, it was Hugh who was our traitor,' Ivan said.

Clement hadn't shared his suspicions with Ivan.

'Not too difficult to work out, Clement. A damaged fold-boat, surveillance flights that continued after the limpet was removed. Seems like the actions of a traitor to me.'

'So it appears.' Clement stared out over the sea. In his mind's eye Clement saw Hugh on the day the Zero had come in low and fast. He'd been on surveillance duty but had been struck with fright at the sight it. Why had Hugh frozen then? Clement tried to think back. Had the Zero started firing as it passed overhead? Or was it after? Hugh had done surveillance duty many times since leaving Timor so why a reaction this time? Clement closed his eyes. His inner vision tried to remember Hugh's expression. He saw again the eyes wide with fright. No, not with fright, Clement thought, with disbelief. And Clement could see his eyes, which meant, although he was looking up, he wasn't looking at the Zero overhead. He'd been looking straight towards the stern of the ship. Hugh had seen something.

'Had you met Hugh anywhere around the islands before this mission, Ivan?'

'Once. Briefly. In Rabaul. But not to speak to. I knew almost nothing about him. Seemed a silent sort of chap. Kept to himself. I knew he was English not Australian. Can you manage without him?'

'One pair of eyes less is never ideal. But we'll manage. If Singapore is still in British hands, we should be in and out quite quickly. If not, well, we do what we can.'

Clement glanced up at the sky. The thick clouds were gathering, white at the top, dark grey beneath. But the rain was holding off. Just. 'Would you mind doing a double shift, Ivan? I want to make sure the lads are all right.'

'Of course, Clement. Happy to. If I may be so bold, Clement, may I say that I think you are a good leader. Able, and you care about your team. It goes a long way, especially in a small patrol. Cohesion is sometimes difficult, especially with recent events. At least, that has been my experience. I'm sorry, I've not asked you about your life circumstances. I've been so preoccupied with my own troubles. Rude of me.'

'Not at all and little to tell, Ivan. I'm a widower, a vicar, a soldier and currently doing things I never thought I would.' Clement smiled at Ivan then went aft. There was a lot he could have said, but experience had taught Clement idle conversation could be dangerous.

He climbed up onto the permanent roof over the engine compartment of the vessel. He wanted to see what Hugh had been looking at. Nothing was there and the heavy rain would make the slightly pitched cover slippery, especially if the sea was rough. Below him, he overheard Tom and Mick chatting near the galley. He turned to listen.

'It just wasn't like him. Not the Hugh I knew. Hugh was good with radios, and he got on with the islanders. But maybe he wasn't a fighter. If he came along with us to the pub in Darwin, he'd sit in the corner. He was a watcher not a doer.'

Clement knew it was Mick's voice.

'Clem's a good man, Mick. Careful. Thorough. Do you know he used to be a vicar?'

'Yeah?'

'She'll be right, Mick. Clem will sort it.'

'You have a lot of trust for someone you've only just met.'

'Men are like horses, Mick. That's what the Station Boss used to tell us. There are the wild ones, the flighty ones, the unpredictable ones and the dependable plodders. But it's the plodders who'll run the course.'

'And you think Clem's a plodder.'

'He'll get us through. He's that sort. Doesn't give up. Just like a horse that doesn't leave you lying in the dirt.'

'Well, I hope you're right.'

Clement half smiled. But as he heard Mick's voice a thought occurred to him. Turning, he retraced his steps and climbed down then went aft to where Tom and Mick were still talking.

'Mind if I interrupt?'

'Cuppa, Clem?'

'No, thank you, Tom,' Clement said smiling. 'Mick, you knew Hugh the best of us here. Did you detect anything unusual in his behaviour lately?'

'He seemed a bit out of sorts. So I asked him but he said it was sea sickness. He said he just wanted to stay in his hammock.' Mick shook his head. 'Never saw that coming. Just not like him.'

'Why do you say that?' Clement asked.

'Lying in a hammock in the fo'c'sle isn't the ideal place if you're feeling sick. Besides that I knew he liked what he did. And he was good at it. He could tap out that Morse code stuff lightning fast.' Mick paused. 'He was keen on one of the island girls in Fiji. Thought he may have, well, you know, taken up with her after the war.'

Clement smiled. 'Did he discuss his life with you?'

'Not really. But sometimes when it was just the two of us rowing a boat into the islands to repair or install a radio with a Coastwatcher, he'd ask about Australia and my home.'

'You grew up on a farm, as I recall?' Clement asked.

'Yeah. Around Narooma, on the south coast of New South Wales. I prefer the Territory. No big brothers telling you what to do.'

Clement smiled. 'Did Hugh talk about his life before the war?'

'Not much, sorry. He said he was born in England although I don't know where. I suppose I didn't know him that well after all.'

Clement left Tom and Mick. He didn't want too much speculation about Hugh's death. But it troubled him why Hugh had not chosen to discuss whatever troubled him with anyone. Clement went for'ard. He wanted to look around Hugh's hammock. Jumping down into the for'ard hold, he stood staring into the space, his eye coursing over everything there. But he found nothing. The man's few items of clothing sat neatly folded in his pack. Clement squatted beside it and felt around the contents. It only contained clothes. He thought back to Superintendent Arthur Morris of Cambridge Police and what Arthur would do in such circumstances. 'Go over what you know,' Clement muttered to himself. He knew almost nothing about the man. Other than the few facts others had told him. Perhaps Hugh had hidden his fear of the forthcoming mission but as time passed, he couldn't face what he may be required to do. Was that it? But the memory of him staring aft and not at the fast approaching Zero troubled Clement.

Clement went back on deck. Ivan was for'ard, the binoculars covering his face. Clement stood on the deck where Hugh had been standing when the Zero had flown over them and looked back along the ship. Clement licked the sweat from his upper lip. Frowning, he cast his mind back. At the time, he'd been in the wheelhouse with Bill. It had been raining hard. Bill had left the wheelhouse and rushed for'ard, grabbing the binoculars from Hugh's hand and pushing him down into the for'ard hold. What had Hugh seen? Had someone else been on deck then? Was it possible Hugh's reaction hadn't been to the approaching Zero but to someone doing something out of the ordinary? Leaving the deck, Clement went to find Bill. He was sitting in the wheelhouse. Clement opened the door and stepped inside.

'Bill, do you remember the evening the Zero flew over when Hugh was on watch, and you grabbed the binoculars from his hand?

'Yeah. He was like a stunned fish, I thought. And could have got us all killed.'

'It was raining heavily, as I recall. Did you see anyone else on deck then?'

Bill frowned before speaking. 'Sorry Clement. I just don't remember. Things were happening quickly. That Zero was moving fast and low and about to strafe us or bomb us, so my attention was on that plane and getting Hugh out of sight. Best to ask the others on deck at the time.'

'Can you ask your lads if they remember anything?'

'If you like.'

Clement left the wheelhouse and stood on the deck looking out over the seas. Spray was coming over the bow and the wind was stronger now making the waves break over the beam and the gunwales awash with salt water. Clement reached for the handrail on the outside of the wheelhouse to steady himself. A theory was forming in his mind. What if Hugh hadn't jumped overboard? Clement closed his eyes as the thought grew in his brain. If Hugh hadn't killed himself, then they had more than a collaborator onboard, they had a murderer.

17

Java Sea - 19th December 1941

They gathered on the deck just as the enormous sun disappeared over the horizon, the evening sky radiant, the darkness settling over the day. Clement recited the words of the burial for the dead at sea as the night quickly closed in around them. The rain had abated during the afternoon, and the wind dropped. José and Juan sang a traditional Timorese song, the quiet simplicity of their voices in the night having a sobering effect on the small group.

Bill broke out some whisky.

'Not the stuff from Darwin, is it, Bill?' Clement asked.

Bill shook his head. 'That stuff will kill you, Clement. This, on the other hand, is mother's milk.'

Bill winked and downed the twelve-year-old whisky in one gulp. 'Just what the doctor ordered in such circumstances.'

'I couldn't agree more, Bill.' Clement walked with him

back to the wheelhouse and closed the door. 'Did you ask Juan and José about seeing anything unusual that day?'

'Yes, I asked them, they said they didn't see anything, but truth is, Clement, one day is much like another at sea so their recollections of who or what was where when wouldn't be reliable. What worries you about it?'

Clement shook his head. 'Just trying to understand, I suppose. Sad, really. When so many are dying at the hands of our enemies; it seems such a waste of human life.'

Clement glanced through the window at his team standing on the foredeck, the red sail long rolled away and the battened shade cloth back in place over the boom. He'd hoped the burial service would help the team move on from the traumatic event of Hugh's death but, in fact, all Clement felt was tension. Confined spaces and heightened expectation for the mission two days away had caused the team to be anything but settled and it was palpable.

Only the daily deluge brought respite from the heat. Twenty-four hours had passed since the service Clement had held for Hugh, and there hadn't been a single Zero spotted since. Clement wondered about that. He hoped it was because of their proximity to Singapore; their mission just over twenty-four hours away. But the strain on board hadn't abated.

Clement sat on the foredeck under the shade cloth.

He'd taken the last watch for the evening but still there hadn't been any surveillance flights.

'Mind if I join you, Clem?' Joe Watkins asked, wandering towards him.

'Not at all, Joe. I'd be pleased for your company,' Clement said and he meant it. A friendly silence settled between them, the only sound that of the engines and the rhythm of the bow waves as the *Krait* seamed ahead.

'I need to confess something to you, Clem,' Joe said.

Clement turned to face the American. 'Sorry, Joe, but I'm not a Roman Catholic priest. I am, however, happy to listen, if you'd like to talk.'

Joe leaned in towards Clement, his voice low. 'I've been thinking about Hugh.'

Clement waited. 'Oh, yes?'

'I can't be sure, but I think I heard a splash during that night. I'm not saying I did; I can't be sure. Hugh and I had had rather a lot to drink that evening. I was just wondering, if it were possible, if maybe he could have fallen overboard. He may have gone on deck to pee and lost his balance. I know I should have said something earlier, I just wasn't sure. I'm still not, but I can't get it out of my head that he may not have committed suicide. It could be just a really dreadful accident.'

'But he left a note, Joe?'

'Yeah. I've been thinking about that, too. Mind if I have a look at it?'

Clement had kept the letter on him. He didn't want anyone learning that Hugh had killed himself due to cowardice, but he suspected Joe had another reason for looking at the note. Slowly, Clement took the folded note from his top pocket and handed it to Joe.

Joe glanced around the deck again then opened the note. He studied it for no more than a few seconds then, folding it, he handed it back to Clement. 'Have you shown anyone else this?' Joe asked.

Clement shook his head. 'What is it, Joe?'

Joe reached into his trouser pocket. 'When Hugh and I were listening to the radio trying to overhear anything the Japs were saying about us, I asked him to write down what I overheard when it seemed it might be pertinent. It was in code so it wouldn't have made any sense to him. Or me for that matter.'

Joe passed the scribbled note to Clement. He'd seen it before when Joe had shown him the transmission and he'd asked about it being JN25B7.

'You told me it's JN25B8.'

'It's not the encryption.'

'What is it then, Joe?'

'Hugh had a strange way of writing 'a'. Look at the transmission. He writes 'a' like the 'a' on a typewriter and not like the '*a*' most people use in handwritten notes. That letter you have, all the '*a*'*s* are rounded.'

Clement held the two notes together.

'For what it's worth, Clem, I don't think Hugh wrote that note.'

18

Java Sea - 20th December 1941

Clement stared out to sea. The wind had picked up and low white crests had formed on the waves. Everyone was on deck, the wind a welcome relief to the heat. Archer was on surveillance duty, the binoculars hanging around his neck. But, again, no Zeros had been sighted. Clement hoped it was because of their proximity to Singapore and that the Allies still held it. He glanced around the men on deck. Joe and Ivan were laughing. While Clement didn't know why, he felt relieved; and the shock of Hugh's death seemed to have abated. For Clement it was small comfort. He felt increasingly sure that a murderer existed among them. He pondered the note and the letter 'a' that Joe had told him about. He looked up at the members of the team. Tom and Mick, Clement believed from what he'd overheard, had developed a respect for him which Clement knew was paramount to a successful mission. Trust was all important. Especially if the team had to separate during the mission. Ivan's inclusion had been confirmed by Long himself as was the presence of Joe Watkins. Bill also had shown his true colours; dependable and discreet but while not part of the team, the mission wouldn't have happened at all without Bill and his boat. And as far as Bill's crew were concerned, Clement didn't think anything worried the boys, José, Pedro and Juan. As long as they were at sea and catching fish, Clement thought they wouldn't care where they were. Perhaps he'd been wrong about Hugh being murdered and perhaps the 'a' thing wasn't important. Clement went to join Ivan and Joe. 'I think it could be a good idea for two people to be on surveillance duty now we are so close to Singapore. One on aeroplanes and the other on patrol boats. Just in case the Japanese are in Singapore.'

'Of course, Clement. If you think it necessary. Tom and Mick will want to be on watch together, so I'll take boat surveillance with Joe,' Lyon said.

Clement stared into the wind, the waves now bigger. The protection afforded by the myriad of islands had gone and as they moved closer to Singapore, the seas were larger and the ocean wider.

Clement joined Bill in the wheelhouse.

'Not long now,' Bill said.

'Do you know when exactly?'

'We'll be in the lee of Blakang Mati Island by late tomorrow afternoon. I'll try to time it with sunset. That way we can sea-anchor off the coast there.' Bill swung around, his eyes on the skies. 'If this weather holds, we should be able to stay there. If not, we'll motor around the area and endeavour to be back in time for your return.'

'Not sure I understand what sea-anchoring is?' Clement asked.

'We drop anchor, but it doesn't reach the seabed. The ship is weighted in position. Of course, there is movement, but in calm conditions in the lee of a land mass, it's surprising just how well it works.'

Clement went over the teams in the fold-boats again in his mind. With Hugh gone, he intended that he and Ivan should take the first, Mick would be in the second and Tom and Joe in the third. With Ivan and Joe leaving them in Singapore, that left more than enough space for Johnny and any equipment he may have with him. If it was large, they could jettison any unneeded weapons into the sea.

The light faded and the brief twilight descended. Clement gathered them on the foredeck and went through the plan.

'Bill estimates that we will be in position in the lee of Blakang Mati Island tomorrow around sunset. It is his intention to sea-anchor, just off the southern coast and towards the eastern end of the island. He'll wait there if he can. If he must move, for whatever reason, he'll be back in place at sunrise on the twenty-second. From the chart, I estimate that it is about five miles from the eastern end of the island to Fort Siloso and another quarter of a mile to Keppel Island Pier. The plan is that we paddle to the south-western point of Blakang Mati then wait there. Once we see the green flash-light signal; three on, two off, we proceed across the strait, then, hugging the shoreline, make our way to the pier, always mindful of where the green light was seen. Try to line it up with a constellation or a distinctive silhouette on shore. It is vital we keep each other in sight as we cross. It will be dark, and the incoming tide strong so it would be easy to become separated. Given the tides, I estimate that it will take an hour to the assembly point under Fort Siloso, then fifteen to twenty minutes to cross the straights and possibly two hours to return to the eastern end of Blakang Mati allowing for the current. It is my hope that we will not be at the rendezvous site longer than absolutely necessary, but no more than thirty minutes. To put us there at midnight, we will leave the *Krait* at ten. I know it's hot, but we'll need to be wearing full kit as well as balaclavas or with boot black on our faces. Mick, Tom and I will each have an Owen gun with one spare magazine, a knife and a pistol also with spare ammunition and one grenade. Mick will have the extra ammunition and grenades with him in the middle boat; that is, the second boat. Tom, you take the limpets with you and Joe in the third boat to act as cover party for the first two boats. As Ivan and I will be first to land, I will act as sentry party for Mick, Tom and Joe, who should all beach as soon as I'm on shore.'

'I can help, Clement, until I leave you,' Ivan said.

'Thank you, Ivan.'

'Do you want me to carry any weapons?'

'Just whatever you brought with you. Please remember, even though we are carrying weapons, this is meant to be a silent operation. The use of firearms is only in an emergency. Once we are in the boats, there is to be no talking. Should you have any questions, please ask them now.'

'Maybe one of us should stay in our boat at the end of the pier and cover the beach as you previously thought?' Tom suggested.

Clement thought for a moment. 'As we are one man down, and it is dark with only a sliver of waxing moonlight, I think it best we all land. With only three of us now, I don't want to lose anyone in the dark.'

Tom nodded. 'Fair enough.'

'Tom, would you find some kit for Ivan and Joe?'

'Leave it to me, Clem.'

They ate a small dinner. Bill suggested that they extinguish all on-board lights except the glass Japanese fishing lanterns Tom had liberated from the Japanese in Timor. These Bill placed around the boat. As the hours ticked by, each man sought solitude, the nervous tension for what lay ahead, unmistakable.

19

The Lee of Blakang Mati Island - 21st December 1941

Clement lay on his bunk. He, with Tom and Mick, had spent the morning checking everything was in order. The fold-boats had been assembled and supplied with their seats and paddles and lay under the foredeck shade cloth, all in readiness for them to be lowered into the sea. Earlier in the day and as it was Sunday, Clement had held a brief service but now it was just a matter of time.

He cast his mind back to Hugh Kearsley. No one had mentioned his name since the service he'd held for the man. If it hadn't been for the note Joe had shown him, he would have believed Hugh had taken his own life. What was it about the questionable circumstances of Hugh's death that disturbed him so? It was like a festering wound that refused to heal. Clement sat up and went to find Joe.

Joe was sitting on deck reading a book in Japanese.

'Interesting?' Clement asked as Joe closed the book.

'Not really. It's about flower arranging.'

Clement must have looked surprised.

'I picked it up in Surabaya from the vendor on the quay. It helps keep my language skills honed.'

'Have you been stationed in Manilla long, Joe?'

'About a year.'

'And you met Ivan there?'

'Yeah. Although, it was a big party at the Brazilian Embassy.'

'But you spoke to him then?'

'Yeah. But it's odd really. He seems to have a recollection of me and others who were there, but I don't really remember him. I do remember my C.O. Rudy Fabian introducing me to a tall Englishman who said he was with FECB. We were working with the Brits at FECB in Hong Kong at the time. Exchanging stuff about the latest cyphers, you know.'

'When Ivan and Hugh went into *The Flying Dutchman* in Surabaya, how did you recognise him if you don't remember his face well?'

'It was arranged for a tall Englishman to enter carrying a rolled newspaper. When I saw him, I was to leave the group I was with, saying I needed to use the john. We didn't speak inside or make any contact. Then we were to meet outside at the end of the row of warehouses. I was a bit concerned about those Japs in the corner of the pub. I thought if I went to the john alone, and one of those Japs followed me, I may not come out.

That's why I pretended to vomit.'

'Have you told anyone else on board about this?' Clement said, remembering seeing Lyon carrying the newspaper.

'No. But I'll be pleased to get off this ship. It's a hunch, I know, but I'm getting a real bad feeling about this mission.'

'Any evidence for your apprehension?'

'I don't trust Mick.'

'Reasons?'

'He always has a gun in his hand. Those two guys are as thick as thieves. Wouldn't surprise me if they were. He never says much, just looks. It's creepy.'

'I, too, have reservations, Joe, if it's any consolation. But we're here to do a job and when it's over, I'll be returning home. Until you have hard evidence, I would ask you to keep your bad feelings to yourself. Everyone's a bit jumpy. It stands to reason; we go tonight. And you'll be in Singapore tomorrow and on your way back to the Philippines by the next day, no doubt.'

'Yeah. You're probably right.' Joe stood. 'It's been a pleasure meeting you, though, Clem. Good luck to you. I hope things work out for you.'

Clement smiled. There was much he could have shared with Joe Watkins, but in view of everyone's misgivings about others, he really didn't know who to trust. However, the one thing he'd learned from working with SIS was that lying was second nature for the career spy.

Hugh Kearsley, however, refused to be ignored. Clement's thoughts lingered on the man. His relatives would be informed of his death. But nothing of the details would be provided. In fact, Hugh's passing, whether by accident or murder was unlikely ever to be investigated. One of millions who had and would die in this global conflict. Clement felt the tragedy of it. If Hugh was innocent of any suspicion, Clement swore to himself that he'd do his best to exonerate Kearsley.

Clement drew in a long breath and gazed towards the far horizon. The world was a big place and humanity mere ants in a vast universe. A shiver coursed through his body. He knew the feeling like the scent of an old friend. Or enemy. He'd felt it before too many times; the apprehension of the mission, the unknown of what lay before him and his team. He could almost feel the cold clammy hand of death. He'd felt that once before, too, in Caithness when a traitor remained unknown and unidentified. But the truth was that nothing could be done about his current situation. They were on a ship in the ocean with no police and no one who Clement could truly trust. If he'd been in England, he would have walked on the downs, his mind open to all thoughts and possibilities and perhaps even have sought out Superintendent Morris. But cramped in a ship with a team of four men and a ship's company he knew little about, he felt completely isolated and surrounded by doubt. Regardless, being alone on a mission was familiar ground for Clement. His mind went back to Caithness. There, he'd trusted one man. A good man whose involvement with him had caused the man's death. Clement didn't want a repeat. Better for him to keep his own counsel and not to expose others to danger by expressing his misgivings.

Clement heard the anchor chain being lowered. It was dark and had been for more than three hours. The men had dressed in full kit; trousers, long-sleeved shirts, jackets, boots and had blackened their faces. Mick wore a knitted black balaclava over his blond hair. He was standing on the foredeck giving out the weapons as Clement had prescribed. Joe and Tom were uncovering the fold-boats. Clement checked his watch. Nerves would be high. Above them, a thin slice of moonlight cast its pale glow over the dark, silent waters. In the distance, Clement could see the occasional light from villagers' fires where fishing boats were tied up along the shoreline. A slight, onshore breeze brought the spicy aroma of cooking from the waterfront to his nostrils.

They waited in silence.

Just on ten, they quietly lowered the fold-boats into the water on the seaward side of the *Krait*. With Tom standing astride in his boat, he reached up for the two limpet mines and carefully stowed one at each end of his boat. Mick passed an Owen gun and a magazine of ammunition to Tom, then Tom settled himself while Joe Watkins climbed down into the fold-boat. Clement waited while Tom reached for the paddle then backpaddled a little distance away from the *Krait* but still in the lee of the boat and obscured from any prying eyes on Blakang Mati.

Mick was the next to descend. His boat would be the heaviest and the most perilous given the amount of weaponry he was carrying should an altercation ensue. Taking the third position, Tom and Joe would, Clement hoped, be able to keep an eye out for any trouble and act accordingly.

Clement passed four Owen guns down to Mick along with some extra ammunition and a box of grenades which Mick stacked carefully around the boat.

Mick then sat, pushed the craft off the hull of the *Krait*, moved away from the ship and paddled out into the water near Tom. Ivan and Clement lowered the remaining fold-boat into the water then descended, Clement sitting aft. Using the oar to push off the *Krait's* hull, they silently regrouped, then paddled away into the night.

The moon was high, and its light made the inky waters barely visible. Leaving the protection of the *Krait's* mass behind them, Clement whispered the stroke, until they swung into a rhythm. Glancing over his shoulder Clement could see Mick and Tom's crafts behind his. Off to Clement's right he could see some lights closer to the shore. They were not bright, neither were they search lights. But they did provide a connection to the land, helping to keep them on course. On the evening breeze he could hear a few locals chatting in some fishing boats tied up along the shore.

Half an hour passed, the stroke of the paddles like a ticking clock. In the distance, Clement heard the rhythmic crashing of waves hitting rocks, the endless splashing carrying on the night air. Above them in the pale light Clement could just make out the long-barrelled canons of Fort Siloso, the two six-inch 37-ton guns that pointed out over New Harbour and the strait of water between Blakang Mati and the main island. Tapping Ivan on the shoulder, Clement indicated for them to veer closer to shore. With only one paddle operating, they slowed and waited in the lee of the dark land mass. Ten minutes passed. Clement wondered about the occupants of the battery on Fort Siloso. He prayed they were British. The waves rocked the boat as they waited for Tom and Mick. Neither man spoke. In the night, Clement heard the sound of the paddles approaching. Tom and Mick's boats appeared out of the darkness and lay just off Clement's port bow. Clement signalled with his paddle that he'd seen them. Ahead was the black emptiness of the straits; Labrador Battery just ahead of them. Reaching for his binoculars, Clement trained them on the point where he could still hear the waves. Occasionally, he could make out the white foam of the breakers glinting in the moonlight. Adjusting the binoculars again, he focused them on the further shoreline, Singapore main island. It was too dark to see any buildings, but he could see some dim lights on the distant shore. He guessed they were from homes or fishing luggers.

In his mind he calculated the times again. He knew the straits were about a quarter of a mile across and Keppel Island Pier a further one hundred yards into New Harbour. While he couldn't check his watch without flicking on a torch, he guessed they'd been paddling for about forty minutes and waiting under Fort Siloso for another twenty to thirty minutes. The crossing, all being well, would take approximately fifteen minutes putting them at the rendezvous within a quarter of an hour after the signal at midnight.

They waited, the boats rocking in the waves.

Then it came.

A green light, three on, two off. The pattern repeated twice. Clement signalled his team and they left the relative safety of Blakang Mati Island, paddling in silence and at a good speed despite the incoming tide. There was no sound but the rhythmic oars dipping into the dark waters. He thought about possible shipping but he hoped that large ships would have some light, or they'd hear the engines well in advance of any impending collision. Nothing came to him on the wind.

Approximately ten minutes later, Clement saw the outline of the pier in the faint moonlight. Tapping Ivan on the shoulder, they slowed, and Clement lifted his binoculars. There was a mud flat beach with an old wooden jetty off to the right. As he studied the shoreline, the green light flashed again, three on two off. The repeat of the signal was unexpected. Clement tapped Ivan on the shoulder again and pointed further east of the green light. Checking over his shoulder that Tom and Mick were following, they paddled hard now, Clement intending for them to beach the boats about thirty yards east of the light and slightly beyond the point into New Harbour.

As they approached a clear patch of sand, they paddled strong and hard straight for the shore, rushing into the mud flat, the bow of the boat sticking into the sand. Clement reached immediately for his pistol and climbed out, the tepid waters filling his boots. Clutching his weapon, he ran towards the thick vegetation that bordered the mud flat as Ivan dragged the boat up the beach, leaving it by some rocks. Clement stood and turned a full 360 degrees, his gaze rapidly scanning the sea and the adjacent area near the beach then further back up the hill and into the thick jungle behind him. Within minutes, Clement heard another boat beaching. Mick jumped into the water and dragged the fold-boat up on the muddy sand then reached for his knife.

Crouching low, Clement ran further along the beach towards the point, his pistol in his grip, and squatted behind some upturned dinghies, his intense gaze scrutinising the surrounding vegetation. He knew they'd landed further east of where he'd seen the repeated green light signal. It was intentional but he hadn't told the others of his decision. He gambled that if everything was all right and Johnny had sent the signal, Johnny would see the boats beach about a hundred yards from where he'd sent the signal and join them within minutes.

Clement could see Ivan waiting on the shore while Mick unloaded the weapons. Five minutes passed and Johnny still hadn't arrived. Clement felt the adrenaline surge. Something was wrong. And Tom and Joe had not beached. He ran back and went straight to Mick. 'Have you seen Tom?'

On the still midnight air Clement heard the muted cracks of several silenced weapons; the rapid staccato cough-like thuds cut into the air then stopped as quickly as they'd started. Clement and Mick rushed for the cover of the adjacent undergrowth. Waiting there, Clement focused the binoculars on where he thought the firing had come from. He saw that Tom's boat was about fifty feet further to the west and almost directly beneath the jetty. Why hadn't Tom followed them to the landing site? Clement held the binoculars and panned the beach and jetty area. But Tom and Joe were not there.

'I don't see them!' Clement whispered.

'Japs?' Mick whispered.

'Can't see any. But they're here, somewhere.'

'What do you want to do?'

Clement thought for a moment. Dead or wounded, he needed to know where Tom and Joe were, and he wondered if Johnny had seen the attack on the fold-boat and remained hidden. 'I'll go and look.'

'What do you want us to do?' Ivan asked, crouching beside Clement and Mick.

'Stay here. Make sure you're armed and protect the

boats and the weapons. I'll be back as soon as I can.'

'And if you don't? Come back, I mean?' Mick asked.

'Wait fifteen minutes and then take one of the boats and return to the *Krait*.' Clement turned to face Lyon. 'Will you stay in Singapore in view of this?'

'I must.'

'Even if it means capture? They'll kill you and Lord knows what else.'

'My wife and child, Clement. I cannot abandon them. If you can manage without me, I'd be grateful. Every minute counts.' Lyon thrust out his hand.

Clement shook it. Lyon's local knowledge was invaluable, and Clement had hoped he'd stay but he understood the man's reasoning.

'I understand and God be with you.'

Clement watched Lyon disappear up the hill, his tall body vanishing into the thick undergrowth within seconds.

Clement checked his watch again. 'In the meantime, Mick, conceal the weapons then wait fifteen minutes. Understand? No longer.'

Clement stayed only long enough to see Mick return to the beach. Staying low, he made his way into the bordering thick jungle. Deciding the beach could be under Japanese surveillance, Clement approached the pier from the land. Hunching low, he crept along a narrow path between the overhanging trees, thick bushes and vines surrounding him. Three minutes later, he crouched at the edge of the beach then reached for his binoculars again. A fold-boat lay on the mud flats. No one was there. Training the binoculars on the boat, he saw the line of bullet holes that ran down the side of the damaged craft.

20

Singapore - 21st December 1941

Clement felt the hollow in the pit of his stomach. He stared at the empty beach, willing Tom and Joe to appear out of the night. In the stillness and from somewhere behind him further up the hill, Clement heard a muffled moan. He stopped, his senses on high alert, his body completely still. He questioned if the noise was an animal of some kind. Silently, he replaced the pistol and withdrew his knife. Crouching down, he crawled slowly up the hillside. About three yards in front of him and surrounded by dense foliage, he could see someone on the ground in a small clearing. He knew immediately it wasn't Tom or Joe, neither did he believe it to be Johnny. The person appeared to be huddled on the ground with their knees bent and feet tucked under them as though cowering in fear.

Clement silently lifted the binoculars and focused it on the crouched figure. The head was bent to one side yet held high, as though in a trance and he could hear the low moaning of repetitive agonised breathing. He knew that sound; the shallow thready breathing of a person in great pain and the final stages of life. It was a sound he recalled from his time in the trenches during the Great War. He steadied the binoculars again. The face was that of a woman. Lowering the binoculars, he edged forward over the damp ground, his hand gripping his knife.

From the periphery of the small clearing, he could see she was bound, almost trussed like a bird ready for roasting. A rope extended up her back, beginning from under her body then wound around her hands and drawn up around her neck. The rope was tight, her head drawn back and high so that should it fall forward, from exhaustion or unconsciousness, she would die from strangulation. Her mouth was wedged open with a gag. Inching forward, Clement checked the area. Rolling on his back his eyes searched for booby traps or trip wires in the branches above his head. He was within a yard now, the dense foliage still concealing him. He rolled over and heard the woman draw in a raspy breath. She slowly opened her eyes.

He inched closer again, still crawling on his belly towards her. He scanned the immediate area around her before crouching down bedside her, then he cut the ropes securing her neck, hands and legs. She fell sideways, one hand reaching for the gag in her mouth, ripping it out. Then she lay on the ground breathing hard, her body still coiled in numbness and pain. Slowly she lifted her head and stretched out her legs. Minutes later, she looked up at him, gasping air, her hand grasping the deep-red, excoriated flesh across her neck where the rope had gouged her throat.

'Dear Lord! Can you stand?' Clement asked, his ears alert to any noise or a presence in the surrounding jungle.

'Give me a minute,' she whispered, her voice hoarse.

Keeping his gaze on the surrounding area, Clement reached down and lifted her to her feet.

Still supporting her, he reached into his webbing and passed her a flask of water. She swallowed several times before speaking.

'Are you the Vicar?' she whispered, still holding her neck.

'I am.'

'Thank heavens! The Japanese have taken Captain Winthorpe. They're looking for you. We should leave, quickly.'

'How many of them?' Clement said, pocketing his flask. Bending, he picked up the cut ropes and shoved them into his pocket.

'It's a small special force, I think. Three brought me here. But there could be some on the beach. They were expecting you.'

'Is Captain Winthorpe dead?'

'I don't know. But I don't think so. I think they're holding him in Labrador Battery. It's a bit further along the coast and higher up the hill.'

'And you are?'

'Evelyn Howard. I was with Captain Winthorpe.'

Clement heard the rustling of leaves behind them. He turned, his knife in his grip.

Tom appeared in front of him. Clement could see blood on his shirt.

Tom eyed the woman before speaking. 'We've got company, Clem. And there are search lights a bit further along coursing over the beach and sea. They've got silenced weapons, they fired on us as we beached. Joe and me rolled into the waves and swam underwater further down the beach.'

'Did you see Mick?'

'Yeah. Mick called to me, so I knew where he was.'

'Is Joe with him now?'

'Yeah.'

'Are the boats well hidden?'

Tom nodded. 'But mine is riddled with bullet holes. It won't be going anywhere.'

One boat damaged left two for the return trip and Clement knew he couldn't leave the woman behind. They would manage somehow. Clement peered into the darkness. Through the vines and bushes he could see the flickering light of torches coursing the beach. And he could hear voices. Although, he thought it odd they weren't loud. Then he remembered he'd heard silenced weapons. He prayed it meant this was a small advance guerrilla force and that Britain still held Singapore. 'We need to re-join the others.'

Clement checked his watch. He'd been away twelve minutes. 'Can you walk?' he said to Evelyn Howard.

She nodded. 'If I can just lean on you for a bit.'

'Of course.' Leading her and Tom through the undergrowth, Clement saw Mick and Joe on the beach. Each man held an Owen gun.

'Mick!' Clement whispered just loud enough for him to hear. They regrouped at the edge of the beach.

'This is Evelyn Howard. She was with Captain Winthorpe. She thinks the Japanese most likely have him imprisoned in the battery just along the coast,' Clement said, his eyes roaming around the immediate area.

'Have the Japanese taken Singapore, Ma'am?' Joe asked.

'Not officially,' she said, her voice slightly stronger. Clement was impressed by how quickly Evelyn Howard had got herself together. The vivid wound to her throat, dishevelled hair and torn clothing were stark reminders of what she had already endured. 'But there are small enemy groups on the island already, coming from the north and west. Our troops are fighting them, but the island is mostly jungle, so no one really knows where anyone is. It's total chaos and Singapore city is no different. People are just trying to get out. Every sea-worthy boat is fully laden. And fresh water is in short supply. It's only a matter of weeks, if not days, now.'

'If he's alive, we have to get Captain Winthorpe out.'

'He'll be alive, although maybe only just,' Evelyn said.

'What makes you so sure?' Clement asked.

212

'They know who he is. I don't know how, but they do. They may hold the battery but not Singapore, so they're not in charge yet. They're still acting covertly. The battery is the only place hereabouts where they could interrogate him and remain unseen. It doesn't bode well for the British soldiers there though. It must be assumed they are either prisoners or dead.'

'Can you fire a pistol, Miss Howard?'

'Of course.'

'First, we move our boats. I want them closer to the battery. Tom, you and Mick carry one, Joe and I'll take the other. If you'd stay to help, I'd appreciate it, Joe?'

'Sure, Clem. Not sure I'd find a ship to take me to Manilla anyway, given the current situation.'

'We carry as much of the weaponry as possible in the boats. Miss Howard, would you carry a pistol and keep watch?'

'I should have a machine gun. And a spare magazine. I'll go first,' she said.

Clement stared at her.

'I can use one, Major.' She turned to face Joe. 'Would you be Joe Watkins?'

'Yes, Ma'am.'

'You won't get back to Corregidor. Best you stay with us and come to Australia.'

Clement wasn't sure what part Miss Howard was playing but now wasn't the time for discussion. He glanced at Joe. He could see a sceptical look on the American's face. But he now understood why Johnny had included her. If the Japanese knew of Johnny's importance, they didn't seem to know her significance. Nor did he, for the moment.

Clement handed her an Owen gun, took his Fairbairn Sykes knife from its scabbard on his arm, and handed that to her as well. She swung the machine gun over her shoulder, raised the knife and cut into the vines above her head, clearing a path. Lifting the boats, the men carried them back along the edge of the beach, moving towards the point as quietly as possible. Clement's ears strained for the sounds of voices carrying on the night air. 'Miss Howard, do you know where this battery is?'

'Yes. It's around the point and up a road about half a mile further on. There's a pillbox on the point, though. It's most likely where the Japanese sent the signal and would be now under their control. If I may suggest, we go over this hill behind us and avoid the point altogether.'

'Agreed. And this battery?'

'It's a large structure. Concrete, of course, with enough space to secrete a small patrol of men.'

'Have you been in it?'

'No. But I know where it is. Best approached from the shore.'

'Surely that would be too exposed?'

'While a naval attack would obviously be expected from the sea, a small guerrilla force wouldn't. Could be how they took it.'

'Are you from Singapore, Miss Howard?'

214

'No...'

A loud spluttering of gunfire coursed through the jungle. Everyone stood motionless, the weight of the assembled fold-boats with the weapons making them stand rigid. The firing continued for a few minutes. Clement looked through the vines, but he couldn't see anyone. From the direction of the gunfire, it sounded as though it was coming from further along the coast and into New Harbour.

'Found me gone, it would seem,' Evelyn Howard whispered. 'Good thing you took the ropes, Major.'

Clement signalled the group and they continued on. Every step was difficult and held the prospect of death. But Clement now believed that the woman wasn't the bait in the trap. The Japanese guerrillas knew they were coming and where the rendezvous would take place. They had expected him to land closer to the point, from where they'd sent the green light signal and where Clement and his team would have most certainly been captured. And Miss Howard, who Clement knew nothing about, had been placed not as bait but to die, in agony and silently without any hope of rescue. At the last minute, Clement had changed the landing site and beached further into the harbour; this decision, he hadn't shared with anyone. He felt his ears go back, like an animal listening in the wilderness. He sensed a traitor's presence, and it felt like the devil was at his heels. He also realised two things; Hugh Kearsley hadn't committed suicide, he'd been murdered. Not because of anything he'd done, but because of something he'd seen that day on watch. And, someone had told the Japanese about the green flashlight signal.

Once over the hill, they descended to the beach again and lowering the boats, crouched in the thick undergrowth. Before them, about fifty yards ahead, he could see a narrow road, the entrance to it cut into the hillside, like a portcullis to a castle. Leaving the boats on the beach and hidden under some vegetation, they ran towards the track and squatted near a brick retaining wall. Holding an Owen gun each, they ran forward into the narrow entry and up the steep road. Clement's ears strained for any sound. Ten minutes later, he could see the silhouette of the large concrete structure of Labrador Battery. It was larger than he'd expected and perched high on the hill overlooking the Singapore Straights below. Through the gun turrets he could see the muzzles of the canons, but he could also hear voices. They were quiet but distinct in the night air. And they weren't speaking English.

Clement bent forward and whispered to Evelyn. 'Do you speak Japanese?'

She nodded.

Clement waited.

'They are talking about the prisoner. Apparently, he hasn't told them anything so most of the patrol are out looking for you, Major.'

'Good.' Clement thought for a moment. 'Who knew you and Captain Winthorpe were coming here?'

She shook her head. 'I don't know. I didn't know until this morning.'

Clement nodded. But someone knew not only the rendezvous signal but also the place. And that had only been arranged through Long while they were in Timor. But whether his nemesis was in the team or in Timor, they would have to wait. There was no time for conjecture. They had to get Johnny out. And it seemed his enemy knew this and were prepared.

'What's the plan, Clem?' Tom whispered, crouching beside him.

'If most of the patrol are out looking for us then we cannot delay. Tom, can you crawl up the hill beside the battery and throw a grenade as far as you can out towards the harbour. Wait three seconds, then throw another into the bunker. Then get out fast and circle the battery to the land entrance. We'll go straight there and wait for you. Mick, you take Tom's Owen gun for him, he'll need it there. As soon as I hear the second detonation, I'll break in the front entry door and, Mick, you, me and Joe will rush the door and shoot any Japanese we find. Miss Howard, can you wait outside the entry door as look-out? Shoot anyone who tries to enter from the front or any returning Japanese. Can you do that?'

'Without a second thought, Major.'

Clement continued. 'I'll go in first, then Joe. Mick, you hang back so you can give Tom his Owen. Remember, he will be unarmed until he re-joins us. Do not hesitate to kill any Japanese you see. Tom and Mick, check the gun turret and any tunnels between that and the entry door. Joe and I will go for Captain Winthorpe. Once we have what we came for, we assemble back here. As soon as we're all assembled, we leave. Keep your eyes peeled and on no account is anyone to leave the group once we're together again. There'll be no time to search for missing team members. Once away, we make straight for Fort Siloso and then regroup there before heading for the *Krait*. Any questions?'

Inching forward over the wet ground, Clement crawled into the jungle with his binoculars to his eyes. He scanned the area and the beach below. Some three hundred yards further to the east, and about fifty feet below them, he could see the torch lights panning over the mud flats. The Kempeitai were still looking for them and their boats. Keeping the binoculars to his eyes, he reached his right arm back and signalled Tom. Tom crawled up beside him. 'Go!'

Tom stood and, keeping to the edge of the track, ran the fifty yards towards the base of the battery. Clement kept the binoculars on Tom and the immediate area around him. Clement could see the large concrete structure with its two six-inch guns pointing out to sea. He crawled back to his little group. Crouching, they ran along the narrow track towards the battery. In front of them he saw some steps that wrapped around the battery and led to an upper entry door on the land side. A second later he heard the detonation.

Clement guessed they had about five minutes before

the absent Japanese, who were still searching for the boats, returned. The second grenade blasted, sending its pounding shock wave through the humid air. The night sky lit up. With two blasts in quick succession, Clement hoped the Japanese would forget about looking for boats. But they were only minutes away.

Rushing up the stairs to the entry door, Clement fired the Owen, unleashing a volley of bullets into the door. With his foot he kicked the shattered wood in and waited one second. From the corner of his eye, he saw Tom return. Clement peered around the splintered door, letting off another round of bullets before Mick and Tom rushed in, followed by Joe.

Inside the concrete battery was a round entry area from which several passageways fanned out. Clement motioned to Tom and Mick to check the two at the front that faced the sea and most likely led to the gun turrets.

'Evelyn, change of plan for you; get inside and shut what's left of the door!' Clement shouted.

Evelyn rushed in. Closing the shattered door, she assumed a position on the floor with her back to the tunnels that led to the gun turrets. She lay sprawled out, her elbows on the floor supporting the machine gun. To the right of these tunnels and off to Evelyn's left was an open door. Clement could see it was the ammunition store, filled with shells and bombs of every type. To Clement's right was another tunnel. This was wider than the others and led downwards. 'Joe, with me!'

21

Labrador Battery - 22nd December 1941

Clement glanced around the internal space. It was surprisingly large. Outside, it looked no more than a concrete pillbox with substantial footings. But this structure went deep underground and had been designed to not only protect and conceal the occupying force but also to allow the soldiers there to hold out against an enemy for an extended period of time. Behind him, Clement heard short bursts of gun fire. He stared at Joe.

'Should I go back and check?' Joe said.

'No.' He had to trust his team would do what was required. And that included Evelyn Howard, whose courage under pressure had secretly astounded him. They ran on, descending a left spiralling passage.

Clement heard a scuffle from deeper in the tunnel. He signalled to Joe and together they stood still, their bodies braced, their weapons ready. There was no cover.

No one came running towards them. Clement fired a short round. The scuffling footsteps stopped. But no one called out. Then more gun fire.

'You right, Clem?' Tom called from higher up the tunnel.

'Yes, Tom. You?'

'Yep. Just get your man and hurry, would you. I'll go back to the main entry. We'll have plenty of company soon.'

In the enclosed tunnel Clement heard Tom's running footsteps grow fainter as Tom returned to the battery entrance. Holding the Owen gun ready to fire, Clement and Joe crept forward. Ahead, the tunnel continued to turn to the left making it impossible to see what lay beyond. Clement let off another burst of gunfire and waited. In the enclosed space the noise was shattering but no one responded. He and Joe edged forward. At the base of the tunnel was a circular space approximately twelve feet in diameter. Off it and around a central control post were three doors, all closed. Four British and two Japanese soldiers lay dead on the floor. Clement could see the British soldiers had been shot in the head with their hands tied behind their backs. The Japanese soldiers lay sprawled where they had fallen.

'Johnny?' Clement called aloud. Had Johnny somehow killed his guards? If so, then one of the three cell doors in front of him was unlocked.

'Here!'

Clement heard Johnny's voice coming from the end

cell on the right. 'Joe, check the other cells would you and be careful.'

'No problem there, Clem. I'll shoot first and ask questions second.'

From higher up the tunnel Clement heard Evelyn call out. 'Company!' she screamed.

Clement ran to the door on the right and tried the door handle. Locked. 'Stand back, Johnny.'

Clement fired several shots into the lock then kicked open the door.

Johnny ran towards him. 'Clement?'

Clement stared at his old friend for one second. The man's face was bruised, swollen and bloodied but otherwise he seemed unharmed. 'Can you run?' Clement asked but before Johnny could answer Clement heard Joe's voice.

'Clem!'

'Are you all right, Johnny?' Clement repeated.

'I'll live, Clement. I don't have a weapon though.'

Clement pulled his Enfield from his belt and handed it to Johnny. Leaving the cell, Clement and Johnny joined Joe. With him was Ivan Lyon.

'Clement! Thank God! I thought you were more Japanese. They caught me in the jungle and dragged me here but before they could have a go at me, I grabbed one of their guns and managed to shoot them. I hid in one of those cells.'

'He almost shot me,' Joe said.

'Can you run?' Clement asked.

'Yes, I'm unharmed. Not sure I would be if you hadn't shown up when you did,' Lyon said.

Running out of the underground space, they rushed up the tunnel. At the bend Clement paused, his hand outstretched to slow the others behind him. 'Tom!'

Clement heard the rapid fire. 'Stay here,' he whispered to the group behind him, then disappeared around the bend. In the entrance to the battery, Clement could see Tom and Mick standing either side of the entry door, their backs to the wall. Evelyn still held her position on the floor by the ammunition store, the Owen gun in her grip and a line of magazines beside her. The firing came from outside the battery entrance.

Clement slowed. Evelyn had seen him. She shook her head, her wide eyes telling him to wait. Then a volley of shots rang out. Tom peered around the door and let off what Clement guessed was a full round of ammunition. Mick threw a grenade out through the doorway.

Then he heard running.

'Stay where you are, Clem,' Tom called.

An explosion roared, the smoke and dust filling the tunnel. Clement covered his mouth. 'Tom?'

Tom appeared through the smoke and dust. 'Time to go!'

Clement called to the others behind him, and they ran forward together, appearing out of the smoke in the tunnel. A minute later Clement joined Tom in the entry space.

'How many, Tom?' Clement whispered.

'Don't know. Another grenade?' Tom said.

'Good idea! But make sure it explodes outside. Evelyn, close the ammunition store door and Mick, drop another grenade out of the gun turret, just in case they're waiting for us on the seaward side of the battery.'

Evelyn jumped up, shut the heavy blast door, then returned to her position on the floor.

'Done!'

Mick ran off. Two seconds later, the double detonations reverberated around the stone and concrete, the noise shattering.

Clement glanced at Evelyn Howard then nodded for her to join him. Slowly the dust cloud from the back draught settled. Through it, Clement stepped outside, Evelyn behind him. Six mutilated bodies of Japanese soldiers lay around the entrance. With the two dead Japanese inside, that made eight. Standing near the steps that led back to the track, Clement waited for his team to join him.

All was quiet but Clement knew the explosions would have any Allied troops in the area on high alert and trigger fingers would be poised. Now they were in greater danger of being shot by their own side.

Keeping to the edge of the narrow road, Clement led the group back down to the portcullis-like entry. Crouching by the entrance, Clement reached for his binoculars and scanned the beach ahead. Focusing the instrument on where they had hidden the boats, they ran across the mudflats towards the beach. Tom and Mick uncovered the two hidden fold-boats.

'Will you come with us this time?' Clement whispered to Ivan.

'I can't, Clement. Especially now the Japanese are so close. But I'm grateful for the rescue. And besides, you seem to have collected one or two strays. No room for me.'

Clement smiled then held out his hand again. He shook hands with Ivan Lyon. 'You're a brave man. May the Lord be with you and your family.'

Lyon smiled then disappeared back up the track and into the jungle.

Clement ran to join the others. 'Is anyone hurt?'

'No,' a chorus of voices responded.

'I don't think I've ever been more pleased to see you, Clement,' Johnny said. 'Not that I can actually see you but I'd know that voice anywhere.'

'I'm surprised you can see anything, Johnny with those swollen eyes.'

'Are you all right, Miss Howard?' Johnny said.

'I'm fine, Captain.'

'Is there anything else to take with us, Johnny? Something you've hidden in the jungle?'

'No. Just us. It's all in the head, Clement.'

'That's a relief. So, nothing for the Japanese to find?'

'Nothing.'

Tom and Mick lifted a fold-boat and carried it to the shoreline.

'If you'll give me a hand, Joe, we'll get the other boat

in the water,' Clement said.

Clement slung his Owen gun over his shoulder and together he and Joe carried the second fold-boat to the water's edge. But he knew with six people and two craft there was no room for superfluous weaponry. Standing in the tepid water, he turned back, his gaze checking the shore and the hillside behind them. He looked again along the beach in both directions. Somehow, he felt someone was watching them. But he saw no one, besides, there was no time to investigate his suspicions. Evelyn pushed the boat into the water and climbed in, her stockinged legs and shoes sodden, her hand still gripping the Owen gun. Clement waded further into the warm water, his right hand on the boat, his left swinging his gun around his chest, the muzzle up and ready to fire should a Japanese ambush them now. Johnny waded through the shin-high water. With Evelyn stabilizing the boat, Johnny pulled himself into the craft and sat in the bow. Clement checked the shore again; he felt completely exposed and vulnerable.

Looking up, he could see Joe wading out behind the other boat. Tom was standing in waist deep water taking the unused ammunition and weapons from Mick and lowering them into the sea. Joe lifted himself into the middle of the boat, then raised an Owen to his eye, the muzzle of the weapon moving back and forth, as he kept a look-out for any Japanese. Within seconds, Tom had hauled himself into the boat and he and Mick were paddling out to sea.

Clement pushed his boat into knee-deep water then lifted one foot into the craft and pushed off the muddy sand with his other foot. Grabbing the paddles, Clement and Johnny commenced to strike out.

No one spoke.

They were not yet out of danger. With the moon now directly overhead, their silhouettes would, at times, be visible from anyone on the shore who may have witnessed their escape. Clement paddled on, trying to keep the rhythm of his strokes matching with Johnny's. Once clear of the point, Clement focused on what lay ahead. But it didn't stop him worrying about a bullet to the back. Of all the places he thought he may die in this war, the Singapore Strait had never been one of them. Ahead, he could hear the paddles of Tom's boat, but he could no longer see them. As the minutes passed, dark night engulfed the small boats.

Clement glanced over the side of the fold-boat. With three people, the craft was sitting low in the water and progress was slow. Once into the Strait's main channel, he intended to jettison anything unnecessary. He stared at Evelyn Howard's back. She was using her shoes to scoop water from the floor of the vessel. Her courage and ingenuity had astounded him. She had proven herself to be not only resourceful but astonishingly brave.

They paddled on. The night was warm, but Clement hadn't felt it until now. Sweat trickled down his neck and back and with every stroke, he felt the overwhelming tiredness of adrenaline withdrawal coupled with the exertion needed to keep forward momentum. Beads of sweat ran from his forehead into his eyes, and he could taste the salt on his lips. They paddled on, no one spoke, with each stroke Clement felt a degree of relief to be away from the shore and the haunting feeling that someone had watched them leave.

Clement glanced back for one second at Labrador Battery. The flames from the explosions of the two grenades had almost gone, the detonations having taken place outside the concrete structure. The blast door on the ammunition store had prevented the whole place from exploding and the small amount of timber in the battery had meant that any fire wouldn't burn long. Despite the feeling that someone had witnessed their withdrawal, Clement hoped that if someone had been there, it had only been Lyon. Perhaps the man had waited to see if they had got away unharmed. His mind drifted to Ivan Lyon. He prayed the man would find his family and that he would explain the damage at Labrador Battery to his superiors. If Clement survived to return to Melbourne, he wondered how he was going to explain it to Commander Long. The mission was supposed to have been silent. Furthermore, taking out a much-needed British Battery at such a time could be seen as treason. Long would not be happy. There was nothing to be done. Clement's one consolation was that Johnny, and his secret were, for now, safe.

They paddled on into the sultry night. The heat hadn't diminished and Clement's shoulders ached; he thought the wind had strengthened. Wind. His mind went to Eric Nave and his *Winds Message. West Wind; Clear.* Eric had been correct about the Japanese intentions towards the British in Singapore. And, apparently, about the attack on the Americans. He wondered what effect that would have on the progress of the war. They paddled on, the looming silhouette of Fort Siloso now black in the night and still about a hundred yards away; its ominous guns still pointing out to sea. Then a light. Clement looked up. He knew Tom would have seen it. A search light coursed over the Straits. But it was brief, one long sweep only and the strong beam lasted only a few seconds before it was extinguished. The men on duty in Fort Siloso would have seen and heard the commotion at Labrador Battery and most likely used the search light to see if a Japanese ship had entered the straits. But seeing none, they'd switched off the light.

'I'm inclined to think the Fort is still in British control,' Johnny whispered.

'I agree,' Clement said.

Clement and Johnny recommenced paddling, the choppy sea filling the small boat. Evelyn continued the back-breaking task of baling with her shoes. Ten minutes later they were in the lee of Fort Siloso, the sound of the waves crashing on the rocks unmistakable. Clement thought about the search light. Doubtless the explosions at Labrador Battery had caused the search light's use. But the garrison at Fort Siloso were seemingly unaware of their presence beneath them.

Clement lifted his head to the skies. He couldn't see any sign of pre-dawn light and while he wasn't sure how long the crossing had taken, he knew dawn was still a few hours away. All that mattered now was that the *Krait* was still where it was four hours ago. Clement listened to the rhythmic crashing of the waves on the rocks below the Fort. 'Slow down, Johnny,' Clement whispered. Ahead he could see Tom's boat. They'd stopped paddling and Clement could see the vessel bobbing in the waves. Something was troubling Clement, but he didn't know what.

'All well, Tom?' Clement whispered as they manoeuvred alongside each other.

'We're fine. Just taking a breather and waiting for you to catch up. See you back on the *Krait*.'

'Not so fast, Tom,' Clement said. It was gut that told Clement they were heading into trouble. He knew all eyes were on him. And he had no way of speaking privately with Johnny, the only person there who he completely trusted.

'What is it, Clement?' Johnny whispered.

'Nothing,' Clement said, realising he had no choice but to continue. 'You go first, Tom. But be careful and don't approach the ship if another boat is nearby.'

'Right you are,' Tom said.

Clement waited until Tom's craft was a little distance away. He didn't want to lose sight of it, but he wanted a minute to speak with Johnny. Even though Evelyn Howard would overhear their conversation, it was a risk he had to take.

'Something isn't right, Johnny.' Clement explained his reasoning.

'It isn't me they're after, actually, Clement.'

'What?'

'The secret I'm carrying isn't in my head. She's sitting between us.'

22

Blakang Mati Island - 22nd December 1941

J ohnny leaned forward, his voice a mere breath of sound. 'The Japanese also thought I was carrying something. When they didn't find anything, they had a go at trying to get me to tell them. When that didn't work, they waited. No one guessed and no one knew that the secret is a person not a document.'

'Did Commander Long know?'

'Yes, but he was under orders not to tell anyone, including you.'

Clement picked up his paddle. 'We need to catch up with Tom. They shouldn't board before we check the ship for mines.'

'Mines?'

'Long story, Johnny, and it will have to wait till we are safely away from here.'

Evelyn shifted on the narrow seat. 'I'll paddle now, instead of Captain Winthorpe. With his injuries, I'll be faster. Besides I'm quite accomplished at it. Although, I haven't done it in years, it's probably like riding a bicycle. It'll be fun.' Evelyn took the paddle from Johnny and held it firmly. 'Ready, Clement?' she whispered.

Clement smiled. Evelyn Howard, Clement decided, was one of those women daunted by very little. He could easily imagine her as Captain of the English Women's Cricket Team or the headmistress of a school of capable, independent young women. Clement began to paddle. Evelyn's pace was indeed quicker than Johnny's and soon they were parallel with Tom's boat.

Ahead, Clement saw the glass Japanese fishing lights on the *Krait*. They were swinging, swaying with the movement of the vessel. But it wasn't the gentle sway of a ship at anchor. Something was causing the vessel to rock more vigorously. Then from across the water he heard raised voices. Above him the first faint hint of day intruded on the dark night, a tinge of pre-dawn light. 'Slow down, Tom,' Clement called quietly.

Tom, Mick and Joe had heard the voices too, their boat bobbed in the water, their paddles lifted above the waves.

Clement laid his paddle across his lap then felt for his binoculars and focused them on the *Krait*. In the lee of the hull was another boat of some size.

'I need to get closer.' Clement turned in his seat. 'Do you have any objections, Evelyn?'

'None.'

Clement grasped his paddle and lowered it silently

into the water.

'You're not doing this without us,' Tom whispered.

Clement paused. 'Change of plan. Tom, can you swim?'

'Like a fish, Clem. What do you want to do?'

'We need to know if they're friend or foe? Can you swim over and back?'

Tom looked out and took in the distance. 'Easy.'

Clement and Evelyn manoeuvred their boat closer to Tom's then drew both together. 'Do you have any weapons still in the boat?'

'You're getting to know me, Clem!'

'Any limpets?'

'Sorry. Too heavy. Grenades and hand weapons only.'

'Right. Here's the plan. First, we need to know who this visitor is. Swim over and find out then come back here. If he's friendly we wait until they leave before boarding the *Krait*. If he's unfriendly, then you and I swim back and check the hull of the *Krait* and the fuel tanks. If it's clear, then we swim back to the boats and wait till they leave.'

'And if we find one?'

'Then you and I, Tom, will remove it and reattach it to a different hull.'

Even in the faint light Clement saw the perfect, white grin.

Mick and Johnny held the two boats close and Joe passed the grenades to Evelyn. Tom then leaned to his right and tipped himself into the water.

'Be careful, Tom. No heroics. Reconnaissance only. Mick, hold your boat together with ours would you? I want to keep my eye on Tom.'

While Johnny held the Owen Guns and Evelyn the box of grenades, Joe held one paddle to steady the two boats in the waves while Mick kept them together.

Tom began to swim away, his head, the only visible part of him, quickly merging with the dark waters and making it difficult for Clement to keep him in sight. But the raised voices from the ship continued. Clement began to wonder if it was Bill's way of letting them know they had company on board.

As Tom approached the *Krait*, Clement saw him edge his way down the land side of the vessel and away from where the smaller boat had tied up to the *Krait*. He lost sight of Tom after that.

Minutes passed. Lifting the binoculars, Clement scanned both ships. He couldn't see anyone, neither Japanese nor Bill nor anyone else. But Clement couldn't see aft and he hoped that's where Bill was remonstrating with whomever was on board. Clement deliberately slowed his breathing, feeling the tension as the minutes passed. At least there were no weapons or fold-boats remaining on board to implicate Bill. He felt his mouth go dry. No one spoke. All eyes were on the *Krait*.

An eerie silence ensured. Minutes dragged by. He couldn't hear the raised voices anymore and Clement began to wonder if Bill and his crew were dead. He lifted the binoculars again and panned both ships once more, then the water between them. Where was Archer? It was taking too long. He began to worry that Tom had drowned or been taken by one of the large sharks he'd seen in the Java Sea. Clement swallowed hard, a deep frown creasing his forehead. Then, through the binoculars he saw the familiar head of his sergeant swimming towards them. The white toothed grin appeared out of the gloom beside Clement.

'Well?' Clement asked.

'Japs,' Tom said from the water. 'Bill's giving them a right serve.'

'Are they in uniform?'

'Yeah! Three of them.'

'And the crew?'

'They're there. Sitting like caught crabs. But Bill's doing all the talking.'

'Any bombs?'

'Oh yeah!'

'Armed?'

'Yep! And set for two o'clock this afternoon.'

'Same place?'

'Yep.'

'Right. You and I go back and remove it.' Clement passed his paddle to Evelyn, then, with Johnny helping to steady the boat, Clement slipped into the warm waters. Following Tom, he swam towards the ship, keeping to the landside and moving to the aft end. Clement could hear the voices above them. Removing the mine this time would not be easy. And it had to be done from the water. Above them he could hear Bill still protesting.

'As I said, we're fishermen.'

'Where you going?' a male voice with a thick accent said.

'Back to Timor, weather permitting.'

'When?'

'Later today, if you ever get off my boat!'

'First, we check holds.'

Clement heard footsteps on the *Krait's* deck. He glanced at Tom. With the Japanese going for'ard to the holds they had a few precious minutes. Clement pointed for Tom to lift himself over the gunwale. Tom pulled himself up and, standing on the proud line of timber just above the water line of the *Krait's* hull, he stepped over the gunwale's edge and disappeared from Clement's view. Clement put his knife between his teeth and waited. Two seconds later, Tom looked over the edge, reached for Clement's hands and pulled him up. He could see the Japanese men standing beside the wheelhouse staring into the radio hold.

Kneeling beside the fuel tank, and using both knives, they prized the mine off. Tom stepped over the side of the ship, using the proud line of timber for support, then lowered himself back into the sea. A moment later, he reached up and took the mine from Clement.

Clement glanced back over his shoulder. The Japanese men were still for'ard. Sitting on the gunwale, he swung his legs over the side and lowered himself quietly into the sea. He and Tom waited under the long, over-hanging transom of the *Krait*. It was the perfect hiding place for them to catch their breath. With Tom holding the limpet, Clement checked the timer and arming switch. All was in place and there was no need to alter anything. He motioned to Tom. Leaving the cover of the *Krait's* transom, Tom swam in a sideways manner, still holding the limpet, Clement about four feet behind him. A minute later, they swam to the ocean side of the patrol boat. Clement tapped the side of the hull. Metal. He looked at Tom. A grin spread over both their faces. With the Japanese men still on the *Krait*, Tom swam along the side of the boat and gently lowered the limpet about three feet down under the water and carefully attached it to the hull.

Swimming to the bow of the patrol boat, they swam towards the land side of the *Krait* and waited amidships and close to the wheelhouse above them. Clement heard a Japanese voice.

'You say you fishermen. Why you have no fish?'

'Sold them all in Java,' Bill answered.

'Do not come back here. If you do, we shoot you as spy, Mr Reynolds.'

'You're not in charge yet!' Bill said defiantly.

A long silence ensued. Clement held his breath then nodded to Tom to swim away from the *Krait*. They had minutes only to get back to the boats. He knew the biggest danger now was being run over by the Japanese boat and getting caught in its propellers. And they needed to get the fold-boats out of sight and behind the lee of the *Krait* before the patrol boat left. With Tom ahead, he and Clement swam as quickly as they could without making any noise.

Clement felt a succession of stronger waves pass over him. He turned to look back. He saw the Japanese step onto their boat, the ship's rocking causing the bigger waves. A second later, a strong and bright search coming from the patrol boat lit up the *Krait*. Then their engines started. The Japanese were leaving but not before making sure the area was clear. Clement could see Tom about six feet away from him.

'Tom!' Clement shouted above the roar of the patrol boat's motor. Archer turned and stared at the beam of light off to his right. Clement could see the wide-eyed expression on Archer's face. Clement pointed downwards and both men inhaled long breaths then dived under the water as the search light coursed over the surface. As Clement dived under the water, he opened his eyes, the warm saltwater stinging and blurring his vision. He could see Archer a few feet away. Both men were using their arms and legs to stay submerged as the water around them became more turbulent from the patrol boat's propellers.

Clement thought of the others in the boats. He earnestly prayed they had seen the search light and taken evasive action. He kept his eyes wide, the churning water around him now making visibility limited. Then in front of him and about four feet away were the rotating propellers. Moving as fast as his arms and legs could manage, Clement swam backwards away from the vortices created by the rotating blades that were drawing him into their deadly whirlpool. He felt Archer's hand grab his belt, dragging him backwards. With almost no air in his lungs, Clement surfaced with Archer a few seconds behind him. They stayed in the water gasping for air, the Japanese patrol boat now heading south away from Blakang Mati and Singapore.

'You alright, Clem?' Archer whispered.

'Thanks to you, Tom I will be,' Clement said, spitting water from his mouth.

'Who put it there, do you think?' Tom asked.

'One of their number would be my guess, while they were talking with Bill, and keeping him busy.'

'So they recognised the *Krait* after all,' Tom said.

'So it would seem.'

Off to Clement's left, he saw the shapes of several fishing luggers drawing nearer. Clement signalled to Archer. If they were Japanese, there would be no escape this time. Clement wondered if the others in the boats had been caught.

'Clement!' Johnny's voice, sharp and clear in the predawn air.

'Here!' he called back.

'Thank God! And your sergeant?'

'Yeah, I'm here,' Tom said. 'We're the lucky ones. Clem and me had a nice swim!'

'We're all on the lugger and it's towing the boats. Hang on to them and we'll pull you over to the *Krait*,' Johnny said.

Bill had already lifted the sea anchor. Johnny thanked the local fisherman and within minutes Bill had poured some medicinal whisky for all on board. As the dawn broke, they left the waters around Blakang Mati Island. Clement felt exhaustion taking hold. And the alcohol was having its effect.

'Johnny, this is Sergeant Tom Archer who saved my life.'

'Just as easily could have been me, Clem, close to those blades. But I've always been lucky.'

Clement smiled back. He'd never believed in luck preferring to think it divine intervention. The Lord had brought him and Sergeant Archer together. Perhaps Archer could come back to England with him after all. The man had shown courage, initiative, and loyalty. All the traits of a man Clement wanted in his sergeant. 'And this is Private Mick Savage.'

'Private,' Johnny shook Mick's hand. 'Thank you for your part in this.'

Mick hung his head, his feet shifting under his more than six-foot frame. Clement thought he saw Mick blush. With a weapon in his hand, Mick was every inch a competent soldier, yet beneath the surface, Clement saw a quiet, humble man. He smiled as an extraordinary sense of pride washed over him. 'And this is Lieutenant

Joe Watkins of the US Navy..'

Johnny turned to Joe. 'I've heard your name mentioned before I think, Watkins,' Johnny said shaking hands with the American. 'And well done all of you. Miss Howard and I are very grateful.'

Evelyn Howard gave a tired smile.

Clement waited. He wanted to talk with Johnny and for that he needed them to be alone. 'Sleep for everyone now. I'll do surveillance duty with Captain Winthorpe for four hours.'

'Two, Clem. You look done in.'

'Thank you, Tom. I won't say no.'

Clement and Johnny stood on the aft deck as the sun lifted over the horizon. 'It'll be too warm for you here soon, Johnny. And your skin is very pale. Very noticeable for any Japanese Zeros that may be about.'

'I hardly recognised you, Clement. You're so tanned. But I'm very grateful as I'm sure is Miss Howard. This surveillance duty, what's that about?' Johnny asked.

Clement explained the precaution and all that had happened since leaving Timor, including the mine from Surabaya. 'I'm just not convinced Hugh's death was suicide. And there's the question who leaked the rendezvous signal and place? That can only have come from someone either in Timor or onboard.'

'Do you have any suspicions?'

Clement shook his head, more out of uncertainty than fact.

'We just need to keep our eyes and ears open, Clement. And inform Long.'

'I know.' He looked around. Bill and his young crew were on the foredeck and the team had turned in for some much-needed rest. Clement spoke in a low voice. 'Is Evelyn that important?'

'Yes. She's found a weakness in one of the Imperial Japanese Naval codes.'

'JN25B8?'

Johnny stared at Clement. 'You have acquired some new skills since we last worked together. But yes.'

'I spent a morning with Eric Nave in Melbourne. Doesn't mean I understand what he's doing. In fact, I'd say I have a very limited understanding of any of it. But I'm impressed she does.'

'Worked with Tiltman at BP. Very clever people who I'm very grateful work for us and not the Japanese or the Germans. As regards Nave; we wanted him back at GC&CS but somehow or rather someone has thwarted our every move there.'

'Really!' Clement said but while he guessed who had, he didn't say anything. From the corner of his eye, he saw Bill approach.

'I can't thank you enough, Bill, that you waited for us,' Clement said.

'When I saw the explosion in the battery, I did wonder if I'd ever see any of you again.' Bill pulled a cigarette paper from his top pocket and stuck it to his lip then reached for his tobacco pouch in his short's pocket, the coarse-grained leaf now being crushed in his left palm. 'I told the Japs I was returning to Timor. Could be a good idea if we didn't. Even though you weren't onboard when they came calling, my guess is that they'll have patrols out looking for you. They'll be stopping everyone but, hopefully, now they've boarded us they'll leave us alone. They did a thorough search before leaving, though. We hid everything of yours we could find so there'd be no trace of you. Cut a hole in one of the water tanks and concealed the stuff there. Had to dump water to do it, so it will be rationed now.'

Clement told Bill about the limpet. 'Right! Well, that will have us back on their list. How did they attach it?'

'My guess would be that one of their number attached it while you were engaged in conversation with them.'

'So, when that patrol boat blows later today, they'll send someone else to come looking for us. Surveillance duty again, I think. And we should work out how we're going to defend ourselves. If that's possible. No stopping now until we reach safe waters.'

'Which way will you go?' Clement asked.

Bill put the cigarette in his mouth and lit it. 'We'll stay close to the land and behind the onshore islands while in the Java Sea. Then take the Sunda Strait, I think. From there I'll chart a course for Christmas Island. It's a British governed island controlled from Singapore, well, last time I looked it was. Hopefully, we can refuel there and reprovision the ship. There's a phosphate works on the island. And we all know that phosphate makes fertilizer and fertilizer makes explosives, so let's hope we don't run into any Japs. But the islanders will be nervous. Christmas Island is a long way from anywhere. And other than one six-inch gun, they are largely unprotected.'

'How far?' Johnny asked.

'About three hundred miles.'

'Can we make it that far without refuelling?' Johnny asked.

'With full tanks we can get to India without needing to refuel.'

'And after Christmas Island?' Clement said.

Bill drew in a long breath then exhaled an aromatic stream of smoke. 'About a thousand miles of endless ocean to Exmouth Gulf on the West Australian coast. Just get your God to keep those waters calm, would you, Clement! That's the Indian Ocean and there's nothing between us and the African coast for thousands of miles.'

'I'll do my best.'

Bill sauntered away. With the heat of the day, Clement and Johnny sat under a shade cloth set up over the foredeck.

'Any thoughts on who leaked the information?' Clement asked.

'No. Not only did they know the rendezvous signal and location, but they knew about me. That has to narrow it down. And despite you thinking it was someone in Timor or onboard, it could be someone in Singapore who'd been keeping me under close surveillance. Or who works at FECB and intercepted the revised instructions to me from Long. With all that's going on, it's going to be hard to prove. By the way, Clement I think the beard suits you.'

'Not too sure about that, Johnny!'

Clement looked up. Evelyn Howard stood before them. Gone was the saturated pleated skirt and buttoned blouse. She was wearing a pair of Tom's shorts and one of his shirts and her legs and feet were bare. On her head was a woven palm leaf hat that Juan and José must have given to her. Clement resisted the urge to laugh. Her short curly brown hair protruded from under the brim of the islander hat and her blue eyes bored into his. For the first time Clement began to wonder about her age. She wasn't young but not old either. He thought her perhaps a similar age to himself. 'How are you feeling, Miss Howard?' Clement asked.

'Considering how ridiculous I look and what we've just been though, that's a bit formal, wouldn't you say?'

'Sorry. May I call you Evelyn?'

She nodded. 'You may, if I may call you Clement.'

'Agreed.'

'Tell me, Clement, how much do you know about Eric Nave's work?' Evelyn asked, settling herself beside him.

Johnny caught Clement's eye.

'Joe told me you'd talked about JN25B8,' Evelyn said.

'Not much, I'm sorry. But I think Eric is onto something that the authorities should take seriously. If the British at FECB have, for whatever reason, decided not to go to Australia, then they should listen to what Eric has to say. He knew about the *Winds Message* in mid-November. Why wasn't that acted upon? Singapore and Pearl Harbour, not to mention the other places that were bombed at the same time, could have been spared, or at least warned.'

'One thing you will learn, Clement is that the Intelligence business is cursed with one, dare I say, several, fatal problems.'

'Surely not apathy?'

'No, not apathy but ego; getting the information to the upper echelon quickly is always difficult. Then it's a matter of getting them to take it seriously. And all this must go through numerous channels in three very different and rivalrous services across more than one nation. You see the problem.'

'No wonder Long wants a combined intelligence unit.'

'And he may well get it. But wheels turn slowly, even during war. And that's assuming others more powerful than him want the same thing.'

'I didn't know you were so sceptical, Miss Howard,' Johnny said.

'Not sceptical, Captain. Realistic. I, of course, have an additional problem. I'm a woman. If it wasn't for John Tiltman, I still wouldn't be taken seriously.'

'Are you working on JN25?'

'Yes,' she paused, then smiled. 'And we've found a weakness.'

23

Indian Ocean - 22nd December 1941

Clement stood on the foredeck as the *Krait* made good progress south. He knew Bill would want to be as far away from Singapore as possible. Despite weaving their way around the myriad of onshore islands, just being in the Java Sea made them a target of Japanese aggression. Clement gazed into the white sky. Johnny had told him, the Japanese advance in the Southwest Pacific was on multiple fronts. They not only were heading for Singapore, but had worked their way down through Malaya, the Philippines and Borneo and were heading directly for the Dutch East Indies and the islands further to the East. It appeared that nothing could stop them but with divine intervention, Clement hoped they could stay one step ahead of the advancing enemy.

Clement checked his watch. Mid-afternoon. He wondered if the limpet on the Japanese patrol boat had exploded. But if the Kempeitai believed the *Krait* had been destroyed, would the regular surveillance flights recommence? Clement prayed that with the different course and destination Bill had chosen, it would be days, if not weeks, before the Japanese learned they'd been outwitted. And by then, God willing, they'd be in safe waters. Clement joined Bill in the wheelhouse.

'Where exactly is this Christmas Island?'

Bill reached for one of his charts and spread it out on the wheelhouse bunk. To Clement the name Christmas Island sounded exotic. Pouring over the chart he found the tiny island; a rocky outcrop many miles south of Java and surrounded by a vast ocean. It was about as isolated a place as St Helena.

Leaving the safety of the onshore islands they headed into the open Java Sea. While Tom and Mick cleaned and stowed weapons, Clement sat with Johnny under the shade cloth and breathed in the warm, salty air. Joe preferred to sit by the radio, listening for news of his former colleagues from the Philippines or any popular music he could find. They had only now to get through the Sunda Strait and into the Indian Ocean. Once back in Australia, he would arrange for a flight to either Melbourne or Sydney then head for England with Johnny.

He thought of his home, although he wasn't sure exactly where that was. As a vicar living in a parish, the vicar's residence belonged to the church. He wondered if old Reverend Battersby was still in Fearnley Maughton. In his mind's eye Clement could see the brown geometric carpet in the hallway in the vicarage there. He hung his head as he felt the tears well up. He told himself that it was exhaustion making him sentimental. Exhaustion or not, Fearnley Maughton could never be home for him again. Not without Mary. And even though the house in Combe Martin in Somerset that Mary had inherited from her aunt was now his, it wasn't his home. He stared at the sea. He chastised himself for becoming maudlin. Besides, it was too soon to be thinking about home or even about England. While his mission to collect Johnny from Singapore had been successful, it had not been without issue. Many things nagged him about this mission and despite successfully rescuing Johnny and Evelyn, Clement didn't believe it was over.

He stared at the hazy white sky wondering about the identity of the collaborator. And possibly murderer. He thought again about the men of his team. Archer and Savage had certainly proved their loyalty and Johnny and Evelyn had been rescued. Even Joe had assisted them and more than that, stayed with them. Lifting his gaze Clement thought on Hugh Kearsley. There he felt real sadness. And if the killer hadn't been a member of the crew, that only left Watkins, Lyon, Archer or Savage. Something about Hugh's death and the watching Japanese man in Surabaya still troubled Clement. He believed the Japanese had known about them and tracked them for most of the journey. This was borne out by the regular surveillance flights. Had the strafing been solely to disguise the fact that the Japanese were watching them rather than trying to destroy the boat? Surely, if they'd wanted to kill them, they'd have sunk them with a direct hit from a bomb. Did that mean the strafing was only diversionary? Had they always known about the mission? While people in Melbourne knew he was going to rescue someone in Singapore, no one there had known how he was getting there. Not even Long knew the name of the vessel. This could only have been told to the Japanese by someone in Timor.

Clement thought back to that time in Dili. He'd been met by Ross and there were three Japanese men there to whom Ross had given whisky. Whittaker had arranged the passage with Bill Reynolds and had time to speak to the Japanese consulate on Timor before they'd even left Dili. Even Tom, Mick and Hugh had spent time in Dili before joining him at David Ross's pink house on the hill. Why had the traitor deemed it necessary to kill Hugh; a nice boy who'd risked his life setting up radios and checking the network of Coastwatchers that Long and his team had set up? Clement's last memory of Hugh was when he'd been standing on the deck, the Zero approaching fast.

Clement stood and walked for'ard to where Hugh had been standing that day. He'd done it before but something still eluded him. Clement imitated the pose. What had Hugh been staring at? 'Not something,' Clement muttered. 'Someone.' Clement had thought everyone was below decks because the Zero pilots were known to count the numbers of men on deck. They'd arranged to have five on deck; Bill at the helm, himself, and Bill's crew. But Hugh had made six. He'd asked Bill about the incident, but Bill's focus was on the Zero, not anyone else on deck. And Bill had said Juan and José hadn't seen anything. But he hadn't said he'd spoken to Pedro. Clement walked aft to where the crewman was preparing food. 'Pedro, can I ask you a question?'

'Si.'

'Try and remember last week; when that Zero flew overhead. Hugh Kearsley was standing for'ard and Bill pushed him down the for'ard hatch. Do you remember that?'

'Si, I remember. Of course, I remember. I was in there too with Senhors Archer and Savage. Senhor Kearsley, he almost land on top of me. But I should be on deck with Juan and José, for the numbers. Senhor Bill was very angry with me later. I'd just went to get my hat.'

'And you came back on deck?'

'Si.'

'Did you see anyone on deck other than Bill?'

'Si, Senhor Lyon was there. He'd said he'd been in the engine bay.'

Clement stared out past Pedro to a flying fish that had surfaced beside them, then just as suddenly disappeared back into the sea. That Lyon had hidden in the large engine bay meant nothing, if he'd been on the aft deck at the time the Zero appeared, it was the closest place to hide.

'He had a torch in his hand,' Pedro added, almost as

an afterthought.

'What did you say?' Clement asked, wondering if he had misheard.

'He have a torch.'

'Why?'

'He say he check bilges for bullet holes.'

'Thank you, Pedro.' But Clement almost couldn't hear his own voice. His mind raced. It was just possible that Lyon had been in the engine bay checking for bullet holes. After all, they had been strafed. But could he have been standing on the permanent engine bay cover signalling an approaching Zero? In his mind Clement went through everything he could remember about the man. Nothing he had done cast any suspicion on him. Even Long had said the man was secure. Trustworthy! Clement stood and went to find Johnny.

'What is it, Clement. You look like you've seen a ghost.'

'Have you ever met a man called Ivan Lyon?'

'Yes. A very brave man. Has been around the Indochinese region carrying out raiding attacks on the Japanese there. I've met him at FECB a few times. Why do you ask?'

'The man who was also being held prisoner in the battery and who left us there, did you recognise him?'

'No. I don't think so. But my eyesight wasn't that good then, Clement, both my eyes were swollen.'

'He came with us, on the *Krait* from Timor. Said his name was Ivan Lyon.'

'Even with my blurred vision, Clement, I'm almost positive that man was not the Major Ivan Lyon I've met.'

Clement felt sick. How could he have been so fooled? Whoever this man was he'd learned a great deal about the real Ivan Lyon. He'd been so convincing; even fooling David Ross and John Whittaker. Were they involved? Clement thought back to the night Ross had brought Lyon from Dili to the pink house on the hill. Clement felt the realisation like a blow to his head. Ross had said he'd never met Lyon but knew him only by reputation. 'We have a problem, Johnny,' Clement said. 'And several people's lives are at stake, not just ours; all the Coastwatchers and, dear Lord, he knows where they all are. He's met David Ross, John Whittaker, all my team, me, you, even Evelyn.' Clement paused. 'He didn't know about Evelyn.' Clement faced Johnny. 'You said no one knew about her. Only Long knew that Evelyn was the secret. That is the only secret *he* didn't know. He thought you were carrying something. Even staged his own rescue, so we wouldn't suspect him.'

'Why didn't he shoot me then when he had the chance?'

'Because he was looking for secret documents. He knew they hadn't found anything on you, and they suspected you'd hidden them somewhere. That's why he allowed us to escape.' Clement remembered the feeling he had that someone was watching them as they left Labrador Battery had headed across the straights. 'He hoped you'd lead him to the documents. And when you didn't, he arranged for the patrol boat to put the limpet on the *Krait*. He knew where the boat was. The Japanese on that patrol boat would have taken you off, leaving me and the others to be blown to pieces that afternoon.' Clement paused, his mind racing. 'But he told me things. Why would he do that?' Clement said half to himself.

'What sort of things?' Johnny asked.

Clement told Johnny about the *Automedon*.

Johnny was silent for a few minutes. 'The sinking of the *Automedon* is top secret. How did he know about it?'

Clement had no answer. How did he know? It was the penultimate question for any intelligence officer.

Johnny looked up, a deep frown creasing his brow. 'But, he hasn't actually told you anything we didn't already know. You may not have known about it, but it's no secret to Naval Intelligence.' Johnny paused then repeated what Clement had already asked himself. 'But how did *he* know? That's what I want to know?'

'That's not all he said.'

'There's more?'

Clement told Johnny about the gold and the *kin no yuri*. 'Were you aware of this?'

Johnny drew in a long breath. 'No. And if others better informed than me aren't either...' Johnny's voice trailed off. 'Do you know Clement, I've learned a great deal about what makes a man, or woman, betray their country, assuming this man is English. But this could be his undoing, I have to wonder about his motivation.'

'I'm not sure I understand you, Johnny.'

'This man may have told you about this *Golden Lily* thing because he believed you'd be dead before you could tell anyone. But it was a huge risk. And one that makes me wonder what motivated him to tell you. Was it just ego? Was he hoping you may try to recruit him as a double agent? Or is it revenge...'

'Revenge!' Clement added surprised.

'Revenge is a powerful motivator, Clement. And it could be for something as simple as being passed over for promotion or not being given the credit for a success of some kind. We need to know who this man is. And I want to know why he chose to impersonate Ivan Lyon. Likely he has certain physical similarities but it's probable he's met Lyon somewhere. And the real Ivan Lyon may not even remember him. It must be assumed that the Coastwatchers network has been infiltrated. Long must be informed as soon as possible. I need to find out how long it will be before we get to this Christmas Island.' Johnny stood and went to join Bill in the wheelhouse. Clement joined him there.

'When do you anticipate arriving in Christmas Island?' Johnny asked.

'Another three days, at least. All being well.'

'Christmas Day! Seems appropriate, given where we're going. Do they have a long-range transmitter there?'

'Not one I'd use for sending private messages, if that's what you had in mind,' Bill said.

'But you and your ship are known there? They'd recognise you on entering the harbour?'

'Not painted like this, they won't.'

'I'll ask the lads if they can paint the ship again,' Clement said. 'I'm sure Tom won't mind. Anyway, gives them something to do during the long hours at sea.'

'I won't mind either,' Bill said. 'And I'll be pleased to burn that damn Jap flag as soon as I can.'

'May I suggest, Mr Reynolds, that you fold it up and stow it away for next time,' Johnny said.

'What makes you think there'll be a next time?' Bill asked.

'Because men like you, Bill are patriots. And there is no better motivation for anyone to do dangerous things.'

'Well, perhaps.' Bill puffed on the cigarette dangling from his lips.

Clement and Johnny left him in the wheelhouse, the enclosed confined space stiflingly hot and sat on the foredeck under the shade cloth. With the ferocious heat, Clement turned his face to the bow, hoping the breeze that the ship generated from its forward movement would bring some relief from the relentless heat.

'Cuppa, Clem?' Clement heard Tom call from the stern.

'Thank you, Tom. I'm sure Captain Winthorpe wouldn't say no either.'

'Right you are.'

'How are you coping with the heat, Johnny?' Clement asked.

'You'd think I'd be used to it, but truth be told Clement, I've lived in London too long. I hadn't remembered how debilitating the heat in the tropics can be.'

'Would you prefer just water?'

'It will be tepid anyway, Clement. More bearable disguised as tea.'

Evelyn, who had been sitting on the bow staring into the water beneath the prow of the ship, joined them. 'Marvellous! Dolphins swimming under the bow. Simply marvellous!' She sat back down beside Clement then pulled a notebook from the pocket of Tom's voluminous shorts. Within seconds she was scribbling figures on the page.

Clement looked at the woman, in those few short seconds she seemed to have moved into a different world, far away, totally absorbed in what she was doing, and he wondered if she even remembered she was sitting beside him.

'Don't mind Miss Howard, she has the highest security clearance, besides, I don't think she'll even hear us.'

'I may look stupid, Captain Winthorpe but it's just the way they've dressed me.'

Clement laughed.

'You realise, Clement that you and your team are the only people who would recognise this impostor. He'll be on your track.'

Joe climbed out of the radio room hatch and joined them.

'Tom has made a brew, if you'd like some, Joe,' Clement said.

'Don't know how you guys drink the stuff in this weather. What I wouldn't give for a soda right now.'

'Dream on, Lieutenant!' Evelyn chimed in without looking up from her scribbling.

'I may be able to add something to your description of Major Lyon, Captain. Sorry, Clement, but with the hatch open I heard you.'

'Well!' Johnny said.

'The *Krait* isn't a big ship so let's not say any more about it. What could you add, Joe,' Clement said.

'Captain Winthorpe, would you remember if the Ivan Lyon you know parted his hair on the right or the left?'

Johnny frowned, the question clearly surprising him. 'I think it was left. Yes, it was a high part but definitely on his left. Ivan has a broad smile and distinctive, rather uneven teeth. The parting is wide and pale against the colour of his hair. I can picture him now. It was definitely over his left eyebrow.'

'You're sure, Johnny?' Clement asked.

'I'm positive.'

'Well, that guy parted his hair on the right, Clem,' said Joe. 'It was quite curly and most days on the *Krait* the wind blows so hair can be any way the wind chooses but when I first saw him in the pub in Surabaya, it was definitely combed and parted on the right. I know because Rudy Fabian in Manilla does the same. It struck me the first time I saw him because other than him and Rudy, most guys part their hair on the left.'

'Thank you, Joe.'

'Well, whoever he is, he has access to some pretty top-secret information,' said Johnny.

'More than you, Johnny?'

'Possibly. But I think he is more dangerous than any Nazi in the North Atlantic right now.'

'Meaning?'

'You might be in Australia longer than you thought, Clement.'

Clement gazed out to sea. Yet another postponement to his return to England? Initially, he felt the frustration that always accompanies delay. He frowned, questioning his reaction. Did it really matter? England held no personal attraction for him at present, nor the furious seas of the North Atlantic in winter.

'I could arrange it for you to remain on Long's staff.'

'I'm a Major in the British Army, Johnny, not in the Australian Navy.'

'Regardless, Clement. Rupert Long is Head of the Combined Operation Intelligence Centre, and he has the ear of Admirals. If he wants you in Melbourne, just like Nave, it will be arranged and there won't be much you can do to stop it.'

Clement saw Tom walking towards him, two mugs of tea on a tray. The young sergeant had more than proven his worth and Clement wouldn't mind working with him and Mick again. Perhaps he would stay in Australia. He half laughed to himself, as if he'd have any say over that!

They drank the hot tea.

'Cuppa for you, Missus?' Tom asked but Evelyn didn't look up.

'That's alright, Sergeant,' Johnny said. 'She can have some of mine.'

From the corner of his eye, Clement watched Evelyn Howard. She held the pocket notebook in her left hand, but her head was lifted to the sky and a pencil was in her right hand. While Clement thought Evelyn would likely spend her days in mathematical conundrums and not earthly practicalities, he admired her fortitude; she was capable and strong and in many ways like Mary, who'd also shown a propensity for mathematics. He sipped his tea. Never in his wildest imaginings did he ever envisage he'd be on an old fishing boat, somewhere near the equator on the other side of the world with a team of men from various nations and a woman wearing men's clothes and a woven palm hat.

As Evelyn pondered over complex mathematical sequences, Clement's mind momentarily dwelt on the vicarage that had been his home in rural England and Mary; her smile, her laugh and her slender ankles, even her apron that hung behind the door in the kitchen. While her passing was only a little over a year ago, so much had happened and the crushing isolation he'd felt had almost gone. Not because he didn't profoundly miss her; he always would, but because the war had dictated his life's path. He looked across at Evelyn again and the unruly mop of curly brown hair that forced its way out from under the woven palm-leaf hat. She was not remotely like Mary physically, but her mind was razor sharp and, from what he'd seen, she was fearless. Clement wondered if she'd been trained for SOE before they'd discovered her talent with figures. But her life experiences in wartime, a bit like his, were a taboo subject.

As afternoon became night, the darkness engulfed the ship. A myriad of stars glistened above them. Clement breathed a sigh of relief that with each passing day, the gap between the *Krait* and the Japanese would grow larger. The setting sun flooded the sea with its orange glow, the enormous sun on the horizon spilling its liquid gold towards them. The only other human presence was the occasional local fishing lugger.

By the following morning, the ship had passed through the Sunda Straits. Bill had timed entering the narrow stretch of water so that they passed through in darkness. Lights on both shores made for an uneventful journey through. If the Japanese, or their spies, were watching for them, they were to be disappointed.

With the morning sunrise, Clement couldn't see any land in front of them. Instead, the vast Indian Ocean lay before them. It would be many hundreds of miles of sea before they saw the tiny Christmas Island. Since leaving Blakang Mati Island, they hadn't sighted a single Zero nor Japanese patrol boat. But while Clement was grateful, he wasn't under any illusion that the Japanese or the impostor Lyon had forgotten them. Clement hoped they thought the limpet on the *Krait* had been successful. He hoped they were waiting in the Dutch East Indies for news of them. But when the *Krait*'s wreckage was not found nor the ship sighted, Clement guessed the Zeros would once again be searching for them.

24

Christmas Island - 25th December 1941

Clement watched from inside the wheelhouse as Bill manoeuvred the *Krait* beside the wharf and Pedro with Juan and José jumped ashore then tied the ship to the massive bollards on the quay. It was late afternoon, and the tropical sun was spreading its astounding glow over the ocean. The heat was still intense, but Clement believed the humidity was less. Two men stood waiting. One wore the uniform of a British Army Captain, the other was an older man dressed in open-necked shirt and short trousers. He wore a pistol on his hip. Neither were smiling.

'Haven't seen you for a while,' Clement overheard the older man say, as Bill jumped from the *Krait* onto the wharf.

'How are you, Kevin?' Bill said. 'Didn't you recognise my ship?'

'Alright. Yeah, I recognised you, but Captain Williams

here isn't taking chances with any ships calling in.'

'Why is that?' Bill asked.

'Have to be careful now. News is the Japs could descend on us any time. Seems farfetched to me.'

'Not at all, Kev,' Bill said, reaching for his cigarette papers.

'If you know this man, Harris, I'll get on,' Captain Williams said then nodded to Bill and left taking the road back towards the few buildings that made up the settlement in Flying Fish Cove.

Clement opened the window in the wheelhouse door to overhear the conversation better.

Bill stood with his hands on his hips, the cigarette on his lips. 'Trouble's brewing, Kev and the Japs are closing in.'

'Yeah! Won't ask how you know this.'

'Best not to. But it could be a good idea to have a bit of extra protection other than that old pistol and one six-inch gun on the headland.' Bill paused. 'Can I refuel and take on some supplies?'

'Sure. We're not rationing anything yet. Just you and the lads?'

'No. Altogether, ten.'

'Ten! What are you running? A cruise?'

'Something like that. Seen any Japs in here, fishing, or pearling luggers even?'

'Come to think of it, no.'

'Right. Some men on board would like to use the island's radio.'

Kevin Harris was silent. 'What sort of men?'

'Army and Royal Navy.'

'Struth! Should I call Captain Williams back?'

'No need. Best these men aren't seen,' Bill jerked his head in the direction of the *Krait*.

'What have you got yourself into?' Harris said.

'Just need to use the radio, Kev.'

Kevin Harris nodded his head. 'Where are they then?'

Bill turned to face the *Krait*. 'Clement!' Bill shouted. 'Says you can use the radio!'

From the wheelhouse Clement nodded and waved his hand in acknowledgement. But for all his skills, radio communication in Morse code wasn't one of them. Leaving the wheelhouse, he went aft to the engine bay where Evelyn was sitting out of sight. Clement wondered how she managed in the stifling heat of the engine bay but she hadn't complained and it gave her a degree of privacy. Opening the hatch, he leaned in. 'Can you use a wireless and transmit in Morse?'

'Of course.'

Johnny joined Clement by the hatch. 'She can't go ashore. Can't be seen, Clement. Take Joe.'

'Wouldn't that have Harris asking how an American got here? And if the Japanese interrogated him, knowing an American had been here could cause all sorts of problems. What if she dressed in Tom's uniform again and that big woven hat?'

'Not ideal but I suppose we have no choice. But, Clement, make sure no one gets a good look at her face.'

'I'll be fine, Captain Winthorpe.'

'I'll ask Tom to bring you some clothes.' Clement closed the hatch and went to get Tom from the for'ard hold.

Clement went ashore, joined Bill and met Kevin Harris. Minutes later, Tom with Mick and Evelyn, disguised again in Tom's shorts and shirt and his slouch hat holding her hair up inside the brim, stepped ashore.

Clement's eyes widened at the sight, but he said nothing. Standing erect, he spoke formally to Tom for Harris's benefit. 'While Sergeant Howard and I are away, you and Private Savage get some provisions.'

'Yes, sir.'

Clement walked away from Harris a little. Tom followed. 'Be careful what you say, Tom. And please pay for everything you take.'

Clement kept Harris talking as they crossed the quay and walked towards some buildings about a hundred yards away. Evelyn lagged behind them and out of Harris's field of vision. It had been decided that Johnny and Joe would remain on board and out of sight. Should the Japanese ever come calling and interrogate Kevin Harris, he couldn't describe Johnny or Joe, or Evelyn for that matter.

'You have a big concern here, Mr Harris,' Clement said striding along a dusty dirt road.

'Phosphate. Makes excellent fertilizer.'

Clement nodded but he knew other uses for phosphate. Uses the Japanese would certainly be interested in. From the corner of his eye, Clement saw Tom and Mick stroll along the wharf heading towards the supply depot.

Inside Harris's office was an old wooden desk that seemed to be covered in grime, the sort that builds up over years and, once congealed with heat, turns black. A whitish dust covered most surfaces in the room. Outside, Clement heard lorries passing, the constant shuttling to the docks, doubtless carrying the precious phosphate.

'There it is,' Harris said pointing. 'I'm guessing one of you knows how to use it?'

'Thank you, Mr Harris.'

Without speaking Evelyn went straight to the wireless, sat and reached for the Morse code key with her right hand. Clement engaged Harris's attention as Evelyn's left hand tuned the frequency dial. Seconds later, Clement heard the repetitive clicking of the message being tapped out.

'I'm surprised the plant is operating today, given that it's Christmas Day?' Clement said standing between Harris and Evelyn.

'Twenty-four hours a day, seven days a week, fifty-two weeks a year. It never stops. Don't imagine it will decrease any time soon now we're at war with the Japs. Besides, most of the people who live on Christmas Island aren't Christians.'

'Really! You've heard the news about the Japanese then, Mr Harris.'

'That thing your sergeant is on is our life-line. Lose that and we lose contact with the outside world. And if you've been at sea a few days then you may not know the latest. Hong Kong has surrendered. Happened earlier today.'

'That is terrible news!' Clement felt a shattering blow. Nothing it seemed could stop the Japanese from coming south. Behind him, he heard the tapping of the Morse code cease. He needed to get Evelyn back to the ship as soon as possible. 'Well, I won't keep you from your vital work, Mr Harris. And, thank you.'

Clement waited until Harris opened the door and they stepped out, Evelyn following them. 'Return to the ship, Howard, no dilly-dallying.'

'Sir,' Evelyn mumbled, her head down and her voice falsely deep.

Outside, he stood with Harris by the roadside as several lorries thundered passed until Evelyn was some distance in front of him. Shaking Harris's hand, Clement left.

Once back onboard the *Krait*, Clement went straight to the engine bay where Evelyn and Johnny were sitting on the bench at the rear.

'Sorry I was so abrupt, Miss Howard, but even the smallest detail, if it's incorrect, can give you away.'

'I understand, Clement. It was fun.'

'What did you send, Evelyn?' Johnny asked.

'Operation Wisdom successful. En route to Exmouth. ETA January 4.'

'In plain text?' Johnny asked, clearly aghast.

'Never, Captain Winthorpe! I did the encryption in my head.'

25

Exmouth Gulf, Western Australia - 4th January 1942

Clement saw the familiar frame of Commander Rupert Long standing on an old wooden jetty surrounded by emerald waters. Behind him, steep rocky hills rose sharply above a pristine sandy beach. There wasn't a single building in sight and although Exmouth reputedly had a naval base, Clement couldn't see it.

Bill and his young crew secured the *Krait* to the pylons, and five minutes later the engine was cut.

'Permission to come aboard?' Long called to Bill.

Clement greeted Long on deck. 'Bill, this is Commander Rupert Long.'

'Guessed as much,' Bill said.

Long turned to Clement. 'Wisdom, well done! Good to see you.' Long's gaze encompassed the motley group that had gathered on deck. 'Although I hardly recognise the man-of-the-cloth who sat in my office in Victoria

Barracks.'

'I'm not surprised, Commander. May I present, Captain John Winthorpe and Miss Evelyn Howard. And this is Lieutenant Joe Watkins. I believe you know Sergeant Archer and Private Savage, who have been of immeasurable service to me and the mission.'

'Good to see you all. I have a Sunderland Flying Boat on stand-by. As soon as it's refuelled, we can go.'

'I wouldn't mind getting some diesel, if the Navy can spare it,' Bill said.

'Of course, Mr Reynolds. You've done your country good service. It's the least we can do,' Long said and shook hands with the *Krait's* skipper. 'Get your things, everyone, and we'll go as soon as you're ready.' Long jumped back onto the jetty.

'Are we going to the naval base in Exmouth?' Clement asked, his eyes looking around for any sign of life.

'This is it, Clement,' Long said pointing to the Sunderland moored in the gulf. 'The flying boat and a tender with a radio is all that's needed here. The Sunderland will take us to Perth then we can fly on to Melbourne.'

Clement stared at the flying boat moored out in the bay then along the beach as he waved away the myriad of flies that buzzed in front of his face. A short distance away, he could see kangaroos sitting under some low-hanging bushes. It was the most barren and remote place he'd ever seen.

While they disembarked from the *Krait*, the tender returned to the jetty and Long stepped aboard. Clement turned to face Bill Reynolds. 'Words will never express my gratitude to you, Bill and your young crew. Will you head back to Timor?'

'We'll take on water and fuel here but then we might sail to Darwin. Given what's happening in the islands, I'll most likely stay there a few months.'

'Wise precaution, Bill.'

'I've got your suitcase, Clem,' Tom said, holding Clement's luggage and pack. Mick stood beside Tom, quiet as ever, Owen guns festooned around his shoulders.

Clement shook hands with Bill and his crew then stepped ashore. He felt the odd sensation in his legs that came after spending several weeks at sea. The land seemed to rock under his feet.

Long stood at the bow of the tender, facing them. 'Once we're back in Perth you can wash and refresh yourselves. I'll arrange the onward flights and you can fill me in on what you've learned.'

Clement stared back at the *Krait* as the tender scooted across the bay. It had been their home for almost a month; and the last place he'd seen Hugh Kearsley alive. There was more than one unresolved issue with this mission and in Clement's heart, he believed it wasn't over yet.

Minutes later, the team climbed into the flying boat. Having been on one before, he knew how loud it would be. 'How long is this flight?' he asked the young captain as he stepped onboard.

'Couple of hours, sir. We'll land at Crawley Bay. You can wash and get something to eat there. Sheila's a bonza cook. She'll look after you.'

Clement glanced across to Johnny. He could see his old friend's face was now almost healed thanks to Bill's saltwater treatments. Johnny had already settled in a seat; his back against the window, his eyes closed. Clement thought he looked exhausted from brutal interrogation and sheer physical exertion. It had been a long war and it wasn't over yet. British troops had been fighting since '39 and the country had been repeatedly bombed but it still clung on. Although Clement wondered how. Grit and determination inspired by the Prime Minister's eloquent speeches had doubtless helped. And now the Pacific was at war for who knew how long. Clement thought of the secret documents taken from the *Automedon*. It was small wonder, the War Cabinet in London thought the Far East indefensible. Fighting on too many fronts exhausted not only men but munitions and supplies. A lesson Napoleon had learned to the peril of his troops. Clement glanced at Long who could move men around like the pieces on a chess board. But would it be enough? The Japanese were conquering all before them and Hong Kong had fallen. He visualised Nave in his small office deciphering Japanese codes. A breakthrough there could ultimately mean victory. Clement was grateful that men like Nave and Long existed. Without them, the Japanese could well be unstoppable. His gaze shifted to Tom and Mick. Clement smiled. They'd settled themselves quickly in the rear of the plane and, despite the noise, were already asleep. Only himself and Evelyn were awake, her pencil and notebook in her hand. He'd never known a woman like her. The sunlight from the porthole settled on her cheek, a wisp of hair across her face. Without disturbing her calculations, her hand removed it, tucking it behind her ear.

The Sunderland skittered over the water then slowed and stopped, the propellers slowing. Once the aeroplane was attached to the mooring and the propellers stationery, the captain opened the door. Long descended to the waiting tender, followed by the others, and they were transported to a small jetty behind which was a large building erected close to the shoreline.

Archer and Savage collected their packs and they followed Long into the building. Inside, it felt cool, and an overhead fan rotated above them. Without pausing, Long led them upstairs to a room with long glass windows that overlooked the main waiting area below on one side and the road on the other. Clement could see a lorry parked there.

Minutes later, a woman brought in a trolley of tea with numerous cups and saucers and a two large plates of sandwiches which she set in the centre of the table. Long stood staring out the window at the waiting lorry before sitting down. 'We'll be here about an hour before our onward flights. I suggest you eat something. It's going to be a long day.'

Clement saw Archer's eyes fix on the sandwiches. Any mention of food had a quick response from Archer. Soldiers, Clement decided, were always hungry. He nodded to the sergeant, who quickly took a handful of sandwiches from the nearest plate before taking a seat on one of the chairs away from the table. He handed some to Savage who, as always, waited for Archer's signal before doing anything.

'I'll play mother,' Evelyn said as the tea lady left the room.

Long waited for the door to close. He looked up at Archer and Savage. 'Sergeant, you and Private Savage will return this evening to Darwin by the regular Qantas flight out of Nedlands airfield. Needless to say, you will not talk about your recent experiences. And nothing is to be said about Corporal Kearsley. I'll get his C.O. to send the appropriate letter to his next-of-kin. You can have one day off in Darwin then return to your former command. There's a truck outside waiting to take you to the aerodrome.'

Tom stood to attention, his mouth half full of tomato sandwich. 'Sir, if I may make a request?'

'What's that Archer?' Long asked.

'Mick, that is, Private Savage and me, sir, we'd like to stay with Major Wisdom.'

Long looked at Clement. 'I haven't decided where Major Wisdom will be posted next. But your request is noted. As soon as you finish that sandwich, you and Private Savage are dismissed. Take your packs and report

277

to the truck driver outside.'

Archer and Savage saluted and, swallowing another sandwich, collected their packs and made to leave.

Clement stood and walked towards them. 'Thank you, Tom for what you did. I wish you both well in Darwin. And wherever they next send you. My sincere thanks to you both for your invaluable contribution to the successful outcome.' Clement thrust out his hand and shook Tom and Mick's hands.

'She'll be apples, Clem,' Tom said, his voice subdued.

'Mick,' Clement nodded.

Mick didn't speak but stood to attention then both Tom and Mick saluted him. Clement stood facing the two young men, returning their salutes. Strangely, he'd miss the odd duo. 'Look out for each other.'

As Archer and Savage left the room, Clement returned to the table. He thought he'd seen Tom's eyes glaze, but Archer was a resourceful young man and, Clement considered, would fall on his feet wherever they sent him.

Clement resumed his seat as Long's words about his own future repeated in his head. He visualised Sir Stewart Menzies. The man had only begrudgingly agreed for him to come to Australia in the first place. But Long had a persuasive manner and Shetland was a long way away. Clement reached for his cup and drank the last of his tea.

'Now tell me about Singapore?' Long said, sitting down.

Clement placed his cup on the saucer. 'Before I do,

Commander, could you bring us up to date on where the Japanese currently are? We've not heard any news for some days, and the knowledge could have a bearing on our experiences. We were told while in Christmas Island refuelling that Hong Kong has surrendered, is this true?'

'Sadly, yes. In the days following the bombing of Singapore, Malaya and Pearl Harbour, the Naval Base on the Philippines was also bombed. By the tenth, the Japanese landed in huge numbers and Guam surrendered.'

Clement glanced at Joe.

'What about the intercept station there, sir?' Joe asked, the concern in his voice evident.

'That's the only good news in the whole scenario,' Long said. 'They did such a good job of destroying their station, the Japs will never know they've even been there.'

'Did they get out?' Joe asked.

'Unknown at this time, sorry Lieutenant,' Long answered. 'By the eleventh, Germany and Italy declared war on us.'

'And Singapore?' Clement asked.

'Both the *Prince of Wales* and the *Repulse* have been sunk. And I understand Singapore is in chaos.'

'That is true,' Evelyn said.

'By December 15th they'd taken the airfield at Victoria Point in Burma, and...' Long paused and looked straight at Joe, 'two days ago the Japanese took Manilla.'

A heavy silenced filled the room.

'Now tell me about Singapore?' Long said.

Clement informed Long of all that had happened since leaving Darwin and especially the events that had occurred in and following Surabaya and the destruction of Labrador Battery. Long listened without interruption during the twenty minutes it took Clement to relate the events.

'I have something to add, Clement, which supports your theory,' Long said. 'I received a message recently from Major Ivan Lyon via Kamer 14. He went to Surabaya to collect Lieutenant Watkins as instructed. However, when Watkins failed to make the rendezvous, Lyon made enquiries and was informed that Watkins had already left.'

26

Crawley Bay Flying Boat Base, Perth,
Western Australia - 4th January 1942

Clement glanced around the faces of those present. He stared at Long, a thousand questions bubbling in his brain, too many to process.

'What!' Joe said. 'You're saying that guy wasn't Lyon? But he had the rolled newspaper. How would he have known about the signal, if it wasn't Lyon?'

'Good question,' Clement muttered, his mind racing.

Long lit another cigarette. 'When Lyon contacted me with this information, I asked him how he got to Surabaya. He said he came by boat from Moresby in a ship called *The Wanderer.*'

Silence settled in the room.

Clement leaned forward, his head in his hands. What he felt was utter confusion but mostly he felt betrayal and it always left a hollowness in the pit of the stomach. It confirmed Joe's suspicions and his own about the man he knew as Lyon most likely killing Kearsley. Pedro had seen the impostor holding a torch. He'd told Pedro he'd been checking for strafing damage, but in fact, he must have signalled the approaching Zero and Kearsley had seen him do it. And Kearsley had been threatened with death if he revealed what he'd seen. Clement thought of the suicide note. Joe had spotted the difference in the 'a's. If this impostor had known about the difference in writing style, Joe would also be dead, and the note destroyed. Whoever this man was, Clement knew for certain now that he wasn't Ivan Lyon.

Evelyn was the first to break the silence. 'If this man is an undercover Japanese spy he may still be in Singapore. What of FECB and the girls at Kranji Station? He could do irreparable damage there. They may all be dead.'

'They started to evacuate on New Year's Day. Let's just hope they're already gone. The ladies at Kranji will be evacuated with other women by sea. I rather hope some of them, if not all, will come to Melbourne. We could use their skills. Especially now.'

'Why especially now, Commander?' Clement asked, thinking of the stolen secret letters taken from the *Automedon*.

'The British are too stretched to assist us. They are fighting on too many fronts. To this end, our new Prime Minister has recalled some Australian troops, but will they arrive in time to make a difference? Let's hope so. Then a few days ago, the Americans arrived in Brisbane.

We will be a motley crew, but I think one that will provide excellent intelligence of our region for the United States Navy. But all this aside, we need to find this man impersonating Major Lyon. The real Lyon is a very brave man, and I won't have his reputation tarnished like this. Perhaps, more importantly, this imposter, by impersonating such a courageous man, could do considerable damage to the Free French Resistance networks in Indochina and Borneo, not to mention other places. His continued existence is dangerous!' Long lifted his gaze then stood again and stared through the window at Crawley Bay beyond. It was a stance Clement had come to recognise Long did while thinking.

'How did he know?' Long muttered without turning around.

'What, exactly, Commander?' Johnny said.

'Many things, Captain. But firstly, how did this impostor know about the *Automedon*. Then there's this *kin no yuri* thing. That, I've never heard of. And if it's true, it would be catastrophic. It would be bad enough if the Japs win in the Pacific, but win or lose, if they had millions if not billions at their disposal, the damage to global economies would be unthinkable.'

'Imagine if it got into the hands of a few greedy men, sir,' Clement added.

'Right. Miss Howard, how close were you and others at FECB to cracking the latest JN25?'

'We've discovered a weakness, Commander. But please be in no doubt; understanding the algorithm doesn't necessarily mean we know what they're saying. The codes the Japanese use are nothing like the German encipher system and, of course, they don't use a Romanised alphabet. Their language is character based so their codes are completely numerical. But like most codes and cyphers, their infallibility becomes fallible when in human hands. And low-ranking radio operators, thankfully for us, will take short-cuts. Despite there being about thirty thousand substitutes for words, only some of which we know, the numbers fall into patterns. JN25 is refreshed every month. But not everything is changed. The code book may remain the same but the additive table changes. This last change happened on the 4th of December, which was unusual in itself.'

'How so?' Long asked.

'Changes usually happen on the first day of the new month.'

'So, what's the weakness.'

Clement saw Evelyn glance around the table. But this was her field, and she was completely absorbed. 'Even though they changed the additive on the 4th of December, they didn't change the code book. We'd been working on that for over a year. But to understand it you need to comprehend the layers of the Japanese codes. Suffice to say that the indicators, which are imposed on the code book cyphers are also five-digit numbers, the first three of which contain the page number in the code book in use, then a daily indicator encryption group which is known to both transmitter and receiver and can easily be subtracted. The fourth number represents the page co-ordinate for the starting place for the message. This is the most important piece of the puzzle. And the fifth could just be padding. Operators will usually use an easily accessible page when transmitting, like the first or last or middle page of the code booklet, so we check those first. Several of us worked with John, that is, Mr John Tiltman, to make this breakthrough a couple of years ago. But that was just the beginning. The really exciting thing was discovering that all the relevant numbers are multiples of three. Mr Turing was marvellous here. With the use of a machine we now have access to and having the digits coloured coded according to the remainder when divided by three, it is possible to quickly assess whether the book groups have digits adding up to a multiple of three by their colours. Only these are relevant to the message being transmitted, everything else is padding.'

'My God! Miss Howard, I could kiss you!' Joe said.

'I assure you, Joe, that won't be necessary. But it is extremely secret and only a few know about it. Which is why only Commanders Long and Nave knew what Captain Winthorpe had in Singapore.'

'It's impressive, Miss Howard and I daresay that Eric and the Professors in Melbourne will be delighted,' Long said. 'This man, this impostor, did he know about this?'

'Of course not!' Evelyn said. 'I haven't told anyone until now. And unless you understand how the code book works, just knowing about additive tables won't help you. But I do need to get back to England. I have work to do there.'

'Of course.' Long sat down again. Everyone waited while he sat staring through the window, clearly once more deep in thought. 'This afternoon, we all fly back to Melbourne.'

Clement's gaze lingered over Commander Long. He could almost see the man's brain cogs turning and he wasn't sure he liked what he saw. Lyon, or rather his impostor, would have to be found and Clement could guess who Long had in mind for the job.

Clement thought of his former friend in England, Superintendent Arthur Morris, and how he would go about locating the illusive impostor. Clement cleared his throat as a way of distracting Long. 'Commander, while the codebreaking is of paramount importance, I think the key to discovering this impostor lies with the real Ivan Lyon. There must be a link between these men. Can you arrange a meeting?'

'Already thought of that, Wisdom. Given where he is currently, it will take a few days to get him to Melbourne.'

27

Long arranged for an RAAF plane to take them to Melbourne.

'Do we leave from here?' Clement asked, his eye on the flying boat still moored in the bay.

'No, I'll arrange a DC3 to take us. We'll leave from Maylands Aerodrome. It's not far,' Long said.

Clement glanced at the Commander, who was lighting another cigarette. He knew firsthand that distances in Australia were immense and Long's idea of *not far* could mean anything up to five hundred miles. Melbourne, however, was thousands of miles away. While flying was something Clement never thought he'd enjoy, it really was the only way to move around this country with any speed. He reached for another sandwich and tasted the strong savoury flavour of tomato and butter. He thought it such a luxury.

Long sat staring at the table before him for several

minutes, a distracted expression on his face. Suddenly the man stood and left the room.

'He's a rare breed, Clement. I wish we had more like him,' Johnny said, still looking at Long through the glass partition.

Clement took the opportunity of Long's absence to talk to Johnny. 'Will the Americans entering the war make a huge difference?'

'Absolutely! The war in Europe grinds on but hopefully now that the Americans are with us, we'll see our fortunes turn.'

'Are you meaning here, in the Pacific?'

'Both, Clement. They have an enormous population, large manufacturing factories and no one overhead dropping bombs on them.'

'What about Pearl Harbour, sir?' Joe said, joining the conversation.

'Hawaii aside, Lieutenant, the mainland doesn't appear to have been threatened. Let's just hope it stays that way, for all our sakes.'

'Couldn't agree more, Captain. What is it you do with FECB, exactly?' Joe asked.

'I'm not with FECB, Lieutenant.'

'But you know Evelyn, sir.'

'Yes. I'm with the SIS in Whitehall but I go to Buckinghamshire quite often, so I am acquainted with the work of FECB's parent in England, the GC&CS.'

'You ever come across this guy posing as Major Lyon?'

'No.' Johnny paused. 'But I wish I'd paid greater attention when we were in Labrador Battery. I didn't even know who he said he was until Clement told me.'

Long returned, the glass door swinging closed behind him. 'We can leave now! Maylands Aerodrome isn't far.'

Finishing the sandwiches, Clement reached for his pack and they left the Crawley Bay building. Outside another lorry waited. They climbed aboard. As it rattled along the dirt road, Clement thought back to the lorry Tom had driven to collect him from Darwin in the pouring rain a month ago. He'd laughed at the rhythmic limping movements of the vehicle with uneven tyres. In his mind he also heard the sound of another mode of transportation, one with a syncopation to the gears; a bus in Caithness. Those memories always reminded him of Reg. Clement screwed his eyes shut forcing those images from his mind.

It was late afternoon by the time they boarded the DC-3. The odd aircraft sat with its nose in the air, parked outside the hangar. Clement climbed the few steps and walked up the aisle to his seat. Beside him was Johnny and across the aisle were Evelyn and Joe Watkins, still talking codes and cyphers. Long sat in the rear, his large feet protruding into the aisle, the inevitable cigarette dangling from his lips.

Leading WRAN McManus was there to greet them on arrival in Melbourne. With her, standing next to a second car, was another WRAN in military uniform.

Clement felt the cool breeze. It refreshed the skin but after a month in the tropics, he felt cold. It was early evening and two days had passed since taking off from Crawley Bay. While they'd stopped in Adelaide, they hadn't left the aircraft hangar there, sleeping on make-shift beds in a draughty building and refuelling in remote locations along the route.

The cars drove away from the airfield, the cows still grazing in the adjoining meadow. Long sat in the front with the driver while Clement and Johnny sat in the rear. Evelyn and Joe were in the other car. But both cars were heading to the same destination, Victoria Barracks in St Kilda Road.

'Miss Copeland has arranged accommodation for your guests at Victoria Barracks, sir,' McManus said. 'She told me to tell you the keys to the rooms are in your office, Commander.'

'Good of her. I'm sure we're all grateful for her initiative,' Long responded.

Clement hoped Long didn't want a meeting at nine o'clock at night. He felt tired and every bone in his body ached. Alighting from the car, he retrieved his suitcase and pack from the boot. A cool wind blew across from the park and he shivered. Climbing the steps, they entered the Virginia creeper-covered building and went straight to Long's office on the first floor. Clement had a headache and a need for uninterrupted sleep.

Long reached for the keys on his desk, each allocated by name then handed them out. 'Please be here at nine tomorrow morning.'

Everyone nodded and, taking their key, left Long's office.

'I'll show you all where to go,' Clement said. He glanced at Johnny, who had the key to the room next to his. They went up a flight of stairs and along a narrow corridor to the side of the building. 'Here it is. The bathrooms are down there,' Clement said pointing further along the corridor. 'Good night, Johnny.'

'Good night, Clement. And Clement, thank you.'

Clement smiled then opened the door to his room and switched on the light. Hanging on a stand opposite him was a khaki uniform. It wasn't strictly British Army but Clement didn't care. It would be warm, clean and dry and he silently thanked Miss Copeland for her forethought. Placing the suitcase by the stand, he closed the door, stripped off his dirty clothes, and fell into bed.

The officers' mess was full of people when Clement walked in for breakfast. He knew he was late, and most likely the last of their number to arrive, but he'd slept well and he'd enjoyed the warm shower. Heaping some eggs and bacon onto his plate he joined the others at the table by the window. 'Morning, Johnny.'

'Morning, Clement. Sleep well?' Johnny said.

'Surprisingly well. You?'

'Like a baby! And what a luxury, bacon!'

Clement smiled then said a silent prayer for his meal. He looked up and caught Evelyn's eye. 'Morning Evelyn,

Joe.' Clement cut into the egg-soaked bread.

Joe nodded but Clement could see worry in his eyes. He knew that look; the anxiety for the unknown fate of his colleagues in Manilla. It tore at the soul and coupled with the feelings of guilt, of being the man who'd survived because he'd been away when the Japanese invaded.

Evelyn, however, looked the picture of health.

Clement smiled at her. She, like all of them, had found some new clothes, doubtless compliments of Miss Copeland and her army of assistants.

Eric Nave entered the mess and walked directly towards them, a beaming smile on his lips. 'How good to see you all.'

Clement stood and shook Nave's hand. 'Eric, it's good to see you too. May I introduce Captain Winthorpe, Lieutenant Watkins, and Miss Evelyn Howard.'

Nave smiled and nodded to the group. 'Thank you for bringing the secret safely to Australia, Clement. Her expertise is invaluable, and I know she will advance our work considerably.'

Evelyn Howard reached for the tea pot as Nave sat down.

'Cocky has asked me to remind you that he would like us all upstairs at nine,' he said.

Finishing the meal, they made their way to Long's office on the first floor. Filing in, Clement took the seat beside Evelyn then glanced around the room. There appeared to be an extra chair. 'Are you expecting someone else, Commander?'

'Eric will bring him up as soon as he arrives which should be any minute, in fact.'

There was a knock at the door. Miss Copeland opened it and a tall man wearing a British Army uniform walked in.

'Ah! And here he is!'

Clement looked up. He could see this man held the rank of major and he carried his cap in his right hand. He had wavy dark brown hair and a boyishly exuberant expression.

'Morning, Cocky,' the man said.

Long stood. 'Good to see you. Let me introduce you. Everyone, this is Major Ivan Lyon.'

All eyes were on Lyon. Clement felt his jaw drop but he saw the similarities immediately.

Long continued, 'I've already told Lyon a little about the man impersonating him, but I imagine he and you have plenty of questions.

Nave took the chair to Clement's left.

'You knew Evelyn was coming?' Clement whispered to Nave, remembering the doubts he'd harboured about Long and Nave concealing something from him, and nodding in Evelyn's direction.

'Yes. Sorry, Clement, really hush-hush!'

'Understood, Eric.'

Long removed his jacket and peered through the nearby windows, then hung it over the back of the chair. 'I cannot tell you what Major Lyon has been doing but he works for us in a clandestine position and does similar work to yourself, Clement. He is familiar with Indochina. His wife and son are sadly in the hands of the Japanese.'

Clement looked up. 'Your wife is French?'

'How did you know that?' Lyon said.

'Your impostor knows you well, Major.'

Clement saw the anguish of deception in this man's face. Whoever the impostor was, he knew a lot about Major Lyon and his circumstances. 'It is possible you've met him, Major, either in Singapore or in Indochina.'

'Commander Long has informed me about this man,' Lyon said. 'I understand you had a camera with you, Major Wisdom. Is it possible you may have taken a photograph of him?'

Clement thought back. 'I did take some shots, but I cannot recall if the impostor was actually in any of them. Of course, he would have been careful not to be.'

'Where is this camera, Clement?' Long asked.

'I have it in my pack, Commander, in my room.'

'We need them developed urgently.' Long leaned forward and pressed the intercom button on his desk. 'Miss Copeland, could you please arrange for someone to collect a camera inside Major Wisdom's pack. It's in his room here, I understand. Also any exposed film, then get it all developed onsite as quickly as possible.'

'Of course, Commander.'

Clement imagined the flurry of activity to accomplish the task Long had requested. If anyone could make it happen, Long and his winning charm would have military staff moving Heaven and Earth to have the films developed and returned to his office with the maximum speed.

'How quickly can it be done?' Lyon asked.

'An hour. Miss Copeland can get most things done with lightning speed. I wish other matters proceeded with such efficiency.'

Clement heard the barb. He knew how bureaucracy worked. Slowly. And wartime didn't seem to hurry it.

Clement cast his eye towards the large windows. The park over the road had been ploughed and vegetables of all kinds were growing there. He remembered the tractor ploughing up the lawns when he'd last been in Long's office. His eye fell on the workmen, their hoes chipping at the clods of earth. Closing his eyes, he saw his garden at the vicarage in Fearnley Maughton. He'd been doing the same thing when he'd received the telephone call from Johnny about joining the secret world. He stared at a bird that had settled itself on the head of one of the statues of the great and famous in the park. Their bronze gaze now looked down on runner beans. Towards the right were several benches, couples seated on some of them.

Long stood, his hands in his pockets. He walked over to the window, his face turned towards the scene outside. 'While we wait, I'll bring you all up to date with some more developments in our region. Rabaul in New Britain was bombed by the Japanese three days ago.

Raids are continuing there, daily. FECB continues to evacuate but I've learned some are going to Colombo and others to Delhi.'

'So, Singapore hasn't fallen?' Johnny asked.

'Not yet. But there is so much bickering between the senior commanders on the island that I fear it might be inevitable. There has, however, been a positive development. On the 4th of January, General Wavell was appointed Head of all Allied Southwest Pacific forces. Although, his job in an unenviable one. He must hold the line known as the Malay Barrier which stretches from Burma in the west to Papua New Guinea in the East and includes part of North-Western Australia. He'll be stationed on Java in Lembang in the mountains and near to Bandoeng where Kamer 14 is located. I believe you know this area, Lieutenant Watkins?'

'Yes, sir. Very mountainous. It's cooler there. It is, however, in my humble opinion, too far away from the Dutch Navy in Surabaya.'

'How far?'

'About two hundred miles, sir. There is a train but it's not a direct line. Several changes are required and animals often stray onto the tracks which can sometimes take a while to clear.'

'When will Wavell arrive?' Johnny asked.

'It is anticipated that he'll be in Java this week,' Long said, sitting down again.

'How is he to get to Lembang, Commander?' Clement asked.

'He'll be coming from Singapore by ship.'

'And which port will he enter by?' Clement asked but his gut told him he already knew.

'He's to inspect the Dutch Navy at Surabaya first, then travel to Lembang.'

'He's there,' Clement said aloud. 'The impostor; could it be that he'll attempt to join Wavell's staff? Or assassinate Wavell? Or take him prisoner along with his entire staff? If that's the case, there'll be nothing standing in the way of the Japanese taking Java and the whole region if this Malay Barrier collapses.'

Long leaned forward. 'Then we must get this impostor before the Japanese take the Dutch East Indies. If Clement is right, we have very little time.'

Here it comes, Clement thought, his gaze on Long. Déjà vu.

'Clement, as you are one of only a handful of people who would recognise this man, I'm asking you to go. You can take anyone you like with you.'

Clement glanced at Johnny. 'Shetland?'

'I think this is more important, Clement. Shetland will have to wait. I'll explain it to Sir Stewart.'

'I want Tom Archer and Mick Savage. I'd also like you, Major Lyon, and Lieutenant Watkins, who would be recognised by the team in Bandoeng. And I'll need a radio operator. Can we get John Whittaker to join us?' Clement asked.

'Why Whittaker?' Long asked.

'Mostly because I know him. I don't want another impostor nor someone who's abilities I don't know.'

'Can't do Whittaker. It leaves Ross without a radio operator, and with the Japanese moving as rapidly as they are, this is not the time for him to be without radio communication with us,' Long said.

'I'll go!' Evelyn said.

'Out of the question!' Johnny, Nave and Long said in unison.

Clement stared at Evelyn Howard. Her prowess with weapons, her determination, and her ability to encrypt in her head had astounded him. She was the perfect person but he knew it would be impossible. 'Miss Howard, I couldn't ask you to endanger yourself in such a way.'

'Commander Long, I am trained in weapons handling, I know Morse code. I can encrypt and decrypt in my head. I also know Kana Morse and I can use a wireless. Most importantly, I can speak Japanese and I'm here. Now.'

Long stood and paced the floor, his hands clasped behind his back. 'I'll try to get Whittaker if no one else is available. But I don't like the idea that Ross is alone on Timor without him.'

Nave and Joe Watkins stared at Long but it was Joe who spoke. 'Sir, she is far too valuable to risk her life on this side show. Sorry, Clement, Major Lyon, but for Miss Howard that is what it is!'

Evelyn leaned back in the chair; her expression indignant, her arms crossed. 'It may be a side show, as you put it Joe, but clever spies can cause more trouble in one day to the outcome of the war than a year spent decrypting enemy messages can benefit it.'

Silence.

Evelyn leaned forward on the table. 'You forget, Commander. The Japanese think I'm dead. And even if they suspect I'm alive, they think I'm a secretary. And a woman can get in and out of places men can't. We're not seen as a threat. And as you said, we have only a few days. And I repeat, I'm here.'

Clement could see Long's hesitation. 'I'll need Bill Reynolds and his crew also.'

'She can't go! She's needed here,' Eric said.

Evelyn turned to Clement. 'How long do you anticipate being away?'

'Two weeks. With divine intervention, maybe less.'

Clement could see Long was wavering. 'I'll protect her day and night. She won't be exposed to any danger. Just radio operation. Nothing else and she'll remain on board the *Krait* and out of sight. She won't be included in any covert activities.'

'Damn the wet season!' Long shouted. 'If I can get Whittaker in Darwin by tomorrow, you take Whittaker. If not...she can go. But no danger. Nothing that will compromise her in any way. And you must have her back here within two weeks or its court martial for you, Wisdom.'

'Cocky!' Nave protested. 'You can't be serious!'

'I have little choice, Eric. No one hereabouts would

299

have the required security clearance for this and be able to understand Kana Morse. Much less encrypt it in their head. She may be our only hope to avert a total disaster.'

A knock at the door broke into the conversation. Miss Copeland came into the room holding a bundle of black and white pictures. 'The photographs, Commander.'

'Thank you, Miss Copeland.'

Long spread the pictures over his desk, his gaze especially on the ones taken of the Dutch Navy in Surabaya harbour. 'If the Japanese capture these, we have a hell of a job ahead of us.'

Clement studied every photograph, but the impostor had been careful not to be in any of the ones he looked at. Then he picked up one of Bill with the *Rising Sun* billowing behind him. It was the first photograph Clement had taken and even then, he'd only taken it to practise using the camera. Off to one side and with his face lifted towards the skies, was the impostor.

'This is him,' Clement said, passing the photograph to Lyon.

Ivan Lyon held the picture to the light and stared at it. He shook his head. 'I don't recognise him. But for him to know about my wife and son, we must have met.'

'Is this him?' Evelyn asked, passing another photograph to Clement. 'It's taken from behind, so not ideal for identification. He's talking to two men in uniform.'

Clement looked at the picture. 'I took it in Surabaya. He said they were Vichy French. And in view of what we now know about him, they probably were. He was passing on information about us to the Japanese. Such audacity, given I was right behind him.'

Johnny reached for the better photograph of the impostor and studied it. 'Sorry, I don't recognise him either, Clement. But if he's only been operating in the Pacific, that's not surprising.'

'May I?' Nave said, taking the photograph. He stood and went to the window, his gaze on the man standing with Bill on the stern of the *Krait*, a frown creasing his forehead. 'I know him!'

'What?' Clement said.

'I'm sure it's him. He's older, of course, but he was in Japan with me at the language school, years ago.'

'Do you remember his name?' Long asked, leaning forward in his chair.

Nave's hand rubbed his forehead for several minutes. He looked at Long before speaking. 'Müller! Hans Müller!'

'He's German?' Long shouted. 'When, Nave, when did you say you met him?'

'It was in Japan in '22. We were both sitting the British Embassy language examinations. As I recall, he was granted permission to take the test there as a gesture of good will after the Great War. He was only a young man then, nineteen, perhaps less.' Nave paused, his mind in the past. 'He had a bit of an ego then and was full of self-confidence, as I recall.' Nave rubbed his forehead again but all eyes were on him. 'He wanted to follow his father into the Kriegsmarine.' Nave looked up at Long. 'He was a very good linguist; fluent in English as well as French and Japanese.'

'How is it he's learned so much about Major Lyon?' Long asked, still looking at Nave. But it was Clement who spoke.

'He travels around the south Pacific, usually by yacht, so his movements are almost undetectable. He said he'd carried out raids along the Indochina coastline harassing the Vichy French.'

'I have been there. And many other islands besides.'

'May I ask what you did there, Major?' Clement asked.

Lyon glanced at Long before answering.

Long nodded.

Lyon went on. 'I've been setting up resistance networks among the Free French there. Some are quite successful.'

'And you're sure about their loyalty?' Clement asked, remembering how Tom had said it wasn't uncommon for some of the islanders to take bribes. 'Japanese persuasion can be brutal, I understand. Perhaps some are as not as loyal as you thought.'

'I would be naïve to think they wouldn't give me away. They are poor farmers and fishermen. But I don't believe it would be done willingly.'

Long stood and paced the room. Clement knew the man's mind operated on many levels, simultaneously processing and sorting information all the time.

'He must be found!' Long exclaimed. 'Sergeant

Archer was in Signals as I recall, Clement. He could be your radio operator.'

Evelyn looked up. 'Does he know Kana, Commander? Because if he doesn't, he'd be useless. Besides, wouldn't Clement need him on the team? He can't be in two places at once.'

Long pressed the button on his desk. 'Miss Copeland. Contact Sergeant Archer and get him to locate Bill Reynolds and engage his ship. Then get Private Savage to Darwin from wherever he is. Tell Archer he is to arrange to have whatever weapons Majors Wisdom and Lyon want loaded on board the *Krait* and get the ship provisioned for at least two weeks.'

'Anything else, Commander?' Miss Copeland asked.

'Tell Archer he's to have everything ready to leave the day after tomorrow.'

Long released the button on his desk.

Clement wondered how Miss Copeland would achieve such an impossible task. He thought about Archer and Savage, hoping they were still in the Northern Territory. Given it was still Wet Season there, Archer's tasks were no less onerous.

But Clement had got to know Archer. If anyone could arrange things quickly it would be Tom Archer. He knew his way around the army and had a knack for sourcing whatever was needed. In his mind, he thought of Reg. The two men were in many ways similar.

'In the meantime, Clement, you and Lyon spend some time together. Anything you can think of to make it faster to locate this impostor would be useful.'

Johnny stood. 'Long and I will attempt to contact Whittaker. It really would be best for Miss Howard to stay here with Nave in Melbourne.'

Clement glanced at Evelyn Howard. He thought he glimpsed disappointment on her face. Her ability with numbers was amazing but right now he needed all her skills. Long and Johnny left the room. Joe Watkins and Eric Nave stood to leave. Clement could see Nave wasn't happy about Evelyn going anywhere other than his tiny office in the red brick building at the back of Victoria Barracks. But Clement liked both Nave and Joe and wanted them to be included in the discussions. Nave, after all, was the only man who knew the impostor and any recollections of him could be useful. And it had been Joe who'd been observant enough to notice the small inconsistency; the side the man parted his hair.

'Eric, would you mind remaining with us. You are the only person here who knew Müller. Anything you can think of would be useful. And any other details you can recall, Joe, would be helpful.' Clement turned to Lyon. 'Could we talk more about your time around the Indo-chinese region. I feel it's where you've met this man.'

Nave and Joe resumed their seats as Clement reached for the photograph of the impostor. He stared at the face. Anger and contempt welled up in him as he looked at the face of this man with his quick lying tongue and evil deception. He'd killed Hugh Kearsley without so much as a second thought. In Singapore he'd even shot two Japanese soldiers pretending that it was self-defence, killing men on his own side. Nothing was morally beyond this man. He remembered Johnny's words about motivation, but this man didn't do things for any patriotic reason. His motivation was entirely selfish. But what drove him to it? Was it simply greed? Clement thought of the *kin no yuri*. But even greed was driven by something. There had to be a reason. Something from the past, this man's past, drove everything he did, and Clement hoped Nave's association with him twenty years before could shed some light on it.

As they talked, Clement learned of the many missions Lyon had made into enemy territory. Already this man had encountered the Japanese and, because he spoke French fluently, the Vichy French who controlled Indochina.

Lyon looked up at a portrait of the King hanging on the wall opposite him. 'The more I think about it, the more I feel it was the Vichy French who've schooled this Müller.'

'May I ask your reasons for this?' Clement said.

'There's a group I've tried to infiltrate a few times. Given what we know now, he may have even been in the next room watching me. Small wonder some of our raids were unsuccessful. But his disguise must be convincing.'

'He's studied you, Ivan, even your mannerisms, although he made a mistake in parting his hair. Perhaps he used a mirror to create the look that would pass for you,' Clement said, then quickly realised he'd crossed a social barrier. 'I do beg your pardon. I don't mean to be familiar. Having spent the last few weeks with a man calling himself Ivan Lyon, I feel we already know each other.'

'Not at all, Wisdom. I only wish it had been me with you. I may have been able to rescue my family.'

'I do apologise. Insensitive of me. But it's an indication of the character of the man.'

'Quite.'

'These Vichy French, were there any in particular who would know you well enough to coach someone about you?'

'Yes, there were some. Two specifically near the border with Laos. As I said, I was trying to infiltrate their group, so I spent some time with them.' Lyon paused. 'Not nice people. None of them are but these two especially treat the locals poorly and thought nothing of taking what they wanted even from the poorest of people.'

'Have you heard of something called *kin no yuri*?'

Lyon's face paled. 'You know about that?'

'He told me.'

Lyon was speechless for several minutes. 'I'm stunned. The Golden Lily raiders and their theft and cruelty towards the local people, especially the Buddhist monks, are the principal reason I felt obliged to do something about them. The Japanese and their Vichy French collaborators have stripped these countries of anything valuable. They must have amassed millions in gold and precious stones, even stamps and all cash reserves.' Lyon paused. 'But why would he tell you about it?'

'Perhaps he thought it gave him credibility. Perhaps the horde isn't destined for the treasury of the Emperor of Japan but for the deep pockets of a handful of greedy men.'

'Whichever, Clement. I think you could be right about him being in Surabaya. From what you've told me, I don't believe he'd think twice about shooting someone if he thought he would profit from it. It could also be that he told you about *kin no yuri* because he believed you'd be dead before you could pass on this information. Have you told anyone else?'

'Long. He didn't know anything about it. Nor does Johnny.'

'You know Captain Winthorpe well?'

'I've known Johnny for years. Why do you ask?'

'I'm too suspicious, I suppose. I suspect everyone until proven otherwise.'

'Not a bad idea given the work we do.' Clement paused. 'There was a death on board before we arrived in Singapore. The radio operator was killed. It was made to look like suicide, but I think it was murder.'

'And you think this impostor was the killer?'

'Certainly looks that way.' Clement glanced at Joe before speaking. 'He did say he knew Joe from Manilla. But Joe says he doesn't have a memory of it. Said they'd met at some Embassy party in Manilla.'

'Manilla?' Lyon said. The brow furrowed and Clement waited. Lyon seemed deep in thought.

Joe leaned forward. 'I went to a Brazilian Embassy thing in Manila with a group of guys I was working with from CAST, our intelligence centre in the Philippines.'

'I'm aware of where CAST is, Lieutenant,' Lyon said. 'I'm sorry, I don't remember the event.' Lyon paused, his head down, his face creased in concentration. 'Brazilian Embassy you say?'

'Yeah.'

'When was this?'

'Last year. About a month before Pearl Harbour, in fact.'

'I didn't go. My wife wasn't well. I sent an apology.'

'Where were you stationed at the time?' Clement asked.

'Singapore. But I was in Manila several times around then, just looking about.'

Looking about. The words rang in Clement's head. 'The impostor used that expression, when I first met him in Timor.'

Lyon was silent for a minute. 'I have to tell you, Clement, that this man could be the most dangerous man in the world after Hitler and Emperor Hirohito right now. Good thing he didn't realise you'd taken his photograph.' Lyon looked directly at Clement. 'And once he learns you are not dead, he'll be seeking you all over the South Pacific.'

28

Clement leaned back in his chair. The perennial intelligence question nagged his brain. *How did he know?* How did this man learn information? Was it just from his own observations when *looking about?* There was no doubt he had to be caught but who was feeding him vital information? He thought about Ross and Whittaker. How did Müller even know about them? And how did he know about the *Automedon* and the *kin no yuri* and the rendezvous details? Surely such information could only come from a top-level source. Were the Japanese reading Allied messages? It had to be presumed they would be trying to break Allied codes in much the same way the Allies were trying to break theirs. Or did Müller have his own network of informants or just one in a very sensitive position? Clement thought back to what Joe had said about the signal for him to recognise Lyon. It had been a rolled newspaper under the arm. Clement frowned. How did *he* know that? Clement stared at the men around him. If Lyon and Watkins had met in Manilla, why would a signal be needed? Even though Joe had scant memory of it, Müller had been adamant they'd met. He had no need for the rolled newspaper. Clement sat up in the chair as though something had bitten him.

'When did you receive the instruction to collect Joe from Surabaya, Ivan?'

'When I was in Moresby. Why?'

'Was it from Long himself?'

'Yes.'

'Does Long send you your instructions?'

'Sometimes. I also get instructions from GC&CS via FECB. Perhaps not anymore.'

'So, from *C* himself?'

'Yes, but Long is the link. I work for MI6 but Long as both Director of Naval Intelligence and Head of the Combined Operational Intelligence Centre is the contact for all intelligence personnel from Britain acting in these regions.'

'So it was Long who instructed you to collect Joe?'

'Yes. As I said, Long is my contact in Australia and would, therefore, be aware of my movements. He has, from time to time instructed me to carry out certain functions in the South Pacific.'

'Looking about,' Clement muttered. 'How do you receive these instructions, Ivan?'

'By wireless. Encrypted, of course. Those from Long

come via Park Orchards. It's the receiving station just outside Melbourne.'

'And Long sends out his instructions to you in the same way?'

'Yes. Although Long wouldn't actually go to Park Orchards. He'd send them from here by despatch rider.'

Clement heard the rain patter the windowpane. A storm had gathered in the hours they'd been in Long's office on the first floor. He stared through the window. But it wasn't like the rain in Darwin or the Java Sea. That rain descended in torrents. In Melbourne, the weather was more familiar to him; more like English rain; gentle and good for growing vegetables. Clement turned to Lyon. 'Do you know where Commander Long has gone?'

'No. But Miss Copeland will.'

Joe stood. 'I'll find out where he is.'

'Thank you, Joe.'

Lyon leaned forward, his voice a mere whisper. 'I think I know what you're thinking, Clement. And if you're right, this impostor will be aware of everything we are currently doing or about to do in the Southwest Pacific. And he'll know about Wavell's appointment.'

'Where do you think *he* is right now?' Clement asked Lyon.

Lyon sat back in the chair, his left hand stroking his thin moustache. 'As soon as he knows you're not dead, he'll be seeking information about you. You'll definitely be top of his list. But I think it unlikely he'll enter Australia.'

'I agree. I think we both know where he's waiting.'

Joe returned with Long and Johnny, and Clement told Long of their suspicions.

The room became very quiet.

'Have you contacted Whittaker in Timor?' Clement asked.

'Yes,' Long replied. 'But we are informed he is away at present, so he would be unable to join the team.'

'Did you mention where we are going or that Miss Howard would be with us?'

Long looked at Clement. 'No. And if there is a leak in Melbourne, then the least said about any of this the better. Asking about Whittaker's whereabouts, though, wouldn't necessarily cause our impostor any concern. He may learn that we've attempted to reach Whittaker, but he won't know why.'

Clement held Long's gaze. 'Could we send a misleading message?'

'With you as the bait, Major?'

Clement nodded. 'I'll go back. Make up some excuse for me to be in the Dutch East Indies if you have to…joining Wavell's staff, or some such,' Clement said.

'You're taking a huge risk, Wisdom.'

'It must be done, Commander if we are to catch that imposter, you know that. And it must be soon. The longer he's at large and pretending to be Major Lyon, the more damage he can do.'

Two hours later Long pressed the button on the intercom device. 'Miss Copeland, I need someone investigated as quickly as possible. Get your blood hounds onto it as a matter of top priority. I want to know everything that can be found on a man named Hans Müller, German Navy, approximate age forty. Contact SIS in London if you must, and make sure they know it's urgent. As quickly as you can.'

'I may not have much for you for a few days, Commander,' Miss Copeland responded.

'Do the best you can,' Long said glancing at Clement. 'And if I'm not in Melbourne, send it to me in Darwin via *Coonawarra* Intercept Station. And tell them to send the same information to Major Wisdom on board the *Krait* currently in Darwin but soon to set sail for Java. This is *Top Secret*, Miss Copeland.'

'I understand, Commander Long.'

'And Miss Copeland, I want the roster for the despatch riders on my desk within the hour.' Long released the intercom button. 'If you're right Clement, we should have someone soon.'

Clement sat with Long, and they worked their way back through the relevant details of the impostor's movements and how they tallied with messages sent out to Clement, Lyon and others in the field. Three important messages had been sent out during the initial two weeks of Clement's mission to collect Johnny from Singapore. The first was from Whittaker who'd sent a message to Long that Clement and the team had arrived in Timor. The second were the updated instructions from Long on the revised rendezvous date, time and place and the green light signal, and the third, albeit unrelated to Clement's mission, was that Lyon was to collect Watkins from Surabaya. All three messages had come via Melbourne's Victoria Barracks from Long's office and the receiving station at Park Orchards then on to the intercept stations of *Harman* in Canberra and *Coonawarra* in Darwin.

Long flipped back through the roster. The message sent by Whittaker informing Long that Clement and the team had arrived in Timor had been sent on Monday, December 8th. As had the message about the change of rendezvous site and green light signal. The message to the real Major Lyon to collect Joe Watkins from Surabaya had been sent to him in Port Moresby on Monday December 1st.

Long checked the dates with the roster. On every occasion the despatch rider was the same, Stephen Munroe.

'Who is he?' Clement asked.

'I need his file to answer that, Clement,' Long said, reaching forward to press the intercom button.

'If I may say, Commander, don't involve anyone. I will go to the records office and check it.'

'You suspect Miss Copeland?' Long paused. 'Sorry, I

314

know, no one is above suspicion, and she does have access to some very sensitive information. I hope it isn't her because I'd be lost without her.'

'Pardon me for saying it, Long, but you'd be lost with her, if she is the leak. Where do I find the records office?'

'Secret files are kept here at Victoria Barracks War Office Records. Go out the door at the back to the red brick building at the rear, as you would to Nave's office. You'll find it on the first floor at the front.' Long paused again. 'Better I come with you. It'll be quicker.'

Long grabbed his coat from the stand in the corner as Clement opened the door to the outer office.

'Just going for a stroll to clear our heads, Miss Copeland. I'll be back soon.'

'Very well, Commander,' the woman said, threading another piece of paper into the typewriter carriage.

Clement followed Long into the corridor outside his office. Pausing a few seconds, he listened at the door. The typewriter clattered rapidly, but he didn't hear the woman make any telephone calls. Leaving the upper floor, they went directly to the red brick building at the rear.

Long requested the file on Stephen Munroe and five minutes later he was handed a thin dossier. Reading the contents, Long passed each page to Clement before returning it to the file.

There was very little information. Stephen Munroe had been born in Melbourne and, following an unremarkable education, studied agriculture which had seen him secure several positions as a market gardener before joining the Army Reserve. Since farming, especially food production, was a restricted occupation, Munroe was employed by the city council ploughing up parks to plant vegetables. But on Mondays, he worked with the Reserve as a Despatch Rider between Victoria Barracks and Park Orchards Intercept Station. His security risk was considered low.

Without speaking, Clement and Long left the red brick building and wandered outside. Long led Clement between the buildings then, taking a side gate, he walked out onto St Kilda Road. Opposite and a short distance away was a large, raised statue of a man on horseback. 'I'll get Munroe checked out. Who he mixes with, any organisations he belongs to. Where his affiliations lie. No stone.' Long lit a cigarette but Clement thought the action automatic, Long seemed deep in thought. 'If he is our man, then his motives for betraying his country don't influence your objectives, Major. We'll deal with him. You need to focus on this impostor.'

'While you may have your man, Long, there may be another traitor. Someone who alerts Munroe to sensitive information in the despatches. And today is Wednesday not Monday. So, he could be somewhere in the park hereabouts. Given the bait we've just sent out, if there is someone on the inside, they'll want to alert Munroe to your discovery as soon as possible.'

'Good! We'll catch them red-handed.'

While Long telephoned the city council seeking to know Munroe's location, Clement removed his army uniform and dressed in a borrowed suit and tie and an ill-fitting hat that belonged to one of the professors currently working with Nave. It had been decided that Clement and Evelyn would enter the park, sit opposite Victoria Barracks and watch who came out and entered the park. Long then telephoned the Military Police and instructed them to secret themselves at various locations around the large park but not to interfere unless requested to by Major Wisdom.

Evelyn entered Long's office, the neat, pleated skirt and twinset giving her the appearance of an office worker.

Clement smiled as she sat beside him in Long's office.

'I took the liberty of helping myself to some sandwiches from the Mess, Commander. If Clement and I are to look like a couple, I thought it would be better to have a reason for us to be sitting in the park.'

'No heroics, Wisdom. I need you both alive. Do you have a pistol?'

Clement shook his head. He'd surrendered his pistol to the armourer on arrival in Melbourne. He had his knife, but this wasn't a situation for stealth. It was, in fact, the reverse: surprise and shock, intended to stun and confuse.

'Take mine,' Long said, removing a pistol from a locked cabinet in his office and handing it to Clement. Clement checked the weapon then placed it into his belt.

Minutes later, Clement and Evelyn left Long's office and took the stairs to the lower floor. Clement walked across the road with Evelyn, and they entered the park.

Long and Johnny were stationed at windows along the front on the upper floor while Joe and Ivan were asked to watch from windows that faced the cross street in case someone left the building from the side entrance.

Clement and Evelyn wandered into the park, picking their way between the runner beans and carrots. The vegetables had grown considerably in the month he'd been north. His gaze settled on the potatoes; his mind transported back to his garden in Fearnley Maughton. 'There's a seat, Mary.' Clement gasped. 'I'm so sorry, Miss Howard. Forgive me.'

'Nothing to forgive, Clement. I'm assuming she is your wife.'

'Was.'

A short silence ensured but Clement noted that while he felt embarrassed, he didn't feel awkward and that surprised him.

'Then I'm flattered. Shall we sit here?'

Clement sat beside the woman he hardly knew. That he'd called her Mary amazed him. He didn't understand his lapse. No one would ever replace Mary. He closed his eyes for one second as though speaking to his beloved late wife, asking her forgiveness.

Evelyn placed the parcel of sandwiches on the seat between them and opened the paper wrapping. It was the most natural and ordinary thing to do yet in that brief second something shifted for him and he felt immeasurably guilty.

Looking up he stared at the door to Victoria Barracks, willing it to open. He needed to concentrate now. A real and deadly leak had been uncovered; one that may already have cost the lives of thousands of agents around the Pacific. A young woman came out and hurried across the road. He stared at the girl, his thoughts of Mary vanishing in a second. Evelyn unfolded the wrapper around the sandwiches, her gaze on the girl. As the young woman ran into the park, Clement knew he'd seen her before. One of Nave's secretaries. No, not a secretary. An assistant. She ran past as though she hadn't seen them.

'You get the police, I'll follow the girl,' Evelyn whispered. She stood and hurried after her.

Clement ran for the statue of the Marquis of Linlithgow, Australia's first Governor General, that stood in the park opposite Victoria Barracks and a little distance from where he and Evelyn had been sitting. It was where the Military Police were waiting for his signal.

Hurrying, he ran along the path and behind the raised stone plinth. 'This way. It's a girl, one of the women from Eric Nave's office,' he said.

Running back along the path, Clement saw the girl standing at the intersection of several paths. She was spinning around, clearly trying to locate Munroe. Clement and the police slowed.

'Stephen!' the girl called.

Clement drew his pistol but waited near some shrubs. They needed the girl to make contact before they could apprehend her and Stephen Munroe. She spun in circles, continuing to call the man's name. Within two minutes, Clement saw a young man approach.

'What is it?'

'They know. They know!'

'How? What did you tell them?'

'Nothing!'

From the opposite direction, Clement saw Evelyn slowly walking towards the agitated couple. Clement held his breath. If Munroe was armed, Evelyn could be caught in the crossfire.

'Do you have the time?' Evelyn asked the man.

Her question seemed to confuse the couple and for one moment their attention was distracted. In that second Clement ran forward, with the two Military Police Officers closing in from the opposite side. The girl seemed to freeze at the sight of the large policemen coming towards her. Her head was darting between Clement and the two policemen approaching her; her confusion rendering her immobile. Clement ran between Munroe and Evelyn, his pistol raised. Munroe dropped the hoe and ran.

'Stop or I shoot!' one of the military policeman shouted.

Clement saw Munroe slow then stop. Replacing his pistol into his belt, Clement rushed to where Evelyn was standing.

'Do you know who the girl is?' Evelyn asked.

'Yes. Her name is Ferguson. She's Professor Room's assistant. She works with the code breakers.'

'Not anymore, I suspect.'

The Military Policeman grasped Munroe's hand and, twisting it behind his back, held his arm high and tight. Within minutes Miss Ferguson and Munroe were led away.

'Shall we finish those sandwiches? Shame to waste them,' Evelyn added.

Clement smiled. Evelyn's composure was extraordinary. 'Why not, Evelyn.'

'Why not, indeed, Clement.'

'A bad business!' Long said, closing the door to his office. 'There will be a thorough investigation. But that's not for you to worry about, Wisdom. We needed that impostor found and removed.'

'Can I speak to Sergeant Archer before leaving Melbourne, Commander? There are some weapons I'd like him to include.'

'Of course. You know you're painting a target on your back, Wisdom?'

'This man must be apprehended and as soon as possible before he does any more damage.'

'I'll get Archer and Savage into Darwin this afternoon, if possible. Then tomorrow, you and Miss Howard will fly to Darwin.'

That evening Clement sat with Johnny in the Officers' Mess. So much had happened and the pace of it wouldn't stop any time soon. 'I'm sorry, Johnny. I haven't asked what took you to Singapore. Was it only war business?'

'Yes. FECB has had to move twice now. Always disruptive. And always a chance that something secret can go astray in the move. But I was really only there to accompany Evelyn. She is vitally important. Tiltman describes her as his right-hand man.'

Clement smiled. 'Yes, I've seen her ability and courage firsthand. Don't worry about her, I'll make sure she isn't exposed to any danger. But I didn't ask, Johnny if your parents still live in Singapore?'

'No. They died within a year of each other. Before the war, I'm happy to say.'

'Did you visit your old home there?' Clement asked, trying to draw Johnny out of his tight self-control.

'No. I have so few memories of that time really. I was sent to school in England when I was six, so I've spent most of my life alone and in England.'

Clement nodded. It explained at lot about the man. 'And you had no brothers or sisters?'

'No, just me. Much like yourself, Clement. Although, unlike you, I have never met a soul mate. I imagine you still miss her?'

Clement was quiet for a few seconds. 'I do. But time is blurring the edges.' He thought about Evelyn and his slip-of-the-tongue. He cleared his throat. 'Mary would be the first to tell me to get on with my life, Johnny. This war can't last forever and if I survive it...' Clement couldn't finish that sentence. He didn't have any idea where he'd be or what he'd be doing. It was too soon. No one would ever replace Mary, he told himself.

'One day at a time, Clement. That's how I get through it. You could always join the Service. With your training and knowledge, you'd be welcomed, I'm sure.'

'No thank you, Johnny. I don't think I'd fit in.'

'Will you return to Fearnley Maughton?'

'I suppose so. If they'll have me.'

Clement finished his tea and placed the cup on the table in front of him. 'But I think it useless speculating about that. We now have a war to win here as well as in Europe. And who knows how long that will take.'

Clement's mind reverted to Hans Müller. 'Do you think this Müller could be turned to work for us?'

'Highly unlikely. We couldn't match or better what this *kin no yuri* can give him. Such wealth would be beyond us and the Americans combined. Money, or rather wealth, is a very great temptation. And given that he isn't English, I don't think he'd work for us at all.'

'I really don't understand such people. So incredibly selfish.'

'You heard what Nave said about him. He has an ego, Clement. But I think it's more that he has something to prove, even if only to himself. It could be that he was held accountable for something he didn't do, so he has a chip on his shoulder. Or he wasn't given the credit for something he did do. Either way, when it comes to spies, especially those who work both sides, it's important to know what motivates them. And with this one, his motivation would be very difficult to learn.'

'I'm pleased to have you along, Johnny. The team are a good bunch, especially Archer and Savage but I don't know what makes them tick. Not like I know you.' Clement glanced at his friend. In his heart he wondered if he did know Johnny. Perhaps he only knew what Johnny was prepared to let him know. 'I trust very few people in this business.' Clement paused. 'But I'll leave the psychology to you. I just want to catch this man before he kills again.'

Clement looked up. Joe had entered the room and was walking towards them.

'Evening, Joe. Won't you join us?' Clement said.

'Thanks, Clem. Nave isn't happy.'

'Really? What about?' Clement asked hoping it wasn't another attempt to stop Evelyn from going with the team.

'Me going with you. I've tried to explain that since the folks in Kamer 14 in Bandoeng know me, it could forestall any issues you may have with co-operation from them. And if Müller can manipulate them as easily as he does others, he could talk his way into convincing the people there that he was the true Major Lyon and have you and the team shot as spies.'

'Good of him. And you, Joe.'

'Happy to serve. Now the Americans are in, I want to

324

contribute. And for the guys in the Philippines who maybe didn't make it out.'

'I understand. And thank you, Joe. It will make it easier for us in Java.'

As Clement walked with Johnny to their accommodation, they met Eric Nave. 'I'll take great care of them both, Eric. I sincerely hope you understand.'

Nave shrugged. 'A few days won't make much difference, I hope. Just make sure she is safe and comes back. And Watkins too. I need them. Currently, we are losing this war, Clement.'

A little later, Clement said goodbye to Eric Nave. He felt badly about Eric whose department desperately needed Evelyn's and Joe's assistance. But if the Japanese advance was as swift as Clement believed it to be, Nave would soon have as much help as he could handle. But first, Clement had an impostor to apprehend. He said good night to Johnny and Joe, the sunrise flight to Darwin dictated an early start.

29

Melbourne - 8th January 1942

Long drove Clement and Lyon to the airfield outside Melbourne. Following in another car were Evelyn, Johnny and Joe. A DC3 sat waiting on the tarmac. Archer and Savage were to join them in Darwin. Whilst Johnny wasn't coming on the *Krait*, he was to stay at the Intercept Station *Coonawarra* outside Darwin and act as liaison between Long in Melbourne and Clement onboard the *Krait*.

'And Wisdom?' Long said before they left, drawing Clement aside. 'If you need to contact me, do so though Kamer 14 in Bandoeng to Winthorpe at *Coonawarra*. Only use the *Krait's* radio to transmit once you have Müller or if it's an absolute emergency. Best not alert him to your whereabouts prematurely. We need to keep him on edge, chasing shadows if this trap is to be sprung. If we hear anything you should know, Winthorpe will contact you from *Coonawarra*. But it will be encrypted. Miss

Howard will know how to decipher it.'

Clement walked with the others across the tarmac and they climbed aboard the waiting plane. The aircraft left within minutes of them taking their seats. There was little in the way of luggage. Everything they needed would be with Archer in Darwin.

Clement was first to step from the DC3 at Darwin. While the heat was immediately noticeable, he was expecting it. To his great surprise, out of the darkness a familiar grin strode towards him. He smiled as Tom Archer approached then checked his watch.

It was midnight but unlike his first visit to the far northern city, Clement saw no lights blazing in the adjoining hangar neither was it currently raining.

'Good to see you, Clem,' Archer said, extending his hand in greeting. Then somewhat uncharacteristically he saluted.

'Good to see you too, Tom. Is Mick with you?'

'Nah, he's getting the stuff on board the *Krait*. Bill's got the same crew. She'll be right!'

'I think she will be, Tom. There are a few familiar faces with me, too.'

Tom glanced at the others as they gathered in the hangar. 'Struth! We went all that way to get them and now they want to go back?'

Clement suppressed a smile. 'Captain Winthorpe is staying in Darwin, but the others will be onboard. And, Tom, this is the real Major Ivan Lyon.'

'Sir,' Tom said. 'I can see the likeness. No wonder those poor buggers in Indochina were fooled.'

Clement glanced at Ivan, Whittaker's words about diamonds replaying in Clement's head.

'Do you have the same lorry, Tom?'

'Yeah. Sorry,' Tom said, the grin returning.

As they walked towards the rear of the vehicle, Clement saw the flash of lightning in the distance. While it wasn't yet raining, he didn't think it was far away. Seconds later, the thunder rolled above like a roaring lion.

Climbing aboard, they hobbled into Darwin, Tom dropping them at the hotel. 'Bert said to take the keys he's left for you on the bar counter. You can work out your own rooms. Said he'd have some breakfast ready for you at five. I'll be back at six tomorrow. Bill wants to be away before sunrise.'

Clement thanked Archer and the group made their way into the hotel. Just as Archer had said, Clement found the room keys on the bar, allocated them, then excused himself from the group. He wanted some time alone and he knew the room would be hot. Saying good night to the other members of the team, he went to sit by the large open doors in The Green Room that overlooked Darwin harbour. The room was empty, the bar long since closed. Even though it was well after midnight, it was still warm but a light breeze made conditions more bearable than a stuffy bedroom. Clement sat on a cane chair and stared out over the bay. He could see the twinkling lanterns on the boats moored there. A gecko lizard ran in front of him, stopping only to stare before hurrying away. Even though late, the amount of movement on the foreshore surprised him. Anxiety must have increased activity and people, mostly military personnel, were everywhere. Northern Australia was quickly becoming the front line. And if Wavell couldn't hold the Malay Barrier, it would be Darwin next on the Japanese target list. An hour later Clement sauntered upstairs and opened the door to Room Two. Turning on the overhead fan, he lay naked on the bed and tried to prepare himself for the coming mission.

Clement woke with the pale light tingeing the sky outside his open window. Lying on the bed in the Hotel Darwin, he stared at the overhead ceiling fan. Sleep had been fitful, a combination of heat and uncertainty for what lay ahead. That an impostor had been so successfully circulating in the region was a major blow to Allied Intelligence and the local resistance groups operating throughout the region. Reliable resistance fighters were hard to recruit and even harder to maintain. And secure networks took a long time to establish. It had to be assumed they were compromised if not already dead. His mind went to the Coastwatchers. That network worked well, but he wondered if it had been infiltrated. Everything relied on secrecy. But if captured, could their continued silence be guaranteed? Theirs was a fate he preferred not to dwell on. With the Japanese moving as rapidly as they were, those radio operators were just as vital as any resistance network on the ground. Even more so, given that the only alternative to radio transmissions in the region was a slow and often perilous sea crossing. But secrecy imposed its own burden; the ever-present danger of network infiltration. And Müller was an expert at it. Clement felt nothing but contempt for the man. But at least now he knew the men on his team and because Joe had previously met members of the Dutch Kamer 14 intelligence group, it would save valuable time in identifying themselves to the Dutch in Bandoeng and limit any resistance to them in Surabaya from the Dutch Authorities there. Furthermore, having Evelyn onboard was a huge help in communications with Johnny at *Coonawarra*.

Rising, Clement went to the shower and stood under the cooling water. The plan was for him to meet the others in the breakfast room just after five o'clock. He packed his bag and went to have some breakfast.

Clement finished the meal as Archer and Savage arrived. Standing, he joined them in the foyer.

'Great working with you again, Clem!' Archer's perfect teeth beamed at him.

'Yeah. Goes for me too,' Mick added, his eyes downcast and his feet shuffling on the timber boards. 'Good to be back.'

Clement smiled at Mick. 'Thank you both for volunteering. Tom, have you been able to get everything? It was a tall order, I know, especially at such short notice.'

'I thought you knew me, Clem. Of course, I got everything.'

'I should never have doubted. I'll go through it with you once onboard. I think it important we get away as soon as possible and before too many people are around to see us leave.'

'Everything is already on board, Clem.'

'What would I do without you, Tom? I'll rouse the others.'

Archer flashed his toothy grin.

Clement arranged for the team to leave the hotel in ones and twos, meeting at the wharf, just in case of roaming eyes on the streets. Archer and Savage were the first to go. As Ivan and Joe left singly for the wharf, five minutes between each departure, Clement said goodbye to Johnny.

Johnny shook Clement's hand. 'Be careful, Clement. Long has arranged for me to be stationed at *Coonawarra* for the duration. And remember, while you can't transmit to me, Evelyn or Joe should always be listening in. If I think there's something you should know, I'll transmit an enciphered message. She can decipher it. Most likely instantly.'

Evelyn joined them in the foyer.

'Be careful, Miss Howard. No heroics, please. We need you back in one piece,' Johnny said.

'I'll be absolutely fine, Captain. You're worrying needlessly.'

Clement reached for her suitcase and together they

walked towards Government House, an attractive neo-gothic place with high-pitched roofs that looked strangely out-of-place in Darwin, then took the steps beside the residence to the lower road that bordered the harbour. Clement could see the *Krait* tied up at the wharf ahead and about half a mile away. 'Thank you again for volunteering for this. And please don't be concerned. You won't be asked to leave the *Krait* and you'll not be exposed to any danger, I promise you.'

'Oh! What a pity!' she said.

'There is no doubting your bravery but involvement would be foolhardy. May I ask how it is that you are so accomplished with a rifle? Did you grow up on a farm?'

'No. I grew up in London, but I went with a group of others to Scotland for some training the-powers-that-be considered necessary.'

Clement's mind went back to January. Reg had told him that he'd been an instructor for clandestine operations training in Scotland. But as much as Clement wanted to ask Evelyn if she'd met Reg, he knew he couldn't.

Climbing aboard, he introduced the real Ivan Lyon to Bill and ten minutes later, the *Krait* slowly motored away from Darwin harbour. As the team settled into shipboard routine, Clement went to the wheelhouse. He wanted to speak privately with Bill Reynolds.

'Thank you for your involvement, again, Bill.'

'In for a penny, isn't that what they say?'

Clement smiled. 'How well do you know the southern

coast of Java?'

'Ports only, sorry, Clement.'

'Is there a port we can put into there?'

'Yes. Tjilatjap. It's not easy though. Narrow, sand bars and shallow water. But I've been there before. I thought you wanted to go back to Surabaya?'

'Yes, well, only some of us. I have in mind that the team will divide. Major Lyon and Lieutenant Watkins will get off in Tjilatjap. Myself, Tom and Mick will go on to Surabaya. Miss Howard will remain on board. I must warn you that it's possible we'll encounter a hostile reception in Surabaya.'

Bill Reynolds looked at Clement. 'I'm beginning to expect it!'

'Sorry. It's important we catch this man impersonating Lyon. From your perspective, do you remember anything unusual about him? Anything at all you thought wasn't right?'

Bill shook his head. 'He was a pretty smooth customer. He moved around a boat like he knew what he was doing. I do remember thinking how personable he was. I mean, he talked to everyone onboard, even the boys. I saw him talking to that poor lad who killed himself. I didn't hear what he said but the look on young Hugh's face! He was frightened. You believe he was murdered, don't you?'

Clement nodded. 'Pedro told me he saw the impostor with a torch, the day that Zero flew over the boat and you pushed Hugh into the for'ard hold. It is possible *he*

333

was signalling the Zero.'

Bill frowned. 'Bad business.'

Clement left the wheelhouse and went to the radio hold. Joe Watkins and Evelyn were sitting by the transceiver. Clement had decided he would vacate his bunk there for Evelyn, allowing Ivan and Joe to occupy the other two bunks. He'd take the single bunk in the engine compartment as it would be too hot for Evelyn, or he'd sleep under the permanent cover on deck. 'Just a reminder, Joe we are to keep radio silence.'

'Understood, sir. Miss Howard and I will cover it. You know, sir, since seeing the photograph of Müller, I've tried to remember anything I can about the guy and the Brazilian Embassy thing. There was a photographer there. If that guy impersonating Lyon was Müller, it's possible he had copies ordered of all those photographs. Why, the guy may not have been an official photographer anyway. He could have been a Jap spy taking pictures of all the Americans in the room. There were several guys from CAST there that day.'

'I heard you mention that name to Major Lyon in Melbourne. I thought he seemed rather quick to stop you talking about it. So perhaps you shouldn't tell me,' Clement said.

'Given everything else you know, Clem, there's no reason why you shouldn't hear. Station CAST is an intercept station with encryption capacity at Monkey Point near Manilla. It also houses the cryptanalysis team in the Philippines and it was where I was based.'

Clement sighed. The impostor's tentacles stretched into every region in the Southwest Pacific. And if Joe was correct about a photographer, Müller could identify the American cryptanalysts. 'He is as audacious as he is inventive. And he gambles. With his life and with the lives of others.' But Clement was beginning to think Müller wasn't spying on the Allies for money or wealth alone. And perhaps not even for personal acclaim. Perhaps the man was a gambler and addicted to high stakes games. Or perhaps it was revenge, as Johnny had said. Whatever it was, it had made him a very dangerous man.

30

During the first voyage, Clement had played chess with the imposter Ivan Lyon. Now he played with the real Ivan Lyon and considered him to be a very brave man with a keen intellect. Despite Clement winning more matches than losing them, he could see there was no bombast about Lyon, no petty jealousies or arrogance; just a courageous man filled with sadness for his captured wife and son. A man, so Clement thought, prepared to act dangerously to avenge their capture and probable death. Clement had also seen the rather large tattoo of a tiger on the man's chest when Lyon had removed his shirt. Something Müller clearly had known nothing about.

Clement stood beside Bill as the *Krait* slowly entered the long narrow estuary at Tjilatjap. It was still hot, and the afternoon sun had disappeared into a heavy white haze that settled over the port. Large ships were berthed along the wharf while others were tied to moorings in the main channel. A strange aroma of salt air, heat and something Clement couldn't name assaulted the nostrils. Bill negotiated the hazardous estuary finding a berth for smaller shipping at a wharf some distance into the port. From where Clement stood on deck, he could see feverish activity. The Dutch appeared to be making hasty attempts to dredge the shallow port. Most likely to increase the capacity to berth large ships and as an alternative port for resupplying Java. It had to be assumed that should the northern coast of the island be invaded, all the ports and cities on that coast would fall into Japanese hands. That included the Dutch Navy, the country's capital, Batavia, and ultimately the intelligence unit in the mountains at Bandoeng. As he stared at the harbour activities, he felt an overwhelming sense of doom for the country. If the Malay Barrier failed, there was only one way out of this island: Tjilatjap. And how long could it hold out?

Bill tied the *Krait* to the wharf and explained to the annoyed Dutchman on the quay that he wasn't staying, just resupplying his ship. While Bill kept the official busy, Clement farewelled Ivan and Joe.

'We'll be in Surabaya at *The Flying Dutchman* in six days and hopefully with a small force of men, should they be needed, Clement,' Ivan said. 'Joe says the trains are good but there are several changes along the way. It's about two hundred miles from Bandoeng to Surabaya and the weather is still rather wet. Let's hope there are no land-slides.'

'God speed, Ivan.' Clement shook hands with him, a man he'd come to know and like. 'And to you too, Joe,' Clement said. They'd been through a lot together since he'd originally met the man in Surabaya and he counted him as a valuable member of the team. He had confidence the two of them would make the agreed meeting. Clement scanned the wharf around the waterfront for anyone taking an interest in them, then stepped back onto the *Krait*.

Three days out from Tjilatjap, the *Krait* experienced bad weather. High seas and storms and the narrow beam construction of the little ship made it roll incessantly with the swell. Waves spilled into the scuppers, causing them to close the radio room hatch in case the precious equipment should be damaged. It made conditions below hot, damp and miserable. While Clement, Tom and Evelyn didn't suffer with sea sickness, Mick had found the going very hard. By dawn of the fourth day, the seas had calmed and finally they could open the hatches, the pungent aroma of vomit finally released.

Lying on the bunk in the engine compartment, Clement thought about the forthcoming confrontation. While he believed Müller would be in Surabaya, he had no idea where the man would be hiding. Clement suspected a look out would be posted to report on their arrival. Then, Müller would make sure the *Krait* was surrounded.

His mind lingered over the man and what motivated him. Now that Clement knew the real Major Lyon, he felt a greater determination to catch the impostor. And because he'd outwitted Müller, Clement felt that for Müller it had become personal. In fact, Clement believed the man was only interested in the personal. The war, whether in Europe or the Pacific, was a game for him. His motivation wasn't for any altruistic cause. Clement thought back on others he'd fought against in this war. For some, they were motivated by ideology. Others had done traitorous things out of fear or blackmail. But for Müller it was always and only about ego. Something had happened in his past and the perceived injustice had simmered within him until he'd found an outlet for his vengeance.

Clement's mind went to Stephen Munroe and the woman, Alice Ferguson. He wondered what Long had learned about their motives and what connected them to Müller. But right now, he needed to find a pernicious enemy and the murderer of a good man and that required his full attention.

Rising from the bunk, he went to the wheelhouse. 'Bill, when we get into Madoera Strait, can you drop me and Archer off somewhere outside Surabaya port?'

'Not easy, Clement. But I suppose we could sea-anchor further out in the bay and row you in.'

'Thanks. Once you drop me and Archer off there, would you wait one day then continue onto Surabaya port and try to tie up where we did last time? You need to be at the wharf in Surabaya port on the 20th. Not a day sooner. Archer and I will go ashore on the 19th and make our way overland to Surabaya.'

'Any particular time?'

'Mid-morning should do.'

'Am I sailing into a trap?' Bill asked.

'Bait in the trap, Bill, but that's all.'

Clement reasoned that Müller would have spies in Bandoeng who wouldn't take long to inform him of Lyon's and Watkins's presence there. Clement hoped that because he wasn't with them, it would create confusion in Müller's mind. Forty-eight hours after arriving in Bandoeng, Lyon and Watkins were to take the train to Surabaya, with or without a small patrol of men following them.

A storm was gathering, the heavy grey clouds massing over the sea, the heat of the day intense. As Bill rowed ashore, Clement glanced at his watch. He estimated it would be raining within the hour. And sunset was about three hours away. Enough time, despite the heat to walk the ten miles into Surabaya.

'Thank you, Bill and see you tomorrow,' Clement said.

'Here, you may need some of these,' Bill said, handing Clement some coins and notes. 'Dutch guilder. If you're going into a pub best to have some local currency. I keep a small amount on board for necessities.'

Farewelling Bill, Clement and Tom jumped from the

dinghy into the mangroves and hurried away from the shoreline. With him, Clement carried his knife under his long-sleeved shirt, a pistol with two magazines of ammunition and a grenade secreted in the pockets of his shorts. In his shirt pocket was a compass and a small telescope. In his pack, he carried a coat, ten sticks of dynamite and a time pencil. Tom carried two grenades, a pistol, a knife and an Owen gun over his shoulder, concealed under a long coat. Clement could see the sweat pouring down Archer's face, but the young man never complained.

Squatting beside a tall crop growing beside a dirt track, Clement pulled out the compass and telescope. Across from them, was a low wet field and in the distance, he could see farm workers bent over planting what he guessed was rice. In front of them, the dirt track showed deep wheel ruts cut into the land, the rain and yoked buffalo carts making the track a quagmire in the wet conditions. Returning the telescope to his pocket he checked the compass. Staying close to the edge of the track they made their way north-northwest, skirting Madoera Bay.

'Got to watch out for snakes in places as wet as this, Clem.'

Clement drew his knife and stepped further onto the muddy track and away from the long grasses. For two hours they walked in silence.

'Wait a minute, Tom,' Clement said. He stopped and

reaching for the telescope, trained it on a group of dwellings about four hundred yards ahead. 'It's a village. Local houses by the look of it. Seems to be some sort of shop there, too.'

'Stay away or go in?' Tom asked.

'It would be good to get some information about Surabaya. I don't think it's the sort of place Müller would frequent.'

'Fine with me.'

At the edge of the village, they paused, and Clement drew his telescope again. But they'd been seen. Local children now ran towards them. Clement replaced the telescope and they walked into the village surrounded by the growing, excited crowd. Clement smiled but he had nothing to give them. Ahead, was an old car parked outside the shop that sold fruit and local produce. A western-looking woman came out of the shop and stared at them. 'Lost?'

Clement lifted his hat. 'You could say that.'

'Are you going into Surabaya?'

'Yes. Do you know the way?'

'Of course. Do you want a lift?'

'Are the Dutch still in charge here?' Clement asked.

The woman walked to the rear of the car and put a box of fruit into the car's boot then slammed it shut. 'For now. But I see what's happening.'

'Why don't you leave?'

'And go where?'

Clement didn't answer immediately. 'I don't want to

inconvenience you.'

The woman scoffed. 'It's no trouble, I'm going that way anyway.'

'Can't hurt, Clem,' Tom whispered, hitching the Owen gun higher on his shoulder.

'It would her if she was caught and interrogated.'

Clement looked at the stern, mature-age woman. 'Well, if you're sure it's no trouble.'

Tom reached for the rear passenger side door handle and opened the door wide. He slid the Owen gun onto the floor behind the front seat then got in. Clement sat in the front beside the woman.

She turned the key in the ignition. 'You from Singapore?'

'Yes.'

'Are they close?'

'Yes. You should leave.'

'My home is here. I was born here, and this is where I'll die.'

'I admire your courage but...' Clement stopped himself, the image of Evelyn trussed like a bird for roasting flooding his memory. 'Well, just don't leave it too long.'

'I heard you the first time.'

They drove in silence for a few miles then the woman slowed the vehicle at a fork in the road. She pointed to the right: 'That's the road into Surabaya. It leads to the markets and port.'

Clement opened the door and got out. 'Do you know anyone by the name of Müller?'

'It's a common enough Dutch surname. It's also German.'

'And you don't know anyone of that name?'

'Not around here.'

'In Europe?'

'Yes.'

'Well, thank you for the lift.' Clement closed the door and joined Tom on the road.

The woman nodded then engaged the gears and drove away. Clement hadn't learned her name and he hadn't given theirs, but he thought it unlikely the woman would tell anyone about them.

'Do you think she knows him?' Tom asked.

Clement thought for a moment. 'I don't think so. Either way, it doesn't matter. He's expecting us anyway.'

Clement and Archer walked along another dirt road, this time in slightly better condition, until they came to the produce markets. The smell of rotting fruit putrid in the late afternoon sun greeted their arrival. The vendors were packing up their stalls and the tracks leading down to the wharves were crowded with carts and bullocks as well as people. With a confrontation looming, Clement worried about the numbers of people about, but the crowded streets and alleyways did provide them with good cover despite both he and Archer being considerably taller than the native Javanese.

Taking a laneway towards the waterfront, Clement saw *The Flying Dutchman* off to his left, about twenty yards away. He paused by the corner of a large building, his eyes fixed on the quay area. Ahead were several smaller craft and further down the wharf were the larger ships. A large yacht was in the process of berthing there. He scanned the people on the quay but he didn't recognise anyone and he couldn't see Lyon or Watkins. With a nod to Archer, Clement led him along the wharf and entered *The Flying Dutchman*. It was filled with men drinking after a long day's work on the waterfront. Sauntering in, Clement waited at the bar until the barman came to ask them what they wanted. Ordering two beers, Clement asked him if he could rent a room for the night overlooking the quay.

'All taken,' the barman said, his gaze slowly coursing over Clement then Tom.

Clement pulled some guilder from his pocket. Among the notes Bill had given him was a twenty guilder note. The man grabbed it then threw a key onto the bar. 'One night. No longer.'

Clement sipped the pale beer but already Archer had finished his. Clement bought another round and they sat at a table in the rear. It had been the table he'd seen the three Japanese men sitting at more than a month ago and he had a good view of the room. Lyon and Watkins were not among the gathering crowd.

Clement glanced at the key number and, finishing the beer, they took the stairs to the upper floors. On the second floor, Clement unlocked a door to the smallest room he'd ever seen. It just managed to contain a wide bed and a chair and he knew immediately what routinely happened there. Tom removed his coat and hung it on the chair as Clement gazed through the small window that overlooked the wharf below.

'Sorry, Clem. You shouldn't have to see rooms like this.'

'I'm not unaware of the principal purpose of this room, Tom. Regardless, it serves our purposes precisely, no matter what the publican may think. You have the bed, Tom. I'll sleep on the floor.'

'No way, Clem. If you don't mind my feet in your face, we'll top and tail. But I'll give the mattress a beating first. Never know what's in it.'

Archer went through the process of battering the old mattress until it yielded its infestation. Cockroaches scurried across the floor and under the door to places unknown.

'Maybe you won't sleep too well, but it's a place to lie down. I slept on my horse once. Figured it was better than crocodiles carrying me away.'

'How didn't you fall off?'

'By not going to sleep.'

Clement laughed aloud. 'Will you return to being a rouseabout after the war, Tom?' Clement asked after saying his brief prayers.

'Don't know anything else.'

'Why not stay in the army. You could become an officer.'

Archer laughed. 'Not me, Clem. Don't want the responsibility. Rather find a good'un like yourself and work for them. Simpler that way.'

'Well, I hope you sleep well, Tom.'

Archer turned on his side and within minutes Clement saw he was asleep.

Clement hardly slept. He wanted to be awake before dawn and from his experience of being in the tropics, dawn was just after five.

Swinging his legs over the side of the bed, he hit the heel of his boots on the floor in case the cockroaches had taken up residence there during the night. The noise woke Archer.

'Everything alright,' Tom asked, rubbing his face.

Clement pulled on his boots. 'I want to have a look about before too many people are on the quay.' *Look about.* The words Müller had used. Clement wondered if Müller was in Surabaya doing exactly the same thing.

Opening his pack, Clement withdrew two sticks of dynamite, two detonators, a length of fuse and two fuse igniters then laid them out on the bed. Taking his knife from the scabbard on his left arm, he cut a length of fuse about eight inches long then pushed it into the detonator and crimped it in place using his teeth. Then he attached the fuse igniter. Reaching for a stick of dynamite, he pushed the detonator into the explosive. Laying the assembled explosive on the bed, he repeated the process with the second stick of dynamite and handed it to Archer. 'Leave the Owen gun under the mattress, Tom, but bring your knife, pistol and three grenades.'

'What are we blowing up, Clem?' Archer grinned.

'Nothing in particular. I want to have a diversion placed around for use later, if we need it.'

Archer pulled on his boots, drew on his dirty shirt and placed the assembled explosive into his shorts' pocket.

'What else do you have in that box of tricks of yours?' Clement asked, seeing Archer's pack under the bed.

'Few things. Never know what you need or when.' Archer opened his pack. Other than the usual array of weaponry and ammunition there was some rope, a torch, a knuckle duster, a telescope and a compass.

Clement smiled, half to himself. Archer may be a good rouseabout but he was a very good sergeant.

Clement and Tom left *The Flying Dutchman* and wandered out onto the waterfront. Only a few men could be seen around the harbour front. Even the publican wasn't in the bar when they left the pub by the front door. A light, almost balmy breeze was coming from the east and if there hadn't been a war on, Clement would almost say it was idyllic. Further down, near to the Customs House he saw a woman with a small child setting up a stall selling baskets.

To his left were several warehouses and outside their still closed doors, leaning against the building were stacks of empty, wooden, cargo crates and general packing debris. He gazed around the area checking who was watching then wandered away from the door of the public house towards the crates. Propping against the stack,

Clement stared along the line of warehouses, Tom beside him. Studying the windows, he couldn't see anyone standing there watching proceedings below. 'Push one stick into the crate, Tom. And make sure you remember where you put it and have the fuse igniter pin easily accessible.'

'When is this diversion happening?' Tom asked.

'Hopefully, we won't need it. But sometime after the *Krait* docks, would be my guess.'

Poking the dynamite into one of the crates, Archer covered it with several crumpled old newspapers and left the pin to the fuse igniter exposed but half-hidden and next to some broken timber planks.

From where they stood, Clement could see all the ships tied up along the wharf and out into the bay. Across from them and on the left was the Dutch Naval Base. A slow, lazy heat-haze was already settling over the waters and with the sun's first rays, the temperature would increase quickly. His gaze lingered on the Naval Base. Several ships and a submarine were still in port there. But with nerves as heightened as they currently were in the Southwest Pacific, he didn't want anyone from the Dutch Navy seeing the explosive and removing it. He reasoned that with heightened tension in the region, the Dutch Navy would want all shore leave cancelled and all the sailors would now be onboard or at the Base.

The waterfront was surprisingly quiet but within the hour the oil refinery workers would arrive and the wharves would become busy. Clement checked the wharf area again, and they returned to *The Flying Dutchman* to get something to eat.

In the hour they'd been on the wharf, the bar had opened. Rowdy Dutch oil refinery workers now filled the area, buying bread and drinking strong locally grown coffee. But in all the groups that came and went in the two hours they were in the bar, Clement didn't see any Japanese. Perhaps they were no longer welcome in the Dutch controlled establishments. Finishing the meal, Clement stood. 'I want to see outside again, Tom. Are you carrying your pistol and knife?'

'Yep. And a grenade or two. Just in case. Anything in particular you want to see?'

'No. But I'd like to be seen.'

'You got a sudden death wish?'

Clement laughed. 'That's been said before. Let's see if anyone we recognise is about.'

'You mean Major Lyon and Joe.'

'Not necessarily,' Clement said, checking his watch. It was just after eight.

Clement and Tom walked outside and strolled along the wharf staring at the ships tied up there. The wharves had become lively with the onset of the day. They weaved their way through the cargo stacks, men and equipment scattered over the wharves in organised chaos. Ahead and about fifty yards distant, Clement saw the two supposedly Vichy Frenchmen standing near to a large pleasure yacht that had just berthed at the quay.

Clement slowed his pace.

'I see them,' Tom whispered.

'Let's just sit here for a while, Tom. Do you have a cigarette?'

'I didn't know you smoked?'

'I don't but it's an excuse to loiter here a while and keep your head down.'

Clement bent forward as Tom struck the match. As Clement breathed in the tobacco, he lifted his head and gazed towards the two Frenchmen about twenty feet away from them. They were talking and laughing. But they hadn't moved. Thirty seconds later a man stepped from the nearby yacht onto the quay. It was Müller.

31

Clement turned away. Time was important now. 'Tom, give me your cigarette packet, would you?'

Archer passed the packet to Clement. 'One smoke and you're a smoker now?'

Clement didn't answer. 'Walk slowly back to the pub and sit by the upper room window with your friend Owen beside you. Don't look back. Remember Lot's wife!'

'What are you going to do?'

'Set a trap.'

'Could be best if I stay with you, Clem,' Tom said, his voice quiet.

'Do as you're told, Sergeant. Now listen and do exactly as I say.' Clement could see rebuked surprise in Tom's face, but he didn't have time for explanations, besides which he needed Tom to do as he ordered. 'Once at the window, keep your eye on me at all times. Timing is vitally important. Then wait for my signal. Once you see me take the cigarette packet from my top pocket, come down immediately and pull the pin on the fuse igniter then run towards me. And have that Owen gun ready to fire. Lyon and Watkins should be hereabouts and when they see the commotion and you running, they'll join you. I'm guessing Müller will do the same. Be prepared to use that gun, Tom, because it may come to that. Don't take your eyes from me until you see the signal. If you do and you miss it, the trap will not work. You may be waiting a while, I just don't know. Understood?'

'Yes, sir. I won't let you down,' Tom said.

'I'm counting on it, Tom.'

Archer left immediately and Clement noted he never looked back.

Clement waited, facing away from the yacht until he saw Archer sitting in the window of their second-floor room. He thought Archer had taken his time in getting there, but perhaps the sergeant had used the time to relieve himself. It could be hours before he gave the signal.

Müller was still on the wharf speaking quickly in fluent French to the two Vichy Frenchmen, his back half turned to Clement. Müller's French was fast and for the most part, Clement didn't understand it. But it wasn't so rapid that Clement didn't hear his own name or mention of the *Krait*. From the corner of his eye, Clement saw the group pointing towards the bay and out into the Madoera Strait. Clement guessed they'd sighted Bill's ship. As Müller and the Frenchmen passed Clement, he bent down and used his favourite trick of tying his shoelace, his back to them. He felt sure Müller hadn't seen him.

Standing, Clement watched Müller and the Frenchmen walking along the quay. Without pausing, they entered the Port Authority and Customs Building located approximately halfway between where Clement was on the wharf and *The Flying Dutchman*. Shifting his gaze to the waterfront pub, he glanced up at the second-floor window.

Archer nodded.

Clement was confident Tom had seen them.

With Müller away from the yacht, Clement decided to walk past the craft and see if anyone was on board. He guessed he had about three to five minutes before Müller or his henchmen would check the wharf from an upper floor window of the Customs House and see him there. Hurrying, he approached the expensive vessel.

A man quite suddenly appeared on deck beside him. He was thick-set, with heavy jowls and although physically strong, he didn't look remotely like a sailor.

'Guten Morgen,' Clement said.

'Morgen,' the man said.

'Ein wunderschönes Schiff,' Clement said. 'Where have you come from?' he continued in German.

'Who wants to know?' the man asked, also in German.

'A friend of Müller. Is he onboard?'

'No.'

Clement gave the man a nod and turned. In his peripheral vision and further along the wharf, he could see the *Krait* berthing. He needed to hurry now. Everything depended on him being in the right place at exactly the right time. 'Auf Wiedersehen,' he said, striding away. Clement hurried towards the *Krait*.

Mick was on deck.

'Mick, grab your weapons and come with me now,' Clement called. He turned and faced *The Flying Dutchman* then slowly withdrew the packet of cigarettes from his top pocket and shoved them into his short's pocket.

Four minutes later, as Mick jumped from the *Krait* onto the wharf, an explosion roared into the hazy air, the detonation thumping in Clement's chest, the smoke billowing into the air.

Clement looked up at the Port Authority and Customs Building. People were running and chaos had descended. Clement knew immediately that the plume of smoke and subsequent eruption was larger than one stick of dynamite. From the size of the smoke cloud, he guessed Tom had emptied a bag of flour into the mix. But while the effect was spectacular, Clement knew it was brief and would burn out quickly. But the timber from the crates had blown outwards in all directions, hitting the stone wall behind, and flying out over the wharf. Smoke filled the air around the damaged crates and carried across the waterfront in the morning breeze. The diversion was impressive and successful.

Clement pulled his pistol as Mick swung his Owen gun around his shoulder holding the weapon ready to fire as they hurried towards the Customs Building.

Mayhem had ensued. People were running and shouting orders in multiple languages. Somewhere a siren sounded. Outside the Customs Building and standing in the doorway were the two Frenchman; above them, standing in the window over the entry door was Hans Müller. A slow grin spread over Müller's face. As their eyes met, Clement felt the shiver of evil.

Clement rushed for the entry door to the Customs House as Archer and Savage charged the Frenchmen from opposite directions. Stunned, they fumbled with the flaps over their pistols but Archer and Savage fired their weapons. Bullets sunk deep into the stone building, and across the front of the entrance where the men had been standing. In a matter of seconds, both men were lifeless on the ground. But Clement could still hear firing. He turned. It was coming from the yacht. 'Behind you!' Clement shouted then ran into the building. Looking back through the open doorway, he saw Archer and Savage turn and run towards the yacht. Someone was firing from an adjacent building and Clement prayed it was Lyon or Watkins. Clement watched Archer and Savage jump aboard the vessel from the wharf, one at either end of the large yacht, both firing into hatchways and below deck. The thick-set man staggered on deck, a machine gun in his hand. Mick held the Owen steady and fired. Clement saw the man fall then heard the splash.

Clement ran up the wooden stairs to the first floor. Outside the firing ceased.

At the door to the front office Clement paused. He had no idea if Müller were alone or if a barrage of weapons would greet him as he stepped forward. As Clement held his pistol steady, he heard the sound of running feet on the stairs, the footfall hard and fast and at least two sets. Clement paused, his heart racing. With his pulse pounding, he paused for two seconds, screwed his eyes tight and waited. If Müller had assistance, he would be caught in the crossfire. From the corner of his eye, he saw Ivan Lyon running up the stairs, taking them two at a time and holding a rifle. Behind him was Joe carrying an American Tommy gun. Clement swung his leg across the door to the upper office and with the heel of his boot, kicked the door in. In that second, he jumped sideways, the sound of the splintering timber causing a volley of shots from inside to be unleashed through the doorway. Joe joined Clement then, leaning forward, fired through the crack behind the open door. Someone fell, the sound hard. No one cried out in pain. Inside the firing continued. Then it stopped.

'It's over, Müller! You will not escape, and your French friends are dead. Throw the weapon into the centre of the room so I can see it. You will not be shot, if you surrender now.'

Clement heard a pistol fall onto the floorboards. But there was no guarantee that the man carried only one

357

weapon. Or that someone else wasn't waiting there in the silence.

Joe stepped forward.

'No, Joe!' Clement called as a shot rang out.

Joe fell backward, sliding down the wall and clutching his arm, his grip on the machine gun slipping.

Lyon grabbed Joe's Thompson and rushed into the room, firing in all directions, the bullets spraying the wall and anything in their way. A series of agonising screams reverberated around the walls.

Clement leaned over the American, 'Are you alright, Joe?'

'I'm ok, Clem. Just a flesh wound,' Joe said through gritted teeth.

Archer and Savage ran up the stairs. 'Clem! Clem!'

'Here, Tom.' Clement left a white-faced Joe and entered the room.

Müller was lying on the floor, his gun on the other side of the room, the screams now reduced to gasping breaths, his face screwed in pain. He'd been wounded in the upper leg, blood was pooling onto the floor. Lyon stood over him, gun at the ready. Clement thought his expression as he looked down at the imposter was the most determined yet contemptuous he'd ever seen. He was certain that if Müller made any sort of a move, he'd be a dead man.

'You are completely loathsome and the lowest form of life. May you rot in hell for all the traitorous things you've done, not to mention your attempts to ruin my reputation,' Lyon said.

Müller stared up at Lyon. Despite the pain, a slow sneer spread over his face.

'He'll not escape justice, Ivan,' Clement said. Under the window was the dead body of a Japanese man. He nodded towards him, 'One of your contacts, presumably.'

Müller didn't answer.

'Can he walk?' Clement asked Lyon.

'We've got company,' Archer shouted, erupting into the room. 'Dutch police, I think.'

'I have all the authority needed with me from the head of the Dutch Military, Lieutenant General Hein Ter Poorten,' Ivan said.

Two uniformed men entered. 'You are Major Wisdom?' the one with more gold braid asked Clement, ignoring both the wounded Müller and the dead Japanese.

'I am.'

'Then you are under arrest! All of you are under arrest!'

32

Surabaya - 20th January 1942

I don't think so,' a calm female voice said. Evelyn held the Owen gun steady, levelled at the two Dutch police officers, her finger on the trigger. The two men spun around at the sound of her voice.

Moving as one, Clement and Lyon grabbed the men's arms from behind, pinning them behind their backs, holding then while Mick removed their pistols.

'I was warned about you. Ter Poorten will deal with both of you!' Lyon said.

Archer passed his Owen gun to Mick, removed a length of rope from his webbing and cut it in half. Mick pushed the policemen's pistols into his belt then held an Owen gun on the pair as Clement and Ivan bound their hands.

'Gags are what we need,' Archer said, removing his shirt and cutting it into strips with his knife.

'And don't take your eyes off that one!' Clement said

to Mick, pointing at the wounded Müller. 'Tom, bind his hands as well and cut some more strips. That leg needs a tourniquet if he's not to bleed to death, which would be too good an end for such as him. Then gag him.'

Ivan laid down the Thompson and took over gagging the Dutch police duo.

'We don't take orders from Ter Poorten,' one of the policemen said before Ivan tied the gag firmly over the man's mouth.

Clement glanced at Müller, his face constricted with pain as Tom struggled to fix the tourniquet. It was obvious that the Vichy Frenchmen were not the only officials in Müller's employ.

'We should leave them here, Clement, for Ter Poorten to find,' Lyon said.

'If you think it's best, Ivan.'

Clement turned to Joe. He could see how pale his face was. Tom produced another strip from his shirt and bound Joe's wounded arm.

'Can you stand, Joe?' Clement asked.

'Sure, I think so. I'll be fine. If someone can give me a hand to stand up. I'll be ok.'

Evelyn helped Joe to his feet.

'We should leave, Clement. The explosion will have people twitchy,' Ivan said.

'Agreed. Tom, take the second stick and place it somewhere between us and *The Flying Dutchman*. And no flour this time!'

'How long, Clem?' Archer asked.

'Ten minutes.'

'Right!' Taking back his Owen gun, Archer turned to leave.

'And Tom, then straight back to the *Krait*. You know where it is?'

'Yeah! She'll be right!' Archer said, disappearing out of the upper room and down the stairs.

Clement glanced around the room then out the window. Below, a crowd of people had encircled the dead Frenchmen. Beyond, where the dynamite had exploded, people were dousing the burnt timber. 'Mick, go downstairs. See if there's a back way out.'

'Right you are, Clem,' Mick said, turning to leave.

'Better I go,' Evelyn said. 'A woman asking for a safe way out wouldn't raise any suspicions.'

Clement nodded.

Without another word, Evelyn handed her weapon to Clement and left the upper floor. Minutes later she reappeared. 'There's a back door. Just leads outside and it's easy to circle the building. Everyone's out the front anyway watching what's going on. But we should be quick.'

'Right. Ivan, will you give me a hand to get Müller downstairs?'

'It'll be a pleasure,' Ivan said and with one arm, wrenched the wounded man to his feet.

Müller screamed under the gag and sagged down. Clement saw immediately that the only way to get him out would be to carry him, which would require all three of their currently able-bodied men. 'Evelyn, you go first and check if the way is clear. Ivan and I will support Müller. Mick, you hold a pistol to his back. If he tries anything, shoot him in the other leg. Joe, can you walk?'

'I think so.'

Evelyn led the way down, pausing at each landing then beckoning them on. Clement along with Lyon carried the reluctant Müller down two flights of stairs, Mick at his back. Behind him and with his right arm tightly bound, Joe carried the Thompson gun under his left arm, his finger on the trigger and his gaze over his shoulder.

Just as Evelyn reached the lowest floor, a door opened and a man stepped out.

'Who are you?' he demanded.

'Where is your supervisor, young man?' Evelyn shouted. 'I demand an explanation for this appalling commotion! Something untoward is happening outside and I demand to know what is going on! Go and see to it instantly!'

'Mijn dame. I don't know. Please wait here in my office and I'll find out at once.'

Clement smiled as the man ran towards the front door. Evelyn waved them down the last stairs. Thirty seconds later, Clement heard the detonation. 'Hurry, we don't have much time to get him to the *Krait* unobserved.'

Once through the Customs Building, they left by the rear door and hurried down the side alley, returning to the wharf further along the quay. People were still rushing in all directions. No one seemed to have taken control. Leaving the commotion behind them, they walked briskly towards the *Krait* where it was berthed beside the wharf, supporting and dragging Müller between them. Clement could see Bill standing on the foredeck.

A minute later, Bill's crew had jumped ashore and were casting off the ropes from the bollards. As they boarded the *Krait,* Bill started the engine. Clement counted the men onboard.

'Where's Archer?'

Running along the wharf came the familiar frame of his sergeant. Archer leapt aboard just as Bill tossed the last rope onto the wharf.

'What kept you, Tom?' Clement called.

'You left your pack in the room, Clem. I went to get it.'

'You could have been arrested or killed.'

'I had to get it, there was a photo of your Missus in it. I knew you'd want it.'

'Very brave and very stupid. Never do that again!'

Archer grinned. 'I said we'd work together again, didn't I, Clem?'

'Well, you and Mick get Müller below, as quickly as you can. Tie him to the bulkhead. And keep that gag in his mouth firmly in place,' Clement called to Archer.

Tom grinned. 'Mick, make sure those ropes are tight.'

Clement glanced around the ship and counted the team. Everyone was accounted for. His eye fell on Joe.

He was lying on the aft deck. 'Ready when you are, Bill,' Clement said through the wheelhouse window. 'Ivan, would you check on Joe. I think he's in more pain than he's letting on.'

Clement turned to Evelyn, already at the radio. 'Thank you, Miss Howard. We owe you a debt not easily repaid. Once we are at sea, would you send a coded signal to Captain Winthorpe?'

'With pleasure, Clement.'

33

Johnny and Long stood waiting on the wharf. Behind them were several Military Policemen waiting to take Müller into custody. A closed-sided van stood on the road not twenty feet away. Clement stepped from the *Krait*, again experiencing the strange sensation of movement where there was none.

'Welcome back, Clement,' Johnny said, grasping his hand in greeting.

Clement smiled. His old friend had dressed for their arrival in full Naval uniform. Beside him was Commander Long.

Bill cut the engines as the group joined Clement on the jetty.

'You've had quite a time of it. Winthorpe kept me informed,' Long said. 'And I'm very pleased to see Miss Howard in one piece.'

'It had its moments, Commander. But I had a wonderful team,' Clement said, glancing at Archer and Savage standing back from the group. He caught Evelyn's eye but he had no intention of informing Long about Evelyn's role in their escape from Surabaya.

'Mr Reynolds. We are in your debt,' Long said. 'Would you like to join us, officially that is? I can always use patriots.'

'Perhaps.'

'Any damage to your boat?' Long asked.

'Some but nothing much.'

'Well, if there is, the Australian government will cover the costs. We are very grateful to you.' Long half turned to walk away then turned back to Reynolds. 'Thank you again, Reynolds. Come to the Hotel Darwin tomorrow and we'll talk some more.'

Bill nodded.

Clement smiled at Bill Reynolds. He thought Bill a brave man. Perhaps Bill Reynolds's war was only just beginning. Clement stepped back on deck and shook hands with him. 'It seems I'm always thanking you for getting me and my team out of trouble, Bill. I'm rather hoping this might be the last time.'

Bill took Clement's hand. 'It's been good to know you, Clement. See you on the other side, if not before.'

Clement smiled. He'd never thought of the hardened skipper as a religious man but evidently Bill Reynolds believed as he did, that divine intervention had kept them safe during some highly volatile situations.

'Major Lyon,' Bill said, shaking his hand in farewell. 'I understand Clement will return to England. But should you have further need for the *Krait*, well, you know where I am.'

'Thank you, Reynolds. I have a feeling the *Krait* and I are not finished with each other yet,' Ivan said.

'Well, we need to debrief you all,' Long was saying. 'I've had the publican at the Hotel Darwin set aside rooms where you can wash and shave and get something to eat. You might even like a swim in the hotel pool. You too, Sergeant Archer and Private Savage. And I've asked one of the local doctors to call by to check Lieutenant Watkins's injuries. Miss Howard, there is a special room for you too; one with a bath.'

'Oh! That will be nice!'

'And Müller?' Clement asked.

'Prison doctor can attend to him,' Long said briefly, then nodded to the military police, who went aboard the *Krait* and took Müller from the for'ard hold.

Carrying their few possessions, the team walked along the jetty and climbed into the waiting lorry. Long had arranged for all the weapons to be taken to the military base in Darwin for safe storage. Now what Clement really wanted was a shower, a shave, and some clean clothes. But if Long wanted a debrief, Clement knew personal wishes would have to wait.

The Hotel Darwin had taken on a look of wartime preparation. Sandbags lined the front of the building and any large area of glass had been removed and boarded up. Bert allocated the room keys. Clement glanced at his; Number Two. The same as previously.

'I've still got your old suitcase, Major Wisdom, if you want it,' Bert said.

'Thank you, Bert. I would.' Clement waited while the man retrieved his battered suitcase from a storeroom off the reception area. Taking it and his pack to his room, Clement opened the door and placed both the pack and the suitcase on the stand at the end of the bed. The windows were open and a gecko sat on the windowsill staring back at him. He smiled at it, knowing how harmless it was. The room contained a simple metal-framed bed with a light blue bedspread and one pillow, but for Clement is was a king's paradise in comparison to the bunk in the radio hold on the *Krait*. Opening his old suitcase, he took out his long trousers and a clean shirt, still folded by Geraldine's hand. Beside it were his laundered underwear and socks and a pair of shoes. For Clement it was like seeing old friends. These were the items of ordinary life. Collecting his apparel, he wrapped a towel around his waist and went to the bathroom at the end of the corridor.

Ivan Lyon was there, taking out his shaving equipment.

'Good working with you, Clement,' Ivan said. 'I suppose you'll be going back to England now?'

'I have no idea, Ivan. But I've enjoyed our chess games. And not just because I won most of them.'

'You're good in a crisis. We could use your talents

here, if you'd stay.'

'If I have any choice in the matter, I'll think about it.'

'Did Long say anything more about the leak in Melbourne?' Lyon lathered his face and began to shave his chin. 'I do wonder who or what connected Müller to Munroe.'

It was a question Clement had thought about himself but until now hadn't had the luxury of time to consider it. For Lyon, however, it had greater significance than mere curiosity. Müller had studied Lyon, knew his mannerisms and about his life. That required either a personal knowledge of the man or a shared relationship with someone well-known to Lyon.

'It will be good to hear what Müller tells them,' Clement said.

'He may not tell them anything. Although, I'm sure Naval Intelligence will interrogate him thoroughly.'

'Then we may never know.'

'Not necessarily, Clement. Munroe had an accomplice, didn't he?'

'Yes. Miss Ferguson. She worked in Eric Nave's department.'

'Ferguson, you say?'

'Yes. Alice Ferguson. As I recall, she said she'd grown up in Singapore. She's fluent in Japanese.'

'Really! I knew a family of that name there.' Lyon sniggered as he worked the razor round his chin. 'In fact, it's rather an odd story. Mrs Violet Ferguson was involved in a very unusual incident. It would have been a little over a year ago now. She was on a British Mercantile ship returning to Singapore when it was attacked and boarded by a German commerce raiding ship.'

'Was she taken prisoner?'

Lyon stopped shaving, as though reflecting. 'I seem to recall she and other passengers were taken off their ship before it was sunk. I think she was taken to Japan. But the oddest thing happened. And this I had from one of the few surviving members of the crew, a Frenchman in Indochina. She pleaded with the German captain to retrieve a tea set from her luggage in the strongroom on the ship before they sank it.'

Clement laughed. 'Must have been a valuable tea set.'

'It wasn't the porcelain that was so valuable. The luggage room also contained over a hundred British Royal Mail bags, some of them containing highly sensitive correspondence from the War Office to the High Commission in Singapore. Apparently the Germans spent hours sifting through it all before sinking the ship. Had she not been so insistent on keeping that tea set, the German's wouldn't have known the documents were there.'

Clement lowered his razor and stared at Lyon. 'Was this ship the *Automedon*?'

'Do you know, I think that was the name.'

Clement put his razor on the basin and left the bathroom. Running through the corridors he hurried back towards the lounge. Long was sitting at a table by the windows, Johnny beside him. 'Long, the leak isn't Munroe. It's Alice Ferguson.'

34

Darwin - 28th January 1942

Clement climbed out of the lorry at the entrance to Darwin airport.

'Good working with you, Clem. Wish you weren't leaving,' Archer said.

'Goes for me too,' Mick added.

Clement placed his pack on the ground, stood to attention and saluted Archer and Savage. Strangely, he'd miss them. They were a good pair and had proven themselves trustworthy and loyal soldiers. But now it was time to return to his life and a Nazi spy who'd infiltrated a recently formed Shetland rescue and resupply mission. Their work had been compromised.

'Take care of each other.'

'She'll be apples, Clem.' Tom grinned. It was how Clement wanted to remember his resourceful sergeant. Picking up his pack, Clement walked across the tarmac with Johnny, Long, Lyon, Joe Watkins, and Evelyn

Howard. The heat of the day was the last thing Clement felt before the aeroplane door closed.

He took his seat. The flight would be long with several stops in remote places to refuel but Clement saw it now as an opportunity to catch up on sleep. He fastened his seat belt and laid his head against the seat rest. Instead of falling asleep he found himself wondering if that in the time it took them to fly from Darwin to Melbourne, Long would have had Alice Ferguson interrogated further and her home searched. Clement wondered what they'd find. He suspected there'd be a radio transmitter at the very least. But her motive perplexed him. She was a British citizen. Why would she betray her country?

After the many stops it took to travel from Darwin to Melbourne, the plane landed at the now familiar airfield. He was beginning to think of it as Cow Pastures Airfield, although he didn't say as much to Long. The same young WRAN, McManus, and another were there to take them to Victoria Barracks in Melbourne.

Stepping from the car in front of the Virginia creeper-covered building, he reached for his coat. People around him were wearing summer attire but despite the warmth of the day, he felt cold.

They met in Long's office.

Long hung his jacket on the stand in the corner then sat in his chair and opened a dossier. 'Well, thanks to Clement and Ivan we now have the real culprit, Alice

Ferguson. Although Munroe isn't getting off Scot-free. Allowing anyone to intercept and read secret documents in time of war is a treasonable offence. But we have learned a lot about Miss Ferguson. When the police searched her small flat in St Kilda, they found a radio transmitter and, perhaps more importantly, they found letters from Müller to her dated from the end of 1940. It appears they'd met on the *Automedon* when Miss Ferguson was accompanying her mother back to Singapore. Müller had been the radio operator on board the German ship *Atlantis* which shelled and boarded the *Automedon*. And it had been Müller who realised the importance of the documents found in the strongroom hold on the ship although the second officer took the credit. This angered Müller but he saw an opportunity and it was easy to convince Miss Ferguson that the British had no intention of coming to the aid of their own in the Far East. She, her mother and many others would be transported to Japan where they would become prisoners of war. Müller exploited her fear, her anger and her vulnerability, persuading her to work for him by coming to Australia and learning Morse code. She would then find employment where her language and Morse code skills would be snapped up and where she was to befriend the hapless despatch rider, Stephen Munroe. Müller even supplied her with the radio transmitter so she could keep him informed of events here.'

'Did you learn this from the girl or Müller?' Clement asked.

'The girl mostly. Once anger is unleashed, it hides little,' Long said.

'And Müller?'

'Defiant. While the letters and Miss Ferguson's testimony will be enough evidence to see him hanged, it appears it was Müller who found the secret cache of documents. However, as I said, the second officer took the credit. Müller then, as a fluent English and Japanese speaker, volunteered to take the prisoners to Japan where he began a new life spying for the Japanese, who were only too happy to have him. Especially when he met many of the Americans from CAST in Manilla. Apparently someone had mistaken him for Lyon. Seeing another opportunity, he exploited it wherever and whenever he could. It is likely that Müller was promised wealth and status when Japan won the war.'

'And the *kin no yuri*?' Clement asked.

'We'll be looking into that,' Long said. 'And Clement, I've taken the liberty of speaking with Sir Stewart Menzies. I've requested you be allowed to stay on here. I can use a man of your talents and I'm sure Major Lyon would be happy to have you with us.'

Lyon turned to face Clement. 'We're setting up an Australian Special Operations group and we need all the help we can get, Clement. I'll add my plea for you to remain here.'

'Am I staying too, sir?' Joe asked.

'Yes, Lieutenant. There is nothing to be gained by trying to get you back into the Philippines. In fact, you will very soon be joined by others from CAST and FECB. Nave is expanding the Secret Intelligence Bureau and we'd like you to be a part of that.'

'I'd be happy to, sir.'

'Now, I'm sure you'd all like to find some more suitable clothes and have something to eat. Miss Copeland will arrange the uniforms, and Eric, would you see that Lieutenant Watkins has all he needs to feel at home?'

'My pleasure, Cocky.'

'And you, Commander?' Johnny asked. 'What's next for you?'

'Like yours, my work never ceases, Winthorpe. I'll continue to co-ordinate fractious intelligence divisions from many countries and for diverse personalities until I'm told otherwise.'

Johnny laughed.

'And, I'll ask Miss Copeland to arrange your flight to Sydney, Captain, then your onward journey to Hawaii.'

'Thank you, Commander.'

'You're going to Hawaii, Johnny?' Clement said.

'Yes. Now the Americans are in the war too, I'm to spend some time with the people at HYPO Intercept Station there, before heading back to England. And Clement, I cannot thank you enough for rescuing me and Miss Howard from Singapore. Her death would have been an immeasurable tragedy for Allied code breaking.' Johnny paused. 'But I'm keen to know, will you stay on here?'

Clement gazed at the blue skies through Long's window onto St Kilda Road. 'I don't know, Johnny. While England is my home, there isn't much for me there except a cold trip to the North Sea in winter.'

'Why not stay here. I'll clear it with *C*. You've found a good team. Men who want to work with you. Did you know Evelyn is staying on?'

'Really?'

'I thought if you knew that it may influence your decision.'

Clement paused. 'No one will ever replace Mary, Johnny.'

'It's time to move on, Clement. Mary would want you to. Between you, you and Lyon could do some good here.'

Standing on the front steps of Victoria Barracks Clement shook hands with Johnny and watched him climb into the car that would take him to the airport. Clement didn't know when he'd see his old friend again.

He felt the hand on his arm. 'I have some sandwiches here. We could eat them on the bench in the park, if you like?' Evelyn said.

Clement turned and smiled. 'Why not. It would be a shame to waste them.'

Acknowledgements

I wish to thank the following people:

David O'Sullivan from the Australian Maritime Museum and the Australian War Memorial Museum for arranging for me to visit and go aboard the *Krait*.

Daniel who advises me on all things to do with explosives and weapons handling.

Andrew who advises me on human intelligence.

Jane who advises me on signals intelligence.

Garry Gallagher whose knowledge about Darwin in WW2 is extraordinary.

Janet Laurence, my wonderful editor.

Ian Hooper my excellent publisher, his assistants and the many people involved in the process of publishing the book.

My husband Peter for the many cups of tea, cooked dinners, and hours of isolation he endures while I write and Harry, the dog, who on occasions kept me company for a while.

Author's Note

While *West Wind; Clear* is largely fictitious, there are numerous real historical events and real-life people woven into this story, all of whom contributed to the Allied successes during the Pacific War of World War II and about whom little is known today by the general public. In order of appearance in my book they include the following:

Commander Rupert Long. Long was a fascinating Australian character. He had the vision to see the need for an overall Intelligence Bureau and strived for its creation well before war broke out. He was an outstanding and charismatic leader and was indeed Head of Naval Intelligence in Australia and the Combined Operational Intelligence Bureau. He was instrumental along with another, Commander Eric Feldt, in the creation and success of the Coastwatcher's networks throughout the South Pacific. These were a true success and contributed greatly to Allied Intelligence gathering in the Pacific.

Commander Eric Nave. Nave was an extraordinary man of huge intellect and ability with code breaking. He was born in Australia, joined the Royal Australian Navy but was then transferred permanently to the (British) Royal Navy. He spent time in Japan learning the language and was employed by the British in China then Singapore. He developed a tropical illness that saw him transferred back to Australia. Bletchley Park was keen to have him in Britain but with the help of an Australian Admiral, Commander Long was able to keep him in Australia. He decoded the Winds Message on 19 November 1941.

David Ross. Ross was an Englishman serving in the Royal Navy and stationed in Dili, Timor.

John Whittaker. Whittaker was also in the Royal Navy and worked undercover in Timor. He was the radio communications officer for David Ross.

Bill Reynolds. In my opinion Bill Reynolds deserves special mention. Reynolds was born in Melbourne and served with the Merchant Navy before the war. During the war, Bill rescued evacuees around Malaya, including survivors from ships attacked by the Japanese and did some work for Australian Special Operations. Despite the *Krait* being owned by Reynolds, and being used in Operation Jaywick, Reynolds was not involved in this successful mission of September 1943 as at the time he was employed by American Intelligence to go into Malaya to recover sensitive information there. Arriving by submarine, he was deposited on a small island near Borneo. He was betrayed by locals to the Japanese and taken prisoner finally ending up in solitary confinement for six months in Surabaya after which he was shot by firing squad on 8 August 1944. He was awarded an MBE on 17 August 1943, but it wasn't received by his family until 13 November 1946.

The Krait. Reynolds acquired the *Krait* in Singapore. It was a Japanese fishing vessel named the *Kofuku Maru*. Reynolds renamed the ship the *Suey Sin Fah* and sailed it around the South Pacific and India with a Chinese crew. The ship is best known for its involvement in Operation Jaywick for which it was renamed the *Krait*, after a thin and very poisonous snake. Even though at the time of my story it would have been known as *Suey Sin Fah*, I decided to use the name *Krait*, as it is best known today by that name because of its involvement with Operation Jaywick.

Major Ivan Lyon – later Lieutenant Colonel Ivan Lyon. Ivan Lyon was one of the truly heroic characters of the Pacific War. An Englishman born into a military family, he had married a French woman and had a son, Clive. Stationed in Singapore at the outbreak of war in the Pacific, he was away undertaking covert operations in Indochina with the Free French when his wife and son were taken prisoner in Malaya. They were interned but did not survive. Lyon successfully set up resistance groups among local populations and later he assisted to evacuated civilians from Singapore by boat in February 1942. Lyon led the highly successful Operation Jaywick in September 1943 which blew up over 40,000 tons of Japanese shipping in Singapore Harbour. A similar mission was conceived a year later, Operation Rimau in October 1944. While the operation had some success in destroying Japanese shipping, the entire team died during combat. Lyon died on Soreh Island on 16 October 1944 while fighting a rear-guard action to assist the getaway of two injured members of the Rimau party. The full story of his inspirational bravery and leadership is well worth reading. After the war his remains were found and reburied in Kranji War Cemetery in Singapore.

Captain Williams. Williams was the officer in charge on Christmas Island. With him were four NCO's and 27 Indian soldiers. The island is rich in phosphate and therefore was a target for the Japanese. The first attack took place on 20 January 1942 by a Japanese submarine followed by some aerial bombing in late February and early March of that year. However, during the night of 10-11 March, the Indian soldiers mutinied killing Captain Williams and the four British NCO's. The island was occupied by the Japanese and by the end of March the radio station there was destroyed. The Japanese occupied the island until October 1945.

Violet Ferguson. This is a really fascinating story. Mrs Ferguson was a passenger on board the *SS Automedon* which was targeted and bombarded by the German commercial raider, *Atlantis* in November 1940. When the *Automedon* was boarded it was found that all the British Officers on the bridge had died during the shelling from the *Atlantis* and only Second Officer Stewart was found to be alive. Stewart, although injured had wanted to destroy the secret documents he knew to be in the strong room hold but during the raid, the key had gone astray. The German boarding party may never have found the top-secret papers had not Mrs Ferguson, who was on her way to Singapore, begged the German captain to retrieve her luggage as it contained a tea set which she prized. Once the strong room was opened, the secret documents were discovered and eventually given to German intelligence who then passed them to the Japanese. Mrs Violet Ferguson could not have known about the existence of these secret documents and is completely innocent of any culpability in their discovery. The daughter, Alice, is completely fictitious and no reflection on any member of the Ferguson family should be inferred.

Other real-life people mentioned in this story. There are references to several real-life people in the story. These include:

Professor Room – one of four professors from Sydney University engaged in code breaking, Lt Commander

Merry, Lt Miller, Jim Jamison, Lt Commander McLaughlin, - all of whom worked with Eric Nave at Victoria Barracks in Melbourne. Rudy Fabian of the American station in the Philippines, Sir Stewart Menzies Head of British SIS and known as *C*. Lt General Hien Ter Poorten head of The Dutch Military in Java, General Sir Archibald Wavell who was appointed Supreme Commander of the short-lived American, British, Dutch and Australian Command and stationed on Java, and there is a nod to Betty Archdale who took twelve Royal Navy women to Kranji Intercept station on Singapore during the war, was later Captain of the English Women's Cricket team, became Head of Women's College Sydney University and finally Headmistress of Abbotsleigh school which I attended.

Made in the USA
Middletown, DE
29 June 2022

68010661R00231